First Class!

Enjoy!

John Mawe

First Class!

John Mower

University of Hertfordshire Press

First published in Great Britain in 2008 by

University of Hertfordshire Press

Learning and Information Services

University of Hertfordshire

College Lane

Hatfield

Hertfordshire AL10 9AB

British Library Cataloguing in Publication Data
A catalogue record for this book is available from the
British Library

ISBN 978-1-902806-90-7

Design by Mathew Lyons
Cover design by Therese Habostad
Printed in Great Britain by CPI Antony Rowe, SN14 6LH

To all the children I taught during my nineteen years in the Primary classroom and to my own children, Nicholas and Megan

Acknowledgements

My thanks go to my wife, Claire, for her support and advice throughout; Kit Thomas, for his belief in this book; Jane Housham, for her critical and professional advice; Kerry Marsh, for her help with the manuscript; Jessica Abbott, Sean Deverson, Andrea Gee, Steven Gobin, Helen Ingram, Matthew Jellett, Natalie King, Alan Moore, Hayley Nice, Amy Orr, Zoe Steeden and Greg Williams for providing an invaluable student perspective on the storyline and characters; and Sarah Cunningham, for her initial comments. I would also like to thank all those who have read and commented on the text throughout the writing and editorial process.

The publication of this novel has been funded by a Training and Development Agency for Schools project: 'Mentoring and Coaching – Supporting Diversity – Men in Primary Schools'.

The novel supports the work of the School of Education at the University of Hertfordshire to recruit and support men in primary teaching.

1.

'Alice.'
 'Yes, sir.'
 Wow! What a start! I don't think I've ever been called 'sir' in my life.
 'Daniel.'
 'Yes, Mr Gray.'
 'Sophie.'
 'Yes, Mr Gray.'
 'Charlotte.'
 'Charlie!'
 OK, first test. Don't panic, she just wants to be called Charlie.
 'Sorry, Charlie.'
 'Yes, Mr Gray.'
 That could have been worse.
 'Miranda.'
 'Yes, sir.'
 Two sirs in one register! The Lord is on my side.
 'Robert.'
 'Yeah.'
 Bollocks.

It was this exact scenario that had had me in a cold sweat at three o'clock this morning. I had learnt the hard way, in my final teaching practice, the importance of the very first registration. While I knew all the theory – establish yourself first, don't be over-friendly, ensure confident body language, etc., etc. – somehow I had thought, in a moment of madness, that if I let them answer the register in a quirky, fun-filled manner, they would instantly proclaim me a cool dude of a teacher and regard me with a cross between hero-worship and reverence.

By the time my first registration in that fateful teaching practice had finished, some fifteen minutes after it had begun, I had already lost control. To my utter horror, 'quirky and jovial' quickly turned to rude, disrespectful and, eventually, completely defiant. It was, by some distance, the worst fifteen minutes of my life, and as the last snotty-nosed kid screeched 'yeeeeeeeessssssss Mr Gay' (met with rapturous laughter) I began to foresee what a nightmare the next six weeks would be. By the end of it my confidence as a teacher was completely shot, and I wondered whether I was cut out for the job. Had I been in the slightest bit cut out for anything else, I wouldn't be here now, in a moment of crisis, barely ten seconds into my first ever proper job, listening to Robert answer, 'Yeah.'

I took a second to look at him and gauge whether his response was a 'cheeky chappy' sort of 'yeah', designed to get a bit of a laugh, but without menace. That first meeting of our eyes confirmed, instantly, that this was no cheeky chappy. Robert was not a big child, nor did he sport a telling crew-cut or stud earring. Indeed, he had rather handsome features, short, well-groomed fair hair, and a clean green uniform. His eyes, however, were steely and daring, causing me to take an involuntary little gasp before issuing the standard response:

'I beg your pardon?'

'I said, Yeah.'

Bollocks, bollocks, bollocks. Any lingering hope of a 'cheeky-chappy-with-unfortunate-steely-and-daring-eyes' swiftly evaporated as Class 6G awaited my response. I knew the protocol. I knew that I could not be seen to hesitate for a fraction of a second, and that I should maintain a calm authority without losing eye contact.

But ... but, but, but. Knowing what to do, and actually doing it fifteen seconds into one's chosen career, are vastly different things. I started to speak but faltered, perhaps for half a second, before saying:

'Let me make myself clear, so you can be in no doubt as to my expectations, Robert. When I call your name, you respond, "Yes, Mr Gray".' (I didn't push my luck with 'sir'.)

'Yes, Mr Gray.'

As a little speech, it was quite well delivered, and I did maintain eye contact, but everybody noticed the half-second hesitation. The moment passed, however, and the rest of registration ensued without incident.

My mother was a primary school teacher for over twenty years. She once told me that the first day of the new school year was her favourite, as everything was clean, the children were well turned out and they presented their work beautifully, writing with their brand-new ink pens and underlining titles with mathematical precision, with their shiny new rulers and sharp pencils.

In my very limited experience, getting children to write a title in pen, and then transferring to ruler and pencil for three seconds, before reverting back to pen, is a bit like forming a New Year's resolution. You are almost anal in your enforcement of it initially but, after a week or so, just as the desire for a cigarette or pint of beer begins to grow, the novelty of the beautifully underlined piece of work begins to wane.

Nevertheless, keen to appear as someone who extolled the virtues of self-discipline in all areas, I watched my class dutifully and silently write their names and the subject title on their exercise books. There is something of a pseudo sergeant major in most slightly insecure young males and I actually found myself striding up and down the classroom, *with my hands clasped behind my back*, checking on my new recruits and virtually ordering them to 'get down and give me ten' if a letter was slightly out of place.

Thus I found myself faced with my first major dilemma. A common mantra amongst my university lecturers was always to be seen to treat all children equally. If you want their respect, runs the argument, they must see you as someone firm but fair. Well, that was all very well in theory but it didn't answer the problem of what to do when, ten seconds after scolding (very unfairly) lovely little Alice for smudging her title when putting her ruler up against it, you view the work of Patrick, the dyslexic dyspraxic. I had been told of the existence of Patrick Collins and been warned that, while he was both affable and intelligent, getting him to write down anything even vaguely legible was nigh-on impossible.

I genuinely felt for the lad and how he must have felt as he watched me marching slowly towards him, chiding those whose quality of writing he could only dream of, and getting closer to the moment when his embarrassment would be subject to my scrutiny. I had also insisted that everybody wrote in pen: 'No arguments – you're in Year 6 now, which means everyone is capable of writing in ink.' The poor lad, in a combination of fear and shame, had kept quiet, and ten minutes' work had resulted in an apparent ink cartridge explosion over his book.

When I first saw his name on his book I thought someone must have been missed off the register, as I couldn't remember the challenge of having to pronounce 'Praitk Cloins'. Looking at his fearful face, I had the good sense to allow for flexibility in the 'firm but fair' rule.

'It's Patrick, isn't it?' I said gently, sitting down next to him. He nodded. 'Would you prefer to write in pencil, Patrick?' Another nod. Without another word, I took Patrick's books away and replaced them with a new set.

Twenty minutes of writing names on books is enough for anyone and, in fear of losing the respectful silence and the high-calibre underlining, I brought them back onto the carpet for the 'Year 6 talk'.

'So, 6G,' I began, 'this is it. Your final year at Green Acre and your most important.' As we began to discuss how Year 6 sets an example to the rest of the school and the importance of SATs, I noticed that Robert and a rather unsavoury-looking child named Allard were starting a conversation at the back of the class.

'Beginner's Guide to the Basics of Teaching', rule one. Never, ever, ever allow children to have their own conversation when you are talking.

'Robert.'

'Yeah?'

I resisted the fleeting temptation to make him fetch a thesaurus, and spoke with the confidence of one who has achieved thirty minutes of relative calm.

'Robert, Allard, you're just getting to know me. I don't know or care what was acceptable in your last class but let me make this quite clear – and this applies to all of you. You will not talk while I'm talking. Is that understood?'

Eyes of steel. Silence.

I could have pushed for an answer but instead opted to move the surly looking Allard to the front of the class. I did this before thinking about the potential stand-off I might find myself in if he blatantly defied me. Fortunately he moved without fuss, but Robert's eyes told me in no uncertain terms that, had I called his name, he wouldn't have budged.

After sending them out, still in relative calm, I took a moment to reflect on my first ninety minutes in charge of my class. In charge. My class. It was quite daunting to know that the safety net of being a student had been removed. The safety net which dictated that, whatever happened, you were not totally accountable for the child. As a student, the class's real teacher was never that far away and, if an awkward incident was to occur, he or she would be there to bail you out. While the head and deputy were there now to bail me out if absolutely necessary, it was still me to whom the irate parent would turn, and it was absolutely my responsibility to ensure that the children in my care behaved well and were prepared well for secondary school.

I felt that the session had gone reasonably well apart from Robert, and even he had basically toed the line. I had got out of a potentially awkward moment with Patrick, and most of the class seemed perfectly nice. In the back of my mind I remembered my mate Rupert, now a veteran in his second year of teaching, telling me not to be deceived by the first week.

'They're sussing you out,' he'd intoned darkly. 'They look for a weakness, then they strike.'

I dismissed this half-thought, and went off to the staffroom. Only one teacher had made it before me, however: Ellie Luck. I've always prided myself on my ability to judge someone's character solely from hearing their name and my success rate had been hitherto fairly high. When I first heard that the Year 5 teacher was called Ellie Luck, I had imagined a young, nubile soulmate with a winning smile, ever ready to exchange amusing anecdotes about the little oiks in her class.

Ellie Luck was fifty-nine, a spinster, and had taught at Green Acre for thirty-four years. She had been in the same classroom for the last twenty and had taught Year 5 or 'third years' as they used to be called, for the last twelve. She was not easy to talk to. She dressed as you would expect a 59-year-old spinster teacher to dress, brown cardigans being her garment of choice. She had actively ignored me when I had been introduced to the staff, and when she overheard me proclaiming, with a devil-may-care grin, that I was lucky to have made the INSET day due to a particularly vicious attack of the squits, the look on her face advised severe caution.

'Hi,' I ventured, judging that pleasantries would be infinitely better than my other two options: unbearable silence, or turning round and walking out. 'Nice class?'

'Fine.' If ever one word said 'shut up, you silly little man', Ellie Luck's 'fine' was it. It was an instant conversation stopper and, as I poured my coffee, I felt the seconds plod slowly by. I thought about excusing myself to the toilet, but the squit comment was still well within living memory, and I judged that she might have thought I was taking the piss.

Fortunately, however, just as I could take the deafening silence no longer, I was saved by the bell, literally. Frank Bell was the deputy head of Green Acre and seemed like a nice bloke. He was about forty, lean and athletic, and, while now married, gave every impression of having once been a bit of a playboy. From the little I'd seen of him he clearly had a fabulous rapport with the children – effortlessly reaching that wonderful state that every teacher yearns for, to have the kids laughing and joking, yet working them hard and enjoying mutual respect.

He asked, as any other teacher in the world would have done, how my first morning had been. When I mentioned Robert, all he managed was a playful smile, and the rather mysterious: 'Oh, so you've met our Robert then, have you? Have fun.'

Out of the corner of my eye, I noticed Ellie Luck, who had taught my class the previous year, visibly twitch at the mention of his name. Further enquiries as to the character of 'our Robert' were put on hold, however, as the whistle signalled the end of break.

What to get Year 6 children to write about on that first morning? I was so desperate not to patronise them, yet keen to give them a theme within their experience that they could write about in some depth.

I eventually decided on 'The best day of my life', which, while lacking in originality, gave enough scope for all of them to provide a decent benchmark. Fortunately Mrs Jones, my teaching assistant, worked with Patrick, leaving me clear to hear some readers and watch them work. After a few minutes spent planning, they got writing and I walked around, looking at their work. OK, if I'm honest, I walked around pretending to look at their work, using this as a ruse to eventually look at Robert's title. I was expecting something along the lines of: 'The day I put Hannibal Lecter to shame' or 'The day I finally finished off my shrink'. He didn't notice me arrive, however; he was too busy writing, in exquisite handwriting, about the day his baby sister had arrived.

'When I first set eyes on Hannah I felt a sudden warmth in my heart' was all I could decipher before having to move

on. I was becoming more and more intrigued by this complex character, and resolved to find out more, as soon as I could.

So lunchtime came without further alarms and I quickly settled to read about the birth of Hannah. '... *and the memory of those beautiful eyes will ensure that the day of her birth will always be, "the best day of my life".*' I read the whole piece through three times. I was in no doubt that Robert was a gifted writer, capable of delicate tenderness so unusual in a boy of his age, so why the attitude? Why the steely eyes towards someone whose only crime was to help him in life?

My first afternoon at Green Acre primary school passed without too much incident. During assembly, Mrs Little delivered the traditional 'new beginnings' lecture, doubtless echoed up and down the country by equally well-meaning headteachers.

At the end of the assembly she introduced the whole school to me, adding that she hoped they would all make me feel welcome. The sea of faces that turned my way at this point was somewhat disconcerting. They clearly expected some reaction and for a horrible second I felt like I should have prepared a Churchillian speech, but in that moment of desperation all I could manage was a rather feeble 'Hi', while lifting one hand in the air and pulling it down rather too quickly.

'They size you up ... then they pounce ...'

An afternoon's art ensued, one of those *let's-make-a-quick-display-but-only-use-coloured-pencils-so-as-not-to-cause-too-much-mess* sort of art lessons, and I was pretty pleased with the results.

Mrs Little dutifully called me into her office after school to enquire about my day. We had talked in safe, general terms for a couple of minutes, when, just as I was about to broach the subject of Robert, her phone rang. It soon became clear that this was to be a long call and when she looked up at me with the words: 'See you tomorrow, glad you had a good day,' I left and returned to my room.

It was only then I realised just how tired I was. Being in charge of twenty-six ten-year-olds for a whole day had been unbelievably draining. So I collected the remainder of the 'best day of my life' stories, hopped into my Peugeot, and went back to my flat. I knew that Liam and Tony were unlikely to be back until midnight, so decided to eat unhealthily and have an early night.

At 9.30pm, I turned on my computer. I'd been casually writing a diary since being at university but had resolved to religiously record my first year as a teacher for posterity's sake. Rupert once told me that after particularly gruelling days, he used to write down what he would have liked to have said, or what he would have liked to have happened. Now that sounds like fun ...

'Robert.'
'Yeah.'
'What did you say?'
'I said yeah.'
'I heard you the first time, you fucking little shit.'
Both Robert and the rest of the class 6G looked at me, open-mouthed, in complete silence.
'And if you're ever disrespectful to me again, I'll string you up. Is that clear?'
'Yes, Mr Gray.' The steely eyes had gone. The defiant, daring

face had cracked and he was looking at me with a mixture of complete respect and unbridled fear.

Now that's better ...

2.

Green Acre Primary is a small, one-form-entry village school near one of the suburbs to the north of London. It was opened in 1955 with the intention of schooling all of the children in the village. These were mainly middle-class kids, with professional parents, although a council estate to the east of the village provided almost half of the school's population in 2007. There were now just over 200 children attending the school, whereas twenty years ago there had been nearer 240. This was no reflection on the school itself; indeed, it had a good reputation and its last Ofsted report, in 2003, had been complimentary, especially about the leadership team. This team was still in place four years later, when I joined the school.

Mrs Little was forty-three and had been headteacher at Green Acre for seven years. My initial impression of her was that she would not look out of place in an executive boardroom. While both polite and courteous, she clearly didn't suffer fools gladly. It was rumoured that when she joined the school in 2000 she had said to the staff, in no uncertain terms, that the quality of teaching and learning, the discipline, the tidiness and the general attitude of the place were simply not good enough. Little treats, such as Friday lunch at the pub, were soon stopped because such jollies were deemed to be unprofessional during school hours. It had become abundantly clear that changes were needed, and she wouldn't hesitate to be ruthless and possibly, as a result, unpopular. Her approach clearly worked. Within three years of her appointment all but one of the existing staff had left, and she had replaced them with professional-looking young teachers who shared her philosophy of how a school should be run or, at the very least, made no fuss and worked very hard.

The one exception to the mass exodus had been Ellie Luck. Ellie Luck did not fit in with the young, modern, professional look at all. She didn't smile or generally give off a relaxed, contented air, as everyone else did, and was very much an 'old-school' teacher, who believed that children should be seen but not heard. She had them lined up in rows facing the front, as she delivered from the board. When I was initially shown around the school my first impression of her class (my current one) was that they had had the life sucked out of them. There they all sat, in meek obedience, clearly bored by the history lesson being rammed down their throats. It was quite clear to me that this history lesson was of the worst kind, in which long extracts about how we lived in Victorian times were read to the children, who then filled in the gaps in the infamous 'worksheet'.

Miss Little had visibly winced when she had seen the worksheets – surely this sort of lesson had been exactly what she had taken such great pains to stamp out, seven years before. The relationship between Sandra Little and Ellie Luck fascinated me. Surely Ellie would have been subjected, like anyone else, to rigorous checks on her teaching style, if not her dour personality? I simply could not understand how the lesson I had just witnessed, albeit for a fleeting minute, could still be allowed to happen at Green Acre. I had heard from Frank Bell that Ellie was due to retire at the end of the academic year and could only assume that, as a result, an uneasy truce had developed between her and Sandra. After all, unless the physical abuse of a child is involved, it is extremely difficult to actually sack a teacher. In 2000, Ellie would have been at the school for some twenty-seven years, and clearly she didn't fancy moving on for the last few years of her working life. As I saw it, she had obviously dug in her heels, quietly fended off all the flack hurled at her, and watched with growing resentment as, one by one, her colleagues succumbed to the Sandra Little approach. She obviously saw herself now as a solitary figure gamely sticking to teaching methods that she believed in, while all around her moved further into the twenty-first century. The appointment of me, a slightly cocky 22-year-old who made squit jokes, would simply have pushed her that little bit further away from everyone else. If she hadn't been so unwelcoming, I might have felt sorry for her.

My own journey to Green Acre had been a stumbling one, to say the least. Leaving school at eighteen, with seven modest GCSEs and three even more modest A Levels, I ended up at teacher training college almost for want of something else to do. One might ask, as many did, why choose such a vocational degree if unclear about where you wanted to end up? The truth is, as an eighteen-year-old, three years seemed such an eternity that I think I felt, subconsciously, that I'd worry about that when it was over. Also, there are very few male primary school teachers and, while I would like to claim some altruistic motive of providing young children with at least one male teacher during primary school, a far greater incentive was that the ratio of men to women on the course would give me a sporting chance of at least one girl fancying me. This premise rapidly backfired, however, when all the girls on my course started dating the impossibly well-muscled lads on the sports science course.

College was not without romance, though. Stephanie, a bouncy, friendly, occupational therapist, and Georgina, a rather serious geography student, both gained my affections for a few months. One-night stands and brief liaisons also registered, rather pathetically, as notches on my bedpost, but, in all my three years, I never met anyone with whom I really fell in love.

My college years passed quickly and enjoyably, with the exception of the teaching placements. I hated these. I hated having somebody watching my every move and writing down all my mistakes; one teacher once tutted audibly and shook her head when I was trying to teach. I hated the endless lesson plans and evaluations, and I hated the fact that the children knew that you weren't their real teacher, and often made my life a misery. My final teaching practice, the one with the jovial and jocular beginning, was awful, and I only just passed it. However, I had a very supportive tutor and headteacher who got me through it and, by the very end, my confidence was slowly coming back.

I was mightily surprised, therefore, to get an interview at Green Acre, with its reputation for having a headteacher who expected excellence from her staff. She would have read my references, which would clearly have stated that I had struggled in my final teaching placement, and yet I was still granted the interview. The reason for this was simple. Miss Sharp, whom I replaced, had handed in her notice on the last possible day, owing to her partner's work relocation. By this time, most newly qualified teachers had been snapped up, leaving the few of us who, for whatever reason, had struggled in certain aspects of the course, to fight over any last-minute slots.

When I was shown around before actually applying, I was checking for one thing in particular: someone on the staff who would make a potential girlfriend. Miss Sharp, in Year 6, was leaving so didn't count. Then came Ellie Luck in Year 5, followed by Frank Bell in Year 4, whom I placed slightly higher than Ellie Luck on my shortlist. Mrs Ryan in Year 3, Mrs Cunningham in Year 2 and Mrs Bradshaw in Year 1 were severely handicapped by their titles of 'Mrs'. By this time I was starting to eye up the teaching assistants, but it is quite clearly a prerequisite of being a teaching assistant that you must be in your 40s, married and with at least two kids. In desperation, I started thinking about cleaners, dinner ladies, cooks and lollipop ladies. Then the door of the reception class opened and there she was.

When I first saw Rachel Sanders I knew, instantly, that she must be the one love of my life. She was not classically beautiful but, to me, she was simply lovely. Petite, with shoulder-length honey-blond hair and olive skin, it was the shine in her eyes as I was introduced that really attracted me. Some people have this way of looking at you which makes you feel totally special and, while I knew she was just being polite, I felt like she was regarding me as a long-lost friend. Her ample bosom and wedding-ring-free finger helped, of course, but these were both secondary to those eyes.

'Rachel Sanders, this is Adrian Gray, a prospective candidate.'

'I'm pleased to meet you,' she said.

'Come away with me, have my babies and never, ever leave me,' I replied. Well, not quite. The actual words that came out of my mouth were 'me too', but I meant the former.

From that point on I was desperate for the job. I was gratified when I got the interview, and ecstatic when I saw my one and only rival for the post. Karen Jenkins was, it has to be said, a plain young lady. More than slightly overweight, she looked at you with her mouth open and head slightly to one side. All she needed was a straw hat and she could have passed, quite comfortably, as a village idiot. Not one ounce of charisma exuded from her and I said to myself that if I was considered inferior to her and she got the job, I would kill myself.

Karen wobbled in for the interview first and wobbled out thirty minutes later with the same lop-sided, inane grin.

'Mr Gray?'

I took a deep breath, stood up to all of my five feet seven inches, and marched purposefully into the headteacher's office.

As well as Mrs Little and Mr Bell, there was Eileen Fisher, the Chair of Governors. Well into her fifties, she had a kindly face and put me at ease very quickly. They started with easy, confidence-building questions about me and my interests. 'Football, rugby, golf, travelling and reading.' Nobody said you had to be honest in these interviews. 'Football, getting pissed with Liam and Tony, watching soap operas while eating Wotsits, and naked women' would have been a much more accurate answer but might also have had Mrs Little running after the village idiot and telling her that all had been forgiven.

'So, why have you chosen teaching as a vocation?' was Mr Bell's question. I knew this one was coming, and I also knew that, in answering, I needed to achieve a delicate balance. I didn't want to sound completely blasé, virtually shrugging my shoulders and chuntering on about long holidays and that it beat packing shelves. But then again, I also didn't want to come across as a desperate Miss World contestant who, while shedding designer tears, extols the virtues of giving a little bit back in society and helping all the needy children on our precious planet.

'I love children. I love working with them and I genuinely feel that I can make a difference to their lives. Also, there aren't enough male primary school teachers and I think it very important that kids should have some male influence before going to secondary school. Many kids out there don't have a father figure at home, and to be able to be that stable male, albeit only at school, must be a good thing.'

Oh well, a bit closer to Miss World than I'd planned, but I think I got away with it.

The vibes in the room seemed to be quite good and I answered questions about classroom management and classroom control smoothly. Then Mrs Little asked why, specifically, I wanted to work at Green Acre. She was watching me intently now, and I somehow felt that my answer would be pivotal to whether I was appointed. I knew, of course, what I wanted to say, but I felt, on careful reflection, that praise for Rachel's breasts would probably not endear me to the panel.

'In the few schools that I've been in,' I began, maintaining cool eye contact with Mrs Little, 'it's been very clear, very early on, what sort of atmosphere they give off. In some schools, tensions, disinterest, and bad behaviour are instantly apparent, but at Green Acre there is a fabulous atmosphere. The staff are all friendly yet hardworking, the children are keen to learn and get through their school day with smiles on their faces. I honestly feel that I could fit in here and would relish the opportunity of working in such a tight-knit school.' *What a load of bollocks.*

However, it seemed to do the trick, as she nodded thoughtfully, in that 'yes, interesting answer' sort of way. I was now really warming to this, and was absolutely not ready for the next question, which momentarily threw me.

'Obviously, we have taken up your references and tried to find out a little about you,' began Mrs Fisher slowly. I didn't like the sound of this. She spoke in a manner which suggested that an awkward subject was about to be broached. It was. 'It appears that you had, er, certain difficulties in your final teaching practice. In fairness to you, you went some way towards overcoming these and eventually passed, but what I'd like to ask is what you feel that you've learnt from this experience?'

I was completely rattled by this. At interviews, as I've been told many times, you need to play to your strengths and only mention the positives. Now here was a question demanding, in no uncertain terms, that I spoke about my shortcomings.

'Er, well, hmm – I think I learnt, erm, that's to say – you know – clearly one or two things went awry at first but by the end I think things were OK.' It was an appalling answer that didn't even begin to broach the question asked, and I knew I wasn't going to get away with it.

'What sort of things?' she asked gently.

I took a moment before answering. 'I think it took a little while for me to gain their respect. At first perhaps, I think, I dunno, I tried to be somewhat over-friendly with them, and maybe I needed to assert my authority a bit more at first. It's an important lesson to learn, but I think I've learnt it.'

She smiled. 'Thank you very much, Mr Gray.'

It's funny, but at that moment I felt certain they were going to offer me the job. One moment of honesty and humility, however hard it had been initially to swallow, had gained me a lot of points. Any cockiness I had built up, however, had instantly evaporated with that question, and I answered the rest of the questions as humbly as I felt. When I finally left the room a great relief surged through me, the pressures of the interview instantly lifting.

Mrs Little phoned me at 4.30 that afternoon and offered me the job. When I hear something which pleases me or boosts my ego, my natural response is to say something which I perceive to be witty, and this occasion was no different. The words: 'so, Tweedledum turned you down then, eh?' were actually on my lips when I decided, prudently, to abort the wisecrack.

My initial elation at being offered the job was tempered somewhat by her next comment. 'The contract will initially be for one year, when we will discuss the possibility of making it permanent. Is that OK?'

No, actually Mrs Little, that is not OK. What you are saying, in thinly disguised terms, is that there was no one better so I will have to do: 'Give us a year to find someone half-decent and you can sod off.'

'Yes, Mrs Little, that's perfectly fair.'

'Very few full-time contracts are offered to first-year teachers,' she went on, as if trying to justify the decision, 'but we have every confidence that you'll still be with us in a year's time.'

'No, no, of course, Mrs Little, I understand.'

'Actually – and I hope you take this as a compliment – we'd like you to take Year 6 next year.'

'I beg your pardon?'

'Year 6. I know it's slightly unusual for a newly qualified teacher to teach Year 6 first up but, with support, I'm quite sure you're up to it.' There was a pause, which I was clearly expected to fill. It may, in some circumstances, be considered a compliment to be offered the responsibility of guiding ten- and eleven-year-olds through their last year at primary school. What with all the pressure of achieving good SATs results, the responsibility of setting good examples to the rest of the school, and the fact that Year 6 are very often complete little bastards – yes, it could very much have been considered a huge compliment and vote of confidence.

On the other hand – and I know where my money lies – it might be that no one else wanted them. Ellie Luck had just taught them, and another year with her would result, almost certainly, in mass suicide among their ranks. Mr Bell, the obvious candidate, had just spent five years in Year 6 and had only just last year changed to Year 4; and all the rest of the teachers were more infant-orientated.

'Wow,' I said at last. 'I didn't expect that, but no, that's fine, I'm sure I'll enjoy it.'

'Thank you, Adrian. I won't pretend there aren't a few lively characters in there, but generally they're a really nice bunch and keen to learn.'

It was only after we'd said our goodbyes that I started having serious reservations about this idea. After all, the problems I'd had with control on my teaching practice had been with Year 4. There is a term that I've heard mentioned by many teachers called 'Year 6-itus' which describes the tendency of this year group, as they approach secondary school, to realise that primary-school regimes are a little beneath them. A surliness and cockiness sets in, which needs skilled and firm handling by an experienced teacher.

No problem there, then.

And I didn't like the phrase 'lively characters' either.

'What an excellent idea, Miss Luck. By re-enacting a Dickensian-style scene you really give them a "feel" of how life must have been like in Victorian Britain.'

'I'm sorry, I don't underst– '

'Miss Luck, this is inspired teaching. Look at the expressions of sheer boredom you've managed to put on their faces. And your Victorian dress sense – that attention to detail, that extraordinary dedication – no wonder you've been here for all these years. No wonder Mrs Little was so keen to keep you.'

3.

'Robert Carlton, now there's a tragic case.'

'Robert? Tragic?'

We were talking in Mrs Little's office shortly before the start of my second day. She grimaced. 'From his first day at our school, back in reception, it was obvious that Robert was something special. He was placed on our gifted and talented register from day one and I listened open-mouthed as this prodigious and articulate young five-year-old introduced himself. His language skills, even then, were on a par with many of our Key Stage 2 children, and now are better than most adults'. While he could be rather awkward and occasionally defiant – not unusual for such a precocious talent – he was essentially a lovely boy.'

'Was?' I was listening to her intently now, waiting for a bombshell that I felt sure was coming. Mrs Little paused for several seconds before she sighed and continued.

'When he was five, his sister, Hannah, was born. I have never seen a child of his age so besotted with a baby sibling. He would not only talk about her constantly, he had even been known to spend entire playtimes looking at his photo album. When she was two years old, Hannah was killed by a hit-and-run motorist.'

I felt a sliver of ice slide down my back.

'His mother was taking her to the shops and, as she turned to lock the front door, Hannah ran out into the road and was knocked over. Despite a nationwide appeal, national press coverage and several false leads, the driver of the car was never found. One can only imagine the effect that something like that would have on a family. Combine that with the unusually close bond between brother and sister and you can vaguely begin to see how Robert's world became totally screwed up. As far as I know, he never shed one tear for his sister. Initially, his defence mechanism was to completely withdraw into himself, and he didn't speak a word for several weeks. Anger and resentment followed and his behaviour in school was appalling. It is a massive dilemma, you know, as a headteacher, to decide how to discipline such behaviour. On the one hand I felt such sympathy for him, and could understand his anger. On the other hand, though, I had the rest of the school to consider. There was one time, a couple of years ago, when he viciously kicked a girl two years younger than him in an unprovoked attack. He looked at me impassively when I tried to question his motives, and I had no option but to suspend him.

'Since his suspension, he has improved somewhat. I think he actively wanted someone to be firm and, seemingly, unsympathetic to his plight. He had had so much sympathy that he had simply had enough of people being nice to him.

'He's still awkward, of course, still bitter and still angry. He can be confrontational for the sake of it and totally unpredictable. He has a great mistrust of strangers, perhaps not surprisingly, and that is how he will view you at present. Give him time to get to know you Adrian, and don't mollycoddle him whatever you do – he'll walk all over you. Be firm with him and he'll eventually learn to respect you.'

I remembered Ellie Luck's wince at the mention of his name.

'How did he get on last year?'

'Miss Luck and Robert did not get on,' she replied simply.

'He's very ready for a new challenge.'

I took a deep breath, remembering the words in his story. *'The memory of those beautiful eyes'* suddenly had a totally different meaning. 'Oh my God!' I said out loud.

'I know it's tragic, Adrian, but it happened a long time ago. Life goes on.'

I couldn't tell her that my 'Oh my God' was not so much an expression of sympathy, but more a sudden recollection of what I had written about his work. *'This is outstanding writing, Robert. Your sister must be an angel.'* The hideous irony of that statement would not be lost on Robert. Nor, when his parents read it, would the fact that his new teacher had not bothered to read his records before starting to teach him. Being keen to establish good relationships with him, I had handed his and a few others back to them at the end of the day. Had he bothered to read the comments I had put? Was there still time to Tippex out the offending line and replace it? How would I find out? I could hardly ask him, as this would only highlight the problem. As my brain tried to conjure up an answer, Mrs Little changed the subject.

'So, apart from Robert, everything else OK yesterday? I'm sorry I didn't really get a chance to speak to you properly. How were the twins?'

'The twins. Oh, is that Shannon and Sean? They weren't in yesterday.'

'Ah.'

In that one word Mrs Little told me that Shannon and Sean Williams were going to be trouble. The intonation definitely said: *'Right, you'd better sit down for this one ...'*

'I shan't pretend otherwise, Adrian, Shannon and Sean can be hard work. They can be quite aggressive at times and we've had many complaints about them from parents whose children have been upset by their – antics. Unfortunately, there's not too much parental support, either. Dad in particular tends to believe their side of the story, rather than ours. You'll have to watch them, Adrian, and if you do have any problems let me or Frank know straight away.'

I was beginning to feel that I had allowed myself to be lulled into a false sense of security, after yesterday's reasonably trouble-free day.

'Don't get me wrong, Adrian, they're not complete monsters – and I'm sure Sean in particular will relate to you as a man. He's a very good footballer and, as you're taking on the football club, that will be an ideal forum for your relationship to grow. If he respects you as a football coach, he's far more likely to respect you as a teacher. For both of them, though, be firm but whatever you do don't put them down in public. They don't respond kindly to that.'

On this rather disconcerting note, I went back to my class and found Robert's English book in his tray. I don't know quite what I was expecting – a note at the front along the lines of '*I haven't had a chance to read your comments on my work yet, although I'm looking forward to doing so.*' What to do? I couldn't even really ask anybody's advice because I blamed myself squarely for not having read his records (a point that I'm sure was not lost on Mrs Little). The bell was due to go in five minutes. It was now or never. If he hadn't read the comment then he would do so in a few moments. I made my decision. After carefully Tippexing out the offending sentence, I changed it, rather lamely, to: '*Your grasp of the English language is excellent.*' I then returned it to his tray and hoped.

I was relieved when, marking the register ten minutes later, there was still no sign of the twins. Perhaps they'd left and gone to mind a different patch. I watched Robert carefully as he read the comments in his book. The quizzical look on his face was not good. He walked over to me and I gulped audibly.

'You've changed your comments on my work. Why have you done that?'

It was a truly horrible moment. I knew that if I didn't justify my actions he might explode, and if he thought I was in some way mocking him (which, given all I'd heard about him, was a distinct possibility), he might physically attack me. I also knew that I couldn't defend myself. All I could do was tell something like the truth – a dreadful thing for a teacher to have to admit to, when trying to establish respect.

'I – well, it's difficult to explain, Robert.'

The expression on his face was impossible to read.

'Er, when I read your work, Robert – and it's excellent, by the way – I wrote down what I thought about it, but then I just thought – you know – calling her an angel might, well – '

'It's just that I thought what you wrote was really nice. She'll always be an angel to me.'

'I know she will, Robert. I was just a little concerned that you might take it the wrong way.'

He continued to look at me for several moments while I tried to assess whether any more explanation was necessary, but then he gave a hint of a smile and went back to the work I'd just set them. This child, as Mrs Little had said, was certainly unpredictable: snarling and confrontational yesterday without a specific reason, yet accepting and verging on showing warmth today, when he could have felt justified in venting his anger on me.

I'd asked the class to work silently and, for fifteen minutes or so, they did, before pockets of discussion broke out. I silenced them again but the noise level quickly got back to a point where I needed to do something. Some of the children were obviously talking about their work – character appraisals from the poem 'The Highwayman' – but a few of the girls had put their pencils down and were clearly talking about something else. Charlie, Kate and Rozinder had produced very little in yesterday's written task and were following suit today.

'Girls,' I said, looking straight at them. 'I asked you to get on with your work silently. Will you do so, please?'

'Yeah, in a minute.' Kate Robinson clearly had no qualms about speaking to her teacher like this and I knew I had to act.

'I beg your pardon, Kate?' I said. Perhaps not the most original reprimand, and one which I had seen used many times, but I usually found it did the trick. I fully expected a passive: 'Sorry sir'.

'This work's boring, I'm having a little break.'

Oh, shit. Shit, shit, shit. I knew that a confrontation was inevitable at some point, but the bookies had stopped taking bets on it being Robert Carlton whom I would meet first in the ring.

'I'm sorry you find it boring, Kate,' I ventured. 'Perhaps I can find you something more interesting to do?' As soon as the words had come out of my mouth I knew that it had been the wrong thing to say. A tutor had once advised me to never use sarcasm as a means to discipline a child and I was about to find out why.

'Oh, thank you,' said Kate, smiling. 'We've just been talking about *Big Brother* – you know, practising our speaking and listening skills. All right if we carry on?' And they laughed – all of the class laughed *with* Kate Robinson, and *at* me.

I'd promised myself I wasn't going to do it, but I couldn't help myself. In a voice that made everyone jump, I roared, 'How dare you speak to me like that! Move your things and sit in front of me where I can see you, and I'll talk to you during your break.'

This was it. This was that defining moment when I would either restore a bit of respect, or she would call my bluff. Kate was clearly quite a confident child and I really did not know what I would have done if she had blatantly defied me at that moment. I don't think I'd have had any choice but to call for Mrs Little and I would have been labelled, on day two, as the teacher who needed to call the Head to bail him out.

Whether it was the shock of hearing me raise my voice for the first time, or simply that she wasn't actually that bad a child, she picked up her work and obeyed my command. The look on her face, though, was thunderous as she loudly slammed her books down – her one gesture of defiance. The rest of the class had been completely silenced by the incident and continued to work silently until break. During this time I felt myself physically shaking at the prospect of having to be a constant authority with the children, never knowing when my bluff would be called.

At break time I called Kate over, determined to establish a truce, even if it was an uneasy one.

'I'm sorry I shouted at you, Kate,' I began, 'but you must understand that you really can't talk to me like that.'

'Sorry, sir.'

I tried to gauge her attitude from those two words. Was this a *'I really am sorry and I don't know what came over me'* sort of sorry, or a *'I'd much rather tell you to fuck off, you stupid little weasel of a man'* sort of sorry? I decided not to probe any further, for fear of concluding that it was the latter.

'Very well, Kate, we'll say no more about it – you can go out to play.' She went without a further word, or any further indications of her true feelings, and I suddenly realised how desperate I was for a very strong dose of caffeine.

Rachel was not in the staffroom again and I found myself exchanging pleasantries with Irene Cunningham, a friendly if rather dull woman in her early forties. She told me in jovial terms about her Year 2 class being a little chatty and I found myself saying something along the same lines. I was feeling, however, rather shell-shocked by the morning's events and, again, weariness took over me. I was so relieved that it was Friday. A two-day opening week was more than enough for me.

'Well, it's like this, doctor. I'm a fit and reasonably athletic 22-year-old who has been a teacher for the best part of a day and a quarter. I'm completely knackered and worried about becoming burnt out. Can you sign me off for a long holiday?'

When I came back into the class I was surprised to see a 16-year-old girl in the cloakroom dressed as if ready to go clubbing. Assuming she was an older sister, come perhaps to pick up her sibling for a dental appointment, I said, 'Can I help you?'

'What?'

'Can I help you? I'm Mr Gray and this is my class. Who do you want to pick up?'

She looked me up and down in silence, with a look of contempt.

'Mr Gray,' said Alice, 'this is Shannon. She's in our class.' I just stood there in stupefied silence. There was no way that this girl could possibly be 10 years old. Not only was she physically very mature for her age, but she had no difficulty in staring me out in a manner that clearly suggested that I was somewhat inferior to her.

Someone had asked me once why I hadn't chosen to teach PE at secondary school, and I had answered, with some feeling, that the thought of teaching a bunch of adolescent girls was my idea of a nightmare. Well, here was that adolescent girl now, cunningly disguised as a 10-year-old. I fully expected her mobile phone to ring at any moment, and for her to then spend the next two hours explaining to Jade how Nathan had dumped her again for that slag Paige.

'Oh, I'm sorry, Shannon; it's just the non-school uniform ...'
'Right.'
No explanation was forthcoming as to why the school uniform was lacking, but I knew I couldn't walk on eggshells for her, even though I desperately wanted to.
'So, where is your uniform, Shannon?'
'It's not sorted yet. We only got back from holiday last night.'
I looked at my watch – stupid mistake.
'Late last night.' She didn't quite say *and what are you going to do about it?*' but she might as well have done.
'OK, I'll look forward to seeing you in uniform tomorrow. Is Sean here?'
She shrugged. 'I dunno. I think he's still in bed.'
The last thing I wanted was another confrontation, so I directed her to her tray, and the class listened as we started our maths work. Thankfully it was a peaceful session and Robert, Kate and Shannon, as well as everyone else, got on well with their work.

I ate my lunch in my room for fear of yet another awkward situation and, just as I finished it, there was a knock at my door and my mood was significantly lifted.
'Can I come in?' smiled Rachel. 'How are the little bastards?' she asked sweetly.
'Bastards.'
And in that one opening exchange a definite relationship had formed. She smiled again as though I had just saved her life.
'I'm sorry I haven't really had a chance to say hello. That reception lot do tend to be a bit clingy, and that's just the mums.'
'So, nice lot?' I ventured, relaxing all the time. Thus followed a pleasant twenty minutes relating our first day and a half. She gasped in a mixture of horror and relief as I related the 'little angel' tale, and seemed genuinely interested in all I had

to say. Her own tales of little Johnny cacking his pants and Danny's mum demanding ten kisses from 'mummy's best soldier' before she left him were equally interesting, and I was just contemplating how I might ask her out for a casual cup of coffee, when she spoke again.

'Lovely as this is, I'd really better get back. I promised I'd phone Alan before one o'clock.'

'Alan?' I hoped the note of desperation was not too obvious.

'My boyfriend,' she smiled as she went through the door. 'See you later.'

All of the disappointments, alarms and concerns of the morning paled into insignificance at this news. I could feel a surge of self-pity go through me as I wondered why I had been naive enough to even vaguely think that she might not only be single, but might actually fancy me. I had been looking forward to the afternoon session. I had always been interested in history and felt I could convey the events of World War II with passion and excitement. After Rachel, however, I simply couldn't bring myself to muster the said enthusiasm and the session limped on.

It was, however, punctuated by one magnificent moment. Mr Adams, the peripatetic guitar teacher, taught on Friday afternoons in a little annexe next to my classroom. He was almost a parody of some terrible 70s disc jockey with his high-pitched, whiny voice (he actually said _'Okeee Dokeeee'_). His hair looked like it had been cut with shears and, such were his facial features, it looked like his whole head had been put on upside down. Apart from this, he was completely tone deaf, but didn't seem to notice. He was busy teaching some poor soul the tune and lyrics to 'Maxwell's Silver Hammer', when Alice came up to ask me about her work.

'Mr Gray, on my sheet it has the word 'atrocities'. What's an atrocity?'

'The word atrocity means a truly terrible thing, Alice. In the war the Nazis committed terrible atrocities all over Europe.' At this moment there came an almighty screeching from the annexe as Mr Adams got to the chorus of 'Maxwell's Silver Hammer'. In a voice that would have done credit to a chicken being strangled, he let out a piercing 'Na-na-na-na-nahhh.'

I shouldn't have done it. It was unprofessional but I couldn't resist it. The timing was just too perfect: 'Talking of which ...'

I caught Alice's eye and the pair of us just erupted in laughter. All around us people were looking, wondering what was so funny, but it was one of those 'you had to be there' moments, and quite hilarious. It really cheered me up.

I suddenly realised, when it was time for PE, that I didn't know the protocol for a mixed-sex class of ten-year-olds getting changed. They obviously couldn't do so in the annexe, for fear of being deafened. There was no alternative but for all of them to get changed together, and I was worried about how some of the girls, Shannon in particular, would react to having to change with their male teacher in the classroom. In the end I took the boys to one end of the room and we all turned our backs, but this did not quell my uneasiness. I was clearly at the mercy of any girl who decided to make my life difficult. If they caused a rumpus, messed about, threw things, shouted, what would I do? Would I try to discipline them with my back to them, or turn round and risk all sorts of reprisals when a young girl told of being spied on by her male teacher? Apart from anything else, I just felt a complete idiot, standing with my back to half the class, occasionally asking if it was OK to turn around yet, as though they were preparing a surprise at a party. Shannon, of course, didn't have her kit with her and the rest of the girls, in the event, got ready without fuss. I was fully aware of the potential for trouble, however, and resolved to discuss the situation with Mrs Little.

By the end of the day, when I wished them an enjoyable weekend and said goodbye, I felt that their respect, for which I craved so much, and which had appeared to be slipping earlier in the day, had, to some extent, returned.

I turned my mind to happier thoughts. Friday night was 'going-out-with-Liam-and-Tony-and-getting-pissed' night, and I had no intention of breaking this habit. When I got home I poured myself a stiff whisky, got into a hot bath, and reflected on things which were not to be ...

'Adrian?'

'Speaking.'

'Oh, hi Adrian. I'm sorry to disturb you at home, but I just had to talk to someone.'

'Rachel! Are you OK?'

'Not really. It's Alan. He's left me for an older woman. Oh Adrian, he's going out with Ellie Luck!'

'Oh Rachel, I'm so sorry, is there anything I can do?'

'It's just – I don't fancy being on my own tonight. I'd just cooked this romantic, candle-lit meal for two when he told me the news. Would you come and eat with me, Adrian?'

'Of course I will, Rachel. I was only going to go out to the pub with the boys.'

'And you'd cancel that for me? Oh Adrian, you are wonderful. And Adrian, as you were planning on drinking anyway, why don't you leave the car here and stay the night with me ...'

4.

'Adrian, you complete bastard.' Liam's voice echoed from the bathroom. 'I know you're a smelly little shit, but does it really take a complete bath full of water to scrub off your scum, leaving no hot water for me?'

As could easily be gleaned from his friendly manner, Liam was my best mate. We had met in our first week at college, being in the same halls of residence, and had quickly found that we shared the same interests in life – football, drinking and women. We shared various flats and houses together from our second year at college. Tall and good-looking, this trainee barrister had infuriated me on many occasions by letting me put in a couple of hours of spadework chatting up a girl, buying her drinks and listening to her go on, while he chatted to mates, danced or got pissed, showing an apparent lack of interest in my gentle seduction. Just as I was ready to suggest to my prospective date that we go somewhere a little quieter, he would saunter in, get chatting and her interest in me would suddenly wane. If I complained to him afterwards that such behaviour hardly befitted a 'best mate', he would just smile and say that it wasn't his fault if women fell at his feet. Too many such scenarios would probably have strained our friendship to breaking point, but luckily Naomi came along and saved it. This womanising man was suddenly completely besotted by the beautiful Naomi and he never looked back. They were engaged a year ago and are due to marry next Easter. Perhaps as some sort of recompense for all his earlier date-snaffling, he has asked me to be his best man.

We got to know Tony well into our final year, when he moved into our flat. George, our previous flatmate, had smoked one joint too many so Liam and I politely suggested he should go. Tony, an English student, immediately settled in and the three of us became inseparable. Slightly overweight and not in any shape or form the male model material embodied by Liam, he made up for any lack of physical prowess by making us all laugh with his closely observed insights into life. While Liam and I were both pursuing our chosen careers this year, Tony jovially announced he wanted to take a year off from thinking, and was now enjoying himself packing books in a factory.

We had been in our current flat for nearly a year now, and it still smacked heavily of being a student pad. Permanent smells of curry and cigarettes as well as an unhealthy collection of tinned convenience food gave any visitor a pretty instant indication of our lifestyle. The sight of mis-matching furniture, numerous old copies of *Viz* magazine and a rather revealing poster of Maria Sharapova hardly detracted from this image. Only a copy of *Pride and Prejudice*, fresh flowers and a bowl of pot-pourri, all in Liam's room, gave any hint of female occupation.

The Coach and Horses was our regular Friday night haunt and we ambled in punctually at 8 p.m. Part of my role as best man, according to Naomi, was to lead Liam away from temptation and, while I was sure he wouldn't be unfaithful to her, old habits die hard. The habit, upon entrance, of surveying a pub for groups of single girls was so ingrained in him that he simply couldn't stop himself. As Tony went to the bar to order the first round, Liam's trained eye quickly took in the three groups of single girls and weighed up all the relevant criteria in a matter of seconds. Looks, body language and proximity of available seats all had to be factored into the equation. It says a lot for our relationship that Tony and I, the two single ones, were never consulted in this process. However, we trusted his judgement, which had often paid dividends in the past. Indeed, since Naomi, there had been a perverse role-reversal in the chatting-up department. Whereas before Liam was not interested in the chase, knowing with arrogant certainty that the catch would happen regardless, he now saw it as his role to use his charms to create an atmosphere where a group of us flirted and chatted naturally. He would then time the moment, usually just before ordering drinks, to casually mention Naomi, hoping that they would not make their excuses and disappear. There was no room for manly pride here. I have studied, on many occasions, the body language of women when Liam removes himself from the situation. There is always disappointment, occasionally a rather brazen and, in my opinion, extremely rude, *'Right, I'm off then'*, but more often a slightly disgusted glance between themselves followed by an equally disgusted look at Tony and me. If they don't actually say the words *'well, better than nothing'*, they may as well do. This is slightly worse for Tony than for me as he is fat and pretty ugly, while I am not without some physical charms, but that we are happy to let Liam set us up like this does show our combined desperation.

Our selected pair today did not look especially promising. The best things they had going for them were that (a) there were two of them and (b) there were seats in close proximity. A far more promising group, younger, more attractive and altogether livelier, sat at the other end of the bar, but there were no available seats. So, short of sitting on their laps, which even by Liam's standards would be a little forward, they were non-starters. The two we sat near were both much older than us, probably in their early thirties, and were silently drinking white wine. Not that our plan was to dive straight in – we always spent the first hour or so getting mildly drunk and exchanging stories from the week, especially, as was now the case, when we saw very little of each other before Friday night.

Naturally, the main topic of conversation was my first two days at Green Acre. I related all the amusing tales, with ample embellishment to increase the comic effect, and was encouraged by lots of appreciative laughter. I then started telling them some of the things that I would have liked to have said, especially to Ellie Luck, Robert, Kate, Shannon, Allard and, for totally different reasons, Rachel. They both chipped in with potential ideas and when Tony suggested that Shannon should have been ordered to do PE in her knickers as she had forgotten her kit, we all roared with laughter.

'Excuse me.'

We all turned to look at the more pompous-looking of the two silent women, who was staring directly at me with a po-faced expression.

'Yes?'

'I couldn't help listening to your conversation, and I have to say that I'm appalled at what I've heard. I'm a special needs teacher, and the way you've been laughing at that dyslexic boy in your class, quite frankly, makes me feel sick. Don't you feel, as a qualified teacher, that you should show a little more professionalism than that?'

I suddenly felt a surge of anger at this busybody, and was about to let rip when Tony chirped up:

'So, I suppose a shag's out of the question then?' This, while hardly original, was perfectly timed and made me laugh out loud.

'Listen,' I began, buoyed up by Tony's quip. 'I'm in a pub, right? On a Friday night, right? With my mates. I'm doing what anybody else on a Friday night down the pub would do, chatting about work. Whatever I say about anyone has got nothing to do with you and if you feel like sticking your nose in 'cos you've got nothing better to talk about yourself, well that's hardly my fault now, is it?'

Throughout this she had looked at me with something like contempt, and her parting sentence stung. 'Well, I just hope you never teach my children, that's all.'

'Yeah, like you're ever likely to have any.'

The reaction to this comment was electric. While Liam and Tony laughed, she whirled back at me, with tears in her eyes and shouted 'What did you say?' She then slammed her drink down and almost ran out of the pub. Her friend followed, chipping in with a terse 'You bastard' as she left.

Tony and Liam thought this exchange was hilarious, and even applauded them out of the pub. I did not find it hilarious at all. I have, as many people keep telling me, lots of faults. I'm untidy, I lose things and I take the piss out of people all the time, but I'm pretty sure I'm not nasty. My last comment to that woman, however much provoked, was downright nasty and it had made her cry. While I still felt strongly that a Friday pub chat should not have to be explained, and while her comments to me were also pretty damning, I made, albeit on the spur of the moment, a comment designed to belittle and insult her. That the comment had succeeded quite so dramatically only made me feel all the more guilty. Part of me wanted to run outside, find her and apologise unreservedly, although she would almost certainly be in her car and out of sight. The other two options were to either make my excuses and head off for an early night, or get totally and completely pissed ...

At 3.30 the following morning, with my head suspended over the toilet seat and my stomach exacting revenge for the eight pints of lager and the chicken madras to the accompaniment of Tristan Adams screeching 'Maxwell's Silver Hammer' in my brain, I experienced a life-changing moment. It occurred to me, while my stomach was preparing for another onslaught, that maybe now was the time to grow up a little and act more in accordance with my professional standing. I didn't mean 'I'll never drink again' – I was just lucid enough to realise the futility of such a resolution, and I was sure I would still have laughs with the boys, flirt with girls and occasionally have further midnight rendezvous with the toilet. But ... *'I just hope you never teach my children.'*

However unsubstantiated that comment was, it had really hurt and I suddenly felt a desire to show the sort of dedication and professionalism that she clearly felt I lacked. I wanted to meet her again in six months' time with a dossier of notes proving what a difference I had made to these children's lives and proving that, under my guidance, Patrick had made remarkable progress and now showed sufficient self-confidence and self-belief to start secondary school with his head held high.

And then there was Rachel. Rachel was only one year older than me but, while she had grown up and become a living credit to her profession, I was still every inch the beer-swilling, adolescent student. I could imagine her evening – a candle-lit dinner party for friends, with just enough wine to create sophisticated laughter and a relaxed ambience. Later, feeling mildly light-headed, she would clear away the crockery, leaving her house looking immaculate, before taking Alan's hand and leading him up to bed. In the morning she would wake without a hangover, ready to begin her hectic weekend.

Her life, as I saw it, was a million miles away from mine. While I held only unlikely dreams of ever sharing that life romantically, I really wanted us to become friends, and to see each other socially. How could I ever invite her back to my flat in its current state, or show her my room which, at present, had chicken madras seeping into the carpet?

I have heard many people talk of life-changing moments or experiences in their life, but a head-down-the-toilet one must be verging on unique. I even managed a half-smile at this and, somehow, this new-found self managed to climb back into bed and fall into a deep slumber.

'You really are one lazy slob.' The words seeped into my waking brain, and as the curtains were unceremoniously swept aside, letting the brilliant September sunshine flood in, I woke with a start. 'Here, I brought you an orange juice. I thought maybe you might want to consider seizing the day, now that only half of it is left.' She handed me my orange juice, smiled, and surveyed the scene of carnage that was my bedroom.

'You know what, Adrian, you really do need a woman. Who's going to mother you and bring you up something eggy for breakfast when Liam and I aren't around?'

Naomi Rogers really was a fabulous human being. Not only was she absolutely gorgeous to look at, she was down to earth and didn't think twice about waking me up at midday on a Saturday, not knowing what state of déshabillé she might find me in. Very much one of the lads, she would have been more than welcome on our weekly Friday night jaunts, and would have thoroughly enjoyed herself, but she was sensitive enough not to want to step into the 'boys only' arena, and we all respected her greatly for that. In fact, had I not just fallen madly in love with Rachel, I would have stolen her from Liam and married her myself. That would have shown him.

I was slightly gratified to see both Liam and Tony looking about as healthy as me as we sat round the brunch table nursing hangovers. After forcing down some toast and tea, dutifully provided by Naomi, I felt slightly better and began telling the three of them of my resolution to grow up.

'This afternoon,' I announced with grim determination, 'the lovely Maria will be removed from my wall, to be replaced by a tasteful Ikea print; new linen will grace my bed and I shall hire an industrial vacuum cleaner with which, out of the kindness of my heart, I will attack the whole of the flat. Those who would like to help are welcome, but by the end of this weekend our flat is going to be a place which we can look upon with pride.'

There was a pause of perhaps thirty seconds as the three of them tried to digest this news. After ascertaining that I was actually me, and not a hitherto unknown identical twin who had implausibly changed places with me, they started to question my motives. As I explained my 'seeing the light' episode in the toilet, their initial shock changed to an 'I'll believe that when I see it' frown. However, I was adamant that this was the first chapter of the new me, and Naomi, for one, seemed pretty impressed. She instantly cancelled her plans for that afternoon and promised to take me to Ikea. Even Tony and Liam agreed that the flat was a contamination area and vowed to work on the kitchen and lounge while we were out.

By Sunday evening I looked back over our labours with real pride. The flat had been scrubbed and dusted, vacuumed and polished and, for my part at least, many ties to the student life had been sacrificed. Maria Sharapova, my *Viz* collection, and even my 'Fantasy league' 2002 winner's trophy had gone, to be replaced by cheap but relatively adult purchases – plants that actually required looking after, matching cutlery sets and candles.

I was under no illusion, however, that this tangible change of scenery would automatically change me as a person. As

Naomi left for her house on Sunday night, the words 'I'll give it three days' echoed menacingly. Somehow, I couldn't see us sipping sherry and eating vol-au-vents just yet, but it was a start, and I went to bed on Sunday night looking forward to school the next day.

'So haven't you got some dyslexic kid in your class?' prompted Tony, clearly keen to provoke some more laughs. 'Isn't that a bit of a nightmare, when you have to try to decipher his homework?'

'Who? Patrick? No, honestly, Tony, Patrick's a great kid. I spend several hours every day planning things for him, talking to him, helping him write. You know, Tony ...'

'Excuse me?' The more pompous-looking of the two girls next to us was looking straight at me. 'I'm a special needs teacher and I couldn't help overhearing you talking about that dyslexic boy in your class. I'd just like to say how impressed I am with your obvious devotion to duty ...'

5.

And so I settled into my new life as Year 6 teacher at Green Acre Primary School. Sean arrived on Monday morning and looked me up and down in a measured, calculating manner, before silently finding his books and sitting where Allard had previously sat, next to Josh. It spoke volumes about the pecking order within the class that Allard, big and potentially quite nasty, quietly sat elsewhere. It clearly never occurred to Sean to enquire whether anyone was already sitting there, he simply exuded a quiet assurance that what he wanted, he got. He stood well over five feet tall and his quiet, mature demeanour was genuinely scary. I would have much preferred a loud, obnoxious joker who could be quietened down, but his careful scrutiny of his surroundings suggested one who was biding his time.

I noticed an instant change in Patrick when he saw that Sean had returned. He looked absolutely terrified and kept his distance as much as he could. While Sean didn't appear to notice him, there had clearly been some previous encounters here, and I resolved to watch out for any further incidents.

As the first full week wore on, I began to feel a little less tense and as though, more or less, the children were on my side. For the first two days I was actively waiting for a time when my authority would be challenged; it made me feel mentally and physically drained. As I relaxed a little, though, so did the class, and the atmosphere improved. This was not to say that everyone behaved perfectly, of course. Robert continued to be unpredictable. While never quite charming, he could produce work that took your breath away. Equally, and for no apparent reason, he'd be awkward, rude and completely uncooperative. I learnt quickly that he was not the type of child to ignore. On Monday, he clearly didn't want to work and sat there arms crossed, virtually daring me to comment. When I ignored him, he started tapping his ruler deliberately, wanting to provoke a reaction. So I reacted. I crossed over to him, stared him in the eye and, mustering all available authority, said: 'OK, Sunshine. I've no idea what you think is acceptable or what you have been used to getting away with and, quite frankly, I don't care. All I know is that this rubbish won't wash with me, all right?' Again, the whole class were listening and, again, it was a defining moment. He looked me squarely in the eye, seemingly knowing that by stalling his reaction he would make me sweat until, slowly, and silently, he picked up his pen and started work. As Mrs Little had said, no mollycoddling.

Kate, Charlie and Rozinder continued to annoy me with their singular lack of interest in anything to do with school. I'd tried the *'you're going to come down to earth with a bang if you think that that work is acceptable'* routine, which had been met with glassy indifference. Kate, obviously the ringleader, wasn't, as I had hoped, 'a nice girl really' and the three of them clearly saw me as some sort of threat to their one and only reason for coming to school – gossip. I hated the way that Kate looked at me whenever I moved them away from each other, several times a week. You could almost hear her hinting darkly about legal proceedings if I took away her civil rights to chat to her mates.

Shannon remained a bit of an enigma. Despite her mature

appearance and self-confident air, the other children seemed more wary than in awe of her, and she didn't appear to have any close friends. She spent some time with the terrible trio but she definitely had the air of an outsider. Perhaps Kate and co weren't quite ready to meet behind the bike sheds for a fag.

On Thursday, I was starkly reminded of Mrs Little's advice not to put Shannon down in public. We had been chatting about imagery in 'The Highwayman' and many of the children had contributed well, with highly insightful comments. Shannon had missed the initial reading and discussion of the poem and clearly had no interest whatsoever in discussing why the description of the moon as a ghostly galleon was a particularly vivid metaphor. Initially she simply looked bored, but when she took out a mirror and started examining her face, I felt like I needed to do something.

'Beautiful as your face is, Shannon,' I began, unwisely, 'I'd much rather hear your comments on the beauty of some of these images. Why do you think Alfred Noyes describes the moon as a ghostly galleon, _Shannon_?' There was too much emphasis on the second 'Shannon' and I received exactly what I'd been warned against.

'Because he's a twat. A moon is a moon and a galleon is a galleon. OK?' There were open-mouthed looks around the class that someone, even Shannon, had dared use the word 'twat' in front of her teacher. Her subsequent raised eyebrows dared me to push her further, but I knew this would be lethal, and that I'd brought it on myself with my sarcastic tone. As I mentally kicked myself for my mistake, I tried to get out of the situation with a mildly wry, 'Thank you for giving us your honest and rather frank opinion, Shannon.' It was about the best I could do, and I quickly turned to Alice who, bless her, had put up her hand with a comment, and the moment passed. However, I was very aware that playground talk might well centre on Shannon's language and how she was able to get away with it.

Perhaps so as not to steal his sister's thunder, Sean waited until the following day to show what he was capable of. I was on playground duty and was using it to get a better picture of group dynamics in my class. The boys were, as usual, playing football, and Patrick missed a relatively easy chance of a last minute equaliser. Sean's response to his team mate's miss was a put-down that really shocked me:

'It's dyslexic Patrick, the dyspraxic spastic.'

While scoring quite highly for alliteration and a contender for the tongue-twister of the year award, it was said with malicious venom. It was made worse by Josh, the epitome of the expression 'sidekick', who burst out: 'Yeah, he's as crap at scoring as he is at writing!'

Now, Josh Robins was not an intelligent boy – in fact, he was on the special needs register for learning difficulties, which made his comment even more reproachable. He had not raised his ugly head until Sean arrived at school, but had gradually grown in confidence as the week had worn on. I stood for a moment watching Patrick Collins, a lovely boy, being laughed at by his peers for missing a goal and for suffering from both dyslexia and dyspraxia. I saw him look at the ground, silently digesting the humiliation and knowing that retaliation would only make matters worse.

I have a deep loathing of bullying. I simply cannot fathom the rationale of deliberately upsetting or degrading someone, especially a classmate, for cheap laughs. I've watched the current trend of 'happy slapping' in horror recently and I'd wondered how I'd react if I witnessed such behaviour at Green Acre. While this was not physical bullying it was, in my view, equally abhorrent, and I had no hesitation in throwing the book at the two little sods.

'Sean Williams and Josh Robins, outside Mrs Little's office, now!' I bellowed, so that the whole of Key Stage 2 instantly became quiet and looked on. Even then, Josh had to look for approval from Sean, which annoyed me intensely. 'And forget about coming to football practice tonight, both of you.' Sean shot me a glance at this which I found hard to read. It was either a *'you complete bastard, I was looking forward to that'* sort of glance or a *'doesn't bother me, I'm too good for this team anyway'* one. It certainly wasn't an *'I'm really sorry Mr Gray and I promise I'll never do it again'* look; that much I was certain of. I decided to let Mrs Little deal with this one, as the nature of the language used was especially offensive. And deal with it she did. When she had finished with them, Josh was in floods of tears and even Sean looked mildly contrite. The promised letter home to their parents and loss of a week's playtime probably had something to do with it.

Despite these incidents, especially the rather unsavoury bullying one, I dismissed the children after my first full week feeling rather pleased. I knew there were some challenging children and that challenging situations would inevitably occur, but I also knew that the way I dealt with them and the lessons I learnt from them, especially at this early stage, were the important things. One thing I had learnt was that children are incredibly perceptive, and can sniff out weaknesses at fifty paces. While I had made mistakes, and they would have noticed these, I had generally managed potentially explosive incidents pretty well and I hoped that this would also have been noted.

It is quite a sad fact of human nature that naughtiness, disruption, rudeness, aggression, defiance or indifference are much more interesting than politeness, humour, warmth, integrity or kindness. The majority of the kids in my class were lovely, several absolutely delightful, and there were moments of shared warmth or humour during that first week that made me sure that I was going to like this job. For example, we'd been out enjoying a game of rounders in the late summer sunshine and it was David's turn to bat. David had been diagnosed with leukaemia when he was seven and, despite having been given the 'all clear' for over a year, was still quite frail and weak. When he connected with the ball and started jogging as fast as he could from base to base, a buzz of expectation arose. As he scrambled over fourth base, exhausted, just before he could be stumped out, the roar of delight from just about everybody, and the hug and kiss he received from Miranda, were incredibly moving. The look of pride on the face of a boy who had suffered for so long was one that I don't think I'll ever forget. It occurred to me, at that moment, that very few jobs would give you the opportunity of witnessing something as magical as that.

After football practice on Friday, I was delighted to see Rachel come through my door. Her smile, as usual, evaporated any frustrations instantly.

'I heard what happened with Sean this morning' she began. 'There aren't many teachers who would have dared shout at him like that, let alone kick him out of football practice. That sort of action, in his mind, is punishable by death. Good for you.'

I didn't tell her that my actions weren't a calculated act of bravado from one whose sole aim is to maintain justice, whatever the personal cost, and that they were simply an instantaneous response to nastiness. If she viewed me as some sort of fearless Clint Eastwood character who roamed around rounding up bad men for the Sheriff, then I, for one, was not going to enlighten her.

We exchanged pleasantries about the week for a few moments, before she said, rather shyly: 'I wonder, if you're not doing anything, whether you'd like to go for a drink tonight. It's just – Alan phoned earlier to say that his sister has asked to come and stay at his place this weekend and – well – she's a bit of a cow to tell the truth and I'm sure you're probably busy – it was just, if you weren't …'

There were at least three things about this rather inarticulate speech that made me believe, after all, that there is a god. First, and foremost, this wonderful creature, who I barely knew, had asked me to go out for a drink with her. Secondly, there was clearly an evil sister lurking maliciously in the background, trying to prise apart her relationship. Thirdly, Rachel had definitely said the words 'his place'. Not 'our place': 'his place'. Up until that point I had assumed that they lived together, but now an altogether more casual arrangement seemed to be the case; an arrangement which meant that she had no qualms whatsoever about organising a drink with a male colleague.

I had perhaps one second to gauge my response. I had to somehow get the balance between sounding too excited – indeed, throwing myself at her and surprising her with a long drawn-out kiss – and sounding too casual. It would have been dangerously easy to shrug my shoulders, check my diary and, after weighing up several better offers, finally consent to the drink.

'No, my social calendar is entirely blank at the moment, and a drink sounds lovely.' I gallantly offered to drive and she told me where she lived. As she left the room I did a little dance around my carpet and did not even mind when I noticed that the caretaker, a grumpy old sod, had been watching this strange routine through the window.

It was difficult to think beyond the evening, but I knew I

needed to speak to Mrs Little and thank her for her support earlier in the day. She too was impressed that I had not shirked responsibility when needing to discipline the intimidating Sean and felt that, long term, it would strengthen the relationship between the two of us.

'I am concerned about Patrick,' I said. 'Not just because he is such an obvious victim, but I'm not sure that I'm really meeting his needs. I know very little about dyslexia or dyspraxia and I feel I should be better informed.'

Sandra Little immediately took out the book showing available courses for teachers, and we were both pleased to see that a day's session on handling dyslexic children was being held in three weeks' time. A quick phone call later, my name was duly added. I left school for the weekend both satisfied that I was actively trying to address the needs of my children, and thoroughly excited, for obvious reasons.

The flat inspection was due at 6 p.m. Naomi, owing to work commitments, had not been around since Sunday night, but we had promised that the flat would remain clean and tidy. In fairness to us, we had kept to our task pretty well. Granted, on Wednesday night we were all too knackered to wash up, but by Thursday evening the kitchen was clean again. I'm not sure I had changed as a person quite how I had envisaged early on Saturday morning, but I felt proud of myself and I couldn't ask for more than that. Had it not been for Rachel's invitation, I'm sure the three of us would have got pissed again that night, but that was fine – why shouldn't we all unwind at the end of a long week?

'Attention!' Naomi put on her best sergeant major's voice as she walked through the door to find Liam, Tony and me standing in a line, duster, polish and toilet brush in hand.

After a couple of theatrical marches up and down the hall,

she came over to me. I kept a serious face as I held my bog brush by my side, even when she went and pretended to sniff it.

'Gray! There are definite traces of turd on this lavatory brush. You are a disgrace to the regiment. Give me fifty.' I assumed she was joking, but when I didn't move she shrieked 'Now!' It was so convincing I actually found myself struggling through fifty press-ups as she grimly looked on.

'If I put my back out, and have to cancel tonight's date,' I groaned, edging slowly into the forties, 'I will sue.'

All silly role play was soon forgotten as I modestly told them of Rachel's invitation, and there was a wonderful buzz in the air as Naomi inspected the rest of the flat.

'So when did you last go for a date with a girl who was already spoken for?' asked Naomi later.

'Never.'

'OK. Basic rules. Be yourself, make her feel relaxed and make her laugh, and resist the temptation to talk in a derogatory way about Alan, even if she does, and whatever you do – don't try anything on. She needs to see that you are a gentleman, especially on a first date.'

'I don't actually think it is a date.'

'Oh, well, whatever. Charm her socks off, and it might soon become one.'

And so it was that, at eight that evening, I arrived at Rachel's flat, well-groomed and sporting slightly too much aftershave. She looked, as ever, wonderful, and we found a cosy village pub to enjoy our drink. We both realised, quite quickly, how little we actually knew about each other and we spent the first hour giving potted histories of our paths to Green Acre.

Rachel had grown up in Leicester, and had studied for her B.Ed in London. She'd applied for the job at Green Acre a year ago because she liked the area, and had met Alan at a party four months ago. I made a surreptitious little fist of celebration underneath the table at this news. If she had said four years, my ultimate goal of prising her away would have been that much harder.

When she said that he was a charity worker, I nearly jumped for joy. I had imagined a corporate financier who would woo her with his fancy cars, country mansions and private yachts. Instead, the worthy Alan was some bloody do-gooder, almost certainly in black-rimmed national health glasses, serving elderly women in Oxfam. It also meant that, almost certainly, she was a *'I don't mind about their looks or how much they earn as long as they've got a nice personality'* type of girl. Which was just as well.

'Actually, he calls himself a charity worker, but that's just him being modest. His official title is "International Development Officer for the Red Cross".'

Bugger.

'This does mean, of course, that he's abroad an awful lot, so I don't get to see him much.'

Hey-hey – things are looking up.

'And of course, when he is at home, much of his time is taken up with his modelling contract.'

Oh, for God's sake. I'm sorry Naomi, I haven't forgotten your advice, but desperate situations require desperate measures.

'So tell me about this old cow of a sister?'

'Oh yes, her. Her name's Florence, which gives you a pretty

good idea before you start. The first time we met she spent most of the evening going on about whingeing teachers and militant unions who don't seem to understand that everyone's taxes pay for the exorbitant holidays teachers get. Which, I have to say, really pissed me off. I'm not a militant teacher at all and I work damned hard for the children, like virtually all teachers. I thought the way she was varnishing us all with the same brush insulted our profession, and I felt pretty insulted myself. It was the first time we'd met, for God's sake, and it wasn't like I'd been nasty to her, I'd just cooked her a bloody meal.'

'What a complete bitch,' I said, warming to the theme. 'Didn't Alan step in and defend you?' OK, a little bit provocative. But you don't miss from six yards.

'Barely, only really when he could see that I was getting pretty annoyed by it, and then he basically got her to shut up.'

'Oh, right. You would have thought, as your boyfriend, he would have stood up for you a little more.'

'Oh God, Adrian don't get me wrong. Alan's a lovely guy and I'm sure he thinks the world of me. I just don't think he realised how frustrating that sort of talk can be to teachers – that's all.'

You stupid arse. You simply can't stop yourself, can you? Naomi warned you, in no uncertain terms, to remain aloof and not to knock Alan, and now you've done it, and probably alienated Rachel at the same time.

'Yes, of course,' I spluttered, backtracking wildly. 'I didn't mean – I'm sure he's a great bloke.'

'He is. Would you like another drink?'

I felt that I never quite fully recovered after that own goal. While we spent the next hour or so chatting amicably enough, there was a subtle and ever so slight switch in the mood, and I felt very awkward. In the end it was me who suggested we should leave, as I had an early start in the morning. I even found myself lying about arranging to meet a friend early in the morning, which couldn't have sounded very convincing.

As I was driving her home I realised that I had blown any chance of accepting an offer for coffee, and none came. We both exclaimed how much we had enjoyed the evening and that we must do it again very soon.

'You must meet Alan, next time; I bet you two would get on really well.'

I smiled but didn't say anything, primarily because I had nothing to say. I could probably have mustered *'Oh splendid. And why don't we bring Florence along as well, and she can stick pins in my effigy while I watch him put his hands all over you.'* But I didn't, wisely. Instead, I said goodnight, and drove slowly home.

I was half-expecting Naomi to be there waiting for me to hear me boast about my conquest, but a silent flat awaited me – she must have taken my seat in the pub – and I was glad of this. I value Naomi's friendship and advice more than just about anything but I was tired, and a little bit down, and all I wanted to do was make myself a sad git's cup of cocoa, and curl up in bed.

'Yeah, he's as crap at scoring as he is at writing!'

'I beg your pardon, Josh?' My tone was so menacing and full of loathing that there was instant quiet on the playground, as they realised he was in trouble.

Silence.

'I said – I beg your pardon. Can you explain what you meant by that comment?'

'It was Sean – he said it – I just – '

'You just copied someone else's joke for a few cheap laughs, is that correct? Not capable of coming up with your own, original method of humiliating someone who has done nothing to you? Oh no, everyone, Josh couldn't come up with anything witty and original, because Josh can't think for himself. Isn't that right, Josh? What's the matter, Josh? Where's all that wit and sparkle of a minute ago gone to, eh Josh?'

6.

I went to bed on Sunday night three weeks later with mixed feelings about the next couple of weeks. The following day was the dyslexia course, and I was really looking forward to it, partly because I felt that it would help me to help Patrick, and also because it didn't start until 9.30, giving me an extra hour in bed.

The next ten days also held in store two potentially rewarding or damning events. On Tuesday, Mrs Little was coming to observe me teach, and the following Tuesday and Wednesday I had to run the gauntlet of my first ever parents' evenings.

It was good, though, that my immediate future held this variety of new challenges and experiences. As the first few weeks had gone by, I'd found myself developing various routines, some of which were enjoyable and some of which were, frankly, tedious. I really enjoyed planning lessons. Whether this was just the novelty or whether it was because I particularly wanted to come up with interesting and inspiring ideas for helping the children learn, only time would tell.

In contrast, I found marking books both time-consuming and hideously dull. We had had it drummed into us at college, and indeed it was part of school policy, that the marking should enrich and enhance the work. However much I wanted to write *'good'* or *'well done'* or *'Rozinder,* _this really is a pile of shite'_, our comments needed to take the work on and suggest ideas for improvement. This took bloody ages, and I wouldn't have minded so much if they took any dammed notice of it. Allard, who despite his surliness was actually quite a bright child, managed to write a whole piece on the causes of World War II without any punctuation, save for a token full stop at the end. I dutifully pointed this out when marking, and even suggested strategies to ensure he checks through work at the end. His next piece of work, written either with total defiance or total indifference, even managed to neglect that one, lone, full stop. It was only when I saw a real difference in children that I felt rewarded by this lengthy process. Sophie, for one, dutifully acted on everything that I wrote and within a fortnight her writing showed a maturity that simply hadn't been there initially.

I had got to know the children quite well by now and was beginning to gauge what made them tick and what turned them off. Needless to say, however, there were still problems, still difficult scenarios and still unacceptable behaviour that needed to be dealt with. I mishandled Charlie quite badly once because I was so fed up with her and felt, for a while at least, that I had lost a little respect. In general, however, things were going well. I could relax and have a few laughs with the kids and some excellent work was being produced.

I didn't see Rachel out of school during this time. We'd chatted on several occasions without any awkwardness and I was sure she was beginning to value me as a good friend, but I couldn't quite summon the nerve to suggest another out-of-school meeting.

Perhaps the most surprising development during these

weeks was that I actually spoke to Ellie Luck for more than a fleeting second. She came in to my room to ask for a favour – could she have my hall-time to prepare for an assembly – and obviously felt that she needed to say something. We then spent an only-very-slightly-strained few minutes talking about her old – my new – class, its characters and their foibles. I even got her to smile when I related the rounders incident and, when she left, I felt that there was a little warmth there, and perhaps now she had actually begun to see me as someone capable of teaching, rather than as just a cocky adolescent, which was certainly the case initially.

I arrived at the Educational Development Centre at just gone 9.30 on Monday morning, having utilised my lie-in to the full. No one had spoken to me about a dress code and I was fed up with wearing ties, so I was a little embarrassed to see all the other males in the room dutifully sporting suits, while I was in T-shirt and jeans. Undaunted, however, I poured myself a glass of complimentary water, sucked on a complimentary mint and settled myself down to listen at a table near the back of the conference room, amidst a group of earnest-looking teachers all several years older than me.

The day would be split into two sections, we were told. The first hour would consist of a brief summary about what was known about dyslexia and a little of the philosophy surrounding why it is believed that people suffer from it. After coffee, and for the rest of the day, we would be looking at general strategies around how we could help children in the classroom and develop their reading, writing and spelling.

The first lecturer introduced himself as Dr Vincent Dobbs, and began the general philosophy bit. I dutifully took some notes but soon started to get bored and let my mind wander. While I had heard, many times, at college that you need to have a philosophical underpinning of a subject to fully appreciate and act upon it, I always found it hard to intellectualise something without basing it on practical experience. Perhaps worthier and more intelligent people than I could relate Vincent's teachings directly to the classroom, but I couldn't. After ten minutes or so I was engaged in a far more interesting activity than listening to the lecture: closely watching all the teachers in the room and trying to gauge their personalities by their body language. I've always considered myself pretty good at this, however difficult it may be to quantify. I suppose I could have gone up to the very earnest-looking lady on my table and said: *'I think you're in your early forties. I think you're married to someone who works in banking and I think you have two children. I think you take your work pretty seriously and command some respect from your class, but very rarely have a laugh with them. I think you have sex every Friday night out of some sort of loyal duty; however, it is predictable and certainly involves no degree of experimentation. I don't think you've ever said the word 'bollocks' in your life. How am I doing?'* Short of this scientific, if rather direct approach, however, I could only surmise, but I still maintain that I'm pretty good at picking up non-verbal signals. I continued this process for some minutes, surreptitiously working my eyes around the room, between the occasional knowing and studious nod in the direction of the lecturer. My trained eye quickly assessed which females looked to be about my age, weren't wearing a wedding or engagement ring, and looked attractive, for the purpose of short-listing girls I might conveniently sit next to during coffee.

I had narrowed it down to two distinct possibilities when my gaze shifted to a corner table and I saw her. I felt momentarily short of breath and a physical nausea enveloped me. As I continued to stare, I decided quickly that she had not noticed or recognised me. Her demeanour was calm, there were no tell-tale twitches or little eye movements, and she was listening intently. My first irrational thoughts were to slip out quietly, find the nearest dressing-up shop, and return with a wig, dark glasses and resplendent beard. If spoken to, I was pretty sure that my well-practised mock Scottish accent would not let me down. *Of all the joints, in all the world* ...

At first, the sheer coincidence of being in the same conference room as the woman from the pub made me think I must have been mistaken. After all, I had barely looked at or spoken to her at all and it was over three weeks ago. But it was her. That short ginger-tinted hair, that slightly pointed nose and those distinctive cheek bones belonged, without doubt, to the face of the woman with whom I had had such an unsavoury encounter, and whom I had thought about, with great regret, many times since. I remembered that she had told me that she was a special needs teacher, so I suppose the coincidence of us both attending a dyslexia conference wasn't quite so great after all.

I felt awful. I knew that, at any moment, she could turn her head and there would be an excruciating moment as our eyes met. I found myself covering my face with my hands to avoid this, but could I do so all day? Did I want to avoid her all day? After all, here was an opportunity to apologise for something which I had felt absolutely terrible about. Even so, avoiding was just so much easier ...

I remember, in an episode of *Little House on the Prairie*, Pa telling little Laura Ingalls that facing up to an awkward situation and forcing yourself to apologise, however difficult that was to do, was so much better in the long run than hoping it would go away. I used to really like *Little House on the Prairie* ...

Any decision about what I might or might not do, whether to heed the worldly-wise advice of Pa or don the fake beard, was taken away from me when I glanced back in her direction. Her lips were pursed, nostrils slightly flared, and she was looking directly at me. I simply didn't know what to do. I didn't want to turn away. I didn't want to smile or scowl. I didn't want to appear indifferent, annoyed, relaxed, angry ... Fortunately, a second later, she turned away and looked down at her papers, clearly deep in thought.

I tried to use my body language expertise to assess her reaction. I was expecting a look of hatred, and possibly a pencil case, to come hurtling in my direction, but the overriding emotion I saw in her eyes was not one of anger. It was a mixture, as I suspect mine was, of sorrow, pain, surprise, embarrassment, and perhaps even a tinge of guilt.

The rest of the session disappeared in a whirl of thought. I knew I had to go and speak to her the moment coffee was announced, but I was absolutely dreading it. She remained seated as those on her table got up, indicating that she was there on her own rather than with colleagues and, if a move were to be made, it was I who would have to make it. Taking a deep breath, I walked over to her and asked her simply if I could buy her a coffee. She nodded without looking at me, and we walked in silence to the canteen. There seemed to be an unspoken agreement between us that we would only talk when we had some privacy and I decided on my opening gambit as I paid for the coffee. It risked a smack in the face, but I felt that lightening the tone immediately was probably the best course, as long as I didn't come across as cocky or unfeeling towards what had happened.

'I'm not sure what to say,' I began after we sat down. 'I used up all my best chat-up lines on our last date.' She screwed up her features somewhat at this incredibly risky opener but there was, thank God, a hint of a smile as she looked up and caught my eye.

'This will probably sound trite and unconvincing,' I continued, 'but I've felt really awful about what happened in the pub and I'd just like to say sorry.' Still she didn't speak, and I was beginning to understand the proverb about the pound of flesh. 'I was a little bit drunk, I was – you know – showing off a bit and, I don't know, I think I just wanted to make it clear that I was just enjoying a bit of Friday night banter – if that's a phrase. It really wasn't a case of me not caring about my class. Especially Patrick, the dyslexic boy in question, who I am genuinely fond of and who is the reason I'm here today. Honestly though, what I said at the end – it was totally uncalled for and I certainly didn't mean it in any other way but as a cheap insult. That probably didn't come out very well, but I am sorry. Oh, and I'm Adrian by the way.'

Again, she was silent for a moment and I was just about to get down on my knees when she finally spoke.

'I'm Alison, and I'm not entirely sure whether you just dug an even bigger hole for yourself, but I certainly accept your apology. To be honest, Adrian, I think it's me who owes you an apology. I don't suppose you even noticed Corinne and me – she's my sister incidentally – but if you did you would have probably seen that we weren't exactly the life and soul of the party.'

I didn't like to say that the only reason that we had sat there in the first place was that the two sisters were the best of a bad bunch on the potential-shag front. I judged, probably wisely, that this would have soured what was rapidly becoming a nice conciliatory moment.

'My father lives in Yorkshire. He's fifty-five and was a foreman for a construction company for many years. That afternoon, he'd phoned me to tell me he had just been made redundant and, at his age, well it was extremely unlikely that he'd ever find any work again, let alone comparable work.'

She paused, and I realised how difficult this was for her,

and how shaken up she must have been at the time.

'He sounded broken when he told me. I felt – I dunno – completely helpless when he asked me how on earth he was going to cope and support my mother – she's wheelchair-bound. He couldn't face having to tell Corinne so I did it for him. We were both, I suppose, still in shock and decided to go for a drink to drown our sorrows. We didn't especially feel like talking – there didn't appear to be that much to say. So we sat, and we drank. Hence I couldn't help overhearing your private conversation and – I don't know – I suppose I just wanted to vent out my frustrations and anger on someone, and the rest you know. What you said at the end – to be honest I probably deserved it, but it just pushed me over the edge. So I'm glad we've met here again, Adrian, so that I can apologise to you.'

By this time, Ma Ingalls would have been in floods of tears and Laura would have been saying something along the lines of: 'Gee, I love you all so much', but you had to hand it to Pa, he knew his stuff.

I think we both had a huge weight lifted from us after our mutual apologies. We then shared a pleasant and chatty ten minutes before the course continued, where I said all the right things about her father and gleaned that she was thirty-one, recently divorced and subsequently slightly wary of men. I quipped something along the lines that her wariness must surely have diminished after our pub encounter, and we returned from coffee agreeing to share lunch together after the next session.

It is astounding how much easier it is to focus one's mind once a burden has been lifted from it. Also, we had now reached the part of the course that I was particularly interested in and it was delivered by a dynamic and amusing young lady. Hence I was fully engaged and switched on to what she had to say.

By the end of the session, I felt that I had enough material to make a real difference to Patrick and, in fairness to Vincent Dobbs, a lot of what he had said during the 'philosophical underpinning' bit now began to make sense. I began to understand some of the frustrations that dyslexic children usually have, and some of the techniques and strategies that I could use in the classroom.

Over lunch Alison told me a little more about herself, and I learnt that she had, this year, come out of class teaching to focus specifically on special needs, and how much she was enjoying the challenge. As the conversation went on, and it was obvious that we were getting on well, I started to think about whether I wanted, or indeed felt I ought, to ask to see her again. In a few minutes' time we would be back for the afternoon session and I might not get a chance to speak to her at the end of the day. As she hadn't mentioned her school name, I would probably never see her again. Still aware of her comment about mistrusting men, I had just about decided to leave it, when she broached the subject first.

'Listen. A few hours ago I would have reckoned on odds of about a million to one of me meeting you and asking you this question, but Corinne's having a party on Saturday night and she asked me to invite somebody if I wanted to. I know this might sound a little forward but ...'

'I'd love to come,' I replied before she could stutter herself into an embarrassed silence, 'if only to see your sister's face when we arrive at her door.'

'I'll warn her,' she laughed, and we exchanged phone numbers and addresses. It was a quite remarkable turnaround in our relationship and I thoroughly looked forward to seeing Tony and Liam's faces when I explained.

The whole situation did make me somewhat confused, however. I had just agreed to go on what I assumed was a date, with a woman nearly ten years my senior, and I was pretty sure that, while we clearly got on, I didn't actually fancy her. Would she try anything on, and if she did, how would I react? I found myself, quite absurdly, thinking about Rachel, who I was completely besotted with, and feeling guilty that I was somehow being unfaithful to my fantasies by agreeing to go to the party. The eternal optimist in me, the one that saw Rachel ditching her special-envoy-of-a-modelling-bastard-of-a-boyfriend in favour of li'l old me, was rather put out by my unfaithfulness.

So the afternoon went by, and with it more good ideas, although it has to be said that my mind was elsewhere for large chunks of it. I spoke briefly to Alison at the end of the day to finalise arrangements, thought fleetingly about giving her a kiss on the cheek but decided against it, and then drove home to prepare my lesson plan for the following day's observation from Mrs Little.

'You what!!' screeched Naomi at the other end of the phone. 'Are you seriously telling me that you've just arranged a date with that girl from the pub? Adrian Gray, you dark horse, you.'

'Well, you know me, I don't bear a grudge. Of course, I did make her sign a legally binding confession taking complete blame for the incident before consenting to the invitation which, I felt, was the least that she could do.'

'Fair enough. Anyway, I don't suppose she's going to want anything to do with you if you are as grossly insensitive to her as you managed to be with Rachel a few weeks ago.'

I had told Naomi of our conversation about Rachel's dinner with Alan and Florence, hoping that she would reassure me that I was unlikely to have done any damage. She hadn't. She had rolled her eyes, given me a hug and said bluntly: 'You know Adrian, next time you go on a date, I'm going to masquerade as your attorney, and stop you saying anything that might be written down and used in evidence against you.' So this time, I vowed, whatever happened I would listen to her advice: 'While she might talk adversely about her ex-husband, she may well still harbour feelings towards him. Whatever you do, don't go down the same road as last time and say that he sounds like a complete prick.'

'Er, excuse me?'

'Och?'

'Er, I know this sounds a little corny, but haven't I met you before?'

'Och Noo, Mahoots lassie, ah've oonly joost arreeved from Bonnie Aberdeeen, where ah've spent ohl ma life up until nooo.'

'Oh, I'm sorry. It's just that you look really like someone that I met in a pub a few weeks ago. Only he didn't have a beard or glasses ... and I'm sure he didn't have bright red hair ...'

'Well, och the nooo, there ya goo then lassie, ya've simply got me confused with some other guy – ah've been grooin' this beard for 12 years noo.'

'Then I must be mistaken. I'm sorry to bother you.'

7.

I left for school early the following morning to get myself fully prepared for Mrs Little's observation. There was a distinct chill in the early October air and, for the first time in many months, I felt the need for a jacket. The extended Indian summer appeared to be coming to an end and autumn was well and truly upon us.

When I walked into my classroom I became aware, instantly, that all had not been well in my absence. I'm not exactly a tidy person, but I do try to instil in children the importance of leaving a tidy room at the end of the day, primarily as this reflects well on their pride in their space but partly for fear of recriminations from our grumpy bastard of a caretaker. Furthermore, if I were a supply teacher, I would feel that the success or otherwise of the day could largely be gauged by how well I had marshalled the troops into leaving a tidy room behind them. First impressions and all that.

Well, clearly Mrs Willoughby did not share this particular opinion. Chairs had been roughly stacked onto tables, which still had books, paper and pencil cases strewn over them. Rulers, glue sticks and scissors were left abandoned throughout the room and, perhaps most telling of all, a paper aeroplane was lodged behind the radiator.

I had met Mrs Willoughby the previous Friday to discuss

75

what I wanted her to teach my class while I was at my course. Our usual, well-trusted supply teachers had all been unavailable and the agency had clearly delved to the very bottom of their pile before producing this specimen. Mrs Willoughby was well into her sixties, appeared to be a little deaf and seemed to show no enthusiasm whatsoever for what I had asked her to do. She was clearly from the school of supply teachers who expected to be able to 'do their own thing' when covering another class. Doubtless there would have been numerous uninspiring and uneducational English worksheets, pages of sums and colouring-in activities filling her bag of goodies, which she had glanced at surreptitiously as I had talked her through the day.

She quite patently had not understood when I explained that, during maths, I wanted my bright, inspired upper set to investigate patterns of triangular numbers and try to put their findings into a formula. She had looked at me blankly when I had asked her to discuss debating skills during English, in preparation for my visit from Mrs Little, and her mouth had opened visibly when I had explained to her that she needed to show the children how to animate their PowerPoint presentations. But, quite frankly, I didn't care. She was being paid to teach a class of ten- and eleven-year-olds which, presumably, she was aware of, and if she didn't feel that she was up to delivering the curriculum, she should have declined. Perhaps I shouldn't have felt quite the sadistic pleasure that I did when I was going through the day with her, but none of us is perfect. I had asked her if she had any questions and, as she had shaken her head, I had decided to let her get on with it.

It seemed to me that both Dora Willoughby and Ellie Luck came from a school of teaching with a philosophy utterly different to that I'd been taught at University. I wondered, fleetingly, whether all teachers of a certain age were so adverse to change. And then I remembered some of the outstanding, inspirational teachers in their fifties and sixties that I had learnt so much from on various placements. Dora Willoughby most certainly was not a 'product of her generation', she was simply unfit to do the job. Just how unfit, I was about to find out.

'Oh, thank God you're back,' said Frank, with great feeling, a few minutes after I arrived in my room.

'So, I take it Mrs Willoughby didn't win any teaching awards yesterday then?'

'Adrian, you have no idea. If it hadn't have been so serious it would have been funny. You can take it as read that the esteemed Dora Willoughby will not be teaching at Green Acre again.'

'Serious?' I said, beginning to feel mildly alarmed. 'Why? What happened?'

'Apparently, it started badly and gradually got worse and worse over the course of the day,' he said. 'I brought my class into the hall to do some mime, would you believe, at 9.15 and I could hear chaos from next door. She had clearly already lost control and was shouting over the noise. I marched straight into the room and was nearly hit by the bag that Miranda was swinging around her head.'

'Miranda?' I said in disbelief. 'She's the nicest kid in the world. What could possibly have happened in fifteen minutes to make her misbehave?'

'I have absolutely no idea. She had her back to me and clearly didn't hear me come in over the noise, and she continued to make this sort of high-pitched whirring noise as I stood behind her and crossed my arms. I tell you, Adrian, it was like something out of a situation comedy. Gradually, the class noticed me and became quieter and quieter and still Miranda tried, seemingly, to take off. When she finally turned round the class was in complete silence; Adrian, you should've seen the look of total shame and horror on her face as I raised my eyebrows. It was a sight to behold.

'Yeah, OK you can laugh now – I asked Mrs Willoughby if everything was all right and she just nodded sheepishly. I let them know, in no uncertain terms, that I wanted quiet for my mime class and shut the door.'

'And things got worse?'

'Just a bit. Irene was in the hall after break but let them get on with it – she said it must have been impossible to learn or teach anything with such a din. But the real trouble happened right at the end of the day, when Mrs Willoughby ran out of the school in tears.'

I closed my eyes. I know there are some difficult kids in my class but I couldn't believe that they had collectively managed to drive her out.

'What happened?'

'Shannon. Apparently she'd done no work all afternoon and Mrs Willoughby laid into her, telling her she was the rudest and laziest girl she had ever known. From what we could glean right at the end of the day, Shannon gave as good as she got and it was too much for Mrs Willoughby. We haven't even been able to get Mrs Willoughby's side of events, as she simply got up and went home. I think Mrs Little tried the agency but there's been no luck there.'

'What's going to happen to Shannon?' I asked thinking, perhaps rather selfishly, about my observed lesson in less than an hour's time.

'She's on a final warning before suspension. The problem is because the incident happened right at the end of the day, we haven't had a chance to deal with it properly yet. That little delight we'll have to sort out today.'

As Frank left to get ready for his day, I sat down with my head in my hands. I was nervous enough about my English lesson today as it was. The prospect, however, of having to deliver it to a class who had just had a real bollocking, just heightened my anxiety. And what about that bollocking? I assumed that Mrs Little would want her say, but I felt that I would be hiding behind her if I didn't say something as well. The main problem, though, was that, Shannon apart, I didn't really blame them for what had happened. Mrs Willoughby had clearly come unprepared in just about every aspect. They had been bored and they'd taken advantage. I was certain I'd have done the same at their age.

It was then I noticed the whiteboard. On it, in large letters, were the words: *'The following children's behaviour has not been good enough today. They need to lose their play time tomorrow.'* Below this were no fewer than twenty of the twenty-six children in the class. It really annoyed me that she had simply stuck names, willy-nilly, on the board, and expected me to dish out the punishment. My first reaction was to simply rub the names off – I could barely see them enquiring as to where they'd gone – but I figured that Mrs Little might want to use this as a starting point to get to the bottom of what had happened.

Out of interest I looked for those children who had escaped Mrs Willoughby's wrath. Five of the six didn't surprise me, but the other one, incredibly, was Robert. I could just imagine him quickly summing up his teacher for the day and deciding that, quite frankly, she wasn't worth it. She would have been, in his eyes, an unfitting opponent, and he'd probably decided just to withdraw into himself for the day, as he was still prone to do.

But all thoughts of recriminations and suppositions had to wait. I had a lesson to deliver, so I went to my flipchart and wrote:

Objectives
· *To understand the format of debating.*
· *To be able to create a persuasive argument, using shared ideas.*

Success criteria
· *You can come up with ideas and justify them in a verbal speech.*

Educationists love buzz-words. 'Objectives' and 'success criteria' are two of the current stock and it was very much the school's policy to share these particular ones with the children at the beginning of each lesson. I had happily done this for the first week or so, but had quickly slipped out of the habit.

So they came in, looking pretty sheepish and, in some cases, a little militant. There was real concern on many faces, though, when they saw Mrs Little in the room.

I had spoken to her first, before they entered, and decided that I would have a brief word about yesterday, but she would speak to Shannon at break time to lay down the law. We both agreed that her presence would be enough to show our collective disappointment and great speeches from her would not help the situation just before my lesson. She had actually offered to postpone the observation but I had written my lesson plan and I had written my learning objectives, and I didn't want to have to go to such extremes again.

Registration went without a problem, and I could see Mrs Little watching me intently to see how I would broach the subject of yesterday.

'In a moment, I want to talk to you,' I said quietly, 'but first I'd like you to tidy this room up – now.'

The effect was electric. In less than a minute the classroom was spotless and they were back on the carpet. I caught Mrs Little's eye and she gave me the briefest of nods – enough to show she was impressed with my calm authority.

By the time I had finished talking to them about disappointment, letting the school down and letting themselves down, I quite exuded authority. I seamlessly moved on to start the lesson, went through the objectives and then my quiet authority got shot to pieces by one screwed-up kid.

'I'm sorry, Mr Gray,' said Robert politely, 'but could you tell me why you're going through the objectives with us today, a process you abandoned after about a week?'

I swear, I nearly hit him. I nearly sacrificed everything with my boss sitting watching. It was just so calculated. Robert had instantly noted the connection between the sudden reappearance of the objectives and Mrs Little's presence and decided that, after yesterday's day off, it was time for a bit of good old-fashioned humiliation.

'Because, Robert,' I said as smoothly as I could muster. 'After yesterday I felt you all needed a little focus.' While the damage had been done, and while Mrs Little would have noted the fact that the objectives were purely for show, it was a quite brilliant answer on the spur of the moment. Gradually regaining the lost impetus, I started discussing the motion they would be debating: Should children have to wear school uniform? As I had hoped, there was immediate vociferous argument against the motion.

'Your first task,' I said, interrupting them, 'is to brainstorm all the arguments both for and against the motion. In pairs, I then want you to compile a persuasive speech to support either side. It would be very nice to see some of you not taking the easy option, and try to persuade us all why school uniform is the sensible option.'

'Boo,' shouted Josh, summoning up all his mental and comical resources. 'School uniform's rubbish!'

'And your task, Josh, is to persuade me that that is a powerful argument.'

There then followed a surge of activity and they all seemed pretty enthusiastic about the task as they retired, in pairs or threes, to brainstorm their ideas. I'd been told of the importance of standing back from these discussions, observing group dynamics and establishing who were leaders, who were active participators and who were passive bystanders. Children who I would have guessed to be fairly quiet or uninterested surprised me: Patrick, Alice and David, for instance, who I would have put in the more passive category, were most animated in their discussions. Even Kate, Charlie and Rozinder, perhaps due to a lull in interesting *Eastenders* storylines, seemed really focused.

After ten minutes or so I asked them to choose a side from their brainstorming and prepare their speech. Two from each side would then be chosen to be read to the class, and after this the floor would be open for debate. Finally a vote would be taken.

As Mrs Little walked round the class discussing their ideas, my eyes turned nervously to Shannon, Sean and Robert, those most likely to cause a problem. But they all seemed on task, which was good. Not that I suspected problems after yesterday, especially from Shannon. However, it is not a good idea to rest on your laurels with that girl, as I was very soon to find out ...

'Time up,' I called, 'You now have two final minutes to ensure you are happy with your speeches, before I choose the first one.'

Kate's hand shot up a few minutes afterwards, and I had no hesitation in choosing hers as the opening speech. In fairness to her, they had clearly worked very hard on it, although the bookies were offering low odds as to which side she would be speaking for.

'The thing is, right. It's all about personal freedom and personal choice isn't it? I mean, we don't go around telling the teachers what they have to wear, do we, so why should they tell us what we have to wear? It's not as though we're all going to come in hoodies or whatever. I agree there should be some rules, y'know. It's just that what we wear is a personal reflection of us, right, our own sort of fashion statement. I mean, you all go on about wanting to make us more independent, yeah, and then you stick us all in a boring green uniform which itches as well, by the way. We wouldn't work any less hard, and we might enjoy coming to school a bit more. So I say vote for Kate, Charlie and Roz and ban uniform.'

This passionate and relatively articulate speech was met largely with cheers of support, and if it hadn't been for the flagrantly rich line about 'not working any less hard', a practical impossibility, it would have been really rather good.

Miranda then stood and gave an excellent and highly articulate counter-argument before David, perhaps surprisingly, spoke against the motion.

'Right, I need one last speech for the motion ... Anyone? Shannon? Excellent.'

'I believe that children should wear school uniforms for a number of reasons.' As she started speaking it occurred to me just how mature this girl was capable of being. Knowing Mrs Little was present, she had begun with the poise of a practised public speaker.

'First, there is class identity. If we all wear the same uniform on a school outing, then we will be easily noticed. Secondly, we look smart. Whatever Kate may say about fashion and independence, some of us are bound to dress badly, or look as though we're about to go to a party and I'm sure that would mean we're not as likely to concentrate as well. Which leads me on to my last point. Some people are rich and some people are poor. If you are rich, you can wear designer clothes and show off to people. But if you're poor, you'll have to come to school in rags, and everyone will notice. Aren't I right, Patrick?'

So that was it. Over the next five seconds of silence, I understood a lot about Shannon. It had become abundantly clear, if it hadn't been beforehand, that she was a very bright girl and that, while she could cope with authority if she felt it was fair, she would have absolutely no qualms in letting everyone know, in the starkest of terms, if she felt she had been wronged or unnecessarily humiliated. The 'twat' incident was testament to that. Also, though, it appeared that her particular brand of getting even was to put innocent people down. God knows what Patrick had ever done to the Williams family — hounded them in a former life, no doubt — but both the twins saw him as easy meat. And that was the principal difference between Robert and Shannon, both bright and both highly unpredictable. There was no way that Robert would ever have been as barbed to Patrick — or, for that matter, to Dora Willoughby. Robert enjoyed a challenge, Shannon didn't care. She didn't care to the extent that knowing suspension was imminent, and knowing that Mrs Little was listening, she had coolly delivered her *coup de grace*. It was quite chilling.

'Shannon, would you come with me to my office, please.' Mrs Little tried to say this calmly, but there was an anger about her that I had never seen before.

This incident rather took the wind out of the sails of what was becoming an enjoyable and thought-provoking lesson. For a debate to function well there must be enthusiasm and lively exchanges. Shannon's comment had sapped the class of enthusiasm, and the rest of the lesson limped along. The debate ended with a narrow vote against the motion, but nobody seemed over-interested one way or another. Even Josh only managed a 'yeah, right now, let's really ban it properly', received without a flicker from the whole class.

I sent out Robert and co and, as agreed previously with Mrs Little, gave the rest a piece of paper and told them to write a page on 'rules and responsibility'. There were many stony faces as they began to write.

I met with Mrs Little at lunchtime for my debriefing. She had had no hesitation, she told me, about suspending Shannon for three days. While the final comment, in itself, could have been viewed as relatively minor, as a culmination of yesterday's events it was revealing in the extreme. I was glad. Shannon had thoroughly deserved it and I was ashamed of her.

'So, how do you think the lesson went?'

That old chestnut.

'Well – I've had better starts ...' I grinned inanely at this pathetic comment.

'OK, enough said. I think you handled the whole class very skilfully at first, and your response to Robert's put-down was excellent. However, and I won't dwell on this, Adrian, engaging with the children about what you want them to learn is very important. You've had lots to take in during your first few weeks and something was always going to give – I'm sure you won't forget again.'

'Point taken.' She couldn't have put this more nicely – she must have been very aware of my embarrassment. Her skill, though, was in the way she still managed to ram home the point all the same. She was generally happy with the lesson otherwise; she felt I engaged well with the kids and motivated them and, apart from one or two minor points, was enjoying it, until Shannon's speech put an abrupt end to her observation.

I left feeling pretty good, to find Rachel waiting in my class, sitting on my chair.

'So then, how did it go, tell me all about it?' She actually patted her lap when she said this, which, without realising it, was about the most provocative thing that she could have done. I resisted the temptation to take her gesture literally, and told her of the day and also about my meeting with Alison yesterday.

She listened intently, with teeth on bottom lip, as I related that first excruciating glance. At the end of it though, when I mentioned the party invite, she said: 'Wow! What a turnaround. Still, it answers my question. I was going to invite you round for some beers and a take-away on Saturday, as Alan's in Africa, but I can't get in the way of your hot date now, can I?'

I quickly thought back to all I had done in the last couple of days, but could not remember murdering anybody, setting anyone on fire, or kidnapping a wealthy businessman's daughter. Surely any lesser crime would only be punishable by several years' imprisonment? Yet here was God, the same one who I was really beginning to believe in, twisting the cruellest possible knife in my back. So many get-out clauses came into my head, such as phoning Alison and telling her I was ill. I even thought, for one ridiculous moment, of running from one place to another in implausible, bite-size chunks.

But the nagging reality was this. I had ruined Alison's evening three weeks ago and I simply couldn't bring myself to let her down again. I don't suppose that she would be especially upset, even if I did cancel – *'Oh, no, Adrian, that's fine. There're loads of people I know going, so it's really no big deal, some other time perhaps'* – but I couldn't do it. However much I wanted to, I would not phone her up and cancel the party.

'Oh, Rachel. That's a lovely offer, and we absolutely must do it sometime. Next time Alan's away, OK?'

It was all I could say.

'Mrs Willoughby? Hi, my name's Adrian, you'll be taking my class on Monday.'

'Yes, I know dear. I'm looking forward to it. I've got lots of nice things for them to do.'

'How lovely. What have you got planned?'

'Well now. Maths first, isn't it? I've got my trusty book of sums with me. What I thought is that I could give them some pages of addition and subtraction to practise for the hour, while I sit at the desk and made sure that they are quiet.'

'That's nice, Mrs Willoughby. What about literacy?'

'Lit– Oh, you mean English? Well, I thought they could write a story of their choice.'

'I'm sure they'd enjoy that. And you would be ...?'

'I'd be sitting at the front making sure that they didn't talk.'

'Right. Bit of a theme developing here. And the afternoon?'

'Um, I'm sure they'll have reading books that they can enjoy for the first hour or so while I sit at the –'

'Yes, yes. Go on.'

'Then – I know it says PE on the timetable but I think it might be a bit chilly outside. I'm seventy-four, you know.'

'Oh, I'm sure we could provide a blanket for you, Mrs Willoughby, and you could get some of the children to bring the desk outside ...'

'That's very kind of you, young man, but I thought maybe they could draw some pictures of their own choice, perhaps using colour pencils to avoid a mess.'

'That sounds like a fabulous day, Mrs Willoughby, I'm sure that the children will thoroughly enjoy it.'

'I hope so, dear. Now, if there's nothing else ...'

'No, I don't think so. If you could just leave the clearly differentiated lesson plans on my desk, together with the *learning objectives.'*

 'Er, the learning what?'

 'Objectives, Mrs Willoughby. You know, what you want the children to actually learn from their hour of silent sums. Robert, in particular, insists that you give him his objectives. Then if you could just link them all nicely to the Primary Framework and the National Curriculum, and comment on how you feel each of the groups have progressed in accordance with their layered targets, that would be just tickety-boo.

 'You're looking a bit peaky, Mrs Willoughby. Everything OK ...?'

8.

My mind, over the next three days, was a muddle of confusion, trying to work out my feelings for the girl-and-the-party-to-be, and the-girl-and-the-dinner-not-to-be. I spent so long trying to decide whether I was excited over the prospect of the date with Alison, until I realised that I couldn't be. By their very nature, feelings are spontaneous and if you have to set up a sub-committee to see if they are there ... However, feelings can grow – the last meeting between Alison and me was always going to be strained, and now that the pub incident was put firmly behind us, who knew what might develop.

I had no such confusion of my feelings towards Rachel. I was, quite simply, in love with her in a way that I've never felt before. But she was unavailable, and however hard I tried to avoid the thought, there wasn't too much to suggest that she was about to ditch the perfect Alan just to be with me.

Life without Shannon was, in fairness to her, not too much different to when she'd been there. I was interested to watch Sean's reaction to her exclusion. As usual, he remained aloof and it was impossible to tell whether he was sorry that she wasn't there or not. I hadn't cracked their relationship with each other yet – it appeared that there was a mutual indifference between them, but I felt sure that there must be some degree of affection or loyalty. This was borne out on Friday when Miranda, a lovely girl but one with no qualms about saying what she felt, said something along the lines of how much nicer the atmosphere in the classroom had been since Shannon's exclusion.

Sean's response was telling in the extreme: 'I beg your pardon, Miss Goody-two-shoes?' The words were fairly spat out but Miranda, to her credit, didn't flinch.

'I know she's your sister, Sean, but she was foul at the beginning of this week. You have to admit that.'

Sean stared at her with steely eyes for a full ten seconds. I should have stepped in to defuse the situation there and then, but I was as wrapped up in it as everyone else.

A menacing smile eventually formed on Sean's face as he said: 'You really do need to be very careful what you say, and who you say it to, is that clear?'

This was now bordering on something out of *The Godfather*, so step in I did, albeit half a minute late. The moment passed, but there was an uneasy feeling in the air and when I looked back at Miranda a few moments later, she was shaking. I watched Sean carefully for the rest of the day to check he didn't put something in Miranda's milk and, at the end of it, after football practice, I made sure that she went safely home without further incident. Shannon was to return on Monday, however, and there might well still have been recriminations if Sean decided to speak to her.

None of us batted an eyelid when, later, Naomi asked to join us for our Friday night out, as her sidekick, Lucy, had come down with flu. While at the pub, we spent an enjoyable twenty minutes or so discussing the worst possible scenario for Corinne's party. I suggested that Alison had lured me there on a ruse, and the place would be filled with politically correct lesbians quizzing me all night about my suitability as a teacher. Naomi thought that I might get off with some hot chick, only to find out later it was Sean and Shannon's mum. Liam's horrifying vision saw Alison and me beginning to make out just as her ex-husband, a Neanderthal skinhead with vacant eyes, stormed in brandishing a knuckleduster. Finally Tony took delight in creating a party where I realised, just after all the doors had been locked, that all the guests, including Corinne and Alison, were actually cross-dressing transvestites and, as 'You Sexy Thing' started blaring from the CD player, the clothes began to come off ...

'Actually, they did look a bit butch,' he continued, revelling in his theme, 'maybe you hit the nail on the head when you said Alison was unlikely to have children.'

What did happen at the party was, in its own way, equally bizarre. I picked Alison up from her cottage at eight the next evening, as arranged. I wonder how many people have ever been invited to a party when the only two words previously spoken to them by the host were 'you' and 'bastard'. Things could only improve from there and Corinne's polite, if slightly stilted, 'hello, Adrian' on our arrival at least splintered, if not broke, the ice.

Corinne lived in a nice three-bed end-of-terrace in the heart of the village. While I had no idea yet what she did for a living, or how old she was – I put her in her late twenties – she had clearly been successful. We exchanged brief pleasantries, although there was not an easy flow to them. I could only guess as to the conversation that had taken place between the two sisters when Alison had explained who she would be bringing to the party, and the inevitable initial tension was certainly in evidence. It was essential, as that great agony aunt, Naomi, had strongly advised, that I played it very cool, didn't try to be funny and showed a little humility.

'You have a lovely house, Corinne,' I said. 'I've brought

flowers for you.' I could almost see Tony in the corner sticking his fingers down his throat, and Liam shaking his head, murmuring 'you cheesy little sod you'. Still, needs must.

'They're lovely, thank you, Adrian. I'll put them into some water – Alison can take your jacket and show you around.' Alison too, had clearly been a little edgy about this initial encounter, but it passed without too much squirming, and I was relieved when Corinne left Alison to give me a brief tour of the place.

My first coherent thought, after these initial exchanges, was how quiet the place was. I had momentarily forgotten that we were at a party, and just managed to stop myself from setting up a game of chess. We walked through the empty lounge, presumably the dance floor, and headed for that great sanctuary of quiet parties – the kitchen. There were precisely five people in there sipping beer and eating peanuts. Fair enough, I thought, it's still early, coach parties don't usually arrive until gone nine.

Alison introduced me to the five revellers. First there were Sally and Roger. Sally apologised in advance if they were a little smelly and mucky, but they'd been painting scenery all day for the local amateur dramatics group and hadn't had a chance to go home and get changed.

'Neither of us like acting,' said Roger, 'but we do like doing our bit. There's nothing quite as satisfying as working up a good sweat painting all day, and it's extremely rewarding when it's done.'

'It sounds wonderful,' I replied, 'but I shouldn't worry about smelling too much around me. I'm a pig farmer and I've been mucking out all day and, well, the farm's just round the corner and it didn't seem worth going home first.'

'Really?' said Sally, without a hint of sarcasm. 'You actually look quite clean, considering.'

'I think he might be teasing you,' said Alison, giving me a

playful punch. 'Excuse us, will you? Adrian, this is Justin and Josephine.'

I just had time to glance at the rather blank, confused and paint-speckled faces of Sally and Roger, and resisted the temptation to ask them if they had any spare ecstasy tablets, before finding myself shaking hands with J and J. After finding out that they were steam rally enthusiasts, I turned, perhaps rather rudely, to the last member of the party, a plumpish woman of about thirty.

'And this is Rachel, she's a teacher.'

There were just too many hideous comparisons between Rachel the teacher here, sipping shandy at a party that closely resembled a wake, and the other Rachel the teacher, who would be at home either alone or, worse still, with another platonic male friend who fancied his chances.

'So, what do you teach?' I said, and if, some three minutes later when Corinne entered, I had been asked anything about what Rachel had just told me, I couldn't have answered.

'Have you got yourself a drink, Adrian?' Corinne asked. 'I'm sorry there aren't more people here, I have invited several others.'

The tone of that sentence, the way it sort of drifted to an uncomfortable end, spoke volumes about Corinne and her life. I had no doubt that she had invited others, but I also had no doubt that they weren't going to turn up. She could almost have added '*I have invited several others, but they're not going to come because they know the sort of friends that are coming*', or '*they're not going to come because they know what my parties are like*', or '*they're not going to come because they know, deep down, that I'm actually rather a dull person*'.

However, I was here. I had no means of escape and I decided, there and then, that I was going to enjoy myself.

'There're more than enough of us to have a great time,

Corinne,' I said cheerfully, 'but first, I need another beer.'

And, to be fair, over the next half-hour or so, as a few more beers and shandies were sipped, everyone did seem to be enjoying themselves. As lively 80s music played, so conversation flowed. The steam rally and scenery painting enthusiasts shared tales with great enthusiasm, as Rachel chatted to Corinne. Alison and I, for the first time, had finally put to bed the pub incident and were chatting easily and openly. Indeed, after half an hour the swing-o-meter was just teetering between 'chatting easily' and 'flirting' when she began talking about Peter, her ex-husband.

'We met at college. He was studying to become a maths teacher and was, I suppose, a bit of a maths boffin. I've never been – er, that lucky with boyfriends and he made me feel really special. I never quite felt he was met with absolute approval from my family and, if I'm honest, I'm not entirely sure I ever really loved him. But we quickly got into a comfort zone which was much easier to stay in than get out of, you know what I mean? When he proposed after our graduations, there was a great sense of security in accepting. I suppose we got on well enough but there was never any sense of real excitement to the marriage and I had long since accepted that comfortable if uninspiring existence before he left me for a German teacher a year ago.'

There was a definite emphasis on the word 'German' here, as if somehow, had it have been a Home Economics teacher, it would have been a fair cop.

'I was more angry than anything else. What right did this slightly nerdy man, definitely below me in the pecking order, have to have an affair? Surely, by rights, I should be the one doing that? That might sound petulant, Adrian, but that's how I feel.'

She was really opening her heart to me now and I felt that this warranted some tenderness back. I gently put my hand on her shoulder and said, with feeling, 'It doesn't sound petulant at all, Alison, I know exactly how you feel.'

She responded by leaning in to me and, before I knew it, we were locked in a warm hug. While this did feel natural, I was wondering where on earth it was heading, as this was patently not one of those sort of parties. I was still debating whether to twist and raise the stakes to a kiss, when the doorbell rang. It was now 9.30 and, all things considered, I was happy for the party to get more crowded. We all heard Corinne run for the door, we all heard her open it, and we all heard the incredulity in her voice when she exclaimed 'Dad!'

'I'm sorry to spring ourselves on you like this,' he began a minute later, after he had wheeled his wife into the lounge. 'I didn't realise you had a few friends round. It's just, your mum and I have been going crazy recently, not knowing what to do with ourselves, and this morning I got another rejection letter. I tried to phone you both a few times but there was no reply. I know it's a long way to come – you know – just out of the blue like, and I know we might have come all this way to find you both out but – we just had to do *something*. I didn't think you'd mind ...'

As an opening speech, it was well crafted and neither Alison nor Corinne seemed the type to say: '*Well, yes, actually we do mind, now piss off you old fart.*' Neither, however, could suppress their slight indignance at the unannounced arrival and, when her Mum asked for the music to be turned down and for a cup of cocoa, there was an audible sigh from Corinne as she dutifully obeyed.

Jack and Rose Crane were both in their mid-fifties, but looked older. Wizened by multiple sclerosis, Rose looked a sorry state indeed, and Jack had sad and defeated eyes. The party had never gone beyond being a wounded animal and now it was stone dead. I clocked the moment when the Nolan Sisters, rather ironically, were abruptly stopped from singing 'I'm in the mood for dancing' at 9.34pm. I was just toying with the idea of phoning the *Guinness Book Of Records* and nominating tonight in the 'shortest ever party' category, when Jack Crane spoke directly to me.

'I don't know you, do I? You Alison's new boyfriend, are you? I hope you're better than that no-good husband of hers. Bit young, though, aren't you?'

Before I could respond to this rather terse inquisition, Alison, thankfully, stepped in.

'No, Dad, this is Adrian, and he's a friend of mine. We met at a lecture recently. Adrian's a primary school teacher.'

'Huh,' came the reply, or, translated: *'What sort of shandy-drinking southern poofter are you?'* Clearly he was slightly wary of men associated with his eldest daughter and I also had a strong suspicion that he was rather uninterested in me anyway, and looking for an avenue to get back to his favoured topic of conversation, himself. Sure enough, his subsequent 'still, it's a job, I suppose' and the baleful eyes invited the inevitable, and he was duly rewarded:

'So, how are you coping, Dad?'

'Not so good, Alison, not so good. I'd never missed a day's work in my life up until last month – you don't know how much pride I had to shelve to walk into that dole office. I've applied for a few jobs but it's pretty obvious that nobody wants someone in their fifties. It's not like we've got any savings either, I'm just not sure how we're going to cope.'

The mood was now so sombre that it had finally been verified, officially, as the least successful party of all time. I tried to think of an excuse to slip into the kitchen to be able to let my hair down and listen to some steam rally stories, but I somehow felt glued to the spot. So he continued telling his immediate family, and me, about his hardships and about his wife's ever-worsening condition.

Any hope of joining the kitchen revellers was soon extinguished when they came in, *en masse*, and announced it was time that they went. It was now shortly after ten o'clock, and there was only me left. I was giving Alison a lift home and was therefore trapped, and the conversation dragged on for a further twenty minutes.

Alison, to her credit, must have realised that this was pretty excruciating for me and so, shortly before 10.30, made excuses for us and we left. She was clearly highly embarrassed by the whole episode and kept apologising for inviting me to such a disastrous evening. I said all the right things – *It was really very nice at first ... Not your fault ... Mix up in communication, Parents seemed very nice* – but these were clearly platitudes and she wasn't fooled.

'If I promise you that none of my relatives will turn up,' she said on arrival at her house, 'would you come and have a cup of coffee with me?'

I smiled, agreed, and we entered her tidy, if unremarkable, house. I sat on the sofa while she made the coffee, allowing her the opportunity to show her hand by either choosing a chair or sitting next to me. And show her hand she did. She placed both our coffees on the coffee table and sat right next to me, immediately nestling her head into my shoulder. I put my arm around her and she moved to kiss me. There was obviously more passion and willingness in her kiss than in my response and she clearly sensed this. She smiled a little sadly.

'What's wrong, Adrian?'

How on earth could I answer that question to myself, let alone her? I really was beginning to like her, a lot, but I couldn't open up to her.

When I was sixteen I'd gone out with a really sweet girl called Jo for a few months and one night, at a party, someone else was flirting with me and I found myself kissing them, partly because I was flattered by the attention and partly because I was showing off to my friends. The look of hurt on Jo's face when she saw us together has never left me, and since then I have gone out of my way to avoid letting people down. And I would let Alison down. If we started dating, if we became close, if she opened herself up again and trusted another man, if she fell madly in love with me, and then if Rachel finished with Alan for me then yes, I would let her down. I would let her down even if it meant her going under. And I couldn't do that.

Yet did that mean I was to remain single because of some ridiculous pipe dream that simply wasn't going to happen? I could picture myself, in my eighties, in the old folks' home, chatting with Doris, and declining her advances. Just in case ...

'Nothing's wrong, Alison, it's just – let's just take it slowly, shall we? Despite what you may think, I have had a nice evening tonight, and I've enjoyed your company. It's half-term in just over a week, how about we go out for the day somewhere?'

She smiled and agreed, and I promised I'd phone her the following week, after I'd got parents' evening out of the way. Then I drank my coffee, gave her another warm hug and kiss on the cheek, and left.

The night was still young, it was a fresh but pleasant October evening, and I wasn't tired. I drove to the canal, found a convenient tree stump to sit on, watched the moon reflect off the water, and let the silence envelop me.

For all my confusions and mixed emotions, I felt happy. I found myself looking forward to my immediate future – teaching the children on Monday, impressing the parents on Tuesday and Wednesday and seeing Alison again at half-term. I was also thoroughly looking forward to relating, with

ample embellishment, the events of the evening to Liam,
Tony and Naomi when I got home.

'So Corinne, do you want the good news, or the bad news ...?
The good news is that I've brought a date with me ...'

'Who? Oh Christ, Alison, you haven't got back together with
that slime ball of a husband, have you?'

'Nooooo. Er, remember that night when Dad phoned with his
news, and we went out for a drink?'

'Oh yes, the one where I nearly decked that arrogant bastard
sitting next to us? Go on.'

'Well, and this is where the bad news starts, maybe the
phrase 'arrogant bastard' is a tiny bit premature. I mean, we
hardly even ...'

'OH-MY-GOD. Alison, please tell me that you have not
brought that horrible little weasel of a man to my house?'

It was time to act. Stepping into view, I smiled as sweetly as
possible, handed Corinne a bouquet of flowers and told her
what a lovely house she had.

That wiped the scowl from her face.

9.

Parents' evening – Tuesday 16th October

6.00	Alice Anderson
6.10	Daniel Brothwell
6.20	Miranda Caldwell
6.30	Sanjay Ganesh
6.40	David Hunter
6.50	
7.00	William Welsh
7.10	Josh Robins
7.20	Mark Baines
7.30	Cherry Michaels
7.40	Rhiannon Salter
7.50	Patrick Collins
8.00	
8.10	Richard Keane
8.20	Charlotte Burrows

'Mr and Mrs Anderson? Please come in. I'm Adrian Gray, Alice's teacher. I'm pleased to meet you. I see the purpose of tonight being to allow me to give you my very early impression of Alice, and then for you to come back with any queries or concerns that you may have. Basically, Alice is an absolute delight to teach. She's enthusiastic, bright and has a lovely sense of humour. However, I don't want to allow her to coast this year, and feel that she will really benefit from being stretched. For instance, I'm trying to get her to read some more challenging fiction to what she's been reading, and trying to stretch her use of vocabulary in her writing. In maths, I'm giving her lots of complex problems to get her teeth into, and in science I'm really trying to get her to analyse why things have happened during her experiments. In summary, if I can really stretch her with the sort of examples I've just given, I think we can expect great things from Alice this year. Does that sound a fair synopsis?'

I'd learnt this speech off by heart, and it clearly seemed to work.

'Definitely,' replied her mum. 'Alice wasn't pushed last year and didn't really enjoy it. She's been really enthusiastic about everything this year, and you've clearly made a good impression on her. She thinks you're great.'

'Oh well,' I said. 'I've clearly paid her enough then. She said she'd say nice things about me if I gave her a tenner.'

And so we laughed, chatted amicably and agreed on some targets for their daughter. It was a thoroughly pleasant way to spend ten minutes and the phrase *'don't know what all the fuss is about'* briefly entered my mind. But I knew I was being broken in very gently, and I wondered whether I'd still feel the same after listening to Kate's, Robert's and Ronnie and Reggie's parents. I somehow feared not.

I had spoken to my friend Rupert the previous evening to get some general tips for talking to the parents and, from just one year's teaching, his advice was good:

'Always start with something positive, even if you have the child from hell. If you know you're about to tell a parent that their child is a psychopathic monster, it sugars the pill slightly if they know that, in a recent story, young Hannibal managed to spell the word 'psychopathic' correctly. Also, whatever you do, don't use the phrase 'oh he's fine, you've got nothing to worry about' for bright kids. Their parents are nearly always keen to know exactly how you are pushing their little darlings on.

'The most important thing, Adrian, is to make all the parents believe that you have really got to know their child. I don't care what anybody says, your reputation at a school is gonna come almost entirely from what the parents think about you. You may not like it, but the mums are going to stand by that school gate at the end of the day, and they are going to talk about their kids' new teacher. Such gossip and rumours – well, you know what it's like, they spread like wildfire. Impress 'em at parents' evening and you'll soon build a reputation for yourself.'

Hence my opening spiel to Mr and Mrs Anderson. This advice was excellent for nearly all children. The Alices, Mirandas and Williams of this world would get the 'specific targeting' treatment, and I was sure that I could think of something vaguely positive to say to the likes of Kate's, Shannon's and, at a push, even Josh's parents. However, when planning my notes, I found it really difficult to make such pertinent comments about Daniel. Daniel Brothwell was the last person in the class whose name I had learnt. He was one of those children who seem to be virtually camouflaged by his surroundings. Slightly below average height, slightly below average ability, he quietly went about his day. He very rarely offered comment or opinion in class and never got into any trouble. He settled reasonably quickly to his work but what he produced was unremarkable.

I found myself telling his mum lots of very woolly, non-committal rubbish that must have sounded very lame. What I would have liked to have said was: *'Mrs Brothwell? My* name is Adrian Gray. I'm Daniel's teacher. I shan't lie to you, or waste your time any further, because the truth is that I simply don't know your child well enough to comment.'

When I asked her if she had any questions or wanted to add anything she replied, uninterestedly, 'not really' and the ten-minute interview was over in slightly under three minutes. It was, from start to finish, most unsatisfactory.

When Miranda's parents entered, I fully expected a repeat dose of the easy-flowing, jovial chat I had had with the Andersons. As soon as I welcomed them in, however, my antennae were raised by their slightly forced smiles and stiff demeanours. I gave them Alice's spiel but their eyes looked at me coldly and when I asked 'does that sound like a fair synopsis?' the words came out lamely, and it was obvious that they patently didn't.

'Miranda is on the gifted and talented register for maths,' Mr Caldwell replied, 'and she was working at a high Level 5 last year. From seeing her homework, and looking in her books, it's clear to both of us that the work is much too easy for her. Those "complex problems" you mentioned? She could have done them two years ago.'

I simply wasn't well-equipped or experienced enough to deal with such an imposing bastard. He was dressed in an expensive suit, was some twenty years my senior, and looked every inch the Chairman of the Board, bullying a recent recruit for poor productivity. I knew that I needed to look him in the eye, and calmly justify the work I was setting her, but I couldn't do it. I stammered out some rubbish about still getting to know her – hadn't realised she was finding it too easy – obviously now I'll give her much harder work, but my body language shouted of one who was being crushed by a much better opponent. He could very easily have turned the screw, but clearly found me unworthy. It was then Mrs Caldwell's turn for a bit of Gray-baiting.

'What are you doing about the bullying?'

This really threw me. 'I – I beg your pardon?'

'Are you not aware that Miranda's being bullied by those Williams twins?'

Oh bollocks. Shit, bugger, bollocks. Quite clearly, Sean had spoken to Shannon at the weekend and the pair of them had quietly worked on Miranda over the last two days.

'Er, I know she had a bit of a to-do with Sean last Friday, but I hadn't realised ...'

'Well, isn't it your job to be aware of these sorts of things, Mr Gray?' she spat.

'Those two nasty pieces of work have taunted, threatened and humiliated Miranda over the last two days, to the extent that she's been in floods of tears and doesn't want to come to school tomorrow.'

Sod this. I'd had enough. A cornered boxer could either lie down and be punched or take a swipe back.

'Unfortunately, Mrs Caldwell, I left my crystal ball at home this week.'

'I beg your pardon?' – the Chairman of the Board's icy response to the spotty recruit who'd dared to answer back.

Shit. Maybe heavy sarcasm was not the best form of defence.

'All I'm saying, Mr Caldwell, is that if things go on in the playground, or behind my back, and nobody informs me about them, how can I be expected to deal with them? Have you asked Miranda to speak to me about Sean and Shannon? Or, if she didn't want to do that, could you have not given me a phone call?' *Take that you bastard.*

'Well I – I assumed – but anyway – you know now – perhaps you'll deal with it.'

'Of course I will – that's my job. First thing tomorrow I'll speak to all three of them and I'll sort it out.'

By now I felt in the ascendancy, and by the time they left –

some seventeen minutes after their ten-minute slot started, I felt like I had at least won back some credibility. However, it had shaken me up. It's astounding how one's confidence can reach such highs and lows depending on whether the parents are pleased or disappointed.

The next few went without incident. Sanjay's and David's parents were very supportive and when I related the rounders incident to David's mum, she had to wipe away the tears. William's parents thankfully agreed with Alice's rather than Miranda's parents' view of my handling of a bright child, and then came Josh's dad.

It was obvious, as he entered the room, that he was struggling to focus, and he sat forward in his chair, staring disconcertingly straight through me. Remembering Rupert's advice, I began with the 'positive', saying that Josh was a 'lively' character. This was such a blatant euphemism to anybody not on drugs for a 'little shit', but it was the only vaguely positive thing I could come up with. As I continued with my rhetoric, it became clear that he didn't want to be there or, just as likely, didn't even know he was. He responded to my points or questions with a throaty grunt, and his response when I said that Josh never handed in his homework was: 'We don't do homework.' It was such a conversation stopper that I simply didn't know what to say next. There were then two people in the room who didn't want to be there, so I flatly ended the consultation by standing and saying 'Unless there's anything else ...?' Unsurprisingly, there wasn't anything else, so I got rid of him and opened the windows.

I really didn't know what I was expecting when I called in Patrick's mum, but my first impression was of someone who did not have too much joy in her life. A single mother of four, she was rather overweight and I felt instantly sorry for her.

I stressed, as much as I could, what a lovely boy Patrick was and went through, in detail, all that I was doing for him, and the provisions that the school was making. She listened attentively enough but there seemed to be a resigned expression on her face, intimating that she knew that Patrick was always going to suffer both intellectually and socially. I tried to tell her that, despite his difficulties, Patrick was a bright boy and she smiled and said 'I guess so.' If there was one parent who could have had a grudge against the twins it was her, but she didn't mention them and, when she left, I hadn't felt like I'd really got through.

I was only fifteen minutes late by the time Richard's parents came in, and had narrowed that to thirteen when Charlie's mum entered. I was a bit concerned about how she might be after I had overreacted to Charlie earlier in the term, but she was, refreshingly, one of these '*I have no illusions about my daughter, if you can shut her up then you're a better man than I*' sort of Mum, and the interview ran smoothly and jovially.

I'd expected that after nearly three hours of non-stop talking, I'd be thoroughly exhausted. However, I felt so mentally alert after having to think on my feet that I felt far more in the need of a drink than of my bed.

I bumped into Rachel on my way out. She gave me her usual radiant smile and asked me how things had gone.

'Fucking Caldwells,' was my frank reply.

She laughed: 'Didn't anybody warn you about them? They've had a reputation all the way through the school and have had more than one teacher in tears. Don't take it personally. I've had a couple of shitty parents as well and I was hoping Ellie might offer to buy me a drink to commiserate. However, it looks like she's gone.'

'Can I help? I think I know where her phone number is ...'
'Ha, ha, I'll meet you in The Crown in ten minutes. I'm dying to know what happened on Saturday.'

So that rollercoaster of an evening had a lovely ending. Rachel laughed in all the right places as I related the details of the party, and then she asked me why I was so reticent about developing my relationship with Alison.
'Because, quite simply, Rachel, I'm madly in love with you.'
'Oh, I don't know, I'm just not sure whether she's right for me, and I don't want to hurt her.'
She said the word 'bastards' in all the right places when I summarised the Caldwell interview, and then told me about her evening.
'Perhaps I'm old-fashioned, but I kind of thought that a parent might be faintly interested if her child messes his pants every bloody day. Mrs Martin's response, however, was to shrug her shoulders and say that Johnny never does that kind of thing at home, and if he's doing it at school, it's our fault and we need to deal with it.'
I listened to this with an open mouth, which widened still further when she told me about the parent who wanted to know why his five-year-old boy wasn't getting regular home-work, and that at home he had taught him how to do long multiplication, whereas at school they were counting to ten.
I left the pub an hour later in much higher spirits and went straight to bed. As I turned out the lights, I remembered an article in a national newspaper entitled 'The real enemy in the classroom', in which the reporter had berated ignorant or pushy parents for the lack of support they gave to schools. At the time I'd dismissed it as excessive journalism, but now, after some of the experiences of the evening, I could see where the reporter was coming from.

I spoke to Miranda and the twins first thing in the morning to try to smooth things over and ensure that there would be no further reprisals. Also, I was worried that Mr Caldwell's lawyer would turn up if I didn't. The twins both shrugged and said, in no uncertain terms, that Miranda had publicly slated Shannon and they were making sure she didn't do it again. This was such a flagrant breach of school rules that I knew I should really march them into see Mrs Little but I judged that this would not be a good idea. These two were intelligent children and if they received any more flak, it was likely that Miranda would be the one to suffer. Even though I made it very clear that she hadn't 'grassed', they would not see it like that. My only concern was that this should blow over.

'If I speak to Miranda,' I said, 'and get her assurances that she won't say such things about you publicly again, can I have your assurances that the matter is now closed?'

'Fair enough,' replied Shannon instantly, and I went to find Miranda.

'Why didn't you tell me they were being horrible to you?' I asked gently.

'I dunno. I just – sort of hoped they'd go away. It wasn't that bad.'

'That's not what your parents said last night, Miranda.'

She just looked down, embarrassed, and I had no intention of making her feel even more uncomfortable.

'Listen. Just promise me two things. First, whatever you may feel about the twins, don't blurt it out in the classroom in future, and secondly – please let me know if you're upset. I can deal with it without making you look like a grass. OK?'

She nodded and walked away. How could such a lovely girl have such horrible parents?

At six o'clock I braced myself for the second round of parents' consultations.

My evening's entertainment was as follows:

6:00   Elizabeth Vaughan
6:10   Marcus Neale
6:20   Rozinder Urzan
6:30
6:40   Sophie Burns
6:50   Donna White
7:00   Robert Carlton
7:10   Allard Mills
7:20   Kate Robinson
7:30
7:40   Prakesh Patel
7:50   Andrew Newton
8:00   Simon Edwards
8:10   Sean Williams
8:20   Shannon Williams

I'd always regarded Rozinder in exactly the same way as I had Charlie – Kate's sidekick, unbelievably chatty and less than enthusiastic about work. I somehow assumed, therefore, that her parents would have the same casual attitude as Charlie's mum. I was grossly mistaken. After routine discussions with Elizabeth and then Marcus' parents, the Urzans came in. They were committed Muslims and valued Rozinder's education very highly. They were also very concerned about her friendship groups and practically begged me to get her to distance herself from Kate and Charlie.

I told them that I had sat Rozinder next to Sophie, a lovely hardworking girl, but they were just as concerned about the social influence in the playground. By the time that this, my first interview of the evening had ended, I not only felt exhausted, but more of a counsellor than a teacher.

I found myself thinking, through Sophie's and Donna's parents' consultations, about the people I would be seeing next – Robert's parents. Such was the enigma surrounding this child that I simply didn't know whether to expect old, young, middle class, working class, supportive, Caldwell-like, emotive or placid. I felt rather guilty as I showed Donna's parents out, as I had been distinctly on autopilot for the last twenty minutes.

Perhaps, if I expected anything at all from Mr and Mrs Carlton, it would have been sad and haggard countenances, but this was far from the case. Two cheerful, intelligent faces met my call.

I had spent ages deciding how to summarise Robert. I wanted to tread a delicate path between showing concern for his situation, but not dwelling on the past.

'I've thoroughly enjoyed the challenge of teaching Robert. He keeps me on my toes in no uncertain terms, and if I show any weakness, he'll let me know.' I then related the tale of the English objectives, but did so with a smile on my face.

'That's our Robert,' said Mr Carlton, with a twisted grin. 'We must say, though, that for the first time since the accident, he seems to be showing an element of enthusiasm, for which we are massively grateful.'

'Well, that's nice to hear. To be honest, I'm never quite sure where I stand with him. One day I feel like we've really connected and the next he's distant and surly again.'

'That's his way. He's received endless counselling and we've been told that he's simply not ready to bond emotionally yet. Even four years on, his defence mechanism is to reject kindness and show apparent indifference. The fact that we can see a very subtle shift in his behaviour patterns, and that he now actually talks about school, must be a step in the right direction. We just hope that it continues this year – we really are worried about secondary school and potential teasing. As you probably know, he finds it difficult to establish firm friendships. He's mentioned a boy called William?'

'William Welsh? One of the first things I did was to try to sit Robert with somebody who would be a good influence – William's bright as well and won't subject him to kind-hearted platitudes. I'd pursue that one if I were you.'

The whole consultation was both fascinating and highly informative. I was also, immodestly, very proud of myself. Here was I, a young teacher in his first year, slowly beginning to have an effect on Robert in a way others had found difficult to do. I held no illusions that his volatile and unpredictable days were behind him, but his parents were really grateful and that was the most satisfying moment so far in my six weeks as a teacher. However, this was, by some margin, the highlight of the evening.

Full of confidence and slightly cocky, I called in Allard's father. I thought at first that his grandparent had turned up, as he was well into his fifties and looked older. The best way to describe him was creepy. He reminded me of a sort of Donald Pleasance character in his most chilling of roles. While he neither breathed heavily and lengthily at me, nor sharpened a sword as I spoke, I felt remarkably uneasy and claustrophobic, and I simply wanted him to go. This was, I knew, grossly unfair on someone who had done nothing wrong. But throughout the consultation he kept up a chilling smile with his head cocked disconcertingly to one side, and only ever breathed 'yes', 'no' or 'I see.' I had planned to take the bull by the horns and broach the subject of Allard's surliness but, to my shame, I quickly went through my spiel and, after establishing that he had no questions, led him out of the classroom. As I physically shuddered, I felt a mixture of relief and guilt: the consultation had achieved precisely nothing because I was too freaked to initiate constructive discourse.

Again, the rollercoaster of emotion had risen and fallen dramatically, and I still had Kate's mother to negotiate, immediately after Allard's father returned to 10 Rillington Place.

If Mr Mills looked like a grandparent then Ms Robinson looked like a teenage sister. She sauntered in, chewing gum, and uttered a cursory 'all right?' as she sat down. I had chickened out of saying what I should have said to Mr Mills, and I wasn't going to with big sis:

She punctuated my speech by saying 'yeah, right' some five times, like the passive listener during a gossipy phone call. I was trying to get across that her daughter needed to improve both her attitude and commitment levels, but all I got back was the stuck-record routine. It was only when I mentioned that she had been disciplined several times for swearing on the playground that I got any reaction.

'Oh for Christ's sake. I'll kill the little shit. I've told her so many fuckin' times that she shouldn't swear at school.'

Quite.

She agreed to have a fucking word with the fucking shit, no doubt to try and establish what fucking influence was making her fucking swear. When she finally left I breathed a heavy sigh, and regained my composure somewhat during successful and rewarding discussions with Prakesh's mum, Simon's dad and Andrew's parents.

There was one other piece of advice that Rupert had given me on Monday night. 'Whatever you do, don't end the evening with a parent who's likely to be awkward or stay over their allotted time. It is so much easier for you to get rid of them if they know you've got someone else waiting.' This would have been excellent advice if the interview times had not already been circulated, and the Williams had not already signed up for the last two slots. I had been dreading these more than any other. There was a cold, calculated yet intelligent air about both twins and I could only assume that their parents would be similar. I had difficult subjects to discuss with them and I had kept them waiting twenty-five minutes. I took a deep breath and called them in.

'I'm sorry to have kept you waiting,' I said. Neither of them replied as they walked towards my door. They were both imposing figures. He was well over six feet tall and very muscular, and she dwarfed my five feet seven inches. Neither of them looked unintelligent and both had piercing eyes that could wilt a man at fifty paces. They did not, however, look like thugs either. Both were dressed smartly, if casually, and were not unattractive to the eye. I would hate to think, though, what would happen to anybody who crossed them.

'I'm sorry to have kept you waiting,' I repeated as we sat down. But if I was subconsciously hoping for a _'no problem – I appreciate these things run over'_, none came.

'As we've got twenty minutes, I'll do them one at a time – so to speak.' _Oh God, did I really say that?_ 'Er – shall I start with Sean?'

'How about you do them both together, as we're late?' came his even response.

'Yeah, well – er – if you like – it's just that – well – they're different of course and ...'

'Please. Just tell us about our children.' It was his calmness that made me so edgy; this huge imposing man calmly waiting for me to tell him what his kids were like.

'OK. Well, both Sean and Shannon are very mature children. They are intelligent and can be articulate but sometimes don't join in as much as I'd like.'

'Are they bored with the work you set them?'

'Er – I'm not sure – sometimes, perhaps. They can switch off easily. They have to understand that this is the curriculum and sometimes you have to grin and bear things if you don't specifically enjoy them.'

'How's his football?' he asked, completely changing the

rather delicate subject that I was braving my way through.

'What? Oh, er, yeah, very good. He's easily the best player in the school, but perhaps not a team player.'

'If he's better than the others, what's the point in lessening our chances of winning by passing to them?'

'Well, it's not quite as simple as that, I mean, after all, it's a game and – er, even if you are the best – '

'That's what I tell him anyway.' This was an interruption of the *'I know what I'm talking about and you quite clearly don't so drop it you silly little man'* kind.

'Well, OK, er – whatever. Can we come back to their work? As I said, both Sean and Shannon are capable of very good work and their efforts, especially their homework, don't usually do justice to their ability.'

'Homework's not good you say?'

'Er no, not usually – really – often – much ...'

'OK, I'll have words.'

This was all excruciating. I was physically squirming in my seat, sweat dripping down my back as he spoke with a calm authority and she looked on silently. I knew I had to bring up the subject of their behaviour and I was absolutely dreading it.

'Good, thank you. As you know both Sean and Shannon are very strong characters and have clear views of right and wrong. Unfortunately they can be rather aggressive, verbally, if they feel they're being wronged.'

'So can I, Mr Gray.'

Oh, shit. OK, forget the euphemisms. 'I can understand them sticking up for themselves and for each other, but there's a difference between that and outright nastiness. Also both of them have been saying extremely unkind things to a boy in our class, completely unprovoked – I can't see any justification in that whatsoever. As you know, Shannon was suspended last week for, primarily, being extremely rude to a supply teacher and – '

'Can I stop you there, Mr Gray?' he said, as evenly as ever but with a slightly icier tone to his voice. 'You're making several points all at once here. First, I heard Shannon's version of events and it seems to me that this teacher got what she deserved. Secondly, if anyone says anything derogatory about my children then they must accept the consequences. I'm sure that's not school policy, Mr Gray, but we've brought our children up to stick up for themselves. Your other point, however, I agree with. Sean's told me about Patrick and he sounds a bit of a wimp. However, as you say, to taunt him without provocation is out of order. That won't happen again.'

'Thank you. Please don't get me wrong. I don't want this to sound all bad – they've both got a really good side to them.'

'Such as what?'

It was only when I was saying this, desperately trying to find something positive, that I realised that it was hard to expand upon.

'Er, as I've said, they're both articulate and intelligent. Also, if they feel that they've proved a point, they're very capable of stopping.'

What the hell did that mean? Fortunately, he didn't pursue it any further and I finally got rid of them. His wife hadn't said a word throughout and I had to stop myself using sign language when saying goodbye. The whole episode, some twenty-five minutes of it, was thoroughly exhausting and I was shattered. I also didn't know if they had been happy with what I'd said or if it was likely to make a difference. I was just glad they had gone.

My alertness of the previous night had been replaced by a weariness caused by the huge range of emotions I had endured on this one. I sat at home with a whisky and thought through my first half term, and my first experience of parents' evenings. It occurred to me that, despite the emotional battering, it was only really the Caldwells, out of twenty-six sets of parents, who had been obviously unimpressed by me, whereas so many others, perhaps because of Ellie Luck's uninspiring methods last year, were really pleased with what I had done. And I was pleased too. I was tired, I was looking forward to a week's break, but I honestly thought that my first half term at Green Acre had been a successful one, and that a platform had been laid for the rest of the year.

I drained my whisky and retired to bed.

'Mr and Mrs Caldwell? Please come through. I see the purpose of this session, for most parents, as letting you know what I think of your child and allowing you to come back with any queries or concerns that you may have. However, that's not what I'm going to do with you. You see, you have a reputation for being bullying, interfering parents who have made many teachers' lives miserable. You have a lovely daughter in Miranda, although, God knows, she must have been adopted.

'So this is not a two-way conversation, it's all one-way. Miranda is a very bright girl but not as bright as you think. You obviously see her as an extension of yourself, some great intellect who's better than everyone else. Well she's certainly better than her parents because she's kind, caring and considerate to others.

'I don't think you give a stuff about people beyond your immediate family, do you, Mr Caldwell? And as for you, you sanctimonious little cow, before you start accusing me of not doing my job properly, how about you get a few facts straight? Now, piss off, the pair of you.'

If only ...

10.

The last two days before half-term passed uneventfully
enough. The spat between Miranda and the twins seemed to
have dissipated and both Sean and Shannon let Patrick be.
Whether this was coincidental or as a result of an order
from above I could only surmise. I fervently hoped it was the
latter – Patrick's life would be so much more enjoyable if
they were to get off his back permanently.

My class left on Friday with mixed emotions – happy at
the thought of nine days' holiday before them, and slightly
miffed that part of that time had to be spent planning their
autobiography as part of an extended piece of homework.

I went to Rachel's classroom after school to wish her an
enjoyable break.

'Are you around next Saturday night?' she asked.

At last! An evening with just the two of us, where I could
slowly unleash my charm.

'I am. What did you have planned?'

'It's just – you haven't met Alan and I wondered if you and
Alison would like to join us for dinner?'

I don't think my face gave anything away. I don't think the
fact that my brain was practically ordering my mouth to tell
her to stuff Alan and Alison showed as involuntary twitches,
as I smiled and told her that that would be lovely.

'I'll have to check with her of course – she may not want to – after all we're not technically an item.'

'Well, maybe a few glasses of wine might help. Let us know, yeah?'

I resisted the temptation to ask if it was likely to be a swinger's party and left, more confused than ever. Maybe I could visit some tribal witch doctor called Mr Wong in the next week and buy some potent love potion. A few drops in Alan and Alison's wine and a subsequent rendezvous in a bedroom would leave two poor, cheated souls desperate for each other's company ...

On Saturday night I met up with Rupert in London. We had been friends for many years and he had been my unofficial mentor this year. He also taught Year 6, but in a large multicultural school in inner-city London.

'You don't know you're born,' he told me, after I had related some of the more challenging episodes of the previous six weeks. 'None of the children in my school are from affluent backgrounds and most of them have woefully inadequate young single mums as their carers. I know of at least four children in my class whose mothers are prostitutes. You'll never believe this but, as a present at the end of the summer term, I was offered a half-price session from one particularly uncouth specimen. I was extremely offended – I'd worked wonders with her little oik and felt I was worth at least a 75% discount, if not a freebie.'

He'd related a few such incidents to me before, but as our conversations this term had, not surprisingly, focused on me, much of this was new.

It really hammered home just how different leafy Green Acre was from his school. Some of the stories he told were quite horrifying, and I felt as though I'd be completely ill-equipped to deal with them. For whatever reason, I'd never been placed in a very challenging school on teaching practice and thus hadn't received guidance on how to handle the sort of scenarios he was relating.

'Take Billy,' he said. 'He's screwed up even by Castle Row's standards. Last week he brought a rope in to school, draped it round his neck and went round shouting: "I'm gonna do it. Why don't you believe me? I'm gonna do it!".'

'And did he?'

'Of course not. He's often making that sort of desperate cry for help though, and has been known to harm himself.'

'So why did you want to teach at Castle Row?' I asked. 'You had excellent teaching practices, you got a brainy swot's degree; surely you could have had your pick of schools?'

Now I've always imagined Rupert to be very much like me – slightly self-deprecating, with a bit of the class clown about him and a penchant for getting out of hard work. His reply not only shocked and shamed me, but introduced me to a side of him that I didn't know existed.

'Is that how you see it, Adrian, as some sort of pecking order? If you're a shite teacher, well you can go to the bottom of the class and teach the shite no-hopers. But if you've got good grades, good skills and a real aptitude for teaching, well hey! The sky's the limit. If you're really good then you may even be allowed the dizzy heights of teaching really rich kids and possibly even in a private school. I'll tell you why I chose Castle Row, Adrian, and not Green Acre. I chose it because the kids here desperately need a decent role model in their lives. Sure, they might throw a few chairs at you initially, but the day they start really confiding in you, the day they ask if maybe you can be their Dad, I tell you, Adrian, you know you're making a difference. That's why I chose Castle Row.'

I didn't know what to say. I hadn't meant my question to

sound the way it did, and I mumbled something to that effect. He smiled and bought me another drink and we continued to share anecdotes. But there was the same sort of uneasy atmosphere as when I first went for a drink with Rachel, and I was quite relieved when I could make my excuses and leave to catch my train.

It was a very thoughtful Adrian Gray who journeyed home alone. I had vowed to myself to 'grow up' on that fateful pub evening and I'm pretty certain that I had done, to some extent. Did I really subconsciously feel that teaching at Green Acre was a cushy option? Would I accept an offer of a job at Castle Row if one came tomorrow? While I flippantly joke that I became a teacher for the holidays, I know honestly that I became one because I wanted to make a difference. I was under the impression that I was genuinely doing so, but now, after listening to Rupert, I wasn't so sure.

I decided not to mention Rachel's invitation when I phoned Alison to organise our day out. If our date was an unmitigated disaster, I could hardly tell her she had failed to qualify for the next round, and we might be left in a ridiculous position in which neither of us wanted to spend Saturday night *chez* Rachel, but both of us were too polite to say so. I could even envisage a situation where I'd be fondly remembering her sister's party. No, play it by ear. If all went well I could phone her later and pretend the invitation had just been made.

She seemed really pleased to hear from me when I phoned on Sunday, as promised, to arrange our day out. I was going to propose something safe, such as a theatre trip or a meal, when she interrupted me.

'We're taking some kids from school to Woodfields Children's Farm in a couple of weeks and I promised I'd do a recce. How about we go there for the day?'

I hate bloody farm animals. They stink, they look at you suspiciously and they always seem to pick me to attack.

'That sounds lovely.' It was only after we had confirmed a time and I'd hung up that I profoundly regretted agreeing. I could easily have claimed to be allergic to farm animals but unfortunately did not think quickly enough on my feet. What sort of chuffing romantic date was stepping in pig shit and holding flea-ridden rabbits anyway?

'What's that perfume, darling, Chanel No. 5?'

'No, Porky Pig's No. 2. Rather alluring, don't you think?'

Also, what the bloody hell was I supposed to wear? I had always taken it as read that dressing smartly and looking one's best were prerequisites for a first date. Yet here was I contemplating the rival merits of Wellington boots or clapped-out dirty trainers, duffel coat or anorak. I very nearly looked up some images of Worzel Gummidge on the Internet to give me some idea of colour co-ordination. Also, unfortunately, my 'best of the Worzels' collection was on vinyl, so we couldn't sing along to 'I've got a brand new combine harvester' in the car to create the right ambiance.

It occurred to me, as I drove to pick her up on Monday morning, resplendent in checked top, jeans and sneakers, that her choice of venue might have been in reaction to what I'd said after the party. However, I only remember uttering the words 'let's just take it slowly, shall we?' If I'd said 'let's arrange the most unromantic, smelly date possible' I could have understood it better. I wondered if she had thought twice about the venue. After all, I still didn't really know her very well. Her sister's best friends were scene painters and steam rally enthusiasts, and Alison seemingly knew them well. Perhaps I was simply going out with a complete nerd from a family of complete nerds.

She smiled broadly as she got in the car. 'I really hope you don't mind this, Adrian. It's just that this honestly is the only day I'm going to get for this recce and I just thought it might be a laugh.' There was a relaxed lightness of tone to her voice and I thought, perhaps for the first time, that maybe, if I too managed to lighten up, we could have a good day. It also occurred to me, as she chatted amiably on our journey, that I had probably never met the 'real' Alison. All our previous meetings had been marred by barbed comments, awkward atmospheres or unwanted parents.

Woodfields Children's Farm was a large working farm with various attractions for young people, such as feeding the animals, hay jumps, tractor rides and bird displays. Being late October, it was rather quiet, and there was a definite 'end of season' feel about the place.

Despite Alison's cheery demeanour, I still felt rather self-conscious walking around as a couple. Everyone else there was in family groups and, perhaps I'm being paranoid, but I'm sure people were staring at us. On several occasions I nearly said loudly 'what time did we say we'd meet the kids for lunch?' There was one young mother who caught my eye several times during the morning and it was entirely obvious to her that we were childless. She was looking at me warily, as though she suspected I was there for more sinister reasons. Part of me wanted to tell her that this was not my idea and that if I had had my way we would have been, at that moment, travelling to watch a matinee performance of a West End show.

So we watched the sheep dog trials, we fed some nasty-looking ungrateful goats and I held a thoroughly vicious-looking snake. Some patronising git took a photo of me with an eagle on my shoulder, while it dug its talons maliciously into me. The git didn't quite say 'smile for granny', but might as well have done. Throughout all of this Alison, smiling broadly, was clearly very relaxed. Indeed, in the short time I had known her this was the first time I'd seen her so carefree and, however grudging I felt, her enthusiasm was beginning to rub off on me. We braved the October wind to eat the picnic Alison had made for us, and she slid her arm in mine as we headed for the boating lake.

'Be honest, now, Adrian, are you enjoying yourself?'

'Well, I was slightly apprehensive about today but actually, yes, I've had a good time. It's not often you get a chance to revert back to your childhood for really justifiable reasons, and it's been a lot of fun.'

It was true. Despite my misgivings, despite the awkwardness of us being childless, and despite the bloody animals, I had really enjoyed her company and we had had a laugh. We took a rowing boat out on the lake and – maybe it was the tranquillity of the moment – I made a decision.

'Are you about on Saturday evening?'

She warmly accepted Rachel's invitation and, before I really had time to think, I found myself kissing her. There was nearly a cheap sit-com moment when I felt the boat tipping, but it simply made us laugh. The mood was lovely.

'How do you feel about – us?' she asked a moment later. 'Do you still feel you want to take things slowly?'

'It's just – I'm very conscious about the fact you've so recently been badly hurt. I'm twenty-two and I'm not really looking for a long-term, serious relationship. I'm just concerned that if things develop between us, but then don't work out, you may be hurt again.'

She looked me straight in the eye for a long moment – but it was not a piercing look; there was much warmth in her eyes.

'Listen, Adrian,' she said, taking my hands. 'I don't expect you to sign any long-term contract with me, and I'm deeply touched that your main concern is not hurting me. If and when you're ready to let things develop between us, with no strings attached, then that's fine with me.'

There was very little awkwardness about this conversation, and it was only when we were walking away from the lake that I realised that I hadn't thought about Rachel once during it.

By the end of the day it was Alison who was mildly embarrassed, as I'd spent the last hour or so being surrogate entertainer to an amiable group of eight-year-olds, leaping the furthest on the hay jump and conducting them vociferously as they accompanied the Worzels during the tractor ride.

Our flat was still in a pretty healthy condition, and Tony and Liam were out, so I dropped her at her place to shower and change, went home to do the same and whipped up a quick stir fry. When she arrived, an hour later, she looked beautiful and we enjoyed a candlelit dinner for two. When I poured her a third glass of wine, it was obvious that she had no intention of driving home and, by this time, I had no intention of suggesting that she should do so. I was still very aware of my feelings towards Rachel, but I also felt that I'd been open and honest with Alison, and she'd given the green light for us to further our relationship, knowing this. I felt it hard to believe that this lady, who so willingly came up to bed with me a little later, had once spoken to me with more venom than anyone else I had ever met.

Alison had various commitments for the rest of the week and I spent a great chunk of time doing schoolwork. First I had the children's PowerPoint presentations to mark. I'd told them that they needed to have completed their slide shows and saved them on their memory sticks by half-term. I would then comment on them before they prepared their speeches.

This was more interesting than most of the marking I did. I'd given them a free rein as far as their topic was concerned, and it was fascinating to see what they had chosen. Kate, Rozinder and Charlie had, naturally, all chosen pop stars and had produced fairly uninspiring presentations. Allard had produced a detailed, informative and well-animated piece entitled 'horror and special effects'. It was a very good slide show, although the words _'chip off the old block'_ did go through my mind.

I had advised them to prepare between one to fifteen slides and was amazed, therefore, to find a staggering seventy-three slides on Josh's presentation. He had chosen _Dr Who_ as his 'research', and all seventy-three slides were images, copied from the Internet, of the Doctor or one of his companions in various different guises, with mind-numbing captions such as _'this is Marfa in seerise four, episoed 4'._

'You have worked very hard on this, Josh' – that great euphemism for _'this is rubbish but I need to write something positive'_ – was the only comment I could think of. However, as I was writing this and forming the put-down in my mind, a wave of guilt swept over me. I had never taken to Josh even though, apart from the occasional nasty, attention-seeking remark to Patrick, his main crime was only that he wasn't very bright and had no parental support from home. My sense of guilt intensified as I realised that I had hardly spent any time at all helping him with this project whereas others, such as William or Alice – who needed much less support – had attracted considerably more of my time. My conversation with Rupert came back to haunt me, and I was certain that he wouldn't have allowed a kid like Josh to copy seventy-three slides without giving him any guidance.

David's work was perhaps the most poignant. His was entitled 'Childhood Leukaemia' and related the effects on a child of the disease over a two-year period between diagnosis and remission. While quite simple in its language, it was written from the heart, had powerful pictures and brought a lump to my throat.

As ever, it was Robert's work that I was most interested in marking. His project was entitled '*Africa – continent in crisis*' and he had written some twenty technically excellent slides about the plight of many of Africa's children, and the economical instability in the region. It was infinitely better written than anybody else's in the class, but it was also remarkably clinical. Whereas David's was simple but heartfelt, Robert wasted no words on dealing with the emotional aspects of the issues he raised. I found this very telling.

On Tuesday morning I spent over two hours in one sitting marking the first batch of their presentations – a record by about an hour and a half – and by Wednesday evening they were all done. While I actively liked marking these, the rest of the week was far less enjoyable. I had been warned by many people that much of a teacher's life was consumed with paperwork, and had spent most of the first half term putting off non-essential stuff. Completing it was a slog but by Saturday afternoon, when I finally finished, I could enjoy the feeling of a huge, lingering burden having been lifted.

I really didn't know what to expect when Alison and I knocked on Rachel's door at eight that evening. I'd decided to play it all by ear and not let my confused feelings for the two people I did know, as well as my irrational hatred for the one I didn't, dominate the evening.

Rachel looked simply stunning as she showed us into her elegant flat, and she and Alison exchanged 'I've heard lots about you's'. When Rachel told me that Alan did occasional model work I had hoped in my sad, pathetic way that he might model shoes or elbow pads or even better, the front cover of 'Freak Show Monthly'. Sadly this was not to be, and he was every bit the chiselled macho man that I had feared. He was also charming, friendly and spent the first half hour making us laugh with amusing anecdotes from his charity work. *Bastard.*

I was very aware at how comfortable the other three were with each other and had to physically force myself to remain cheery and relaxed. For there was no doubt about it; for all Alison and I were getting on and our relationship was growing, I was madly jealous of Alan. Everything he stood for – looks, success, sense of humour and, most of all, Rachel – I could only aspire to. He was being the perfect host and it was all I could do to remain civil.

I was horrified, then, that when Rachel and Alan went to prepare the dinner Alison asked me what was wrong.

'Wrong? Nothing's wrong.' I could feel myself flush. 'I'm just a bit tired, that's all.'

'You don't quite seem yourself – don't you like Alan or something?'

Oh shit. Was it that obvious? What must they think of me?

'What gives you that idea?'

'Well, you're not being very responsive, that's all. That tale he told us about that Kenyan boy was hilarious. I'd have thought that you'd have laughed out loud at such a story, but you barely raised a smirk.'

It is amazing how difficult it is to force yourself to react in a positive manner when you have negative vibes seeping out of every pore. I quite clearly had to try harder. I muttered something incomprehensible to Alison and went into the kitchen under the guise of getting more drinks.

'Wow, something smells fantastic,' I said, a little too enthusiastically. 'What are we having?'

'Oh, this is Alan's speciality. It's his own, highly secret variation of 'Duck à l'Orange' and it's quite delicious.'

I bet it is, you perfect bastard.

'I'm so looking forward to trying this, Alan' I said, patting him on the shoulder, all matey-matey. 'He really is a clever little bastard, your fella, isn't he Rachel?'

'He certainly is, aren't you, darling?'

Now the good part about my last comment was that it allowed me to call Alan a bastard to his face, albeit in a cunningly disguised jokey manner. The bad part, however, was that as a direct result of the said comment Rachel called him darling and kissed him on the cheek.

I got some wine and left the room.

During dinner — and I found the orange sauce just a tiny bit tart — Alan politely enquired about Alison and me and we answered politely, but without panache or witty asides. Somehow my quick one-liners had deserted me and the conversation soon revolved around him again. I laughed slightly too loudly at his next anecdote and Alison's sideways glance at me said, in very clear tones, 'you're being a prat'.

We'd agreed to take a taxi home and by this stage I had sunk perhaps five or six glasses of wine. While the room wasn't spinning around, I was beginning to feel distinctly light-headed and was aware that I was ever so slightly starting to slur my words.

'So how long have you worked for the Red Cross?' I asked, feigning interest.

'About five years. I've always wanted to work in the charitable business. Don't get me wrong. It's a good job and I get well paid, but what we're doing is making a real difference in Africa, and I'm very proud of that.'

This was the second occasion in one week when I had been stung by someone proudly saying that they made a difference and I reacted before thinking.

'Yeah, well teachers make a difference as well, you know.' It didn't mean to come out aggressively – I'm sure that was the wine – but there was a horrible silence for a moment.

'I'm sorry, Adrian; I wasn't implying that they didn't. I know from Rachel just what a great job you all do.'

His words hung in the air for a moment, and I could feel Alison burning with embarrassment. Rachel, to her credit, quickly held up a glass and said as brightly as she could: 'Hell, we all make a difference, and I'll drink to that – cheers!'

'Cheers!' we all echoed, but the damage was done. Rachel has this fabulous ability to make light of anything and Alan was so damn charming that he would probably have accepted responsibility if I had have punched him, but Alison's body language was much more transparent. She was clearly disappointed in me and I felt dreadful. Yet again I had this desire to leave a situation that was dragging along, and by the time our taxi finally arrived and we said our thanks and goodbyes, I was dreading Alison's debriefing.

I was half-expecting her to rant at me, but all she did was look out the window of the taxi, which was even worse. I couldn't leave it like this.

'I'm sorry if I spoilt your evening, Alison. It's just, I don't know – I just wasn't myself tonight.' It was lame, but it was all I could come out with. She remained silent for a while, looking pensively out of the window.

'I don't understand you, Adrian. You've been a perfect gent the last couple of times we've seen each other, but tonight – you let yourself down and I don't understand why.'

It was, perhaps, just as well that she didn't understand why, and I blamed it on the wine, tiredness and just one of those things. She nodded her head and smiled but it didn't seem to pacify her and, tellingly, she didn't invite me in for coffee.

'Do you want me to call you again?' I ventured – I wasn't going to leave not knowing if I had completely blown it.

'Of course I do. Just show me your nice side next time, OK?'

'Point taken. Good night, Alison.'
'Good night, Adrian.'

I strolled into the lounge carrying two glasses. 'Who's for wine? Alan? Alison? Excellent. I'll get you yours in a minute, Rachel.'

When I came back with the next two drinks there was a strange glint in both Alan and Alison's eyes, and she had moved up closely to him on the settee. I went to sit next to Rachel, who was looking more and more bewildered by what was happening.

'Has anybody ever told you how beautiful you are?' crooned Alan, as he stared soulfully into Alison's eyes.

'Oh, Alan, do you really mean that? I was only just thinking how fabulous your elbows are; you're not a model by any chance, are you?'

'You're so perceptive, Alison. I went for loads of auditions, but everyone just said I was too ugly – then someone noticed my elbows.'

'Come upstairs with me now, Alan. Run away with me and leave these two to suffer on their own.'

We watched in silence as Alan dramatically picked her up and marched off into the setting sun.

'Oh, Adrian,' cried Rachel. 'What are we going to do?'

'Never you mind, my dearest, I'll look after you, but first I need to make a phone call.'

'Mr Wong? Good evening. My name's Adrian Gray. I came to see you this week? I just wanted to say thank you very much …'

11

So time went by. I went to see Rachel on Monday morning to apologise for Saturday night. 'Don't be ridiculous, you haven't got anything to apologise for, we had a lovely evening.' She really is an angel. We agreed a date three weeks hence when they could come to us. Any frostiness between Alison and me was rectified when I took her out to a slightly-more-expensive-than-it-looked restaurant the following Friday.

The bill was some twenty pounds more than I'd anticipated. Like most graduates, I was facing many years of debt and this sort of extravagance took up most of my weekly budget, but it was worth it. When I told Alison about the rematch at our flat she didn't, to her credit, make me sign any sort of contract stipulating better behaviour; instead she just smiled and said that it would be nice to see them again.

And so it was, as winter was rapidly squeezing out autumn, that I finally laid the ghost of Rachel's dinner party by acting the part of perfect host as well, in my opinion, as had Alan. My lamb shanks were more tender than his duck and I finally found a bit of form on the amusing anecdote front. Had Tony not sauntered in, pissed, at 11.30 and marched upstairs with a rather insalubrious girl he had picked up from somewhere, and had they not then proceeded to actually rattle the wine glasses with their subsequent session, it would have been a perfect evening. I had had time to digest all that Alan stood for by now and, partly because I was thoroughly enjoying life with Alison, I could grudgingly accept his relationship with Rachel.

In the classroom, the children were now firmly set within the routines of the week. I noticed, as time went by, subtle changes in my relationship with the class as a whole, and with specific children.

I was very thankful that I had, primarily, quite a mature class and, while this could cause problems of its own, it at least meant that there were precious few childish squabbles. However, there were a group of four rather immature kids who had kept quite a low profile before half-term. In the few weeks after it, though, Simon, Marcus, Elizabeth and Andrew began to show their true colours. Whether it was because they were being taught by a male teacher for the first time, or they simply hadn't had anything specific to moan about before, I don't know, but I do know that soon after the holiday they really started getting on my tits.

'Mr Gray, he's got my pencil.'

'No I haven't, he's lying to get me into trouble.'

'Mr Gray, Elizabeth's been drawing on the desk.'

'My shoe's gone missing, sir, and I saw Andrew kicking it earlier.'

At first, I calmly talked to them about not telling tales and told them to stay away from each other if they couldn't get on. When it continued, however, I just started to get really annoyed and told them, in no uncertain terms, to grow up.

Mrs Vaughan, who'd been fine at parents' evening, came in to complain that her darling little Elizabeth was being bullied and that I was picking on her. She was one of these parents who believe everything their child tells them. When I pointed out that I had actually seen darling Elizabeth deliberately wind up Andrew and Simon to get them into trouble she told me that I must be mistaken, as little Lizzy would never do that sort of thing. I have very little patience with doting, blinkered parents and even less with their spoilt offspring. So I told her that, in my opinion, Elizabeth needed to grow up. Mrs Little received a written complaint from Mrs Vaughan the next day about my apparant apathy towards her daughter and I got a lesson in the art of diplomacy. Next time the doting parent comes in, I'll bake a cake.

There were many children that I'd always got on well with, such as Alice, Miranda and William, and I was slowly starting to get to know other children better. I found myself liking Kate far more than I had at first. If you got her on a subject of interest such as soap operas or pop stars she could be good company and on several occasions we laughed together, which was lovely. I'd also started doing daily lateral thinking quizzes with the kids, which they all enjoyed, but Kate, in particular, showed the sort of enthusiasm for these that I had never seen in her for any other aspect of school life.

I also started getting on quite well with Sean. Our mutual obsession with football was proving, as Sandra Little had predicted, a useful bonding agent and he scored winning goals in both our league matches after half-term. One of these, a last-minute screamer against our local rivals, prompted a 'high five' with me and a particularly warm moment.

I was not allowed to forget, however, how volatile he could be, and one of my worst experiences at Green Acre concerned his mobile phone. We have a very strict rule at the school that if children are found using their phone, for any reason, during the day, it is confiscated and returned, with a letter, at the end of it. When I tried to confiscate Sean's for texting someone during maths, I had the closest thing to open defiance yet.

'All right, I'll put it away in my bag.'

'I'm sorry, Sean, you know the rules. Give it to me and I'll return it at 3.20.'

'I said I'll put it away!' This was said vociferously and I knew another authority-defining moment was upon me.

I so much wished to allow him this compromise but the whole class was watching and, if I did, they would perceive it for exactly what it would be: a cowardly teacher backing down to a stronger pupil.

'It's not open to negotiation, Sean' I said, as lightly as possible, but I could feel my legs begin to quiver slightly.

He thought about it for an agonising couple of seconds before uttering a face-saving 'stupid bloody rule', and plonking it on my desk with as much force as he dared without damaging it. I muttered a thank you – and he had no idea how thankful I was – before putting it in the top drawer of my desk.

While he scowled and mooched about for most of the day, and told Josh to 'shut up' quite viciously after another of his attempted witticisms, there wasn't anything like the recrimination that I had feared. At 3.20 I called him over to collect his phone, opened the drawer and it wasn't there. I stood staring at the place where I knew I'd put it, hoping, I suppose, that it would suddenly appear. It didn't. As a chill swept through my body, I muttered something incomprehensible and started hopelessly looking through all the drawers.

'Have you lost my phone?' His voice was measured.

'No – er, I'm sure it's er, well – er, you saw me put it in here and, er, I'm quite sure it will ...'

'Did you lock the drawer, Mr Gray?'

Oh, shit. He knew perfectly well that there was no lock on the drawer and the manner of his question suggested all sorts of sinister reprisals.

'No, Sean – if there was a lock I would have – er, look it's obvious somebody has hidden it for a joke – we'll sort this out tomorrow if I can't find it now.'

'That cost £150 – it's new.' He left the words floating, but their meaning was very clear.

'As I said, it will turn up.'

'And if it doesn't?'

'Let me talk to Mrs Little. I can assure you, Sean, that this will be sorted.'

He nodded slowly and left with Shannon, who had been standing watching and clearly enjoying the show. I immediately sought out Mrs Little to explain.

'First of all,' she said, sighing deeply, 'if you confiscate an expensive item – and you were right to confiscate it – you must make sure you lock it away. We don't have many thieves in this school but you have thrown yourself wide open.'

'Point taken – what do we do now?'

'I will phone up Mr Williams and explain – if it doesn't turn up we're going to have a very awkward situation, but I'll sort it out.'

'I see – thank you.'

I had to endure just under twenty-four hours of agonising wait, searches of bags, and strong words to the whole school by Mrs Little before the phone reappeared in my drawer. When I thought through the whole incident later it became pretty clear to me what must have happened. Everyone in the class had seen me confiscate the phone, everyone had seen Sean's face, and no one would have dared to steal it. Recriminations from the school would have been mild compared to recriminations from the Williams clan. I have absolutely no doubt that either Sean or Shannon took the phone with the express intention of making me sweat. The twins rarely walked home together, and Shannon's waiting when the loss was discovered was not out of any brotherly affection, but to enjoy seeing their scheme reach fruition. Of course, I had absolutely no proof of this but it was another example, in my mind, of their calculated determination not to let anyone get the better of them.

So November turned into December, and with it came thoughts of Christmas. Most people seemed to think that Christmas is a time of goodwill, giving and high spirits, although to Ellie Luck it appeared that it was a time of endurance. We were discussing Christmas arrangements in a staff meeting and I suggested putting on a staff panto for the children on the last day of term. Everyone, including the teaching assistants, thought it a great idea. Even Ellie Luck, to her credit, agreed to take a small role, although she clearly felt that this was not a fitting part of the teacher–child relationship. Secret Santas and staff Christmas meals were also agreed upon, and the atmosphere was jovial. Rachel, however, was not especially looking forward to Christmas as she had been asked to produce the foundation stage nativity play and felt that she couldn't really refuse.

It is a universally acknowledged fact that nativity plays performed by five-year-olds are unmitigated crap. It is also a universal fact that, however bad they are, parents and, more especially, grandparents absolutely love them. An uncle of mine once told me, after watching his grandson perform, that when the children make mistakes it doesn't make it worse, it makes it better, because you think: 'Ah, bless 'em.' While that may have been a grandparent's take it certainly wasn't Rachel's, who was a perfectionist and wanted everything to run smoothly.

'The whole thing's a bloody nightmare,' she said two weeks before the opening night. 'None of the kids have a clue what they're doing and most of them just stand there grinning inanely. If the real Mary had had to wait so long for an answer from the inn-keeper she'd have given birth on the doorstep. Then of course there's Mrs Key.' She said this with a shudder. Gwyneth Key was Rachel's teaching assistant and entirely useless. She showed no initiative whatsoever and had no aptitude for dealing with four- and five-year-old children.

'I felt it was safest to put her in charge of making relatively simple sets. I can only assume that her desired effect was to make them look as though the children had painted them themselves, although no self-respecting five-year-old would have put their name to such rubbish.'

The whole production was clearly wearing her down. However much granny might 'bless 'em' when they buggered up their lines, a poor show would reflect badly on Rachel and she knew it.

While rehearsals for the nativity were happening during school, secret rehearsals for Cinderella were happening after school. I scoured the script several times to double check whether my 'Buttons' got to passionately kiss Rachel's 'Cinderella' and it seemed a complete waste that Mrs Jones, my teaching assistant, aka Prince Charming, got to dance with her and even peck her on the cheek. I decided, after some thought, that it was better that I hadn't got to play Prince Charming as I couldn't totally trust myself to stop at a kiss on the cheek, even with 200 children watching. The standard of the acting was really quite awful, although I was quite sure Robert and Shannon would be sitting at the back saying 'Ah, bless 'em.'

I was fortunate enough to pick Ellie's name out of the hat in the 'secret Santa' draw and, despite her relative acquiescence on the panto front, the opportunities presented by this caused great merriment. The beauty of 'secret Santa' is that the presents are given anonymously. However, if she received a vibrator – and, my God, I was tempted – it wouldn't take Hercule Poirot to work out whodunnit.

The performance of the nativity play went, as they always do, better than had been expected. With the stage up, spotlights on, newly repainted scenery in position, dressed-up cute-looking children on stage and a very forgiving audience, the whole thing passed reasonably smoothly, and it was all very sweet. It wasn't perfect of course – the inn-keeper, a special needs kid who would have been much better cast as a tree, cheerfully told the happy couple that there was indeed room at the inn, causing confusion for a full minute. One of the wise men managed to drop Jesus, who fell with a sickening thud onto the stage, and a strange smell started emanating from the direction of the angels towards the end of the final scene. This mystery was soon cleared up, literally, when Mrs Key, rather unsubtly, marched across the stage, took Johnny's hand, and quickly frogmarched him off.

I took Rachel out for a well-earned drink after the show, where we met up with Alison, Naomi, Liam and Tony. It was the first time we had all been out together and we had great fun. Rachel and I embellished the events of the early evening, causing great merriment throughout. I saved my *coup de grace* until other conversation had dried up, and they all rubbed their hands in glee at the prospect of coming up with the best possible 'secret Santa' present for Ellie Luck.

We agreed, there and then, to compile a top five of most unsuitable presents. My vibrator snuck in at number five. At four came tickets to see the Chippendales; at three, matching skimpy bra and crotchless panties, and at two the latest Eminem CD. The winner, however, suggested by Alison, was a one-way ticket to New Zealand. It occurred to me that this sort of conversation was not too far removed from the sort of pub banter that Alison had taken such offence to on that fateful night but I decided, wisely I think, not to risk souring the mood by mentioning it.

The final day of the autumn term is an enjoyable one for several reasons, and it is particularly gratifying when smiling children come in with presents under their arm. Though it was nice to receive anything, opening many of them tested my acting skills to the limit: 'Mmm, Liebfraumilch. My favourite. Thank you, Charlie.' Or: 'Now that really is a rather super paperweight, Daniel, thank you very much.'

There were some fabulous presents. A bottle of single malt whisky from the Andersons and a £20 gift voucher from the Carltons, were the pick of the bunch. There were countless boxes of chocolates: 'Oh, more Roses, I am going to get fat, thank you Allard.'

The most telling present, however, was a small packet of jelly babies, unwrapped, from the Caldwells, with a card reading: *We live in a house worth well over half a million pounds. We're both successful in business and Miranda has thoroughly enjoyed herself in your class. However, as you know, we're complete bastards, so we've given you a small, unwrapped packet of jelly babies to show you, in the most ironic manner possible, exactly what we think of you.*

Perhaps the best moment, however, was when Patrick stood up, rather awkwardly, and announced: 'I'd just like to wish you a Happy Christmas and thank you very much for teaching me this term.' I thoroughly expected to see some giggling at this but it was said with such sincerity and generosity that even the likes of Shannon and Josh remained nonplussed.

I would have liked to have told him that such a sentiment meant so much more than a packet of unwrapped jelly babies, but I contented myself with: 'Thank you very much, Patrick, what a lovely thing to say. I hope you have a wonderful Christmas as well.'

The staff panto was a fabulous success. It started with Sandra Little who, as Prince Charming's father, had plenty of time to change, march out into the playground and shout at the children in a most convincing manner. She was, she said, more annoyed with the school than she'd ever been, and they were to walk, in silence, into the hall before she spoke to them. The faces on those 200 or so children, as I calmly marched out of the staffroom dressed as Buttons, was worth all the rehearsal time on its own. In about three seconds, their expressions changed from sheer worry to bemusement and finally to a gradual realisation that Mrs Little's diatribe had been nothing more than a ruse to get them into the hall. They cheered and applauded heartily as, one after another, all of the teachers and teaching assistants appeared in resplendent costume and make-up and acted out, however poorly, the story. We all carried clipboards with our scripts – there was never any suggestion that we would learn our lines – but this did not distract from the entertainment. The only exception to this was Irene Cunningham, an ugly sister. Irene decided that it would look more professional if she were to cut out her lines and stick them on various parts of her costume, to avoid obviously reading from a script. Then followed the quite hilarious spectacle of her not only having no idea of when she needed to speak but, as she had attached them in a random order, no idea of what she had to say either. In fairness to her, though, even she was laughing, and it was one of the highlights of a thoroughly enjoyable hour.

I received one of the biggest cheers of the term when I told my class, at the end of the day, that their homework

over Christmas was to relax and have a fabulous holiday.
When they had gone, I found Rachel to offer to drive her to
the restaurant later on for the staff Christmas do.

'I will more than happily drive you, pay for your meal and
do all the washing up if you promise you'll sit next to me at
the table. The thought of finding myself between Ellie and
Irene fills me with dread.' She agreed totally with the
sentiment but insisted on driving, as it was her turn.

So Rachel picked me up at 7.45 and we managed to sit at
the more rowdy end of the table, with Frank Bell, Julia
Bradshaw and Theresa Ryan, the Year 1 and 3 teachers, both
of whom were in their late twenties and were good company.

After dinner, and plenty of wine, it was time for the secret
Santa presents. I knew that, had I bought any of our top five,
Ellie would simply have got up and walked out, but there
was never any serious question of my being allowed to have
my fun. In the end, I had asked Alison to choose something
sensible and Ellie seemed very pleased with the ornate
picture frame she received. Whoever bought me the comedy
stress balls in the shape of women's breasts was quite
inspired and, perhaps it was the drink, but I couldn't resist
placing them in position and giving a provocative wiggle.
That wiped the smile off Ellie's face.

Eventually Mrs Little stood, with the obvious intention of
making some sort of speech.

'While I'm here I'd just like to say a few things, if I may.
First of all I'd like to thank everyone for their hard work this
term. I feel very lucky that I can lead a team who are so
hard-working most of the time, yet can have the sort of fun
that we all had today – which leads me to my next point.'

There was a definite tone to this sentence, making us all
listen intently.

'Only Frank knows this so far, primarily because it's all
happened so quickly. Last week I was approached by our

county advisor, who asked me to spend next term leading another school. Apparently, they had a poor Ofsted report in October and the head has finally walked out on the school, just two weeks before the end of term.

'His sudden departure has completely thrown the school into a state of confusion and it was felt that they needed someone with er, some experience, to steady the ship for a term before they find a permanent replacement. I thought it over briefly – such was the time factor here – and have decided to accept the post. Frank has also decided, for his own reasons, that at this stage of his career he doesn't want to be acting head. Consequently, next term, the advisors and governors have found a temporary replacement. Mrs Sheila Warnock will start on the 2nd of January.'

There was a long pause while we all took in this information.

'Do you know her?' asked Julia. 'What's she like?'

'She's – er, competent in her job, yes, I don't think any of the children will mess *her* about.'

That last sentence spoke volumes. The slight hesitation, the emphasis on the second 'her', all suggested an old battleaxe. From the faces around the table it seemed that everyone else had the same thoughts and the relaxed mood of the whole day disintegrated into a more sombre and subdued one. You couldn't share too many rude jokes with Sandra Little, but she was professional, friendly and had been extremely supportive of me this term, while skilfully guiding me through my mistakes. I would miss her.

We all said our goodbyes and Rachel took me home. We were both concerned about what January had in store for us, especially as we wouldn't even meet Mrs Warnock until the INSET day. Rachel was going back to Leicester for the holidays and I wouldn't see her for two weeks – this also added to the sombre feel. I kissed her on the cheek, took her parents' number and promised to phone her on Christmas day.

'Thank you, Rachel. I can't tell you how much easier this term has been, knowing you've been around to give me advice and to have a laugh with. Happy Christmas.'

'What is it?' queried Ellie, with a strange look on her face. 'It looks like some sort of big finger. Do you use it to stir soups or something?'

I looked straight ahead of me, avoiding Rachel's face. I could see, out of the corner of my eye, Rachel's whole body shuddering, trying desperately to avoid the inevitable. I screwed my face up and shut my mouth firmly but I couldn't stop the involuntary snorts forcing their way out of my nose.

'It's er, it's just a joke, that's all,' said Sandra, ever the peace-maker, but even she was trying hard to suppress her laughter.

'I still don't understand. What exactly does it do?'

A huge uncontrollable snort escaped from Frank Bell's nose as he ran for the sanctuary of the toilet.

'Why don't you – er – read the instructions?' suggested Theresa, with admirable control. Still with a bemused look on her face, Ellie turned over the package and began to read. As her face turned from bemusement, to shock, to horror and finally to anger, I could hold it in no longer. With an explosion of noise, I started laughing uncontrollably. This started everyone else off as well, and great gales of laughter enveloped the room.

With as much dignity as she could muster, Ellie Luck, that cantankerous old spinster, stood slowly and walked out of the room.

'Don't forget your present,' I shouted after her. 'That cost me a tenner!'

12.

When I was sixteen my father died, suddenly, from a heart attack. We had always been close and it was largely his influence that led me into sport, especially football. He taught me the importance of being active, and it seemed so incredibly unfair that he should die so young when other people, unfit and inactive smokers, lived for so long. My father was forty-two when I was born and only fifty-eight when he died. My mother, four years his junior, never really got over his death. Like him, she had always been keen on sport and was still playing tennis in her fifties. My brother, Andrew, is seven years older than me and was studying for his finals at college in Plymouth when our father died and, while he helped with the funeral arrangements, he returned to Plymouth soon afterward, where he has been ever since.

I think, subconsciously, that I have always resented my brother for being away. My mother, despite being only in her early fifties, never seemed to recover from her husband's death and became rather reclusive. When she was diagnosed with breast cancer a year later, she didn't seem to want to fight it. She died shortly before I went to college and I felt rather insecure when I began my course. I could have easily gone off the rails but, fortunately, I built up strong friendships, especially with Liam, who helped me through those difficult days. I even gave up my sport for the best part of a year, clearly as some sort of backlash against what had happened to my parents. With very few family ties – I saw my brother perhaps once a year – my friends became especially important to me, which is perhaps another reason why I'm so concerned about not letting people down.

Over the past couple of months, Alison and I had let each other into our respective pasts and this had strengthened the bond between us. When she invited me to stay with her over Christmas my initial concern was having to endure the woes of her father. 'Oh, that's a shame', I answered, pathetically, when she told me that her parents had decided to stay in Yorkshire and mooch together over the festive period. She was not fooled then, and neither was she when I replied 'that would be lovely' to the invitation to visit them in January instead. I simply didn't want to go, and I'm sure Alison saw through me, but I clearly called her bluff sufficiently for her to eventually announce 'well, OK, if you're sure. I'll phone and tell them we're coming.'

Shit. By then, of course, it was too late and I resigned myself to a weekend of gloom and doom. Corinne joined us for Christmas Day and, while we had a nice time, I still felt a slight uneasiness in her presence. I would have had no problem asking Alison to borrow her phone and make the promised call to Rachel if it had just been the two of us, but somehow I felt awkward doing so with Corinne there. I ended up, ridiculously, trying to sneak a call on my mobile phone when they were in the kitchen. Just as Rachel's mother answered the phone, Corinne walked into the room and, I can't say exactly why, but I panicked.

'Hello?'

'Er, hello, could I speak to Rupert please?'

'I beg your pardon?'

'Could I speak to Rupert?'

'Rupert?'

'Er, yes.'

'I'm sorry, I think you must have the wrong number, this is Leicester 264–'

At that moment, Rachel, who must have grabbed the receiver from her mother, spoke:

'Hello, who is this please?'

By now Corinne was looking at me, as the moment got worse and worse. She must have noticed my face colouring – I certainly felt it burning, and I was just about to hang up and start blaming useless bloody modern technology when things took a turn for the worse.

'Is that you, Adrian?'

Bugger, bugger, bugger. By now hanging up was out of the question, as a quick 1471 would reveal all. Oh well, in for a penny ...

'Rupert, how are you doing, my old mate?'

'I beg your pardon. I think you must have the wrong – Adrian? Is that you?'

'Yeah, course it's me, I just phoned up to wish you a Happy Christmas.'

'Adrian, why did you just call me Rupert?'

'Yes thanks, mate, nice and relaxing, you know, how about you?'

'Please, Adrian, this isn't funny, what the hell's going on?'

'Good, Good. Listen, mate, you know that problem you wanted me to help you with? If I phone you tomorrow after all the festivities and all that, I'll explain it to you then.'

'What the hell are you on about?'

'As I said, I'll explain tomorrow – look, I think my credit's running out. Speak to you tomorrow, yes?'

'Tomorrow?'

'Excellent – see you then, mate, have a brilliant day, bye.'

I switched off the phone as casually as I could, murmured

'Rupert, an old friend – promised I'd help him with something,' to Corinne, who still looked a little unsure about everything, and headed to the toilet.

I always thought it was only done in cartoons, but I actually found myself banging my head against the wall. What sort of ridiculous insecurity was this, that I had to go to such insane lengths to avoid letting Corinne know that I was phoning a friend to wish her a Happy Christmas?

Would I be letting Alison down, somehow, by doing this? Was I simply feeling guilty? With my mind racing as to how I was going to explain this to Rachel in the morning, I flushed the loo and rejoined the girls. Fortunately, if Corinne was suspicious about the call, she barely showed it and the rest of the day was spent drinking and enjoying Trivial Pursuit.

On Boxing Day morning, I found an excuse to return to my flat and repair some of the damage from the previous day. It was a testament to our relationship that I felt I could explain everything to Rachel without having to alter some of the details in order to save face. She thought the whole situation hilarious, and any potential awkwardness very quickly evaporated.

I was undoubtedly, after three months of our relationship, feeling a great deal of affection for Alison, but when I hung up the phone it occurred to me just how much I had missed Rachel. By the time Christmas and New Year had come and gone, I found myself really looking forward to returning to school. Curiosity surrounding our temporary headteacher and anticipation at seeing all the children again were, of course, reasons for this, but the main incentive, beyond doubt, was the knowledge that I'd be seeing Rachel again.

Sheila Warnock was, it has to be said, a larger than life character in more ways than one. Physically commanding, she was several inches taller than me and powerfully built. Behind her constantly smiling face were eyes that suggested that she expected that she would always get her own way. As she introduced herself and gave a potted history of her path to Green Acre, I found myself watching Frank Bell, who was sitting next to her. My finely-tuned reading of body language suggested that he, for one, was not glad that she was here. He was smiling a little too much, nodding a little too enthusiastically, and nervously running his shirt material through his fingers. He had always come across as a relaxed, laid-back, yet hard-working man who skilfully remained approachable while emanating authority as deputy head. I resolved to study the relationship that developed between the two of them while Sandra Little was on secondment.

After her rather lengthy and slightly too self-important summary of herself, Sheila Warnock introduced the two ladies who had sat like lemons waiting. Gloria Rhys and Amanda Madison were both well into their fifties and looked very matronly. We had been told, on the last day of term, that we were having a first aid course for the morning of our INSET day, for which we should wear loose-fitting clothes. I had completely forgotten this and was slightly over-dressed in my suit and tie, while all those around me had donned tracksuits. The rather fetching little number being sported by Ellie Luck had probably not seen the light of day for thirty years – she was very much one to tell children during PE to kick a football, rather than demonstrate a complex sequence of keepy-uppy. Still, she didn't look as much of a prat as I did. We were told to convene in the hall by the more vicious-looking of the matrons, who promptly asked me where I was going with a hot cup of tea.

'You've come here to learn the theory of first aid, young

man. We're not risking any real-life practical by you scalding yourself.'

As I opened my mouth to protest, Mrs Warnock, still smiling falsely, looked at me and said firmly, 'put it back, Adrian.'

This really pissed me off. I felt like I was being treated like a child who couldn't be trusted not to spill his drink, and I found myself sitting cross-armed at the back of the gathering like, I suppose, a sulking child.

My mood was not improved when I was chosen by Big Bertha to be her unconscious model for the demonstration of how to put someone into the recovery position. Every time she reminded me that I was supposed to be unconscious I found myself stiffening more and she ended up tutting, telling me I was an unconvincing dummy and instructing me to put her lifeless form into the recovery position. I looked at the tub of lard sprawled in front of me and very much did not want to touch it. I had also been concentrating so hard on being unconscious that I had completely forgotten what to do. I vaguely remembered something about lifting an arm and hence putting her on her side, but as soon as I did this she flopped, a little over-dramatically I felt, straight onto her belly, smashing her face on the mat. Her slightly nicer colleague then told me that had this been on a road, I would have already damaged her face.

'Good,' said the sulky child. *'She deserved it.'* I was then faced with trying to haul this huge deadweight back onto her side, knowing that if I pulled too far the other way she would flop back on her back and crack her skull open. I gently tried rocking her while pulling on her arm, but nothing happened and by now I was seriously hating the exercise. It was obvious to anyone watching that I didn't have a clue what to do and, without waiting to be asked, Rachel came forward and helped me. She clearly knew how

to position the arms and legs and very soon we, or in reality she, had succeeded in the task. After delighting in shaming my appalling effort, Glorious Gloria then put us into pairs to practise. I know she did it deliberately. She had clearly taken an instant dislike to me and delighted in pairing me up with Sheila Warnock. I then spent a further excruciating ten minutes manipulating, and being manipulated by, this falsely smiling woman.

My hopes rose for about a second when we were told that, after coffee, we would be practising the kiss of life. The lovely image in my mind was very quickly dispelled when we were shown the rather evil-looking dolls that were to be our subjects. As a slightly childish protest to all of this, I decided to drink my coffee in my room, under the guise of preparing it for the children's return.

I was gratified when, a minute later, Frank Bell came in, shut the door and said, confidentially: 'Bloody woman!'

'Isn't she just? I swear if I had been allowed to keep my cup of tea, I'd have thrown it all over her when she was spread-eagled on the floor. That would have made her conscious again.'

'Oh, right. Yeah, she's horrible as well,' replied Frank. 'But I didn't mean her, I meant the Little Hitler who's going to make our lives miserable all term.'

'Mrs Warnock? Is she that bad?'

He sighed deeply. 'Quite frankly,' he began 'I shouldn't be telling you this. I'm deputy head and all that, and my loyalties should, in theory, be with her. So I'd appreciate it if you didn't – you know – man to man – bit of sticking together against the women – yeah?'

'Absolutely – what do you know about her?'

'Last night I got a phone call from an ex-colleague who worked under her for a while last year. He had somehow heard she was coming to Green Acre and felt he needed to ruin the final day of my holiday by warning me about her. Apparently, she's a complete megalomaniac whose basic philosophy is that if the children and staff fear her sufficiently, they will be putty in her hands. She's developed a reputation for barging her way into schools and running amok. Ted, my mate, said that the first thing she did when entering his school was to insist on observing all teachers within the first week, would you believe? Ted told me that three of the teachers failed the inquisition and were then subjected to weekly checks for the rest of the term. Two of those three left soon afterwards and the mood in the place was horrible, as people just stopped enjoying teaching there.'

'I hope I'm not talking out of turn,' I said, 'but isn't that effectively what Sandra did when she came here?'

'That was different. Green Acre needed a shake up then. The SATs results were poor, there were too many Ellie Lucks not moving with the times and Sandra did what she had to do. I don't know what your opinion is of her, Adrian, but I think she's a great leader and a nice person. She hated being confrontational, and she confided in me many times about her dread of having to let someone know that they needed to pull their finger out. The difference between Sandra and Sheila Warnock is that Sheila, by all accounts, enjoys rattling the cage. As I said, she's extremely egocentric and seems to love the power. I'm not looking forward to this term.'

'Have you spoken to her yet?'

'I was summoned to see her at seven this morning,' he said, his tone decidedly depressed. 'I assumed she wanted to ask me about the school – how it runs, strengths and weaknesses, and all that – but she wasn't interested in any of that. She basically said "You're my deputy, Frank. As far as I'm concerned that means you're my eyes and ears. I'm only here for a term but I have every intention of giving this school a lift. You can help me with that." I swear, Adrian, she was asking me to be her fucking spy. I tell you, if she thinks I'm going to lose all the respect I've gained from everybody by sniffing around for her then she's got another thing coming. I tell you, Adrian – '

At this point he was cut off, mid-rant, as the object of our discussion came in and sweetly told us that we were beginning the next part of the session.

'Oh, and Adrian, can I suggest you lose that tie?'

'How about I string her up with it?' I muttered to Frank as we made our way back to the hall, 'Then Gloria can show us how to save a sweetly smiling fat cow who's thrashing about in mid-air.'

The evil doll was waiting for us when we returned, ready for us to perform the kiss of life. Rachel, Julia and Theresa were definitely ahead of the doll in the pecking order of who I'd want to kiss, a few of the classroom assistants and Irene were about on a par with it, and everyone else was definitely below. Sheila Warnock and Gloria Rhys would probably fight it out in the 'you've got to pick one of them' stakes, with Ellie Luck a definite last. If I did meet Ellie unconscious and turning blue in a street, I'm sorry to say that I think I would have to wait for the ambulance driver to arrive and let him perform the unpleasant procedure.

The session went without too much alarm, although I was surprised at the amount of force that we were expected to use when pressing the breast bone between puffs. No wonder we had to use dolls ... By the time we'd covered deep gashes, gaping wounds, head injuries and broken limbs I'd been rather put off my impending lunch. I've never been good with blood or thinking calmly in any emergency and the morning's session, rather than reassuring me, just made me more acutely aware of my shortcomings. If someone had collapsed on me, even during the rest of that day when the various treatments and procedures were fresh in my mind, I still think I would have panicked and shouted 'Help!'

With the Red Cross girls gone, the afternoon session was to be a business meeting and then individual planning time. Even though the painted smile was still in place, there was a more formal and less friendly air to Sheila Warnock's opening spiel after lunch. She announced, graciously, that she felt that the school was running pretty smoothly under Sandra Little's leadership, and she did not foresee having to make widespread changes. The surreptitious look that Frank gave me at this point said, very clearly, _'see what I mean? She thinks she's doing us some sort of bloody favour by not making too many changes. Who the hell does she think she is?'_ And while their faces didn't entirely show it, it was very clear to me that everybody else felt something along the same lines as she continued:

'I do like order in a school, and I shall be making this very clear to the children tomorrow. However, order must start from us. I've been around all the classes and had a good look and I'm sure there's room for improvement. If you leave those paintbrushes in that sort of state, Adrian, how can you expect the children to take care of them?'

It was a rhetorical question, and she certainly didn't pause to let me answer, which was just as well because not only did I not have a clever riposte but I was also unbelievably pissed off that this woman had been inside my cupboards. Such was my indignation that my response would have probably have got me sacked.

'Anyway, enough said, I'm sure we were all lost in the chaos of Christmas and things will return to normal by the end of the week. Clearly, as I've only got a term with you I want to get to know you and I want to be able to offer you all the benefit of my experience, in a way that can help you as teachers. The best way to do that, I think, is to actually watch you teach. Hence I've put a list of times I'm available over the next few weeks – if you can sign up for one of them I'd be grateful – and after your lesson, I can give some feedback. Is that OK?'

It is often said that the most egocentric megalomaniacs cannot notice or respond to criticism if it punches them on the nose. Nobody actually hit her, nobody ran out of the room and nobody emptied a bag of soot all over the room screaming 'bollocks to your tidiness', but the atmosphere was tangibly frosty. The silence was so complete, the eyes were so cold and mouths were so pursed, that anybody with even an ounce of sensibility about them would have realised, very forcibly, that no, it was not OK ...

'Excellent. I'll take that as a "yes" then. I do expect my staff to work hard but never let it be said that the schools I'm in aren't happy ones. My main aim is that by the end of the term we'll all be exhausted, but we'll be proud of what we've achieved and, most importantly, we will have thoroughly enjoyed it.'

This was clearly the end of her speech, and I was half-expecting a full-size painting of her to suddenly appear from behind a curtain amid a fanfare of fireworks and welcoming anthems. All she got, however, was another silence that lasted for about five seconds but seemed to last for half an hour.

To his credit, and because he must have been damned sure that no one else would, Frank got up and welcomed her, on behalf of the school, to Green Acre.

'Sandra and I have always been extremely pleased with the wonderful staff we've got here,' he said, in a clear attempt to show everyone whose side he was on, 'and I'm quite sure you will be too.'

'Well, let us hope so.'

There followed a brief business meeting and diary dates for the term. During this time it felt a little like we were playing 'wink murder', that game you played as a child where people have to wink at each other without the detective noticing. All the staff so clearly wanted to let off steam and whenever I caught somebody's eye, a furtive baring of the teeth or widening of the eyes passed between us.

When we were eventually dismissed, Rachel and I managed to force ourselves out of the staffroom, through the hall and the dining room and into her room in silence. As I shut the door we simultaneously gripped each other's shoulders and screamed loudly. It was such a release of tension and the number of swear words uttered over the following five minutes, words that I never thought I'd hear from Rachel's mouth, must have set some sort of record. 'Bloody, bastard, bloody, shitty cow, who the bloody hell does she think she is?' was one of her more eloquent and repeatable efforts.

Frank went to each class in turn over the next hour, promising all of us that things would not be quite as hideous as they must have sounded.

'She's got an unfortunate manner,' he said. 'Honestly – her bark's worse than her bite.'

His efforts were much appreciated, although this last sentence was a master of the understatement. When we had finally calmed down, I decided that I would do last-minute jobs, like naming the paintbrushes and putting them in alphabetical order, in the morning. For some reason, I just wanted to go home.

'OK, young man, so you've just seen how it's done, even though you clearly have no concept as to how floppy a person's body is when they're unconscious, now it's your go. I'm going to lie on my back, clearly unconscious, and I want you to put me in the recovery position. Off you go.'

'Yes, of course, but do you mind if I remove these mats first, it's just that I'm allergic to rubber and I can feel the back of my throat tingling ... Thank you. Now, what was first? Oh, yes, is the subject still breathing? – well let me just ch– Good grief! No doubt that you're still breathing love – perhaps a little mouthwash next time, OK?

'Now what next? I'm sure you yanked me on to my side. Listen love, I'm not sure whether you can hear me or not, but as you're so overweight I'm going to have to pull your arm quite hard and tip you onto your – whoops. Right, OK. I'll mop you up after we're done. Again I'm going to have to gently ease you back from your tummy onto your side ag– Oh dear. Now you're not going to believe me but that really was an accident. Shit, is that a dent in the floor?'

13.

I was feeling distinctly nervous when I arrived at school the following day. Not only was I now fully expecting the Spanish Inquisition to charge in at any moment, but I was perhaps irrationally nervous because I hadn't seen the children for two weeks. I couldn't really put my finger on why – I wasn't expecting them to have changed into a bunch of wild animals but, for whatever reason, I found myself taking deep breaths at five to nine.

I had also heard, some twenty minutes previously, that a new boy, Timothy Reeves, was to be joining the class. Whenever any teacher hears this news there is always a moment of concern. If a ferocious-looking skinhead with tattoos and body piercing appears at your door, staring vacantly and frothing at the mouth, you know that the delicate equilibrium of the classroom is about to be seriously threatened. Part of the nervousness comes from the not knowing. I was pretty sure, however, that the moment he walked through the door, I would be able to make certain assumptions, and be able to use these to decide who to sit him next to.

The word that instantly sprang to mind when the secretary brought Timothy through was 'superior'. He was quite small and plumpish, and had an uncanny ability, presumably using some sort of hidden periscope system, to look down his nose at me when talking to me, despite being about half my height. His slightly pursed lips suggested that he felt he was doing everybody a favour by deigning to grace us with his presence.

'Hello, Timothy. My name is Mr Gray; I'll be your teacher while you're in Year 6.'

'*Enchanté.*'

Oh, please. In that one word, he had cut out a huge banner reading '*I'm a supercilious twat, please bully me*' and stapled it quite firmly to himself.

'Right – er. Well, Timothy. Let me show you your peg and your tray. Do you have a pencil case?'

'I do. Am I allowed to write in italic pen?'

'Of course – I try to encourage the children to write in fountain pen when they're ready for it.'

'Oh good – it's just that it's a Parker and it cost £80.'

'Well, make sure you take good care of it – staple it to your forehead or something.'

'Why would I want to do that?'

I could see he was going to be hard work.

'Oh, never mind. Give yourself a minute to sort yourself out, then when the rest of the class arrives, I'll introduce you.'

Timothy stood stump-still as the class filed in, whispering, giggling and pointing. After I sat them down, I turned to Timothy who still, worryingly, wore his holier-than-thou expression; I could tell, from the looks on many of the faces, that the class had already formed its own first impressions.

'As you can see, we have a new boy who is joining us today. This is Timothy; his parents have just moved into the area and so he doesn't really know anybody yet. I'm sure you'll all make him feel very welcome. David, I'm going to ask you if you will look after Timothy today – show him the ropes and all that. Will you do that for me?'

'Yeah, OK. Shall I move to another table so that he can sit next to me?'

'That's very kind of you, David, but I'm actually going to mix you all up this morning anyway. As you all know, you've got your SATs coming up in just over a term and we're going to really knuckle down to some hard work. We'll be doing lots of old practice papers and from now on there'll be three pieces of homework each week. That's the good news. The really good news is that I'm going to be sitting you boy/girl, boy/girl at your tables so that you won't be tempted into distraction.'

I said this with a broad smile and the collective groan that followed was actually quite good-natured.

'Do we still get to do lateral thinking quizzes?' said Kate, hopefully, 'if we promise to work really, really hard?'

'And since when have you done anything but work really, really hard, Kate?' My slight raised eyebrow and her subsequent laugh was another lovely snippet in our developing relationship.

'Absolutely. That's the least I can do. You work your socks off, and I'll make sure there's a bit of time each day for some fun.'

So I read out who was sitting where, to more groans, and set them off with their first task, which I thought might be revealing: *'What things do I need to improve on this term, and how am I going to go about achieving these improvements?'* I impressed upon them that this piece of work was going to act as a benchmark; that they were going to discuss it with me, type it up, get it signed by their parents, laminate it and place it prominently in the room. Some of them went about this task with more enthusiasm than others. Robert appeared to be in one of his defiant moods and was looking out the window. I had also noted the look of contempt that had passed over his face when I had introduced Timothy, and I resolved to watch this.

I looked at David carefully showing Timothy which book was which and felt that I had made a good decision by appointing him as unofficial mentor. I had considered Patrick but felt that that might get them labelled as the 'victim twins'. David was, like Patrick, a thoroughly nice lad but, despite still being rather frail and small, appeared to be both liked and respected by everyone. Even Sean, Shannon or Josh had never, to my knowledge, teased him, when it would have been extremely easy to have done so.

The children apparently found this exercise quite hard, especially the 'what am I going to do about it?' part, and the session struggled along until ten, when Mrs Warnock was to announce her presence in assembly. As we all filed into the hall, she sat, like some sort of hideous Greek goddess, enthroned in her chair. I nearly went searching for a large vine leaf with which to fan her. When everyone was seated and she had done the dramatic pause to well past its effective best, she stood slowly up, and began.

'Well, little ones, welcome back to school. As you have probably worked out, I am not Mrs Little. She has been asked to be the headteacher in another school this term, and so I have come here. My name is Mrs Warnock, and I hope we are going to have a lovely term together. Now, who can tell me what we must do to make sure everybody has a nice term?'

As soon as I saw Robert's hand go up, I knew that there was going to be trouble. I'd seen that confrontational mistrust-of-strangers look in his eye, and I hoped that she wouldn't ask him. There were enough hands in the air, and the odds were pretty good ...

'Yes, the little boy at the front here?'

'Work hard, miss.'

'Excellent, that will make me very happy. Anyone else? Yes. The girl in the middle with the glasses – yes, you – sorry dear, I don't know your names yet.'

'Behave, miss.'

'Ah, yes, good behaviour. You'll find me very strict about that. What about the boy at the back? What must we do to make sure we have a happy term?'

Dear God. I know I haven't been to church for a long time but if you could just talk a bit of sense into him then I'd ...

'How about if we don't patronise Year 6 children by referring to them as "little ones"?'

Bollocks.

'I beg your pardon?'

'I thought I spoke clearly enough, but I'll repeat myself. How-about-if-we-don't-pat–'

'What's your name?'

For the first time since I'd met her, the sickly smile had disappeared from her face, and she just looked terrifying.

'Robert Carlton.'

'Well, Robert Carlton, I'm afraid you've picked the wrong person to be insolent to. Go and stand by my office. I'll deal with you later.'

He looked at her for just long enough to show continued defiance, before calmly standing up and walking out. I thought there was every possibility of him marching out of the school, and stood up to follow him.

'Mr Gray?'

'I think I'd better – you know – just in case.' And without waiting for her approval, I followed him out. I sat down next to him and for a long time neither of us spoke. He was scrapping for a confrontation with somebody, and he wasn't going to get it from me.

'I could see that you were struggling for ideas when we were writing back there. How about you putting as a target to try to stay in Mrs Warnock's assembly for at least two minutes in future?'

I got a half-laugh, which was as much as I could hope for.

'Why, Robert?' I asked gently.

He shrugged. 'Dunno.' Another long pause followed and I was determined that he was going to be the one to break it.

'It's just – I dunno, she just wound me up, that's all – "little ones", for God's sake.'

'Listen, Robert. She's going to come in here all guns ablazing in a minute. What are you going to say to her?'

'Well if she thinks I'm gonna apologise she's got another think coming.'

I suddenly felt a little out of my depth. I was pleased with myself for defusing his initial anger, but I could see no way of avoiding the inevitable. Frank Bell could have done it. I'd watched him talk round children many times and I was forever learning from him. In the end, I decided, perhaps weakly, to change the subject.

'So, anyway, how was Christmas?'

When she returned, Sheila Warnock had a look about her which said 'so now to show this snotty-nosed little upstart who's boss around here'. I knew this approach would be disastrous so, before she could speak, I intervened.

'Mrs Warnock, could I speak to you, please?'

'In a minute, Mr Gray, I need to ...'

'Please, Mrs Warnock, it's important.'

Such was my obvious consternation that even the master of the 'I'll do things my way' approach stopped short.

'Very well. In my office. I'll deal with you, Robert Carlton, in a minute.'

As the rest of the class were now at break I knew I had a few minutes. In fairness to her, she listened intently enough as I gave her a quick summary of Robert's past, although she flared her nostrils slightly when I suggested that if she wanted to gain his respect, she wouldn't do so by shouting him down.

'To be frank Adrian, I am not looking to gain his respect. However, you were right to speak to me first but I'll deal with him now. You get yourself a coffee.'

The look that I got when entering the staffroom was usually reserved for a family gathering, when the eighteen-year-old is just about to announce his A level results.

'Well?' said Theresa. 'Out with it. Has she put him in the chokey?'

I relayed the little I knew and noticed, with certain satisfaction, that even Ellie Luck was showing unconcealed interest.

'So what happened in the rest of assembly?' I asked. 'Did I miss a treat?'

Frank gave a snort. 'Huh. Suffice it to say that nobody even breathed out of place by the time she marched them out to play. I've had my ups and downs with Robert in the past, but you've got to hand it to the lad – I wouldn't have had the balls to say that.'

Robert's expression when he returned after break was, as I had expected, devoid of any clues. I'd sat him next to Miranda who wasted no time in trying to work out what happened. Normally, as I sat them down after break, I would use that time-honoured teacher's favourite: 'Come along, settle down. Let's have some quiet now.' Instead, however, I pretended to be busy so I could listen in.

'What happened then, Robert? Are you going to be expelled?' A lovely girl, Miranda, but not a diplomat.

'Nah – she didn't say much really.'

'Oh come on, she must have done. I think you're brilliant by the way. I'd never have had the nerve to say that. What does it mean, anyway, "potrinise", or whatever you said?'

It was pretty clear that, despite Miranda's protestations, and she was pretty persistent, he wasn't going to reveal the upshot of his conversation with Mrs Warnock. So I, too, conceded defeat and quietened them for maths.

My concerns that Timothy was going to be a problem were confirmed when David asked to speak to me after lunch. Had it have been Marcus or Elizabeth, who delight in telling tales, I would have been a little more doubting, but I had no reasons to disbelieve David.

'It's Timothy,' he began. 'I don't want to tell on him or anything, but – it's just, he's upset a few people.'

'It's all right, David, go on.'

'Well, he was being a bit – you know – posh – talking about his old school and saying – kind of – that it was better than this one. Then Prakesh – I'm sure he was only joking – said "Why don't you go back there again?" and Timothy said "Why don't you go back to your country?" and Prakesh said "This is my country" and Timothy said nothing but carried on looking all posh and Miranda said that's racist and Timothy said he didn't care what silly girls said and ...'

I'd heard enough. This boy clearly thought he was better than anybody here and if he said that sort of thing to Shannon or Sean they'd crucify him. Also, all racist comments had to be officially logged which meant talking to Mrs Warnock, which meant ... I sighed. Had we really only been back one morning? I decided I needed to teach Timothy some home truths, and see just how thick his skin really was. So I got the others reading and took him quietly to one side – but not before I noticed the disapproving glances from most of the class. I was really worried about a mob culture developing amongst them. I needed to nip things in the bud pretty sharpish.

I thoroughly expected him to be bullish and was therefore

slightly taken back when he started crying as I broached what had happened at lunchtime. This really wasn't in the script and it threw me momentarily.

'They're all being horrible to me,' he whined, 'just because I'm new.' I tried to explain that if he came across as a clever-clogs who went on about his old school being better, then this was likely to happen. Whether I got through to him or not was pretty difficult to determine, but he agreed to think things over, and sat back down.

Towards the end of the day I was reminded of the expression about leopards and spots. While she'd started the afternoon well enough, Kate had spent most of the latter part of it shamelessly flirting with William. I gently warned her three times and on the fourth, told her in no uncertain terms that if she didn't settle down the class would miss out on their lateral thinking quiz at the end of the day. She was quiet for a couple of minutes but when I looked up again, she was openly chatting and laughing.

'I'm sorry, Kate, but I warned you. There'll be no quiz at the end of the day.' As soon as I said this, I realised I'd made a mistake. The groans and protestations of 'it's not fair' echoed around the class and I realised, for the first time in a long while, that they weren't on my side. I couldn't take back what I'd said and had to brave it out, but the mood wasn't good, especially when Sean muttered, 'Don't like those stupid quizzes anyway – they're rubbish.' I was also really upset with both myself and Kate that this incident had soured our relationship – and the look on her face said, in no uncertain terms, that it was soured – and I kicked myself for not handling it better. By the time I dismissed them at the end of the day, I had to remind myself that I was still new to this game and if I felt at the beginning of the day that I'd somehow cracked it – well, then, I needed to think again.

As the week wore on things began to settle again and Timothy blended in a little better. While he most certainly had not made any friends to speak of, there was a bit more of an acceptance from all sides, and an uneasy truce developed. However, leopards and spots and all that. At the end of the third day he reminded us all, in spectacular fashion, just what a first-class pillock he could be.

'Suppose you are a bus driver. The driver's job is to take children to school each morning. One fine day, the driver picks up twenty-four children at 8.30 and then at 8.35, drops off two and picks up another five. At 8.40, he drops off twenty and picks up a further three. At 8.45 he drops off another four before realising he has left his lunch at home. Here is the question: What is the colour of the bus driver's eyes?'

This quiz always gets an initial look of puzzlement and today was no exception.

'How are we supposed to know that, you never mentioned his eyes?'

'By thinking laterally, Josh, by thinking laterally.' I'd repeated the quiz three times before Timothy put his hand up:

'Are they – azuooerr?'

'I beg your pardon?'

'I said, Are they azuooerr?'

I should have deflected it. I should have simply said, 'No, Timothy they're not azure, any other guesses?' but I couldn't resist it.

'Please, Timothy, I'm intrigued. Why do you think they may be azure?'

'Well.' Oh God, here comes the superior look and supercilious voice: 'You mentioned that it was a fine day so, presumably the sky was blue. I think I'm right in saying that the reflection of that in his eyes would have been azuooerr.'

I was so stunned by this outrageously stupid remark that I simply couldn't speak. Fortunately Shannon stepped in for me:

'You really are a twat, aren't you Timothy?'

OK, *un*fortunately Shannon stepped in. This was the second time that Shannon had used this particularly descriptive word and the second time, to my shame, that I didn't act on it.

'That's enough, Shannon. No, Timothy, the answer is not azure.' The moment could have turned rather awkward had not Kate, in a far friendlier mood, shouted: 'I've got it! They're whatever colour eyes you've got! You said, "Suppose *you* are a bus driver ..."!'

All the 'oohs' and 'ahs' and 'of courses' went a long way to diffuse Shannon's comment and help the class momentarily forget that Timothy was, indeed, a complete twat.

My concerns about him intensified still further, though, when he handed in the 'what I'm going to improve' task: '*I really don't think there's anything I need to improve on. My private tutor says that I'm good for my age at all subjects, and I think I am too. I hope I'm not given work that's too easy for me.*'

Part of me wanted to read this conceited rubbish to the class and ask them if they had any suggestions as to how Timothy could improve: '*Well, Timothy, thank you for that most illuminating account. But remember the task is to think about things to improve on, even if we can't at first think of any because we're so bloody perfect. So everybody, let's help the new boy. Who's got some ideas as to how Timmy can get even better than he is now? David?*'

'*He could be a little more grateful when people are helping him.*'

'*Yes, good one that David. A little humility, Timothy. Any more? Prakesh?*'

'*He could stop being racist, sir.*'

'Miranda?'
'He could stop being sexist.'
'Shannon?'
'He could stop being a complete twat.'
'Thank you. Is that helpful at all, Timothy?'

While such ruminations brought a wry smile to my face, I had to remind myself, as I had done with Josh the previous term, that I was his teacher. If I didn't particularly take to him, and the early signs weren't good, I had to be careful that that didn't detract from my sense of responsibility towards him. One of the hardest things about teaching, which had struck me from day one, is the maintenance of calm and order amongst children who simply don't get on and, crucially, stopping yourself from unwittingly taking sides because of the personalities involved. The spat between the Williams twins and Miranda, which I'm sure I should have dealt with better, came to mind.

But I could see, after just three days, that the relationship between Timothy and many of the other children was likely to become inflammatory because, fundamentally, he was so different to the rest of the class. Timothy Reeves, for sure, was going to test my fledgling skills to the limit.

'So, Robert Carlton. What have you got to say for yourself?'
Silence. Eyes of steel.
'I see. I've spoken to Mr Gray and he's told me all about you but, quite frankly, none of what I've heard excuses the sort of rudeness that I just received from you. I don't care what you might have got away with before Christmas, but let's get one thing straight, young man, if anyone here thinks that they can be rude to me and get away with it then ...'
'I wasn't rude.'
'I beg your pardon?'

'*I said I wasn't rude. I just answered your question, quite politely I thought. No, Mrs Warnock, that wasn't rude.*'
'*HOW DARE YOU SPEAK TO ME LIKE ...*'
'*This, however, is rude. When some fat cow storms into our school like she owns the place, speaks in a patronising voice to Year 6 and then is too stupid to realise she's made a mistake, she can't really expect to gain too much respect. OK?*'

Attaboy!

14.

'Monday Morning Moan. I don't like doing it; I'd much rather start assembly with a smile and praise for good things, but sometimes these things need to be done. Now, you can all work out what my Monday Morning Moan is this week simply by looking in front of you. Lost property. Everybody has things which annoy them, and one of the things that really annoys me is lost property. Do you know how many items are here? Oh, put your hand down you silly boy, I'm not actually asking – over fifty things! So that means that one out of every four of you has something on this bench that you haven't taken care of. And not one item here is named. Look at these shoes. They're brand new and must have cost well over £20. You must know if they're yours. Look at them. Does anybody recognise them?'

Had the shoes that Sheila Warnock was now brandishing been solid gold and worth a small fortune, nobody would have claimed them. There was every possibility that if a child sitting in the middle of the floor had put their hand up, they would have been dodging a low-flying size 3 in the next few seconds.

It was the start of the third full week of term and already the fun of predicting Sheila Warnock's Monday Morning Moan had seeped into the staffroom. It was a good job that she was not looking at Frank Bell when she announced 'lost property' for her specialised subject this week, as she would have wondered why he had given a little triumphant punch in the air. Frank, Rachel, Theresa, Julia and I had started off a sweepstake the previous week. A fiver, per person, per week. Whoever correctly guessed the Monday Morning Moan won the pot. I'd been quite confident with my suggestion of litter this week and had even considered tipping the odds in my favour a little by decanting the waste bins around the playground and outside her office.

'Mr Bell, could you tell us what you're doing, please? You look like a footballer who's just scored a goal.'

'And I feel like one as well. I've just won fifty quid! Cheers, kids!'

It was quite laughable to everyone in the room that Sheila Warnock said that she didn't like doing it. I bet she stayed awake every Sunday night desperately trying to think of an excuse for her to wield more power, not to mention a shoe or two, with her Monday Morning Moans.

At the end of assembly she made a great fuss about making every child parade past all the items as they filed out of the hall and pick out what belonged to them. It was like some sort of ridiculous identity parade, with Mrs Warnock getting more and more agitated as child after child refused to pick anything up.

'Oh, for Pete's sake, this stuff must be somebody's,' she expostulated as the poor little reception children edged their way out. 'These plimsolls – they must be someone's in reception.'

Finally a brave little girl recognised a jumper and picked it up. You could almost sense everyone hold their breaths to see what retribution would befall her. Fortunately our esteemed head opted for sarcasm rather than violence – 'Jolly good, well done. One down, forty nine to go' – and afterwards others were more inclined to pick out any of their belongings.

Rachel's face, during all of this, showed growing concern, and not just for the safety of her kids. It was her dreaded observation immediately after assembly and, with Mrs Warnock clearly in a bad mood, it didn't bode well. I had put off my observation until the very last day – a week on Friday – for the simple reason that it increased the chances of one us dying in the interim, or of her simply forgetting. I whispered a 'good luck' to her as she left the room, and waited for my class to run the gauntlet. When there was only Year 6 left to inspect the clothes, well over three-quarters of the original lot were still unaccounted for. The look on Mrs Warnock's face suggested that this was entirely Year 6's fault, and if every offending article was not removed by them, there would be reprisals.

'It's obscene, isn't it,' I said to her as I passed. 'All this lost property. Mind you, have you noticed all the litter around the school ...?'

My class, generally, were responding well to the 'let's knuckle down' regime that I had impressed upon them at the start of term.

I had become increasingly strict in expecting homework completed on time and found myself getting quite shirty with offenders. However, this was another example of me finding it difficult to maintain consistency. I found it extremely easy to get really annoyed with the likes of Charlie and Andrew, both of whom handed in work late more often than not:

'How many times have I told you the importance of deadlines?' I bellowed. 'If you were a journalist who needed to get your report ready by 10 a.m. and you said to your editor "Oh sorry, I forgot. Can I stay in at lunchtime and finish it, please?", would the whole country happily wait an extra few hours before their newspaper arrived?'

It was much harder though, to speak so abruptly to Alice or

Robert. Alice's face, when she told me that she'd forgotten her homework, was filled with guilt and concern, and it was clearly a one-off lapse.

'Don't worry, Alice,' I found myself saying. 'We're all entitled to one mistake. Bring it in tomorrow, OK?' Now while this was a perfectly reasonable response to a genuine mistake, I did catch the eye of several of the class when I said it and I could almost see the words 'teacher's pet' forming on Charlie's lips. This whole issue of how I spoke to children I really liked compared to ones who annoyed me – and any teacher who tells you they like all their class equally is unlikely to be telling the absolute truth – was one that I hadn't cracked yet and I was very aware of what the children must think about this. Do I treat all children the same and be considered fair and consistent, or do I respond to the given situation and treat each individual in the way that I deem is fair and suitable for them? This intricate and delicate issue of child-management both worried and fascinated me – I'd chat to Frank and ask his opinion.

Robert's case was different again. If I spoke to him in the same way as I'd spoken to the passive Andrew, God knows how he'd have responded. Yet Andrew needed a good kick up the backside because he simply couldn't be bothered.

There was still an uneasy truce between Timothy and the rest of the class. I'd received his records from his previous school and it was evident from these that he had had similar social problems before. A few comments were still volleyed across the playground and I was very conscious that I was sitting on a timebomb. Robert and Sean, in particular, held a special hatred for him, and I could see Sean holding back from unleashing a tirade of abuse. He knew, though, only too well, that the annual football tournament was just around the corner, and didn't want to jeopardise his participation for one quick fix of Timothy-bashing. For his part, Timothy had formed an unlikely friendship with Elizabeth, Simon, Marcus and Andrew. None of them played football at breaks either and perhaps this is what drew them to him; but, on the other hand, none of them was especially bright and they were all pretty immature. This seemed at odds with this precocious little brat. Still, if they were happy, who was I to demand justification for the friendship? I hadn't had any complaints from Timothy, as yet, that the work was too easy for him and I put him in the 'A level' maths homework group along with Robert, Miranda and William. It soon transpired that he wasn't quite as bright as he thought he was and when I marked his homework on the probability of picking out various combinations of playing cards, most of which he got wrong, I thoroughly enjoyed writing on his book: *'Please see me, Timothy. Clearly this work is a little hard for you.'*

I knew that I wouldn't get to see Rachel during the day – infant playground duty and a de-briefing lunch would see to that – but I'd promised her that I'd buy her a beer after school and let her use me as a punch bag to offload any lingering fury.

Instead, during lunch, I found Frank, who was merrily leafing through a weekend breaks brochure, wondering how to spend his sudden windfall. I told him of my dilemma over how to deal with different children committing similar crimes.

'As you are no doubt learning very quickly, Adrian, children, especially by Year 6, are amazingly perceptive. If you rant and rage at a little shit for not bringing in homework – and believe me I've done it many times – then say "there, there, never mind, I'm sure you didn't mean it, have some smarties", to someone else, they're going to perceive that as being unfair. Equally, as you say, there are some children who need different handling to others. Some need a lot of help, some need gentle reminders and some need the proverbial rocket up the backside.

'The trick is – and you're not always going to get this right – the trick is to give the impression that you're dealing with them fairly, certainly by not varying your tone of voice. For your example, use language such as "everyone can forget things occasionally but this is the third time in a row" or "fair enough, we all forget things occasionally, make sure it is only once". This is a really difficult thing to teach, Adrian, it's simply something that you will learn from experience. The fact that you've identified it as an area for concern and are trying to deal with it is good. You may not be aware of it, but you've come on a great deal since September, but you'll always be learning. That's the nature of this job.'

'Thanks, Frank,' I smiled. 'That's reassuring.'

'Oh, don't get me wrong, Adrian. I'm only giving you advice and being nice to you because I took money from you this morning. Had the school been spending lunchtime picking up litter, I'd have given you an official warning and have had you on report in a jiffy. Incidentally, know of any nice country cottages?'

Rachel had her usual queue of parents waiting for her after school, followed by a dental appointment, and so I didn't get a chance to speak to her until I picked her up at 6.30 from her flat. We exchanged pleasantries in the car until she took her first, large swig of beer in the pub.

'So then, how did it go?'

She gave me a twisted grimace before replying. 'Not only is that woman an old bag, but she has absolutely no idea about reception teaching. At their age, they don't have the concentration span to sit through long maths or English sessions, so I tend to rotate them in small groups with myself and Mrs Day and I organise a group of parents to do things like listening to readers. It takes a bloody long time to organise, I can tell you, and the system usually gets shot when Johnny Shitpants gets going.'

For the first time, I think ever, I saw a frown on Rachel's face and what looked like real annoyance. It had never occurred to me just how much work Rachel must put in to organising her day and ensuring that her children were challenged all the time. I suppose that I had always subconsciously thought *'well, all they do is play, how hard can that be ...'*

'I've no idea how you manage it,' I chimed, in a rather pathetic attempt to rectify my shameful misconception. 'I'd last about ten minutes in your class before running out screaming. So what happened?'

'Nothing, really. It all went pretty much as planned. I was working with a group in the play area, Gwyneth was doing basic spellings with the special needs group, there was handwriting and reading sessions going on and – basically – it went well.'

'So what was her response?'

'First of all she thought it was too noisy and that it was hard for the children to concentrate. Well, I'm sorry, but that's just rubbish.'

'Did you tell her that?'

'I certainly did. I said *"Mrs Warnock, you're talking out of your backside."* Well, words to that effect. The point is that unless you're talking to the whole class or reading them a story, a reception class is always noisy. You simply can't expect quiet in the way that you can in Year 6. She was also going on about a lot of them not being on task. Again – welcome to the world of reception teaching. You know what she's like. If she forms an opinion about something you're not going to shift her on it. I tried arguing my corner but she wasn't having any of it. Her most annoying comment was when she said "It was quite a good lesson really" – you could almost see her biting her lip to avoid adding: _"for a beginner"_. Patronising cow. I'd love to see her teach them for a morning, I bet she's never set foot in a reception class in her life.'

She paused for a long swill of beer.

'I knew, as soon as she came in the class, that she was positively looking for something to criticise. She was clearly pissed off about the lost property. If she'd opted for good manners, my MMM guess, she'd have got it off her chest quickly and wouldn't have felt let down because nobody dared to pick up their stuff. It would have also earned me fifty quid.'

'It doesn't sound like it went too badly,' I said, thinking it might be helpful. It wasn't.

'Of course it didn't go too badly,' she snapped. 'It went bloody well. It just really annoys me that she clearly sees me as someone who's still new to teaching and who hasn't quite got it right yet. I'm sorry, Adrian, but you said you'd be my punch bag, and I'm punching.'

'D'you want another beer?'

'Yes, I bloody do, and make it snappy.'

This last remark, said with a lot of affection, suggested to me that she'd now got her frustrations off her chest and by the time that I came back with her beer, her usual smile had returned. She looked at her watch. 'Actually, I've got a bit of a confession to make – I just – you know – what with planning my lesson and all that, didn't have time to tell you.'

'Tell me what?'

'Well, Alan phoned late last night and asked whether I was up for a drink tonight – you know – just like you. And I told him I was already coming here with you and ... well, I didn't think you'd mind.'

'If he joins us? No, of course not – what time's he coming?' I wanted to sound as cheery as possible about this and, in fairness, I had actually come, rather grudgingly, to like him. I had long since got over the rather adolescent idea that if he wasn't around she might decide to be with me. My feelings for her though, despite my relationship with Alison, remained as strong as ever.

'Yeah, well, that's only half of it.'

'Go on.'

'Apparently, Florence is working around here this week and she's staying with him ...'

'What, his sister? The teacher-basher? That's fine with me – I'm more concerned about you putting a bottle through her neck.'

'Hmm. There's every possibility, the mood I'm in. Anyway, they won't be here for half an hour or so.'

With the mood visibly relaxed, we enjoyed some casual chit-chat, before I brought up what had been on my mind since Christmas:

'You know I told you about going to stay with Alison's parents? Well, it's this weekend.'

'Oh, God, do you know what you're doing when you're there?'

'I've no idea. I expect we'll all enjoy fun-packed days at the seaside and the funfair and perhaps go clubbing till the small hours. Either that or we'll all sit in silence all day awaiting her father's hourly bemoaning of his life. Happy days.'

'Surely you and Alison can get away for some of the time?'

'I bloody hope so. If I'm not in school on Monday you'll know that we didn't and that I chose hanging myself as a preferable option.'

We then spent another ten minutes enjoying our favourite game of inventing the worst possible scenario for the weekend, before Rachel called out 'Hiya!' I turned around to see Alan and what must have been his driver walking towards us. Well, if she wasn't his driver and was actually Florence, and all the evidence seemed to be pointing that way, she must have been adopted. Never have I seen two siblings look so different. While he was tall, muscular and handsome – the bastard – she was shortish, with mousy-brown hair, a pointy nose and an altogether plainish appearance.

So we did introductions and I found out she was in sales, and rapidly climbing the ladder. I caught Rachel's 'see what I mean' glance, before Florence spoke to me.

'So, you're a teacher, as well, is that right? Isn't it slightly unusual, in this day and age, to be a male primary school teacher?'

'Yes and no. There's still quite a few of us about.'

'Right. Can you see yourself staying in teaching or – you know – doing something ...' She left the sentence dangling, but the subtext was obvious: *'doing something a bit more worthwhile or a bit more befitting a real man.'*

'I've no idea. I'm also a qualified brain surgeon but I've always found the whole neuro-surgery thing a bit – you know – humdrum. Not much job satisfaction.'

She looked at me for about a second – a glorious second of vexed confusion, before saying, simply, 'Yeah, right.'

Rachel's slight, furtive smile was worth the entrance money alone and it almost encouraged me to continue the theme, until I remembered Naomi's warning. If she had been here, at this moment, she would have told me in no uncertain terms not to overdo it. After all, Alan was here as well, and to alienate his sister in front of his girlfriend would have been a stupid thing to do and caused a lot of embarrassment. I quickly, but sensibly, simmered down.

'No, seriously, Florence, I love teaching and I think it's so important that primary kids have a male teacher for at least one year. Whether I'll be teaching in thirty years' time, who knows, but for now, I'm really enjoying it.'

Alan then asked Rachel how her observation had gone and she recounted the events of the lesson once more.

'How often do you have appraisals?' asked Florence.

'Well, it depends, usually about once a term, but with this old cow, who knows.'

'Just three a year? Wow! In my job I'm being appraised all the time. It really keeps you on your toes.'

Again, this comment seemed designed to just give a little dig, to just subtly suggest that her sales job was somehow better, somehow more important; and it was pretty obvious to me that Rachel thought the same thing. I was very interested in Alan's take on this. He must have been aware that Florence had really upset Rachel before and must surely then be sensitive to any hiccups in their relationship. While Florence's comments were very subtle jibes, rather than unsubtle onslaughts, both Rachel and I saw them for exactly what they were. Alan's calm demeanour suggested he had no idea that there were any tensions in the air and this, from an obviously intelligent and astute person, seemed very strange indeed. I actually found myself enjoying the 'us and them' feel of the show. *Don't worry Rachel, I'll console you later* ...

The conversation then took different departures over the next hour or so and, while there were no arguments as such, Rachel's usual sunniness was definitely clouded, and I'm certain that this was Florence's influence. Again, though, the adolescent in me felt like I was scoring points. This pathetic idea was firmly shot in the foot when Alan and Florence got up to leave, and Rachel went with them.

'Thanks very much for the beers, Adrian, and allowing me to vent out my frustrations on you. I'll see you tomorrow, yeah?' And with that she kissed me on the cheek, I said my goodbyes and we all left. I tried to put away any thoughts of self-pity. It was entirely natural for Rachel to leave with her boyfriend. After all, I had my own girlfriend, who was about to serve me up a wonderful weekend ...

'Right, can you see yourself staying in teaching or – you know – doing something ...'

'Doing something what, Florence?'

'You know – doing something – different.'

'And why do you ask me that, Florence, when I'm less than six months into my career?'

'Er, well, I don't know really, I just thought ...'

'Just thought what, Florence? That a man should be doing something a little bit more worthwhile than teaching kids their tables?'

'Well, it's just a bit unusual, you know, for a man. Most professional men go into business, or something that pays well and really tests their abilities – you know.'

'So business tests your abilities, and teaching doesn't, right?'

'Well, I wouldn't quite say that, but surely it can't be that difficult – you know – teaching a bit of maths and English.'

'And what about reception children, eh? Five year olds – they must be even easier. After all, Florence, all they do is play.'

'I'm sure they do a bit more than that, eh, Rachel? But assuming you've got some patience, no, it can't be that difficult, I guess.'

Smoke was beginning to come out of Rachel's ears now – everything was going to plan.

'So Alan, you're keeping pretty quiet. Your sister's effectively saying your girlfriend's got a cushy little job playing with kids. What's your take on that?'

'My take? No, I'm sure Rachel does a really good job. You've

always liked playing with kids, haven't you love? Messing about in sand and all that. What's wrong?'

'Come on Rachel, you can do it. Raise that right hand, bring that glass down ... there's a good girl.'

15.

'So, how's it all been this week, then? Kids OK?'

It was just gone 4 p.m. on Friday, Alison and I had made an early start to get up to Doncaster by early evening, and already we were stuck on the M1. The chilly late January winds were swirling around outside as darkness began to fall. The thought of spending several hours having to make polite conversation in a traffic jam would have been of great concern to me with many people I knew, but it was a good yardstick of our growing relationship that I felt entirely comfortable in this environment with Alison. And, to be honest, four hours in murky drizzle on a motorway was likely to be more fun than the all-singing, all-dancing Jack and Rose show awaiting us.

'Oh, I don't know, I'm getting a bit concerned.'

'In what way?'

'Well, towards the end of last term I was beginning to feel that I had the class where I wanted them. They were working hard and didn't complain much. Now, they're working even harder and still not complaining much.'

'And the problem is?'

'The trouble is – there doesn't seem to be any enjoyment on their faces – oh, we have a daily quiz which they still like and the occasional joke, but it's all got a bit serious with our SATs preparation and well – where's the fun in that?'

'Everyone knows that this is the term for working hard, Adrian, you're not a entertainer at a children's party, you know.'

'I know – it's just – well, there are so many children who last term always had a smile on their face and a bit of spark. That smile doesn't seem to be there any more and – well – it's still three months to their exams – I'm just worried that I'm gonna – you know – lose them somehow. I'm not really making much sense.'

'Yes you are. You've built up a lovely relationship with the kids and you're concerned that you're going to turn into some hard taskmaster who they're not going to respect. *"Oh God, he's metamorphosising into Ellie Luck. Quick, let's hurry up and leave"* – that sort of thing?'

'Exactly. Robert's another one. I was definitely getting somewhere with him last term and now he seems to have gone all surly again. Perhaps it was a mistake giving me Year 6 in my first year.'

'Oh, for Christ's sake, listen to yourself, will you? If you carry on like this I'm going to sit you in a small room with Dad later and see who can out-self-pity the other – if that's a phrase. It sounds like you're doing a marvellous job there. What did that Frank say to you on Monday? Well, then. Stop being such a whingeing old git.'

That's what I was really beginning to love about Alison. She had a wonderful talent for cutting to the chase and rudely aborting self-piteous rants.

'OK. OK. Fair enough. I'm just being over-sensitive. You know how fragile us men get. So how was your week?'

'Well – you might call me a hypocrite in a moment when I start getting into whingey-old-git mode, but you've never met Christian.'

It occurred to me suddenly that I didn't really know too much about Alison's job. I knew she took out the special needs groups and I'd heard various names banded about – but I'm sure I must have bored her with tales from my school more than she'd bored me with tales of hers.

'Christian Day is a complete pain in the backside. I'm supposed to take out the children with learning difficulties, you know, and help them with spellings, reading, that kind of thing, but I'm sure his teacher only sends Christian out to get rid of him for half an hour. I mean – take today. He quite clearly didn't want to come out to me so decided to make my life as difficult as possible.'

'What did he do?'

'Oh, you know, the usual. Putting his hands over his ears and singing when I'm talking to him. Playing drums on the table and then – God, I hate this – repeating everything I said. What do you threaten a child with who doesn't want to be there in the first place? Keeping him in during break doesn't help – he's so odd no one plays with him anyway. What would you do?'

What would I do? Again my mind went back to my conversation with Rupert as I contemplated asking her why she chose to do this and come out of the classroom.

'I've absolutely no idea, Alison, but it does put my "Oh, I'm feeling depressed because a few kids aren't smiling quite as much as they were" rant into perspective.'

As the conversation gradually drifted to other subjects, and eventually silence fell, I started thinking about the likes of Christian Day, or some of the nutters that Rupert had to endure. I'd come close to experiencing defiance a few times, with Robert, Kate and Sean in particular, but I'd never had anything like that – yet there were teachers, thousands of them, who had to put up with classfuls of Christians every day. I'm really not sure, I thought to myself, that I could cope with that.

It was a miserable journey – all three and a half hours of it – before we finally arrived at Alison's parents' house, just about escaping a bout of deep vein thrombosis. They lived in a working class area in a three-bed end-of-terrace which was looking distinctly unkempt. Flaking paint, broken pots and grass left to grow too long the previous summer evidenced a lack of care, and the inside looked both dark and gloomy.

Jack Nettles opened the door to us, hugged his daughter and shook my hand.

'It's good to see you again lad, I trust you're looking after my girl?' This was said in better humour than I'd experienced before, and I wondered whether he'd had better news on the job front. Rose also welcomed us with a smile and I felt slightly self-conscious bending over her wheelchair to kiss her on the cheek. There was a horrible moment when I thought I wasn't going to reach and would have to actually tilt the chair towards me to perform the task, but fortunately I managed a brief brushing of our cheeks and this seemed to do.

'You're sleeping in your old room, pet, if you want to take your things up.'

As Alison went upstairs with her bag and I returned to the car to fetch mine, I began to wonder what that comment meant. There was a distinct emphasis on the word 'you're', which suggested that the next part of the sentence may have read *but that man who you are seeing out of wedlock can sleep on the couch*. The last thing I wanted to do was to boldly follow her upstairs, effectively shouting out *let me through, 'cause I'll be shagging your daughter tonight*, so I decided to saunter in slowly and wait for clues.

Jack shut the door after me when I got back in the house and there then followed an agonising few seconds of silence with the three of us in a very crowded space, me not daring to move and them wondering why I didn't.

'Are you going to ...?' said Jack, nodding upstairs.

'Er, yes – er – where ...?'

'Oh right, well, Alison's room is first on the right, upstairs.'

'OK – and is that where ...?'

'Sorry?'

'Er – am I – er – you know – er – going there too?'

'Well, unless you'd rather share our double bed with Rose –
I sleep in the spare room these days.'

This was getting more horrible by the moment.

'Oh Christ, I certainly wouldn't want to do that!'

'I beg your pardon?'

'I – er – well obviously – she's your – you know. I'll take
this stuff up to Alison's room, shall I?'

He didn't say anything more as I started climbing the stairs,
hopefully out of just about the biggest hole I had ever dug.

'All OK?' said Alison casually as I entered her room.

*Oh, hunky dory – apart from showing to your dad obvious
revulsion at the prospect of having to sleep in the same bed as
his handicapped wife. Tell you what: I'll instigate a jolly sing-
song when we get downstairs to really lighten the mood. How
about: 'If you're happy and you're working clap your hands?'*

Fortunately, there didn't appear to be any lingering
awkwardness as we came down a few minutes later, me
following sheepishly in Alison's wake. Indeed, the mood
seemed almost jovial and I realised just how hungry I was
when I smelt dinner. I still managed to score another own
goal when the casserole was served.

'Oh, right, so no black pudding then?'

There was a second of blank faces during which, if given
the choice, I would have happily accepted death, before Jack
laughed.

'Oh, yeah, good. Yorkshiremen, black pudding – very good.'

Thank you, God. I really, really, really promise not to do it
again.

'You seem in a good mood, Dad, how are things?'

'Well – touch wood – I had an interview yesterday for a
six-month project putting up some office blocks in town.

What's promising about this one though is that they said they're looking for someone with lots of experience and well – I don't want to count any chickens but the interview went really well and at the end the guy gave me a huge smile and said "I'll let you know soon." This'll make such a big difference pet, if I can land this.'

I didn't like to say that in my extremely limited experience of interviews, a charming final smile could mean several things.

'So pet, what are your plans for the weekend?'

'Well, we haven't really got any yet. We've had a long journey up here so we thought tonight we'd just have a quiet ...'

'Nonsense, Alison. Your mum's really looking forward to having a girl's chat tonight and you know I always go down the club every Friday. What do you say, eh, Adrian?'

'Er, what – sorry – what club?' Nightmarish visions of a randy pensioner and his boy being laughed out of the local nightclub flashed through my brain.

'The club – the working men's club. Been going there every Friday for donkeys. Fancy a game of pool and a drink – let the ladies talk knitting and flower arrangement?'

'Er – yes. That sounds great. I love a pint of Yorkshire – er, real cream of – best.'

'Ha, ha, very good. You'll do the dishes, won't you love? Me and your fella's got some drinking to do.'

Mostly I was glad that he was so obviously in a good mood – for a start he took my appalling attempt at being a pseudo-Yorkshireman who knows his beer as a deliberate joke, and it was also considerably more pleasant than the gloomy depressive who had gate-crashed Corinne's party. Yet part of me felt uneasy – this was new territory for me, going drinking with the father of the girlfriend, and I'm sure that beneath all the blokey camaraderie there was an element of sizing-up in his mind. Still, to refuse would have been extremely rude, so twenty minutes later the two of us left

Alison and her mother and began the short walk to the club.

The working men's club was pretty well exactly how I had envisaged it: twenty or so working class men, predominantly in their fifties or sixties, enjoying a drink at the end of the week. Jack accepted my offer of a beer and we sat down. After the regulation pleasantries – work and football mainly – Jack brought the conversation around to his daughter.

'So how's it going then, lad, between you and Alison?'

'Yes – well, thank you. We're taking it easy for the moment and seeing how it all goes.'

'Hm. Well, however much of a prick you might turn out to be, you can't be worse than that bloody no-good waste of space of a husband of hers. I never knew what she saw in him, but whatever it was he hid it pretty well. Have you ever met him?'

I resisted obvious sarcastic responses to this and replied that I hadn't, but that Alison had told me a fair bit about him. I was a bit unsure where this was all going but I found out in a rather sudden fashion. He gripped my arm and his eyes opened wider as he said:

'You're not gonna be like him, are you, lad? You're not gonna run off with some little tart and break my girl's heart?' By now his eyes had a slightly manic look and it occurred to me, that had I not been in this dingy club with a very slightly deranged man telling me in no uncertain terms not to let Alison down, I'd probably have been at the pub with Liam and Tony casually chatting up girls.

'As I said, Jack,' I replied as evenly as possible, 'It's still pretty casual between us, but if it does get more serious, then I certainly wouldn't let her down like that, you have my word.'

He patted me on the arm and added, 'You're a good lad, Adrian, you're a good lad.' This was verging on another *Little House on the Prairie* moment, so I decided to down my pint and order him another, before one of us started crying.

Unfortunately, there was a tiny bit more in my glass than I could reasonably drink in one go but, call it foolish manly pride if you will, I was determined to manage it and give the empty glass that satisfying 'real man' thud on the table. By the time I took the last couple of gulps, I knew it was a mistake and ended up splurting back a mouthful, choking and gasping for breath.

'Another?' I said finally, watching him wipe away the flecks of spittle from his face.

'Same again, thanks.'

Despite this being a regular Friday night routine, it soon became apparent that Jack Nettles was not very good at holding his drink. As we got well into our third pint, he began to slur his words somewhat, and after he'd started on his fourth, despite my useless protestations that it might be nice to go back for a cup of tea, he was clearly getting pretty drunk. This brought about an attack of the 'woe is me's' and I listened as sympathetically as I could to the stories of his redundancy and of his wife's downward spiral.

'Since Alison and Peter split up she's gone downhill really fast. I'm not sure how long she's going to be able to cope on her own, especially if I get this job. Have you ever had to care for anybody, Adrian?'

'Well, when my father died, my moth—'

'Have you ever had to wipe someone's bum or clean them up when they've wet themselves? I tell you it's no fun, Adrian – but we gotta stick by 'em, haven't we? It's all too easy walking away. I mean, I could have run off with some blonde dolly bird anytime I wanted, like that little bastard, but that's not how it's done, is it?'

What an image.

'Oh look, the pool table's free, fancy a game, Jack?'

Watching him trying to hit the ball in vaguely the right direction without tearing the baize was marginally better than listening to that last conversation. He was really quite drunk by now and at one point ended up on his hands and knees when he tried to lean on the table but missed. It was extremely telling that none of the regulars took much notice of his embarrassing exploits; the obvious deduction was that this was quite a regular event. After a very one-sided game I managed to persuade him to leave, and said my thanks to the barman.

'Good luck,' he replied, raising a slight eyebrow as Jack leant heavily on me.

'A bit of fresh air, Jack, and you'll feel fine by the time I get you home.' The final embarrassment of the evening was the singing. The fresh air seemed to rejuvenate him somewhat and he began a loud and tuneless version of 'Let's face the music and dance', causing several heads to be turned. Finally, at about 11.30, we opened the front door and he staggered in. Alison and her Mum were finishing a cocoa and I looked at Alison with a 'don't blame me' expression on my face. I suddenly felt incredibly tired, which Alison must have sensed, for within a few minutes she suggested that we went up to bed.

Fortunately, she too was tired and it was mutually agreed that we would go straight to sleep. The thought of Jack storming in and asking us to keep the noise down would just about have rounded off the evening's embarrassments perfectly. Despite all of this, though, I was glad to be here with Alison. I was glad to have a weekend away from thinking about school, and I was glad to feel her warmth as she cuddled up to me, and we both slowly drifted off to sleep.

I awoke in the middle of the night, as I always do after a few beers. Feeling dazed and nursing the beginnings of a headache, I stumbled out of bed, out of the door and into the bathroom. Whether it was the effects of the alcohol or just plain tiredness, it took me a good second more than it should have done to realise that Rose was already in there, sitting on the loo. She didn't say anything; she just glanced rather awkwardly at me. I, however, yelped, hastily apologised and shot out of the room. Had there have been more than one loo in the house I would have quickly retired there but there wasn't, and by now I was absolutely desperate to go. I could hardly bang on the door and shout 'get a move on will you, what the bloody hell do you think you're doing in there?' My only other option was to creep downstairs, unbolt all of the locks and make use of one of the broken pots. But it was pouring with rain and the thought of Jack looking through his front window and witnessing such a spectacle negated that idea. Just as I was contemplating the kitchen sink, I heard a shuffle and a groan from inside the bathroom, as Rose struggled to get up.

'Adrian,' she called quietly.

I froze in complete horror. Oh my God, no. I can't do it. Please, please, please God, don't make her say what I think she's going to say. She's putting me up in her house for the weekend and I probably owe her a favour ...

'Yes?' I answered, in about the same tone of voice as the convict when asked if ready to be executed.

'Sorry to take such a long time, pet, I'll be ready in a moment.'

'Oh, honestly, no problem – whenever,' I answered. The mixture of utter relief and utter desperation was one that I don't think I'd ever experienced before. After what seemed an eternity, and by now my legs were well and truly crossed, the door slowly inched open and she hobbled out, clutching on to the specially designed rail. I smiled as much as my aching body would allow, and asked if she needed any help.

'No, it's all right pet; I just need to go slowly, that's all.'

Aaagghhh! Go any slower and I promise you that I will piss all

over your carpet. Eventually, there was enough room for me
to squeeze through and I practically dived for the toilet. As I
stood there, relief surging through me, I contemplated, with
a huge shudder, just how much worse that scenario might
have been.

I awoke at just gone eight with a nagging headache. Alison
was asleep so I decided to have a quick shower, find an Anadin
from somewhere and surprise her with breakfast in bed.
Slightly invigorated by the shower, I went downstairs to the
kitchen, thoroughly expecting to find no-one there. I could
only see Jack's back, but I sized up everything in an instant.
The stillness of his position, the slightly hangdog posture and
the opened letter discarded on the table. Part of me wanted
to creep back upstairs like the total coward I am in this sort of
situation, but he must have heard me, hence I had no choice.
  'Morning, Jack,' I muttered as casually as I could.
  Silence.
  I walked over to the kettle and started filling it.
  'Can I make you a cup of tea?'
  Silence.
  I realised that I had now completely used up all acceptable
pleasantries and that I had to mention what neither of us
wanted to talk about.
  'Not good news?'
  'No.'
  I had absolutely no idea what to say next. Mindless
platitudes such as 'never mind, I'm sure something else will
turn up soon' would sound both hollow and patronising. In
the end I plumped for simple honesty.
  'I don't know what to say Jack, I'm sorry.'
  There was a long silence while he continued to stare at the
floor. Eventually, I gently touched his shoulder in the only

act of solidarity I could think of and said, 'I'll make the tea.'

I made a cup for everybody, left his next to him and went upstairs. While I didn't want to feel like I was passing the buck, if anyone was going to initiate a heart-to-heart it should be Alison or Rose, not me. It was clear that Rose was unaware of the news when she said 'Oh, bless you, Adrian, what a lovely surprise' upon receiving her tea and I wasn't going to say anything to her.

Alison was awake now and I quickly told her that her father had not got the job.

'Shit. Oh shit. This is going to knock him back a long way. I'd better go and talk to him.'

I sat on the bed thinking, rather selfishly, about how morose the rest of the weekend was now likely to be. I had witnessed Jack's dejection once before, but at least on that occasion I could get up and go home. I thought, and perhaps secretly hoped, that Alison would return and announce that we were going home but when she came back in several minutes later, it soon became clear that that wasn't to be.

'He's pretty depressed, Adrian, as you can imagine. I suggested that we go but he said he'd rather we stayed.' After she'd relayed their conversation, I said:

'So what are we going to do today? Go out somewhere?'

'Oh, I don't think so. Let's just stay here and see what happens, eh?'

So followed the longest and dullest day of my life. Jack seemed content to sit and do nothing all day, allowing self-pity to set in. Any attempt at conversation by the rest of us was cut short and quickly died a death and I found myself spending most of the morning reading a local paper. If nothing else came from the morning at least I was now secure in the knowledge that Benji the cat had been found safe and well after a three-week absence.

Alison was acutely aware of the awkwardness in the

atmosphere and insisted that the two of us go out for a while after lunch. However, her father's mood had clearly been catching and our walk through the park was hardly electric entertainment. The hardest part of the day was that it was impossible to say anything even vaguely optimistic. If he couldn't even land a job to which he was so suited, what chance did he have?

I have a particular aversion to Saturday night television but I jumped at the suggestion that we should watch it. Even the compulsory celebrity-based reality show was strangely appealing for the simple reason that it broke the silence. I was actually looking forward to *Match of the Day*, as I hadn't dared to listen to the football results earlier, but at that point both Alison and Rose announced they were going to bed. Naked-Scandinavian-Nympho Match of the Day wouldn't have tempted me at that point, as the thought of spending the next hour in the sole company of Jack was just too much to face. I quickly concocted a yawn and went up with Alison.

When I eventually climbed into bed, I noticed that she was trying to stifle back tears, and I felt a great wave of affection for her.

'I'm really sorry, Adrian, it's been a shitty weekend. You must think that we're all a bunch of miserable bastards – how can you want to keep on seeing me after this?'

'Now who's being the self-pitying old git, eh? Listen. I can assure you that I feel so much closer to you now than I did on Friday. You're in an impossible situation – none of which is your fault – and you've known that just being with your family had to be your priority today.'

And for the first time in the months that we had been together, as she held me close and held back the tears, I felt more than merely casual towards her. Had Rachel walked in at that precise moment, improbable as that would have been, and asked me out, I would have turned her down.

Jack was slightly more lucid in the morning and promised, with admirable dignity, that he would continue his search for elusive work on Monday. He even suggested that the two of us went for a swift half before lunch but, fortunately, both his wife and daughter insisted that he helped with the preparation. I expect they did this for my benefit, rather than for theirs.

When we came to say our goodbyes in the afternoon there was a lot of emotion ricocheting around, and I found myself caught up in it. I had gone through a lot with them over the previous two days, and it felt as though they now saw me as a member of their family. While this was a clearly a compliment, I really wasn't sure how I felt about it.

The journey home was considerably quicker and as we neared our junction off the M1 Alison asked me, bluntly, if I would stay over with her. Up until now we'd never stayed together with work the following day, and it felt like a new juncture in our relationship. It also felt entirely right, and I found myself packing a small bag before heading to her house.

'Have you ever had to wipe someone's bum or clean them up when they've wet themselves? I tell you it's no fun, Adrian. I mean, I could have run off with some blonde dolly bird anytime I wanted, like that little bastard.'

Fortunately, the 'dolly bird' bit of this sentence took my mind away from the 'bum wiping' bit. By now though, I was feeling distinctly uneasy with this conversation and I just wanted to get away from this depressing club and this depressing man. Just as I was beginning to accept another two hours of his increasingly drunken rants, though, a miracle occurred. Into the bar came a young nubile blonde dolly bird and without hesitation Jack sidled up to her.

'Evening lass. I'm 58 years old but I fancy a bit of young skirt tonight, as I've had a bit of a tough evening wiping my wife's arse. You'll have to buy all the drinks 'cause I'm unemployed, but I thought maybe we could run away together. How about it?'

As they departed, dreamily staring into each other's eyes, I sighed with relief, sauntered up to the bar and ordered a pint of Yorkshire real cream of best.

16.

Whenever the staff, in any establishment, are summonsed together at very short notice for a meeting it invariably suggests that something major is about to be announced. The Thursday after the weekend in Doncaster, just before midday, a memo went round that everyone had to meet in the staffroom at 12.30. As soon as the kids went out for their lunch break I went to find Rachel to see if she had any clues.

'Maybe somebody's died,' she suggested cheerfully, 'or the Prime Minister is coming over to announce that Mrs Warnock is to be made a dame. Who knows?'

There was an air of expectation, mixed with anxiety, as Sheila Warnock made her dramatic entrance to the staffroom at just gone 12.30.

'I'm sure you're all wondering why I've called you here at such short notice. Well, at 10.30 this morning I got *the* phone call.'

It was clear that she expected us to know the difference between *'the'* phone call, as opposed to *'a'* phone call, which would obviously require further explanation. Maybe she *was* being made a dame.

'There's no easy way to put this, but we are having an Ofsted inspection, beginning on Monday.'

There was a horrible silence as everyone digested this news. Up until a few years ago, schools had had about six weeks' notice of an inspection. This gave you adequate time to prepare everything and get your paintbrushes arranged in alphabetical order, but the stress of waiting and worrying for such a lengthy period of time had proved too much for many neurotic teachers. The philosophy behind the three-day warning was that it was much harder to paper over the cracks, and the inspectors would see you for what you were, warts and all.

'In three days we can't do much. The registered inspector is coming to visit me at ten o'clock tomorrow morning, and he'll want to see the school. If nothing else, make sure that your classroom looks tidy ...' She glanced at me here. 'And if you have any displays ready to put up, it might be an idea to do so tonight. You will need to have lesson plans for all sessions from Monday to Wednesday ready for Mr Rankin by 8.30 on Monday. We'll meet again briefly tomorrow lunchtime and I'll report back on anything else he wants, or that he is specifically looking for. Oh, and Adrian, I'm afraid I'm going to have to cancel your observation tomorrow.'

'Oh, that's a shame. I was looking forward to it.'

'Well, never mind. I'm sure we'll fit it in later in the term.'

'I'll make sure I remind you, Mrs Warnock.'

I've often found that people who are obsessed with their own importance have no sense of irony whatsoever, but at least that little exchange produced a few stifled giggles as everyone tried to digest this news.

'Oh, and one more thing. Please keep this news completely secret for the moment. I'll announce it to the children in assembly tomorrow and a letter will go home to the parents after that. Can we meet back here please, same time tomorrow?'

In fairness to Mrs Warnock, if she was filled with consternation, as the rest of us were, she hid it very well, and delivered her bombshell calmly and evenly.

I was intrigued by what she would tell the children in assembly the following morning, but all she said was that we would be having some 'special visitors' who would be here the following week to look round the school and maybe talk to them to see how they were getting on. It was a very brief, woolly message, and wasn't good enough for Year 6.

'So, who are these visitors we've got next week?' asked Shannon, shrewdly, when we were back in class. 'Are they coming to inspect how well you're teachin' us or somethin'?'

'They're called Ofsted inspectors, yes Shannon, and their job is to look around the whole school and see how well it's running. But make no mistake,' I lied, 'they'll be inspecting your behaviour and your work as much as how well I teach you, so I reckon we all need to show them next week just what a fab class we are. What d'you say?'

By the end of that speech I was aware that I was beginning to sound like an American college kid, and I thoroughly expected a few whoops, high fives and 'get on downs' from the masses. Instead I got a few thoughtful nods and very British 'OKs'. I figured that, by bending the truth a little – Ofsted most definitely would not be criticising the children, only our handling of them – I was more likely to get enthusiasm and hard work from them next week. The obvious exception to this was Robert, who would be very likely to see through my ruse and deliberately be a complete git simply for the sport. Perhaps he'd go on holiday next week, or contract some rare disease over the weekend.

Halfway through Friday morning, Mrs Warnock brought round Mr Rankin, the registered inspector. He was a small comedy figure of a man, in his mid-forties. His unfortunately large ears were accentuated by the lack of hair concealing them. Despite this, his eyes looked most shrewd and I had the feeling that he was internally digesting everything he saw with a view to performing an initial hypothesis which he would then test the following week. Fortunately the class were working on an interesting maths problem and were reasonably on task when he came round. I glanced uneasily at Robert, to check that he wasn't about to set fire to something, before walking over to introduce myself. He seemed rather shy and overwhelmed to be there, but I wasn't fooled. Those eyes were piercing and they kept flicking around the room, memorising everything. He stayed for perhaps two minutes before he was ushered out to the next classroom.

'Is he the one who's inspecting us, then?' asked Kate, a little disbelievingly. She had obviously formed a vision of an imposing giant of an inspector who could wither by his very presence. A small baldy with big ears was clearly a disappointment to her.

'Yes, Kate, that was Mr Rankin, and I promise you that he will not miss a trick next week, so when I ask you all for your homework first thing on Monday morning, I'm quite sure that he'll be here with his clipboard, ready to name and shame anybody who's forgotten theirs.'

There was a real look of anguish from some of them at this comment, and I was a bit concerned that I'd gone over the top. I could quite easily visualise Elizabeth's mum barging in on Monday morning, in front of Dumbo, complaining that her little darling had been traumatised by my comments. So I toned it down a little and duly set their maths homework, which they all wrote down with nagging accuracy. Perhaps the inspectors should come more often.

Fortunately I didn't have too much planned for the weekend, so I could devote it to writing lesson plans, although I wasn't going to miss out on our boys' night out on Friday, or indeed my romantic meal for two on Saturday. We're not especially original on our Friday nights, but we were kept amused on this night by competing to invent the worst thing to happen during the inspection. In fifth place was Tony's scenario in which Shannon collapsed and I made a complete hash of trying to put her in the recovery position, at which Sean officially complained, to a nodding Mr Rankin, that my attempts at administering cardiac massage were akin to sexual assault. My suggestion, that Patrick mistakenly called the inspector Mr Wanker, was awarded fourth place, while Liam came in third and second with his contributions, which, respectively, involved Timothy correcting Sean's grammar once too often and ending up in hospital, and the whole class, conducted by me, singing a chorus of 'When I see an elephant fly' to ease the tension during a quiet moment, only for Mr Rankin to emerge from the stock cupboard, where he'd been inspecting the paintbrushes unnoticed. The winner was dreamt up, perhaps inevitably, by Tony, who suggested this nightmarish situation: upon Mr Rankin asking for a volunteer to read their 'letter of complaint' English task, Robert's hand shoots up:

Dear Sir,
Over the past few weeks I have been undergoing treatment at your surgery and I am most displeased with the results. First, the anti-balding agent seems to have made me lose even more hair. Secondly, when I asked for my ears to be repositioned, I rather assumed that they would be pinned closer to my head, rather than be pushed further away from it.
Yours faithfully,
Mr Rankin

Alison pulled out all the stops on Saturday night, after I had spent the day writing lesson plans. Her juicy steaks went some way to temporarily relieve the nerves I was now feeling. She'd been through this process twice before and, although the topic was banned on Saturday evening, had insisted that the three-day treatment could only be better than the slow trauma of waiting for it to happen. Lovely as the meal was, there was a sense of 'The Last Supper' about it, a final offering before the inevitable doom.

I had stayed at Alison's house all week and had enjoyed being there. However, as the week wore on, it became clear to me that I wasn't ready for this on a semi-permanent basis just yet. I still enjoyed the blokey feel of our shared flat, and I wanted to make the most of the six weeks that the three of us had left until Liam and Naomi got married. This was quite an awkward subject to bring up with Alison. Last weekend at Doncaster had certainly upped our relationship a notch or two, and my guess was that she'd have been happy for me to move in. To announce completely the opposite – that I effectively wanted to spend most nights at the flat still – may well have upset and confused her. Perversely, though, Ofsted gave me the opportunity to do just that, at least for a few days, as it was entirely reasonable for me to want to base myself at home during this time. I mentioned this casually as I was leaving on Sunday morning to sort out my planning file and if she was disappointed, she didn't show it.

As Sunday slowly passed, my sense of nervousness gradually developed into one of panic. After all, this was my induction year. In early June, Sandra Little would decide whether to offer me a permanent contract, and my performance during the next three days would be paramount in the decision she and the governors would reach. Even though she wasn't here, I had no doubt whatsoever that she would very quickly glean how everyone was doing.

I slept fitfully, but the adrenalin levels on Monday morning easily outweighed the lack of sleep, and I arrived at school at 7.30 feeling wide awake. We were to have a meeting at 8.30 during which we would all be introduced to the inspection team and, because everything by then was so well planned, I spent the next hour mooching around, going through what I was going to teach in the morning in nearly as much detail as an actor having a final run-though of his lines before his first entrance.

At 8.30 Mr Rankin introduced us to the other two inspectors. Mrs Rush looked professional and astute, but her body language gave little else away. Mr Burnham, the lay inspector, on the other hand, looked rather nervous about the whole event. He was rather twitchy and his darting eye movements suggested anything but calm. I decided that, given a choice, I would prefer Mrs Rush as the first visitor to my room – I felt that the likes of Kate and co. would be more likely to respond to her and therefore give their best.

We'd been told, on the previous Friday, to expect to be observed about once a day for the three days, and Mr Rankin reiterated this.

'Please expect us at any time – it is possible that you might be seen more than once, so don't get too perturbed if that happens. While we are here to inspect you, and we're not going to hide behind anything that we might find, we are human and we appreciate that you are too. We would expect you to be a little nervous this morning, and we'll be very sympathetic to that. My best advice would be to teach as normally as possible. If you try to put on a special show for us, you will only confuse the children.'

Unless of course you are Robert, who will delight in showing you up in front of the inspectors.

'We'll be joining you all for assembly at nine and then we'll approach those of you that we'll be visiting immediately after that, and go with them to their class. If you could leave all your lesson plans I'd very much appreciate it, and I wish you all the best of luck.'

There were some anxious looks on the children's faces as they filed quietly and calmly in at nine. Their glances around the room were hardly subtle, and Josh even opened the stockroom door expecting, presumably, Mr Rankin to jump out with a loud 'Surprise!'

'When you've finished checking every corner of the room,' I said, 'would you please get your homework out and sit down ready for registration.' Unsurprisingly, everyone had finished and brought in their work and there were some rather disappointed looks as they handed it in. Andrew, who was notorious for forgetting his homework, slowly walked up to the homework tray, all the time looking at the door, clearly hoping that Mr Rankin would walk through and dish out a tube of smarties for its successful completion. It was a bit like that moment in 'pass the parcel', when you deliberately take as long as possible before passing it on in the hope that the music would stop. You could almost hear him muttering 'dunno why I bothered'.

'Where are the inspectors, then?' came the inevitable question, from Sophie.

'There are three of them, and we can expect at least one of them at some point today. After that, who knows?'

One could easily have mistaken the school for a deaf and dumb institute, such was the silence that was observed by everybody as they walked into assembly. The looks that some of the younger children gave the inspectors as they gave them a wide berth on the way to sitting down suggested that their teachers had hinted darkly about terrible reprisals if they were to breathe out of place. Had Mr Rankin suddenly turned into the child catcher out of *Chitty Chitty Bang Bang*, very few of them would have been surprised.

With her most ingratiating smile, Sheila Warnock introduced the three musketeers, and gave a lively and thought-provoking assembly, full of props, overhead projections and child participation. Curiously, there were no Monday Morning Moans. Part of me wanted Robert to ask her why she had chosen this morning to give such an assembly, rather than read yet another uninspiring story from a book.

At the end of assembly the inspectors got up and started walking towards their first victims. Part of me really wanted to get it out of the way quickly, and I was pretty confident that my impending maths lesson would go well, so I was slightly disappointed when they walked towards Theresa, Irene and Ellie.

I was amazed at how much my class had embraced the whole Ofsted thing, probably helped by my bending of the truth the previous week. There was, therefore, a certain flatness to the morning as first maths, then ICT and finally English passed without a visitor. During lunch I rather assumed all the staff would converge and compare notes, but either they were all being debriefed or doing last-minute preparation for the afternoon, and the staffroom was eerily empty throughout the break.

I took a deep breath as Mr Rankin walked through my door at the beginning of the afternoon. None of the children had been a pain in the morning – Robert, in particular, appeared to be on my side – so I had no reason to assume that they would be any different in the afternoon. Registration passed smoothly enough and I went on to explain the afternoon's science activity. We had been told the previous Friday not to 'play safe' with straightforward lessons that involved the children working silently from textbooks or worksheets. So I'd decided to take the bull by the horns and give them an activity that could go either way.

'How many of you can tell me, with confidence, exactly what the function of the heart is, and how it works?'

As I had hoped, only a few hands went up, with perhaps three appearing confident.

'So this is what we are going to do. We'll first have a discussion and double-check that we're all clear on the vocabulary and then I'm going to put you into groups of six or seven, take you into the hall and your task will be to produce a stylised improvisation explaining exactly how the heart works.'

Oh look, he's writing something down – hopefully something along the lines of 'children seem keen on this idea, good kinaesthetic approach to cementing a concept', rather than 'sounds like a pile of hippy claptrap to me'.

The conversation went well and there was a real buzz of excitement as I put them into mixed groups and took them into the hall. I suggested that each group elected a narrator who would lead us once around the circulatory system, and gave them twenty minutes to plan their improvisation. I had thought carefully about group dynamics and made sure that Timothy was kept well away from Robert, Sean, Shannon and – it has to be said – about three-quarters of the class.

The session seemed to go well, despite a few minor arguments along the way. I wonder if the phrase 'I don't want to be an artery, you always get the best parts,' announced vehemently by Josh, has ever been uttered before.

During all this, Mr Rankin wandered round chatting to the groups, until I finally brought them together to show their improvisations.

The first group was excellent. They had come up with the idea of using an analogy of the underground train system and William skilfully talked us through how the arteries and veins were the tunnels, the blood was the trains and the oxygen the passengers. I could see Mr Rankin nodding as they all got a well-deserved round of applause.

The second and third groups were also good, if not as inventive, and Sophie and Allard narrated them well, and I was just mentally ticking the 'outstanding' box on Mr Rankin's form, when the last group stood up and Josh began to speak. The other members of his group had clearly had enough of his whingeing and said something along the lines of *'well you bloody narrate it then, and make a fool of yourself'*. I had very nearly chosen the narrators myself, and now I wished I had.

'Right, so this is the heart and er – it sort of bleeds out blood into the veins.'

'It's the arteries, you pillock,' hissed Shannon as she mimed, rather provocatively in my view, the heart pumping blood.

'Oh, yeah, arties. Er, so this blood right, you know, sort of dribbles its way along the arties until it gets to your arm.' He looked around desperately at this point but nobody was going to bail him out. Meanwhile, Shannon's pumping was getting more and more stylised and people were beginning to laugh.

'So, er, when it reaches the arm it rushes all the way to the fingers and then the, er, passengers get out.'

'Had they paid for their tickets?' called out Sean, as everyone started to laugh harder and Josh froze in embarrassment. It was time to act:

'OK, thank you everyone, let them finish. Miranda, perhaps you'd like to finish off the narration?'

'But Josh is the narrator. How can I be a narrator and oxygen?'

'Well, you've got off the train now, so it doesn't matter,' chirped Sean, who was clearly enjoying himself.

'That's enough, Sean. Shannon, *please*!'

By now Shannon was performing some grotesque ritual dance, turning around and wiggling her bottom to the audience, who were clearly loving it.

'OK, everyone, stop,' I shouted, my voice slightly quivery. 'Everyone sit down.' I tried to restore some calm to my voice and at least they all had the decency to obey me and quieten down.

'Now, this is a shame. This has been a lovely session and you've all worked so hard. I don't expect such silliness from this class. Now, silently walk and line up, we'll finish off the discussion then.' Mr Rankin had remained impassive during all this and God knows what he must have thought. Maybe he enjoyed ritual tribal dances ...

The closing discussion went without event, but it had clearly lost the early spark. Eventually Mr Rankin smiled, thanked us all and left for his next visit. I knew I needed to speak to them at this point but to just get annoyed again and alienate myself would have been a mistake, and it was hardly everyone's fault that the session had degenerated in such a way.

'I think we need to be a little calmer for the rest of the afternoon,' I began. 'It seems that some of you have had your fill of lively and interesting activities for one day.' I left it at that, and most of them had the decency to look sufficiently chastened.

'So, how do you think it went?' asked Mr Rankin, after the children had gone home.

'Well, up until the last few minutes I thought it was going well but I'm afraid it was somewhat ruined by the last group.' I had felt rather depressed for the second part of the afternoon, and so was a little surprised by his answer:

'They got a little bit silly and a bit carried away, but that's what can happen in that sort of lesson. You could have got them to fill in a worksheet instead and that wouldn't have happened, but they really enjoyed it and learnt so much more than they would have done by filling in gaps on a piece of paper. My only criticism is that you should perhaps have stepped in a bit earlier. Whether he deserved it or not, that poor lad was being laughed at by his peers, and it was obvious that his group weren't going to finish successfully. Also, it might have been an idea to nominate the pivotal part of the narrator. However, it was a good lesson, well done. Oh, and incidentally, I thought that Shannon's beating heart was quite hilarious – that bit's off the record, though.'

Much buoyed by these comments, I went to find Rachel, but she had a tearful Theresa Ryan with her and was administering some TLC. Her quick shake of the head told me to go away, which I duly did. I was going over my lessons for the following day when Rachel came in.

'Sorry about that, Adrian, but Theresa's in an awful state.'

'Shit. What happened?'

'Mrs Rush. She's just really slated Teri's lesson – she said it was slow and that the children weren't on task and that it was unsatisfactory. Apparently, according to Teri, she actively enjoyed telling her that.'

This rather soured my upbeat mood, especially as there was every possibility that Mrs Rush would observe me within the next couple of days. Also, it rankled me slightly that I had misread her body language. I'd put her down as a supportive inspector who looked at the cup as being half full rather than half empty. I'd better make sure that my cups were full to the brim by the morning.

Memories of our Friday night predictions haunted me when Mr Burnham, the lay inspector, came to observe my English lesson the following morning. As ever, he looked a bit twitchy and nervous and a few glances shot his way as he walked in.

Fortunately though, the letters of complaint did not live up to Tony's creation. Indeed, the only really vociferous offering came from Sean, who wrote to Arsenal Football Club demanding, with something verging on menace, his money back due to a 3–0 home defeat. The session went fine, but it rather lacked any spark and was branded by Mr Burnham that most damning of terms, 'satisfactory'.

I think she did it on purpose. I think she deliberately waited until the last lesson, on the last day, when the finishing line was within sight, before paying me a visit. A smiling Mrs Rush accompanied us to the computer room and I rather nervously went through the activity – to use search engines to research life in Tudor Britain. Most of the children were computer literate, and all of them could log on and get online easily. The session seemed to be going merrily enough until Sophie put her hand up.

'Er, is this supposed to be here, Mr Gray?' My blood froze. Sophie had innocently typed in *'Tudor Sailor Boy'* to the search engine and a particularly hardcore porn site featuring men dressed as sailors had appeared. At that precise moment I was far less interested in protecting Sophie from such filth than I was in making sure that Mrs Rush didn't see it. I nervously glanced over my shoulder but, to my eternal relief, Mrs Rush was discussing something with Daniel and I quickly got rid of the page. Such websites are usually pretty stringently filtered out of the system but the occasional one still gets through.

'Er, no, Sophie. That absolutely should not be there – I'd appreciate it if you didn't bring it up again.'

'Oh, I'm sure that inspector would like to see it, wouldn't she? Shall I call her over?'

'If you call her over and show her that site, Sophie, I shall strangle you.'

She smiled good-naturedly and the moment passed, but it did get me thinking what other horrendous images of Tudor depravity were but a mouse-click away.

With fifteen minutes of the session to go all the computers

and lights suddenly went off as a power cut struck with deliberate malice. Twenty-seven faces, including Mrs Rush's, looked my way, and I knew that I was about to be tested on how well I could think on my feet.

'Right, well, that seems to put an abrupt end to our research, so let's pick up our bits and return to the classroom.' In the end I got them to tell each other, in their own words, what they had found out and Mrs Rush, later on, was pretty pleased with this. She said that the lesson could have been better differentiated and have a little more actual teaching, but by now I didn't care. She was soon to leave our school forever and I felt a huge burden had been lifted.

Mrs Warnock spoke to us briefly the next morning to say that preliminary findings were pretty good and that we'd get detailed feedback the following week.

'So well done everyone, that's that over with for a couple of years. I know it must feel like a holiday now but remember there's still over a week until half-term – don't ease up on things please. Oh, and Adrian. That observation we had to cancel last Friday? How about tomorrow morning at 9.30?'

'Now, I'd like a volunteer to come up to the front, someone who can do really exciting, hands-on things that will make you all gasp in wonder. Robert Carlton, your hand was up first.'

'I don't want to come up, miss.'

'Then what – er?'

'I just wanted to know, Mrs Warnock, and this is me being rude again incidentally, why you chose today to have an interesting hands-on assembly when normally you are a grumpy old bag. What's happened to the boring stories this week?'

'Oh, I don't think that's fair, Robert, why I – er love doing assemblies and er, you know, telling you lovely stories, and – '

If ever there was a demonstration of the dictionary definition of the word 'squirm' then this was surely it, and it was too good to miss.

'I have to say I agree with Robert,' I said. 'The little I've seen of your assemblies is enough to show us just what an uninspiring story-teller you are.'

'Really, Mr Gray, now you're being – '

'And what happened to the Monday Morning Moan this morning? Have you no idea that this is the only part of the assembly that we actually enjoy? What about the state of the cloakrooms this week?'

'Er, well now you mention it, the cloakrooms in many classes have got rather messy recently. Can I suggest ... '

'Objection!' Frank Bell was beside himself with rage. 'She's having words put into her mouth. If you think you're winning the pot with blatant cheating, Gray, then you're mistaken. And besides, what about all the computers that were left on last week?'

As Rachel, Theresa and Julia stood up and started complaining about chewing gum in school, improper PE kit and dirty footprints everywhere, I looked over at the faces of the three inspectors. They were looking at Mrs Warnock with a mixture of contempt and disbelief as she tried to regain some order from a very immature and rowdy set of teachers.

17.

As Mrs Warnock had predicted, there was a definite flatness to the last seven working days before half-term. The older children, in particular, who were very aware of the significance of the visitors, felt, I assume, very much as I did and while I tried to give it the 'don't let up before half-term' bit, none of us were on particularly good form. The class had worked so hard since Christmas, and a short respite from the demands of cramming for SATs was probably not too bad a thing.

In the end, I never had my observation from Mrs Warnock. When she left the room after announcing the rescheduling of it, there was a mood of solidarity that boarded on the militant.

'What an absolute bloody cow!' fumed Irene, with perhaps the most vehemence I have ever heard from her.

'Frank, you have got to see her and let her know how unbelievably unfair it is to have an observation two days after the end of an inspection,' said Rachel. 'Surely even she can see that.'

'And everybody's really tired as well.' We all turned to check that these words of support for me had really come out of Ellie Luck's mouth. I felt really chuffed that everyone, including Ellie, was speaking so vehemently on my behalf. Frank was virtually shoved out of the room to voice the deputation, muttering, 'If I should die, think only this of me ...' He returned five minutes later, every inch the heroic soldier, after persuading Sheila Warnock to cancel, or at least postpone, her observation.

We had further feedback from the inspection just before half-term. The school was branded 'good with some very good elements'. When Mrs Warnock was going through the summary sheet with us, however, she somehow omitted to read out the part stating that her leadership could be somewhat didactic.

Half-term was also unremarkable. Alison and Corinne were going skiing – booked many months before I'd met them, and Alan was whisking Rachel away to somewhere exotic. I was jealous of both holidays for differing reasons and I allowed myself one tiny moment of self-pity as they all left. Rupert was also away and just about all my other acquaintances were either married or at work. I did ask Ellie Luck whether she wanted to accompany me on a long-weekend's white-water rafting, but even she was busy. I was determined to do as little work as possible, after Ofsted, and hence spent most of the week sleeping in late and enduring the mind-numbing experience of watching day-time television.

When the children returned I noticed a better feel to the atmosphere in the classroom almost straight away. The week's break had clearly done them good and they seemed refreshed and ready to go. Robert seemed a different child, for reasons I had long since given up trying to work out. He was producing outstanding work and his poem in the style of Rudyard Kipling's 'If' was exceptional.

Timothy, on the other hand, was still a concern and I had resigned myself to his never being fully accepted by the class. He hid behind Andrew and co. and was rarely troubled by the others, but didn't seem very happy.

Kate and Allard continued to become more likeable by the

day and even Rozinder and Charlie began to take their work seriously. The greatest change, though, was in Sean, who was almost Uriah Heapish in his desire to please. I was not fooled that he had somehow seen the light and renounced his wrongful ways, but I had told him, in no uncertain terms, when he was being a pain shortly after half-term, that if it continued he would miss the impending 7-a-side. While Sean usually quite enjoyed calling people's bluff, he'd clearly decided that this prestigious event was not worth jeopardising.

The annual 7-a-side football tournament took place each year at Green Acre School. Twelve local schools competed in two leagues of six, on three different pitches, over the course of an afternoon. The winners and runners-up from each group then competed in a semi-final and final. Frank had told me how enjoyable, yet incredibly competitive, past tournaments had been. Green Acre had traditionally done quite well, but had not won the event for five years, despite reaching the final in the last two. I was thoroughly looking forward to the event, not least because it gave me an afternoon away from the classroom. I was also pretty confident that we had a decent team. We'd been training for several weeks for this event and my prize team was as follows:

Goalkeeper	Miranda Caldwell
Defenders	Prakesh Patel
	William Welsh (Captain)
Midfielders	Allard Mills
	Jordan Caines
	Mark Baines
Striker	Sean Williams
Sub	Josh Robins

When I had initially announced that Miranda was to be our goalkeeper there was a look of sheer disgust on the faces of

Sean and Josh, especially as it relegated Josh, who assumed
he would be keeping goal, to sub.

'Are you allowed _girls_ in the team?' he'd asked hopefully,
putting a distinctly disapproving emphasis on the word 'girls'.

'Absolutely, Josh, and Miranda is there on merit. Not only
has she been to every practice this year but her shot-
stopping is excellent.'

It had taken Sean many months to get over the fact that I
had named William captain at the beginning of the season.
Sean's simple logic was that if he was the best player, which
he undoubtedly was, then he should be captain. He was also
put out that Jordan Caines, a very promising Year 5 boy, had
been chosen to play, when he had been told the year before
that only Year 6 children would be considered. But these
were minor niggles and by the time the competition was
due to begin, they were forgotten.

Fortunately, the mid-March weather was more akin to
early spring, rather than late winter, although there was still
a chill in the air. When I called the team together at 1.30 for
the pre-match team talk, I was gratified to see that so many
parents had come along to watch. I was especially surprised
to see Mr Caldwell, who had taken the afternoon off to
watch Miranda play. No doubt some multinational company
would grind to a halt without his presence, but he seemed in
a jovial mood. 'Miranda's been looking forward to this for
weeks,' he said. 'Let's hope we do well.'

When I had initially picked her for the team, I had expected
them to write back complaining that Miranda would be
missing an afternoon's schooling and that she had an
entitlement to her RE and Geography lessons.

Green Acre weren't playing in the first round of matches,
but I was refereeing one of them. It was a rather one-sided
affair between a large two-form entry school and a tiny
village one, who had barely enough players to choose from.

One of these kids, a small curly-haired waif who had clearly never played before, saw the ball coming in his direction and promptly caught it. Had he been named Webb-Ellis, he could have run with the ball and invented a new game. Unfortunately, his name was Billy, so neither of these things happened. He just looked bemused when I awarded a free kick and briefly explained some of the more basic rules. It had been, up until this point, a very friendly game, due to the lack of competitive edge; thus I was amazed to hear one of the parents from the winning team bellow, in total earnest: 'Oi ref!'

I gave him a disbelieving look as I remembered Frank's warning about how competitive and serious these games could get. Despite his son's team eventually winning 10–0, he still felt that he needed to speak to me.

'You do know, don't you, that deliberate hand ball is a sending-off offence? He really should have walked.'

I told him in no uncertain terms that I wasn't going to send off a lad for not understanding the rules properly, but he was so obviously a believer in the letter of the law, rather than the spirit of the game, that he simply couldn't see this argument.

We won our opening two games in relative comfort, primarily due to Sean's goal-scoring prowess, but also with some excellent saves from Miranda. The whole tournament was, at this stage, still rather friendly, but I was beginning to notice a few niggles and tensions developing, especially in the tight matches. It was really interesting, especially in the matches I wasn't involved in, to sit back and observe the different team coaches, and see how they approached the games.

There was one guy, clearly a frustrated physiotherapist, who had a huge first-aid bag with him and seemed to be almost hoping for an opportunity to use it. When eventually one of his team fell under a tackle, he was almost rubbing his hands in glee at the prospect of performing a miracle and bringing the boy back from near death to ace goal-scorer with a few deft touches from his magic sponge. What followed was hilarious. The boy clearly wasn't that badly hurt and obviously just wanted to get up and get on with it. But Mr Physioman was having none of it. He started meticulously rubbing the boy's ankle, while constantly asking where it hurt.

'It's OK, honestly, I can play on now.'

'You stay there, lad, I want to make absolutely sure you're all right.'

He then delved impressively into his bag and administered some sort of ankle spray to the boy, who was now looking distinctly embarrassed.

'Can I play on now?'

'In a minute. How many fingers am I holding up?'

'What?'

'How-many-fing–'

'Three.'

This terse and vociferous response beautifully conveyed the message _'just piss off and let us get on with it'_. At this point, two of the boy's team mates, with admirable humour, actually started a slow hand clap, and it finally took the referee to intervene and send the coach packing before, presumably, he began amputating.

In stark contrast to this zealous manager was the woman, well into her fifties, who quite clearly did not want to be there and was not even bothering to watch her team's performance. She'd obviously drawn the short straw among a staff which had no interest in football and had now resigned herself to a cold and miserable afternoon.

It was only when I refereed a tight match between two of the favourites, Lodge Farm, our local rivals, and Fisher Heath, that I became fully aware of how much passion is involved in these matches. The manager of Fisher Heath was their caretaker and had a previous conviction for GBH. He was an absolute nutcase. From the start of the game he was shouting orders at his troops, shouting orders at me and expressing his opinion on everything. He found it highly amusing when Lodge Farm's striker blazed over the bar, shouting 'dear oh dear, that's well wide'.

He moaned at me for playing advantage when his player was felled and then, two minutes later, for not playing advantage for a similar incident. I was finding the whole thing really intimidating and then, at 0–0, with two minutes to go, the inevitable happened. One of Lodge Farm's players was upended in the penalty area by a clumsy challenge. Totally drowning out the calls of 'penalty' was Psycho's screaming: 'Dive! He bloody dived, ref! Send the bloody cheat off!'

I then had a horrible second as everyone waited to see what I would do. Had it not been for him I would have blown for a penalty instantly but I was seriously worried about being subjected to more verbal abuse. I knew, however, what I had to do, and listened to his tirade as I awarded the penalty. The guy who had blazed over earlier stepped up, amid more taunts, and calmly struck the winner. As the final whistle blew Mr Andrews, an imposing-looking teacher who was in charge of the whole event, took Psycho to one side and, I assume, warned him about his conduct. This did not prevent him from giving me the most withering of glances as I passed, and I was visibly shaken by his outburst.

'Well done, Mr Gray,' said Miranda's dad, as I went back to the team. 'Never let yourself be influenced by bullies.' I almost choked on the gulp of water I'd just taken at the sheer hypocrisy of his statement.

A couple of shaky matches later, we suddenly found ourselves in the situation of having to win our final round-robin game to ensure our place in the semi-final. The manager of the Ferns, our opponents, was clearly a master tactician and

I was amazed to see him actually take out a mini blackboard and give a few last-minute instructions to his bemused team. By now, tensions were running high and I found myself getting carried away with it all during the match, loudly exhorting my team to give their all. With five minutes to go, and the score level at 2–2, Miranda made a fabulous reaction save which prompted Sean, forgetting all his macho sexism, to run over and smack a solid kiss on her forehead.

'That was bloody brilliant Miranda, my son. Keep it up.'

A quick glance over at Mr Caldwell confirmed that he, too, was caught up in the excitement of the match, so I chose to ignore both the 'bloody' and the 'my son'.

Immediately after this, Mr Tactician suddenly bellowed: 'Right! All change!' at which point his team obediently switched positions, so that the defenders became strikers and vice versa. He looked remarkably proud at this tactical masterpiece and I heard him telling a bored-looking parent that such a manoeuvre completely threw the opposition. Everyone else just looked mystified, and it made no difference whatsoever to the game, which limped to its anti-climactic conclusion. In the end, Miranda's save was crucial – the other final round matches went our way and the draw saw us through to the semi-finals.

While the amount of people was reduced significantly at this point, with eight of the twelve teams mooching home dejectedly, the atmosphere was clearly hotting up. Also, as it was now 3.30, Green Acre got a sudden huge advantage as swarms of children, classes finished, came out to watch and support.

Josh was not happy when he was announced as sub, for the third match running, against Fisher Heath in the semi-finals. It was testament to how poor he had been in the two matches he had played that nobody tried to argue his case for him.

If Psycho had been wound up in the match that I had refereed, he was positively bursting a blood vessel now. Mr Andrews had opted to referee this match himself and had probably taken out extra life insurance for the task. I'd heard him talking to Psycho just before kick-off, but he could have threatened him with life imprisonment and it would have made no difference. *'Football's not about life and death,'* Bill Shankley had once famously remarked. *'It's far more important than that ...'*

As soon as the game started, Psycho began barking his orders. He soon worked out that Sean was our star player and instantly set this huge manic-looking child to man-mark him. There were not many eleven-year-old kids bigger than Sean Williams but this guy was one of them. Suddenly, Psycho's whole raison d'être was to ensure that Wilf did not stray more than a foot away from Sean.

'Oi, Wilf. 'E's getting away from yer. Stick to 'im like glue. That's m'boy.'

Unsurprisingly, Sean was getting more and more wound up by both Wilf's marking and Psycho's instructions. Just before half-time, with the score at 0–0, things erupted. As Wilf clumsily bumbled into Sean once too often Sean turned, looked him squarely in the eye, and shouted:

'Will you get off my arse, you stupid, lanky git?' In fairness to Sean, this was a pretty good description and the stupid lanky git looked back and forth from Psycho to Sean, clearly trying to weigh up who was the more dangerous.

'Oi, ref! That's bloody 'arassment, that is. Send 'im off!'

Exactly what happened in the ensuing skirmish was impossible to say, but it ended with the referee blowing the half-time whistle and demanding that both Psycho and I substituted the two offenders, otherwise he would send them off. This gave Fisher Heath a distinct advantage and Sean was so irate I thought he was going to hit somebody. I knew how he felt; it took all my self-control to channel the injustice of the situation into a morale-boosting team talk.

'Let's do it for Sean,' were William's last words as the second half started and a goal apiece for Jordan, Allard and, astoundingly, Josh, sent us into the final. My joy at our victory was tempered slightly by the looks of sheer terror on the faces of the Fisher Heath team, as they awaited the inevitable reprisal.

In contrast to many of the managers on show during the afternoon, Mike Malloy, the team coach of Lodge Farm, was an affable, laid-back chap. I knew him reasonably well from consortium meetings and we got on well. However, there is something about a final, especially when it's the local rivals competing in it, that brings out the more base elements in men. As I wound up my tired team for one final push, I could hear this mild-mannered man expostulate just as vividly to his kids. Any semblance of tactics had by now gone out of the window and both of us were resorting to the game's oldest clichés in a desperate attempt to fire the kids up for one final thrust. I actually heard myself saying: 'It only takes a second to score a goal,' and by the time the game began I had them frothing at the mouth, in the hope that we would eventually be over the moon and the opposition would be as sick as parrots.

Sean was now playing like a man possessed, and his superb opening solo effort was cheered heartily by the partisan crowd. But Lodge Farm were in the final for a reason, and goals either side of half-time gave them the advantage. I could see our heads going down, and with five minutes to go, their star striker, now on a hat-trick, had a clear run at goal, with only Miranda to beat. With most of the crowd holding their breaths, I distinctly heard a woman's scream, presumably his mother's, echo across the pitch:

'Go on, Jack! If you score, I'll give you a tenner, and I mean it this time!'

It seemed that Jack had heard this empty promise several times before and his shot, struck weakly, was easily saved by Miranda. With less than a minute to go, William scored a wonderful header to set up extra time, and the excitement levels were now so great that I was actually losing my voice.

When Prakesh volleyed in the winner a few minutes later, the sense of jubilation was so great that I began to well up inside. By this time most of the staff had come out to watch and even Sheila Warnock joined in the celebrations.

My cup was completely filleth when Mr Caldwell, with a huge grin on his face, came up to me, shook me by the hand and said 'That was such an enjoyable afternoon, Mr Gray. Thank you, and well done.'

I've always loved the thrill and the emotion that sport, like nothing else in life, manages to conjure up. I've played in reasonably successful football teams in my life and I've shouted at the television often enough as I've watched our national football and rugby teams in major championships. But I don't think I've ever enjoyed any of that quite as much as I enjoyed watching the faces of my team as William lifted the cup, proclaiming Green Acre as champions for the first time in six years. Had I ever doubted that I was in the right profession – and I had, many times – had I ever yearned for the normality and predictability of an office job, then the sheer emotion that I felt during those few minutes firmly diminished such thoughts.

'Could I see both you lads, please, and your managers?
Right. That scuffle between you two would be enough, in normal circumstances, to have you both sent off. However, this is a friendly tournament and nearly everyone has treated it as such, so I'm going to offer a compromise.'
The look on Sean's face as Mr Andrews said these words was murderous.

'That sounds fair,' said Psycho. 'I substitute Wilf, and they can take off their little thug. I think that's totally fair.'

'I haven't finished yet. As I said, nearly everyone has treated this afternoon in a friendly, but competitive way, the one exception being you, you psychopathic yob.'

'What? I'm only cheering on my –'

'No, Psycho, you are not cheering on your team. You are ranting at anything and anybody who comes near the ball. You are a complete nutcase and I am sending you off.'

'You can't send me off! I'm the manager. Send off their mouthy little yob instead.'

At this moment – and I never thought I'd be pleased to see him – Sean's dad arrived. He was infinitely bigger than Psycho and rivalled him in the 'who's got the wildest eyes?' stakes.

'Is that my son you're referring to, you bloody Neanderthal? You don't want to be sent off? Well, let's try throwing you off ...'

Even as he was unceremoniously hoisted in the air and carried away, Psycho still had time to bark one last order:

'Oi, Wilf! I wanna see you even tighter on him this half. Stick to his arse like glue!'

18.

The atmosphere in 6G, and indeed the rest of the school, was given a tremendous boost by our success in the football tournament. Mrs Warnock made a big thing about it in assembly the following day, and there was triumph in the air. I'd noticed before how the mood within the class echoed the mood of the Williams twins, and this time it was tangible. Sean quite clearly saw himself as the hero of the school and strutted about with a champion's swagger. His goodwill even extended to lessons, and he worked hard for the rest of the week. There were only four weeks to go now before the Easter holidays and I felt that I had the class, more or less, where I wanted them.

These four weeks passed without a great deal of incident, although I did notice the tension and stress levels rise in a number of children as that all-consuming monster known as SATs began to get closer and closer. It was the conscientious children who were palpably affected by this; they would double-check things with me and get genuinely fretful if they didn't understand. But by far the biggest change was in Alice, who had never been anything but bubbly, friendly and vivacious. She was so determined to do well that it was actually making her ill and rather withdrawn. Indeed, her mother came in to discuss it with me and, while we both tried to play down the importance with her, Alice wasn't having any of it and would spend upwards of two hours every evening learning maths and science vocabulary, or practising styles of writing.

This was not what I'd had in mind at the beginning of the year, when I'd tried to find a balance between the demands of SATs and the enjoyment of their last year at primary school. After speaking to Alice's mum shortly before the end of term, I resolved that, assuming I was still at Green Acre teaching Year 6 the following year, I would play down the importance of these tests, regardless of the pressure on me to achieve target levels. These kids were ten and eleven years old, for heaven's sake.

If I was beginning to feel a little down during this time about my handling of the preparation for SATs, several things going on around the school kept me amused. Tristan Adams, the peripatetic guitar teacher with the upside-down head, announced that there would be a concert at the end of term for all the guitar players. What was fabulous about this announcement, though, was his intention to play a couple of songs himself, so that non-players might be inspired to take up the guitar. If inspiration is to be found in an out-of-tune howl and consequent untold mirth and merriment, there would be a mad rush of takers. I, for one, intended to queue through the night if necessary in order to secure a front-row seat for this extravaganza.

For the last four weeks of term, Frank Bell had a postgraduate student working in his class. It took me several moments before I realised who it was that Amanda Maitland reminded me of. That open-mouthed, hang-dog expression, that slight tilt of the head, those vacant eyes, the overweight bumpkin look – if she wasn't a relative of Karen Jenkins, my rival at interview, then the resemblance was uncanny.

Our Monday Morning Moan pot was currently standing at

a healthy £75, and to add a little extra spice, we all chucked in another fiver to try to guess what Amanda could possibly have graduated in. Rachel went for sociology, Julia for media studies, Theresa for leisure and tourism and Frank, perhaps rather boldly, chose computer science.

'Some of these tekkies,' he argued, 'are so wrapped up in computers that all personality has been drained out of them.' My bold guess of 'the history of gurning' was, admittedly, a bit of a long shot and a complete waste of a fiver, but it made Rachel laugh, which more than compensated for the waste of a guess. Frank actually asked Amanda one day, and then relayed back her answer – psychology – to disbelieving gasps from the rest of us.

Frank was an outstanding teacher and man-manager and I knew that he would have been incredibly supportive and helpful to Amanda, who had struggled from the beginning. Indeed, I spoke to her on several occasions and could empathise with her entirely as, less than a year ago, I'd been in the same situation as her. This did not stop Frank, however unprofessionally, from closing the doors at the end of the day and relating some of the most memorable moments from it. I laughed heartily at these, although it did occur to me that those supportive staff on my final teaching practice probably closed their doors at the end of the day too …

Such stories became commonplace in the last few weeks and I did feel a little guilty laughing at her shortcomings, albeit behind closed doors. Losing control of and respect from a class is about the worst thing that can happen to a teacher, and I did feel for her. It took Frank fully three weeks before he dared leave Amanda on her own with the class. When he came back, supposedly during a quiet writing session, there were two kids actually playing table tennis, using books for bats and a bouncy ball. She'd never stood a chance.

Another memorable event in these last few weeks was the second round of parents' evenings. To some extent, these were more nerve-wracking than the first lot, as there was, or should have been, discernable progress in two terms from which the parents could judge the quality of the teaching. The exception to this was Timothy's parents, whom I had never met. While Mrs Reeves looked relatively normal, Mr Reeves was an enlarged version of Timothy. Not that enlarged, mind you; yet even at five feet four, he still had Timothy's uncanny knack of managing to look down his nose at me. He didn't smile throughout and, as I spoke, all he could manage in response was a cursory 'hmm'. There's nothing like a good 'hmm', I've always found, to register disapproval. I was very glad when they, clearly dissatisfied, left, but at least I'd now solved the mystery of why Timothy was so goddamn weird.

Fortunately, memories of the football tournament were still strong in Mr Williams and he seemed to be on my side when I gave my opinions and targets for both his children. The rather chilling calm was not in evidence, but I was to find out, in the summer term, that it had not gone away permanently.

The Caldwells' appointment was immediately after the Williams', and I naively assumed that the feel-good factor generated by the football would be in evidence with them, as it had been with Mr Williams. The jovial laid-back football Dad, though, had been replaced with the all-too-serious-chief-executive one and, again, I got a grilling about how I was meeting Miranda's targets. It was only after they had gone, after fifteen gruelling minutes, that I realised that they had voiced no particular concerns about their daughter at all. They clearly believed that parents' evening was an opportunity for them to make the teachers as uncomfortable as possible, rather than a forum in which they could engage with the education Miranda was receiving.

On the whole, though, the parents' evenings were a success, with some especially nice comments thrown in. Kate's mum managed to get through the whole consultation without swearing; she didn't know what I'd done but, for the first time ever, Kate was actually showing enthusiasm for school. Rozinder's parents seemed far less concerned about her and Robert's mum was positively glowing about how he was beginning to come out of himself. Again, I finished the sessions mentally very alert and relatively pleased with how they had gone.

During the time since Doncaster, Alison and I had been staying with each other on a rather ad hoc basis. Things were still good and the arrangement suited us well but, as the last week of term began, we both knew certain decisions needed to be made.

Liam and Naomi were getting married in under two weeks and we had not considered his replacement in the flat yet. Was this the time, now Liam was moving out, for us all to go our separate ways and start again? It was the grown-up thing to do, to move in with one's girlfriend, but I was far from sure that it was what I wanted.

Frank, as deputy, had been charged with the responsibility of speaking on the evening of the last day of term at the dinner to celebrate Sheila Warnock's departure. Both Sheila and the rest of the staff had used the term 'celebrate', but I suspect that our interpretations of that word would have been vastly different to hers. Frank had fretted over his speech for ages and still hadn't perfected it by the start of the last day.

'If I say loads of nice things about her, I know you lot will be putting me off by sticking your fingers down your throats, and you won't let me forget it afterwards. On the other hand, I can hardly say *'Sheila, you've been a complete cow all term and we're so glad that you're now off to piss on someone else's parade.'*

Before the heckling of Frank, however, we had the heckling of Tristan Adams to enjoy. In the last assembly of term, prior to the guitar playing, Sheila Warnock talked emotionally about how much she had enjoyed her term at Green Acre and what a pleasure it had been to work with such lovely children. It is amazing how easy it is to put on the rose-coloured spectacles at the end of a working relationship. The children sat there passively enough during her speech, but they must have been thinking *If we're so lovely, why have you been so completely horrible to us?* I would have loved to have seen the sort of reception she would have got from a more challenging lot.

Rachel and I had reserved seats at the back of the hall for one of the most eagerly anticipated events of the term. Tristan Adams was obviously quite nervous about speaking in front of a roomful of people, and this came across, magnificently, in his opening speech.

'Er ... hellooee. Er, good afternoon children and, er, welcome to our special little concert. Well, no – er, perhaps concert is a teensy bit of a grand – er – you know – ha ha. Anyway, the kiddiwinks have worked really, really hard to become the next Paul McCartney, ha ha, only he's left-handed and most of this lot are – er – anyway. Without further ado – er, I hope some of you are inspired to take it up so, er, anyway. Right. Okeee-dokeee, first up is Gemma Pick, who will be using her "pick", ha ha, to help her play "Over the rainbow".

I had bet Frank, at fairly generous odds of 5–1, that Tristan would use the term 'okee-dokee' in his opening speech. At least three children looked round and must have heard him say 'shit' as he realised he'd just lost twenty-five quid. Rachel was already beginning to get the giggles, and it was only at this point that I realised that if I needed to leave the room I'd have to struggle past about fifteen children on the way.

For the next twenty minutes or so we listened to a disparate collection of children play the guitar, some of them pretty well and some of them cringingly badly. Then came the moment we'd all been waiting for.

'Righty-ho. Now I've got a little treat for you to end with.'

Oh Mr Adams, you have no idea how true those words are.

'Now, how many of you have heard of 'Yellow Submarine' by the fab four? Most of you? Excy-lonty! Well, if you know the chorus, you're welcome to join in.'

The difference in body language between the staff, who knew what to expect, and the parents, who didn't, was evident. While the parents were relaxed, there was a stiffness in the posture of most of us; we were steeling ourselves to maintain control. It was almost like a scene in a bad sit-com when the archetypal German announces *'Ve aff vays of making you larf.'*

So he began. At first, he was just a little wobbly and mildly out of tune but, like any good comedian, he was building up slowly. By the time the chorus arrived, there were many parents, teachers and children who were beginning to suppress giggles and, though a few obedient children half-heartedly joined in, it was still very much a solo. I knew I wasn't going to last until the end of the song, and was already planning my exit route.

Oblivious to the reactions, which were steadily growing, Tristan Adams was clearly beginning to enjoy himself, and upped his noise levels so that the full limitations of his vocal prowess became gloriously apparent. I finally lost it during the line: '*and our friends are all aboard*'. God knows what he was attempting on the word *'friends'*, but the squeaky noise that emanated from his mouth finished me off. In a moment of complete loss of control, I snorted so loudly that three rows of children turned round. I had no choice. I stood up, shaking violently, and trampled across feet to the sanctuary of the hall door. Once outside, my uncontrollable spasms of laughter were so great that, when I finally began to calm down, I was gasping for air.

It was a very sheepish Adrian Gray who sidled back into the hall five minutes later. The concert had finished, the children were about to file out of the hall, and Tristan Adams was sitting down, looking remarkably pleased with himself.

I was greeted with mocking and accusing taunts by my class as we got back into our room at the end of the day. I had intended this moment to be poignant, with me congratulating them on their hard work over the term, telling them how proud I was of them, and perhaps shedding a little tear as I wished them a relaxing holiday. This idea was shot down in flames very quickly.

'Ah! We saw you sneaking out! You were laughing at Mr Adams, weren't you?' The children had a field day for several moments, but it was all good-humoured and I played along.

'Not at all, Kate. I have this medical condition that makes me laugh for no apparent reason. I had to rush outside to take my anti-laughing tablets.' I just about managed to restore enough control to tell them to have a good rest ready for the final push next term, and then they were gone. I had to peer through the keyhole of the staffroom before entering to ensure that Tristan Adams was not sitting there alone, but fortunately he had had to leave immediately after the concert and we spent the next twenty minutes reliving every wonderful moment of the last hour.

At the restaurant that evening, Sheila sat majestically at the head of the table and Frank sat dutifully, and rather nervously, by her side. At the end of the meal Sheila stood and made a predictable speech about being proud to have led us through Ofsted, and a promise to come and visit us sometime next term.

'While you're here, you can give Adrian his lesson observation,' said Frank. 'He's been looking forward to it all term.' I had, actually, spent the last few weeks fully expecting it to happen, and on many occasions Frank had threatened maliciously to remind her.

'Yes, of course, Adrian, your observation. We both forgot about that, didn't we?'

'Slipped right out of my mind, Mrs Warnock. Anyway, Frank, enough about me. Didn't you have a few words you wanted to say?'

He didn't quite say 'touché' as he rose, but he might as well have done.

'I'd just like to say, Sheila, on behalf of everyone, a big 'well done' for a successful term and, obviously, for Ofsted. I was amazed to read in the report that it said your leadership was 'didactic'. Well, I've chatted to all the staff and none of us could see that at all.'

This was vintage stuff. By playing to her ego and keeping a totally straight face, he was telling her what she wanted to hear, while telling us what he really meant.

'I, for one, will miss your Monday Morning Moans, Sheila. Indeed, I'm going to suggest to Sandra that she keeps them on next term. I think, by the end, the children were really responding well to these, and I think they were determined to act on what you said each week, as they wanted to please you and make the school a better place.'

Sheila beamed. I beamed.

'But most of all, I'll miss your dedication to Green Acre. It would have been too easy for you to passively lead an already productive team yet, right from day one, you were offering help and advice, spending time observing us teach and feeding back. And those weekly evaluation forms you instigated – OK, it was a bit more work for us, but Adrian was telling me only yesterday how much spending two hours each week evaluating his lessons was helping him with his planning.'

God, this was good. My actual words, when Sheila had introduced these pointless, time-consuming forms were, and I think I've remembered them correctly, *'bloody witch'*.

He ended by inviting us all to charge our glasses; the applause we gave was hearty. Sheila clearly thought it was aimed at her, but Frank knew it was in recognition of a truly inspired speech.

It's funny, but as we were leaving I realised how much I would miss her. Well, not her, exactly, but her presence. Whether one of her intentions had been to create a bond amongst her staff I doubt, but this is certainly what had happened. Up until Christmas, I had hardly known Theresa and Julia, but this term, primarily due to Sheila, we had shared loads of laughs. Even Ellie Luck, who had never been on my side in the first term, had joined with us in our universal condemnation of Sheila Warnock.

But by far the greatest change in relationship had been between Frank and me. From that first INSET day, when he had chosen me to confide in, we had become great friends. Last term I had seen him as a nice bloke, but as a deputy head who had deliberately maintained a slight distance between himself and the rest of the staff. This term he had been full of fun, mad bets and practical jokes. I was very interested to see what his take on things would be when Sandra Little returned.

'Okeee Dokeee, I can see that you all enjoyed that. Lots of smiley-smiley faces. Smashing!

'Now, before I say toodle-oo I have a little surprise for a

certain member of staff who we're saying goodbye to today.
Come on, Mrs Warnock, ha, ha, there's a good girlie, that's
right, on my knee.

'Well, kiddiwinks, as a leaving present, Mr Gray has kindly
rewritten the words to 'Yellow submarine' which – yes you've
guessed it, I'm going to sing for the lovely Mrs W.

'Now, join in the chorus all of you …

In the schooool where I was from
Lived a witch, who said to me,
I will turn this happy school
To a hellish misery.

So she marched into the room
In a sea of lost property
And she moaned and made our lives
One hellish misery.

We all live in a hellish misery, a hellish misery, a hellish misery
We all live in a hellish misery, a hellish misery, a hellish misery

And her frieeeeeends can take no more
Many more of them have gone abroad
And the band begins to shriek;
NA-NA NA-NA NA-NA NA-NA
NA-NA NA-NA NA-NA NA-NA

Now she's off and we're all free
Everyone of us, wants her to leave
Sky of blue (sky of blue) and Acre Green (Acre Green)
No more hellish misery

'Altogether now …

We all live in a hellish misery, a hellish misery, a hellish misery
We all live in a hellish misery, a hellish misery, a hellish misery

'Not joining in, Mrs Warnock ...?'

19.

It has always intrigued me how customs and traditions evolve and enlarge over time. Thirty years ago, in the vast majority of cases, a 'stag' or 'hen' party would entail a couple of drinks with friends the night before the wedding, with maybe a mild headache first thing in the morning. These days, Liam's day at the races and Naomi's weekend in Barcelona are very much the norm. I foresee a time, in thirty years or so, when couples will kiss each other goodbye and look forward to their reunion at the altar after their eight-week world cruise.

I had never been to a race meeting before and had absolutely no idea what to expect. We arrived at Windsor racecourse early on the first Saturday of the Easter holidays, a week before the wedding. I'd brought £50 cash with me – I'm not too much of a gambler, I thought to myself, so that should cover it.

As we approached the gates from the car park, a rather shady-looking man came up to me. 'Excuse me, sir,' he said, in a broad Irish accent. 'Would you loik any tips fer t'day?' He waved an envelope at me, presumably with the names of a couple of horses that he fancied during the course of the meeting. Now call me naive if you will, but I just thought he was being nice.

'That's very kind of you. Thank you very much,' I said, taking the envelope. I did wonder, vaguely, why he'd gone to the trouble of writing them down, and didn't just say, '*I really fancy Red Rum in the 3.40'* or whatever, but it was only a fleeting thought. I was just about to leave to catch the others up when he gently put a hand on my shoulder.

'How 'bout somethin' fer me kids, sir?'

'I beg your pardon?' I had no idea what he was going on about and started thinking of a good joke that he could pass on to his children.

'Somethin' fer me kids. We gotta eat tonight. A tenner should cover it.'

I looked at him blankly for a second before realising that he was expecting payment for his tips. I was so dumbfounded that I found myself giving him ten pounds. It was only when he had gone that I realised I could have simply returned the unopened envelope.

Liam, Tony and Kevin, Liam's brother, found this hilarious.

'Welcome to the world of racing, Adrian,' said Kevin who was, by all accounts, a bit of a gambler. 'Anyway, what is his fabulous tip?'

At this point I started to shield my envelope like a kid who's taken his ball away because he's been made to play in goal.

'I don't know. Maybe I'll sell it to you later.'

Their continued laughter clearly indicated that they did not value the contents of my envelope any more than they would value the result of sticking a pin in a list of names. So I opened it and inside, on a scruffy piece of paper, were the words:

2.10 – Fairy Queen
3.00 – Rollercoaster Lad

'Is that it?' laughed Tony. 'In my *Racing Post* this morning there were dozens of tips, and you've got two for a tenner!'

I suddenly felt this ridiculous urge to defend the tipster.

'Well, anyone could pick out loads of names at random. The fact that he's only written two suggests he's mightily confident about them.'

This mindless banter continued until we reached the gates and I read 'Adults — £18.50'.

Again, rather naively, I'd assumed it would be free to enter, and that they'd take your money on the betting and in the bar.

So we drank some beer and chatted about the first race. Kevin narrowed it down to three horses for us, and I plumped for Clueless, rather appropriately, at 10–1.

'Er, I would like to put a bet on, please,' I said to the brute of a man at the Tote.

'What?'

'Er, I'd like to put a bet on. Please.'

'You would like to put a bet on?'

'Yes, please.'

'And on which horse would sir like to place this bet?'

If I'd been pretty sure that he was taking the piss with his first comment, now I was certain of it.

'Three pounds on Clueless.'

'To win, or each way?'

'Er, each way.'

'Six pounds, then sir.'

There was no way I was going to ask him why it was six pounds and not three. I was feeling distinctly uncomfortable in a completely foreign environment and just wanted to get away.

'You're making two bets,' explained Kevin patiently, 'three pounds to win and three pounds for him to finish in the first three.'

I'd never seen the purpose of horse racing, or dog racing, or motorbike racing, or three-legged racing. As a spectator sport, they had always appeared completely dull, presumably because I couldn't care less who won. But suddenly, now that

I'd staked the princely sum of three pounds each way on Clueless, this race meant everything. I found myself getting caught up in the emotion of it all, as I had at the football tournament, and when Clueless came from behind to scrape a narrow victory on the line, I was shouting myself silly.

Somehow, this victory altered my whole demeanour. Up till then, I'd been a nervous novice who, quite clearly, couldn't distinguish one end of a horse from the other. With the win, though, I found I had a bit of a swagger about me and, when I went to collect my winnings, I went with the air of a seasoned pro. I hadn't, however, forgotten the piss-taking bastard who'd taken my bet. So, in my poshest possible voice, I said to him:

'I'd like to collect the money I've just won, please.' The look he gave me was like thunder, as he virtually threw my winnings at me, but he lacked the wit to say anything.

My cocky swagger rapidly diminished as I soundly lost the next two races. The fourth race, however, generated much interest among us, as the inimitable Fairy Queen was about to run.

Out of something approaching loyalty, I placed £10 to win at 12–1, despite Kevin's warnings of less-than-convincing recent form. I so much wanted to wave my £120 winnings in the faces of my cynical friends, and was feeling irrationally confident when the horses paraded. When I saw the number five, Fairy Queen, my look of disbelief was more than matched by the squeals of raucous laughter around me. Fairy Queen, and I kid not, actually had a hole in the side of its neck, with a tube running through it, presumably to let it breathe. It looked physically exhausted by the time it had cantered to the starting gates, and its trainer had a shifty, embarrassed look on his face. Still, at least my friend's kids would eat tonight ...

The race was just over two circuits in length, and by the

time the winner passed the finishing post, he had virtually lapped Fairy Queen. Never had anybody laughed quite as much at my expense and, despite feelings of unbridled hatred towards the guy who by now must be dining out on this, I just about managed to see the funny side of it.

Liam's laughter abruptly stopped during the next race. His horse, a 5–1 shot, was winning by miles coming down the home straight. Now, Windsor racecourse is shaped in a figure of eight and, just before the finishing post, Mighty Joe somehow managed to take the wrong turn, veering left instead of speeding straight ahead. Liam's protestations were greater even than the jockey's as he tried in vain to right his course. It couldn't have happened to a nicer chap.

By now, of course, all eyes were waiting for the horses to come out for the final race and I, wisely, decided to wait before backing Rollercoaster Lad, in case he came out clutching a white stick in his mouth. He was actually the 3–1 joint favourite, and looked a handsome and well-muscled beast. However, either the Irishman had simply picked two names out of a hat, or was deliberately having a laugh at my expense and knew something that I didn't. Either way, it was hardly expert advice, so I went for the other favourite. Needless to say, Rollercoaster Lad, backed secretly by both Tony and Kevin, romped home. When Tony suggested drinking a toast to the Irishman, I nearly threw my drink at him. I'd now lost far more money than I could afford and was feeling distinctly fed up with proceedings.

'I never want to come to this stupid place again. All I want now is more beer, and a photograph of a naked Liam on a stripper's lap, so that I can enlarge it and show it off to Naomi's grandmother at the wedding.'

So we left and my spirits rose as we tried to humiliate Liam by making him go up to strangers and insist on a bridegroom's kiss, but this backfired on us when a queue started developing. We finally staggered in at just gone midnight and thoroughly deserved the subsequent hangovers the following morning.

By the time the girls arrived back from Barcelona on Sunday evening, looking distinctly sheepish, I had just about recovered. It would have taken a skilled lawyer or, more probably, a skilled torturer, to get them to admit what had actually gone on and, such was Naomi's skill at winding people up, Liam eventually crawled off to bed muttering about divorce proceedings.

I stayed at Alison's, who had felt really chuffed to have been invited to Barcelona. I didn't manage to extract any of the sordid details from her either. Tony and I had decided the previous day to advertise for a new flatmate, and I was unsure how to bring this up with Alison. She had never actually suggested that I move in with her and so I was perhaps being ridiculously paranoid, but I felt like I was somehow letting her down by getting someone else to take Liam's room. I finally plucked up courage late in the evening and her 'Oh, right,' was horribly difficult to read. To elaborate any further would have smacked of somehow trying to justify the action, and I managed to divert the subject back to the wedding. By now I was really beginning to fret about my best man's speech, and had already had one nightmare where I stood in front of a hundred people with a blank piece of paper in my hand and ended up singing 'Yellow Submarine' as the guests ran out with their hands over their ears.

We were pleasantly surprised to receive three enquiries for the vacant room, and conducted interviews on the Thursday before the wedding. I had only ever been an interviewee in the past, so the role of interviewer made me feel very important.

The first guy was in his early fifties, and was easily old enough to be my father. He was recently separated, he said, and needed a stopgap for several months before finding a permanent place. Pleasant as he was, I could not bring myself to live in the same flat as someone who was likely to tell me to be sure to be home by ten o'clock when I went out because I had school in the morning.

The second guy was about thirty, and had never lived away from his parents. While this might not have been too bad in itself, my suspicions were aroused when he turned up with his mother. Again, he could have just about got away with this had she not answered all his questions for him:

'Stephen's 31 and he's a bank clerk.'

'Stephen likes films, reading and the occasional game of badminton, don't you darling?'

'We felt it was time that Stephen became a little more independent, didn't we, love?'

If this was an example of this puppet exercising independence, God knows what he'd been like before.

The last guy looked infinitely more promising and we both took to him instantly. Graham was from Auckland, and was planning to stay in the UK for six months or so while working behind a bar. He was twenty-five, taking a couple of years out after graduating, and seemed a man after my own heart. We offered him the room there and then, and he agreed to stay for three months initially.

Tony, Alison, Liam and I drove down to Bath, Naomi's home town, on the Friday night. There was a strange quiet on the journey down, as if we were all contemplating a time of change. At our hotel, although we ate and drank merrily enough, I felt that Alison was slightly less animated than usual. She did manage a laugh at my expense, however, when she tried to talk to me later on in bed.

'Sh! I'm going through my speech in my head and I'm

timing it. I'll talk to you in a minute.'
  'You really are a sad git, Adrian,' she laughed. 'Good night.'

A glorious April morning welcomed us to the biggest day in
Liam and Naomi's lives. Liam's calm seemed to have
deserted him for once, as he paced around all morning
before we all dressed up and I drove him to the church. I've
never quite understood nerves before a wedding. I can
understand it before an exam, or a football match or
before going on stage, when the result is up in the air.
Unless you live in soap opera land, where wedding
massacres, dramatic reappearances of wronged former
girlfriends or aliens stealing the bride are the norm, things
are not likely to go wrong.
  'So, then,' I began, on our journey to the church. 'What are
the five worst possible scenarios that could happen in the
next hour?'
  'Fuck off!'
  I'd been told by Rupert, who'd been a best man before, to
mentally note amusing little moments during the day, as
they always went down well in the speech. While Liam's curt
response to my suggestion made both Tony and Alison
laugh, I was not too sure that Auntie Mabel would
appreciate it quite as much.
  By the time that we were standing by the altar, waiting for
Naomi's entrance, he was an absolute wreck. I checked
outside the windows for him, but there were definitely no
UFOs in sight. When the bridal music started, we both
resolutely stayed facing the front, resisting the temptation
to look back, until Naomi joined her husband-to-be. To say
she looked beautiful would be akin to saying the Taj Mahal
looked quite nice, and it was a full minute before I could
take my eyes off her.

Of course, the wedding went perfectly. Of course they both looked the picture of happiness when they sipped champagne in the Rolls Royce, and of course the subsequent meal was wonderful.

Both Naomi's father's and Liam's speeches hit the mark, but their emphasis was, correctly, on the emotion of the event, rather than on humour. As I stood up I sensed that, certainly among the younger fraternity, there was a hope that I would make them laugh.

'I have known Liam for three and a half years, since we met at college. Since that time, we have been through much together, and our relationship has gone from strength to strength. He has pulled me out of the gutter when I've been too drunk to stand, and I've repaid him by being sick on his foot. We've enjoyed the company of a wild rat in our first flat, we've narrowly avoided arrest for sharing a house with someone who smoked pot for a living and, for the last year, we've let a fat Geordie slob enter our happy home. And now he's leaving me, and I can't for the life of me understand what he sees in this girl to make him want to turn his back on all of that.'

Apart from a few elderly faces who looked vaguely troubled by this opening gambit, it went down pretty well, especially when Naomi rose from her chair and hit me, a little too hard actually, on the back of the head. I started warming to my theme:

'Actually, Naomi's arrival on the scene gave both Tony and me a sporting chance of attracting young ladies while in Liam's presence. You can picture our faces pre-Naomi, when all the girls completely ignored us two and made a beeline for him. Mind you, you can probably also picture the faces of the said girls, post-Naomi, when they realised he was off limits and they saw the alternatives.'

I continued on for several minutes with anecdotes

designed to embarrass and humiliate Liam as much as possible, before turning to his wife.

'And so to Naomi. Not only has she come into Liam's life and tamed him away from the adolescent student that he was but, probably by default, she has managed to do the same to both Tony and me. I'm quite sure that I would still have been stealing traffic cones for no apparent reason had it not been for the influences of both her and Alison and, for that, I suspect everyone who knows me is grateful.'

Both Liam and Naomi's father had already eulogised, at length, about her warm-hearted and fun-loving nature, as well as how stunning she looked today. My comments, therefore, seemed a little like a repeat performance, but they were still heartfelt and she clearly appreciated them. I ended by drinking a toast to them, and I was flattered to receive a particularly generous kiss from the bride. When I glanced at Alison, however, she seemed to be looking a little thoughtful and I began to feel very slightly uneasy that I had overdone the accolades a bit in front of my girlfriend.

Later, when everyone had reconvened for the evening, I spoke to her.

'You OK, Alison? You seem a little quiet. There's nothing wrong, is there? I didn't go on too much about Naomi in my speech, did I?'

'Oh, don't be silly, Adrian. Of course you didn't – it's her wedding. She's entitled to have praise lavished on her. I'm OK, honestly. Just a little tired, that's all.'

So the dancing began, and soon grown, sensible men were doing the actions to the 'birdie song' and 'Agadoo' and actually smiling while doing so. One thing that Alison and I had in common was a dislike for disco dancing, especially mindless movements to novelty records, so, although we did a bit of token shuffling after the rubbish had stopped, we sat and drank most of the evening and chatted to Tony, who was an even worse dancer than me.

Eventually it was announced that Liam and Naomi were leaving, and it would be a full two weeks before we saw them again, with a honeymoon in Antigua awaiting them. It was a highly emotional moment when we said our goodbyes, and then they were gone.

Alison was still very quiet as she got changed and into bed. She did look tired, as she had said, but her face showed more than tiredness. There was a thoughtful, almost melancholy look about her and, when I joined her in bed, we were both silent for a few moments. She would never be described as a beautiful woman, but she had looked lovely today and now, stripped of make-up and false expression, she was certainly beautiful to me. I had an uneasy feeling that something was wrong, and wondered what I might have done to upset her.

'What's the matter, Alison?'

She remained quiet for a few seconds more, as my words hung in the air. 'Oh, I don't know – us.'

It is amazing how one two-letter word, said after a brief pause, can mean so much and threaten so easily to alter the shape of one's life.

'Us? What about us?' I tried to say it as gently as possible, but there was a discernible crack in my voice.

'I – I'm not sure where we're going, that's all.'

'I thought we agreed that we'd take it easy and see where things led us.'

'I know, I know, and that was totally right – at first. I was still getting over Peter, and I didn't want to rush into anything, and I know you didn't either. It's just – well, we've been together for nearly six months now, and I'm not sure where things go from here.'

'What do you mean?' Again, she was silent for a while as I

thought through my decision, my desire, to remain in a boys-only flat for the immediate future.

'I'm nearly 32, Adrian. I've had one go at marriage and it didn't work, but I do want to settle down. I want children and I don't want to wait five years for them. You're young, you're enjoying life and you're not ready for that commitment.'

I noticed that she didn't actually ask me if I was ready for that commitment, which was just as well, as I would have stuttered out a non-committal response which would have verified her thoughts unambiguously. I did feel a lot for Alison. I got on well with her, I felt a great affection for her and, quite definitely, these feelings had grown since Doncaster. But I'm not sure that I loved her. I was sure, however, that I wasn't ready for a long-term commitment and the thought of children, while not quite abhorrent, seemed a million miles away.

'What's brought all this on?' I asked.

'The wedding, I suppose. It's been at the back of my mind for a while, but seeing Naomi looking so stunning and so happy – I need to feel that again, Adrian, and I need to sooner rather than later. Whether I can go out and find somebody of my age, who I fall deeply in love with, and who wants the same as me – whether that man's out there, I don't know. I just think – it's just not going to be us, that's all.'

Part of me wanted to talk her out of it, wanted to suggest we move in together, wanted to propose even. But I knew, deep down, that that would be to appease her rather than what I really wanted.

'So, what now?'

'I don't know, Adrian. I think – maybe – I'd like a hug.'

'Hello?'
'Hello, is that Mrs Giles?'
'Speaking.'

'Oh, this is Adrian Gray here, from the flat?'

'Oh yes.'

'I wondered if I could speak to Stephen, about the result of the interview.'

'Er, he's a little busy at the moment.'

'A little busy?'

'Yes, a little busy.'

'Practising for a speech competition, or ...?'

'Perhaps you could let me know?'

'OK, then. We had three people come for interview and we're delighted to say that we thought Stephen interviewed the best. So, assuming he's still interested, the room is his.'

'Oh, that is good news. I think this will do him the world of good, and you two did seem like such nice boys – Stephen doesn't really have many friends, you see.'

'Indeed.'

'It will be so nice for him to be a little more independent. I mean, at his age, he shouldn't really still be living with Mummy and Daddy, should he? Obviously I'll still come round and cook his meals for him some days ... well, most days at first, until he can cook for himself.'

'Obviously.'

'And, naturally, I'll collect his washing for him each week, and do his ironing ...'

'Naturally.'

'And, of course, I'll phone every night.'

'Of course. Would you like me to let you know when his bottom needs wiping?'

'I beg your pardon? Oh, I see. Ha ha. No, I expect he'll be all right there.'

'Good, good. Well, just a few details we need to sort out before he moves in: dates, contracts, house rules, that sort of thing ...'

'Yes, of course.'

'Now, first and foremost, he is gay, isn't he?'

'I beg your pardon?'

'Stephen. He is gay?'

'Er, no – I don't think so – er, gay, you say?'

'Yes. Oh well, if he's not, it doesn't really matter. He'll just be the odd one out, that's all.'

'Odd one out?'

'Yes. Then, of course, there are the parties.'

'What parties?'

'I didn't mention them? Tony and I have parties on Friday and Saturday nights for all the boys.'

'What boys?'

'Oh, I'm sure Stephen will be all right if he just serves drinks or nibbles or something, and perhaps keeps to the kitchen, you know, to play safe ... Mrs Giles? Mrs Giles?'

20.

As I lay awake in bed that night, contemplating the range of emotions I had experienced that day, I envisaged a horrible, awkward atmosphere during the journey home. However, when we chatted in more depth in the morning, there was only a sense of fondness between us, rather than awkwardness. We agreed that we would remain 'just good friends' – that clichéd term used so often to soften the pain of separation – and told Tony our news at breakfast. He seemed totally shocked, to such an extent that his trademark witty riposte completely deserted him.

The journey home, therefore, had less of an awkwardness about it, and more of a feel that the air had somehow been cleared. I dropped Tony off at our flat before taking Alison home. I helped her with her luggage but had resolved not to stay, so turned down her offer of coffee.

'I really must get on, Alison. I've barely done a thing for school tomorrow.' I've no doubt she saw this answer for the pitiful excuse that it was, but I also suspect that she'd only offered coffee because she thought that she should.

'Goodbye, Alison. Keep in touch, OK?'

'Of course. Bye, Adrian.'

So I left. And as I drove away, I wondered whether I'd see her again. After all, we had no common links, and I couldn't foresee too many 'just good friends' evenings out. My mind was a whirl for the rest of the day, and I couldn't focus on schoolwork. Luckily, there was an INSET the following day, which required no preparation on my part, so I resolved to plan Tuesday's lessons on Monday night and, until then, let the sea of thoughts wash over me.

Such was the common sense of relief at Sandra Little's return the following day, it made the prodigal son's homecoming reception look like he'd just nipped out to buy a paper. It's strange, but when someone is gone for a lengthy period and their replacement has been universally disliked, one's memory of the original gets distorted. Sandra Little had taken on the unwitting mantle of hero and saviour. It wasn't until we started bombarding her with stories of Sheila Warnock's foibles that I remembered that Sandra was not the sort to join in with raucous tales. She smiled grimly, and occasionally allowed herself an 'Oh dear', but remained remarkably restrained. We then insisted that she told us all about her term at Farnden School, and sat back with an air of children waiting excitedly for their teacher to tell them a story. Sandra was clearly a little uncomfortable talking about colleagues and children at her seconded school, but I think she realised that we were going to down tools until she did. The problem with Sandra Little, however, was that she was simply too damn professional to tell, and embellish, a good story. It was not too difficult, though, to read between the lines and gain an insight into the characters and situations that she had to cope with after the previous headteacher had so suddenly left. There had quite clearly been a lot of disquiet amongst the staff and her descriptions of them suggested an angry, militant, 'I'll-see-what-my-union-has-to-say-about-this' lot. With a bit of coaxing, we managed to establish a little about them.

One of the teachers, a hard-line union's dream, was soon

referred to by Frank as 'Millie Tant'. Apparently, she was short, with spiky hair, and knew her rights on everything. The 'us and them' feel between staff and management was stirred up by Millie, and it led to a really awkward atmosphere in the staffroom.

Another problem was that the difficult Year 6 children were being taught by the weakest teacher in the school.

'No change there, then,' muttered Frank, quietly.

While Sandra didn't quite state as much, it seemed pretty clear to me that Miss Wilson, the Year 6 teacher, had a *laissez faire* attitude towards school, and that the children were effectively running riot.

'If Shannon or Sean joined Farnden,' said Sandra, 'they'd meet their match in that class.'

By the end of her tale, I found myself glad that I was at Green Acre and full of admiration for the amazing man-management job that Sandra Little had clearly undertaken. I had not really considered whether I had aspirations to be a headteacher in the future, but the thought of trying to cope with the sort of shit that had clearly been flung at her filled me with dread.

The INSET day that followed was a desperately dull affair, full of mind-numbing policy reviews, and I spent most of it thinking about Alison, or picturing myself being massaged on a beach by an Antiguan beauty.

During our coffee break, Sandra asked to see me.

'I feel rather guilty that I haven't been around to ask you how you're getting on, Adrian. I know that teaching Year 6 can be a demanding task, especially in your first year – how's it going?'

I briefly went through some of the more memorable moments of the term and she laughed heartily, a rarity for Sandra Little, when I mentioned Shannon's physical exertions in front of the registered inspector.

'I know the next few weeks are likely to be stressful for the children,' she continued, 'I'll have a chat with them tomorrow, but at least they've got Wales to look forward to.'

'What's happening about the school trip?' I asked. 'I know that the medical forms have come in and the activities are booked but, beyond that, I don't know. Am I in charge?'

'Absolutely not, Adrian. I can't come with you, having just returned, but Frank has agreed to lead the trip. Is that OK? There's no way I'd expect an NQT to lead a school journey.'

'Frank sounds great. Anyone else coming?'

'I think ideally I'd like four adults to go, three of them teachers. Mrs Jones has agreed to come with you, as she'd be helping your class anyway. I don't really want to ask Julia or Theresa, as they've got young children, and Ellie won't want to go, which leaves Irene or Rachel. What do you think?'

I assumed this was a serious question. I assumed she was genuinely asking me to assess the rival merits of Irene Cunningham and Rachel Sanders for the week in Wales. If it was laced with sarcasm, then it was extremely dry indeed.

OK, Adrian. Ponder it over for a minute. Put your finger on your chin; raise your eyes and say, 'Hmmm. Let me see. Irene I'm-not-very-intelligent-and-really-rather-dull Cunningham, or Rachel I'm-quite-the-most-gorgeous-girl-on-the-planet-and-Adrian-needs-my-ample-bosom-to-cry-on-because-he's-just-lost-his-girlfriend Sanders.'

'I don't know; I'm sure they'd both be great. Actually, I do remember Rachel once saying that she'd like the opportunity of working with the upper school – you know, to get a bit of experience. Why don't we ask her?'

Fortunately, Sandra's response of 'that sounds like a good idea' sounded like a 'that sounds like a good idea', rather than a 'don't think you can fool me, you randy little bastard'.

The thought of spending a week with both Rachel and

Frank raised my spirits immensely, and I desperately hoped that she'd be able to come.

It was lunchtime before I finally managed to speak to Rachel alone. She asked me how the wedding had gone and I explained, trying to strike the balance between sadness and self-pity, how Alison and I had separated. She was wonderfully sympathetic and insisted, after twisting my arm mightily hard, that she take me out for a drink to drown my sorrows. This felt like a good time to strike.

'You don't fancy coming to Wales with Year 6 next month, do you? Frank and Leah Jones are coming. It should be a laugh. Sandra's going to talk to you about it.'

I don't suppose she noticed that I was literally holding my breath while she checked her diary, but she would certainly have noticed my broad grin when she said that there was nothing else on that week and she would love to come.

My sorrows were well and truly drowned later that evening as we shared a drink.

'Was Alan OK about you coming to Wales in May?' This question was designed to casually test the lie of the land, and her response exceeded all expectations. She actually huffed when she replied.

'I don't suppose he'd notice. He's never in the country long enough to notice many things these days.'

This was, by some margin, the best huff I'd ever heard in my life, and the actual sentence probably also made my top twenty. I could, however, hear Naomi screaming 'Play it cool' and, although I would have liked to have said, 'Well, why don't you ditch the smarmy bastard and marry me instead?' I settled for an admirably restrained, 'Oh, why's that, then?'

'He's working on some major project in Africa, and it's taking up a huge amount of his time. Hopefully it won't be for too long.'

Even though this last comment was considerably more conciliatory towards him, the tone of the first one had been noted and stored, and I began to really look forward to Wales.

Beforehand, of course, and for the next three weeks, there was the tiny matter of last-minute preparation for SATs to negotiate. I was even more conscious now of trying to achieve that elusive balance between taking them seriously and not taking them too seriously. I'd chatted to Frank, who'd suggested a framework for the final three weeks of preparation. So when I saw the children on Tuesday morning I told them that we were going to push the revision in the mornings, with past papers and exam technique exercises, but take things easier in the afternoons.

Mrs Anderson came to see me first thing on Tuesday morning with Alice, who looked less stressed than two weeks previously. A hastily arranged Easter break with no revision books allowed had probably helped.

The class, on the whole, seemed keen to knuckle down and didn't raise too many eyebrows when I told them I was upping their homework for the next two weeks. Even the likes of Sean, Shannon and Josh seemed to be taking things seriously. My greatest concern, during these weeks, was Patrick. He seemed to be rather withdrawn and Leah, who worked closely with him everyday, voiced her concerns:

'He seems to have lost belief in himself,' she said. 'Even though he knows that I'm allowed to sit with him and read the questions during maths and science, he seems to feel that he is just not going to succeed. I don't know what to do.'

I wasn't sure either. Patrick had had a major impact on my life this year both directly and indirectly. Without him I would never have met Alison in the pub, been stung into action by her words and subsequently gone to the dyslexia course. Perhaps I felt that I owed him something, but I had spent more of my time preparing for him or directly helping him than I had anyone else. Leah and I had created a programme for him based largely upon the ideas suggested on the course, and he had generally responded well to this. His confidence had certainly risen. However, now SATs were imminent, his confidence was waning, and I didn't really have a plan B.

I spoke to Irene, who was in charge of special needs, and she was singularly unhelpful. Her attitude was that this was probably just a blip, things had been working well up to now, and that an extra dose of praise and encouragement would probably be all that was needed. I also spoke to his mum, who looked as weary as ever, and she felt that he was quieter at home, but couldn't put her finger on why.

I wondered whether Sean or Shannon had been up to their tricks again, and tried to speak to him about it, but all he would say was that everything was fine. I resolved, finally, to take Irene's rather lame advice and keep an eye out for him.

Things didn't improve, however, as the first three weeks of term went by and, as we finished school on the Friday before the tests started, the positive and confident air in the majority of the children only highlighted further his disconsolate one.

It came as no surprise to me, then, when on Monday, the day of the first test – his strongest subject, science – Patrick did not turn up to school. I had had no doubt whatsoever that, with Leah reading the questions for him, he would achieve the national expectation of a level 4, but the rules are ridiculously strict: if someone misses a test, for whatever reason, they cannot redo it on a subsequent day, and would effectively, therefore, fail it.

When we telephoned his home at nine, with the test due to start in half an hour, his mother told Sandra, very sheepishly, that Patrick had a bit of a headache and was still in bed. When Sandra asked her to fetch him to the phone, he apparently refused to come. Sandra Little's next gambit was as commanding as it was surprising.

'Mrs Collins. I don't think that Patrick is too unwell to come to school and he needs to be here within half an hour. If he will not give you that assurance now, while I'm listening, could you tell him that Mr Gray and I will drive to your home and fetch him?'

She waited for a moment before saying, 'I see. We'll be round in a few minutes.'

I'm not entirely sure that what we were about to do was legal, and if I'd had Millie Tant's number I'd have phoned her to check, but five minutes later I found myself driving a grim-faced Sandra Little to a tiny grim-looking council house. When I remembered how many children Mrs Collins had, I could only assume that this house was Tardis-like.

Sandra must have seen my face as we knocked on the door.

'Don't worry, Adrian. I'll do the talking to her. If she thinks she can let him stay off school on a whim on a day like this, then she's mistaken. It might be an idea if you can have a quick word with Patrick, though. You've built up a really good relationship with him.'

It was a rather haggard-looking Mrs Collins who opened the door a moment later. She wasn't angry or indignant, she just seemed at a loss, and I really felt for her.

'Could we come in, please, Mrs Collins?' asked Sandra.

Slowly and unwillingly, Mrs Collins inched back the door and let us in. I deliberately tried not to look around as we climbed the stairs of the tiny two-up two-down – that's not what we were there for – but it was impossible not to get a feel of the place.

There was a darkness throughout, but this could not conceal a combination of clothes, toys and various incongruous items making up the unruly mess that was their home. An unpleasant sour smell, made up probably by dampness and overflowing bins, added to the depressing scene. Mrs Collins must have been aware that we were taking all this in on our way to one of the two small bedrooms.

'Patrick, it's Mr – er – your teacher.' This comment in itself was telling, but thoughts of shaming her for not knowing the name of her son's teacher were well down my list of things to do in the next few seconds.

The first thing I noticed, as she opened the door, were three sleeping bags touching each other on the floor, with a very weary-looking Patrick sitting resolutely in the central one, staring at the wall.

'What's wrong, Patrick?' I asked gently, as we stood there.

His response, perhaps predictably, was to shrug his shoulders and maintain his fixed gaze.

'I think I know you well enough, Patrick, to know that this isn't about a headache. You worked really hard for these tests – I've been pleased with you, your mum's been pleased with you, and how do you think Mrs Jones is feeling at the moment, striding up and down the classroom, wondering whether all the work she's put in with you has been for nothing?'

Again, silence.

'Just tell me this, Patrick. Is this about a headache?'

He was quiet for a moment before he shook his head.

'And is it because you don't think you're going to do well in the tests? Because I think you are going to do well, and so does Mrs Jones, and so does Mrs Little.'

I could feel that I was beginning to get close to the root of his concerns and it was abundantly clear from his expression that this went beyond a worry about the results of the tests.

'Has someone been teasing you about them? Sean? Shannon? Josh?' His lips were now beginning to purse and I knew I was approaching the truth.

'Who is it, Patrick? Who's made you unhappy?'

There was a silence for a full thirty seconds and I prayed that neither his mother nor his headteacher would break it. Eventually, I got the word I was waiting for.

'Timothy.'

I hadn't really known what to expect when I had arrived at this house, although for the last week or so I'd suspected that it was someone rather something that was getting at him. I'd scrutinised his classmates' dealings with him and while the usual suspects, Sean, Shannon and Josh, hadn't been openly hostile, they were still the obvious candidates to be behind a cynical and nasty bullying campaign, if this is what had happened. Timothy, I was fairly certain, had kept his head down in the classroom and looked every inch the victim rather than the bully, making this revelation that much more of a surprise.

'Timothy? What's he done?'

The greater the pent-up emotion, the greater the outburst, and his reaction to my question suggested weeks of suffering. Tears cascaded down his cheeks as he struggled to control his gasps for breath.

'Do you want to tell me?'

I was acutely aware that my class, supervised by Mrs Jones, were waiting to start something that they had worked towards for months, but I also knew that there was a little leeway in time and, at this precise moment, coaxing Patrick to join us was more important than a few minutes' anxious wait for the rest of them.

'He's never liked me. Ever since he's come he's called me thick. And then this term, well it's just got worse and every playtime he's said I'm gonna fail my SATs and I wouldn't be able to go to secondary school. He said I'd have to stay here until I passed them which would take forever.'

And so he continued. Slowly at first but then more quickly,

as he felt it safe to expand, he told of a systematic campaign by Timothy to dent his confidence. It was jaw-dropping stuff and even though both Sandra and I were well aware that this was only one side of the story, neither of us had any doubt that he was telling the truth. The obvious motivation for Timothy in all of this was to deflect the mantle of 'victim' onto someone else. Timothy was a victim because he acted so superior. Patrick was one due to circumstances beyond his immediate control. His dyslexia, his poor background and his patent lack of confidence would have seemed to Timothy to be more worthy of cruel jibes than his own superiority. Patrick, as ever, would have taken anything that Timothy said to him without fighting back, and this would have made him an easy target for someone who had always been picked on himself. Timothy was also intelligent enough to be subtle and careful and one could only imagine what his parting shot would have been last Friday:

'You do realise that everyone's going to laugh at you next week, don't you? You'd be much better off staying at home ...'

It was now 9.30 and Sandra phoned the secretary to tell all concerned to put back the start of the test by twenty minutes. As soon as Patrick had opened his heart and had been given my assurances that I would talk quietly to Timothy, he seemed to have a weight lifted from him, and he got dressed very quickly. Munching on a piece of toast, he walked without fuss to the car and, by the time we began the exam, we were only fifteen minutes behind schedule.

Fortunately, Patrick was working in the music room with Leah anyway, so there was no awkward atmosphere to put everybody off. I glanced surreptitiously at Timothy from time to time – I wasn't going to openly stare at him – and I felt pretty sure that he was aware that the game was up. There was a nervous, twitchy demeanour about him which went beyond pre-test nerves, and I hoped he was suffering. Sandra and I had discussed, briefly, when it would be best to confront him and we both agreed that it needed to be sooner rather than later. Patrick's well-being during the tests was the priority at the moment.

So, at break, as the class were buzzing about the science test, I called him over and we went to see Sandra Little. I rather assumed that she would begin by giving him a chance to give his version of events but she clearly decided that a more direct approach was needed.

'We know what's been happening with you and Patrick over the last few weeks,' she began, 'and it's got to the point where he refused to come to school this morning and we had to fetch him. Is that what you wanted, Timothy?'

A shrug.

'I haven't got much time, Timothy, and neither have you. Either you tell me why you've done this now, or I'll phone your parents and get them up here.' If she was bluffing, it worked.

'Because people were being nasty to me.'

'Was Patrick?'

'No. But everyone else was.'

'So you thought you'd pick on the one person who wasn't being horrible? I don't understand.'

She did understand, as did I, but Timothy had nothing further to say. In the end, due largely to the delicate stage of the year, Sandra agreed not to tell his parents on the understanding that he would never bully Patrick again. None of us had any doubts that the systematic name-calling was now over, and I left her room promising myself that I would never put myself in a position where she had to cross-examine me.

I talked to all of the children at the end of their second paper about how it had gone and there was a general feel of optimism in the room. When Josh announced that it was easy, to more than a few raised eyebrows, I found myself relaxing for the first time that day. There was also excitement in the air as I'd promised that we would spend the afternoons beginning our auditions and rehearsals for *Oliver!* which would be taking up much of our time from now on. When I had told Sandra about this ambitious project she had tried to talk me out of it, arguing that it was much too big a production to attempt in my first year, but I was resolute and, eventually, she had given in.

I loved auditioning for plays. I'd directed a couple of times at college, and I was thoroughly looking forward to doing so with children for the first time. Sophie's mum had agreed to play the piano for me, and we spent an enjoyable afternoon learning some of the more well-known songs. Over the course of the week I had planned to have a series of auditions, both with and without singing, and have it cast by Friday, so the leads could begin to learn their words.

The rest of the week followed a similar pattern – SATs exams in the morning, singing and auditions in the afternoons. The general consensus was that the science and maths papers were OK, but the English one was difficult, especially the writing, which had given them a thoroughly dull topic to have to be creative about. But they did it and by Friday lunchtime there was this wonderful feeling of freedom, as they knew that their exams were behind them and Wales and *Oliver!* were waiting around the corner. There was also much excitement as they knew I was going to cast the play in the afternoon.

Both Patrick and Timothy had recovered well by the end of the week. Patrick, knowing that the bullying was over, looked a totally different child; Timothy, having messed up his science paper and, probably, his pants on Monday, had gradually lost the guilty expression during the week, and his superior expression was well and truly back in operation by Friday.

By three on Friday afternoon I had made my decisions, and the class waited, with bated breath, as I told them the cast. Allard, who had been quite brilliant in auditions, I cast as Fagin; and Alice was perfect as Oliver. Miranda made for a raucous Nancy; and Sean, rather predictably, got the part of Bill Sykes. William got to play the Artful Dodger, and Cherry, Richard, Donna and, I was pleased to announce, Robert, also had main parts. I wanted to cast Timothy as Scrooge, but I had a horrible feeling that someone might notice that he didn't actually appear in the play.

I congratulated a smiling and excited 6G on an excellent week, wished them a restful weekend, and looked forward to seeing them, bright and early, on Monday morning, ready to get on the coach.

Fagin:	Ah, my boys, my boys. It's good to see you all back in one piece. Now, what've you got fer me t'day? Dodger, is that what I think it is?
Dodger:	Only the best leather, Fagin, and 'ankerchiefs made of the finest silk.
Fagin:	That's m'boy! That's m'boy! And 'oo's this mighty fine gentleman you've brought back with you?
Dodger:	This is Ebenezer Scrooge, Fagin. Nobody likes 'im coz 'e's a miserable old sod. And 'e's also weird.
Fagin:	Well, Mr Scrooge, what've you managed to get fer me, eh?
Scrooge:	I have this eighty pound Parker pen that Father purchased for me from Harrods. It writes in azuuuer, and is far superior to anything that these urchins have procured.
Fagin:	Twat.

21.

There was a great feeling of excitement as we all assembled on Monday morning, ready to depart for south Wales. A heady mixture of a week away from their families and being at school in civvies made for priceless pictures of anticipation on the children's faces. They had been told to wear something old and warm, as we were to be visiting a disused coal mine on the way to our guest house. Most of the children had followed this advice. Shannon, however, clearly not listening beyond the 'non-uniform' bit, had donned a belt masquerading as a skirt, and a rather-too-tight-for-her top. Sandra and I exchanged raised eyebrows at this, but such was the jovial atmosphere that we simply couldn't be bothered to challenge her.

The only exception to the sea of excited faces was Elizabeth, who clung to her mother with a look of sheer dread. Mrs Vaughan had warned me beforehand that her daughter had never been away from home before and she had actually said the words 'delicate little flower', to which I had just resisted replying 'pampered little pansy'. Mrs Vaughan looked as distraught as Elizabeth and it was clear that an industrial-sized saw would be needed to separate them when the time came to board the coach.

Otherwise, the parents looked as happy as their children did at the prospect of a child-free week. Ms Robinson was virtually shoving Kate on to the bus. As a young, single mother-of-one, she had clearly lined up a week of clubbing and revelling which seemed, apparently, to be starting in the next few minutes.

And so the coach prepared to leave. There were last-minute waves, kisses blown and celebratory jigs of delight as the children jostled for position on board. The only way that Elizabeth was going to get on the coach was if her mother went with her. As she sat down, doing a passable impersonation of a limpet, the histrionics began. The coach driver, a miserable git of a jobsworth called, remarkably, Sunny, started muttering about M25 traffic and EU directives regarding the length of drivers' lunch breaks.

'If you want to reach the guest house this side of tomorrow,' he growled, with unbelievable insensitivity, 'you'll get that woman off my bus right now.' Eventually, it took both Frank and me to prise Mrs Vaughan away from Elizabeth and, while he ushered her off the coach, I took the full force of Elizabeth's continued outburst. If I hadn't known that this was fundamentally the right thing to do, I would have felt awful about actively separating a mother and her only daughter.

Ironic and heartfelt cheers echoed around the coach as we pulled away from the school and there was a party-like atmosphere until Sunny took up the microphone and addressed the children as if they were new recruits at a high-security prison.

'Just so's you're aware,' he barked, 'there's to be no litter on my coach, so no eating or drinking. Nobody is allowed to take off their seatbelt for any reason.'

Perhaps a 'Hello children, my name is Sunny and I hope you have a fabulous holiday,' would have been nice, but he clearly deemed this pleasantry superfluous.

Rachel, Leah and Frank sat at the front of the coach, and I was more than happy to join the throng at the rear, doing quizzes and playing games, as much as anything to avoid being shouted at for breathing by our esteemed driver.

Watching the children take out their packed lunches was an education in itself. Most of them, with a few quite remarkable exceptions, had been given the time-honoured combination of sandwiches, crisps, chocolate bar and drink. I thought that Patrick's 'whole-Swiss-roll-and-nothing-else' lunch would be unbeatable until I saw Josh unwrap a plate of cold fish and chips, clearly purchased the day before. Still, waste not, want not. Timothy, of course, picked gracefully at his plate of sushi and prawns and, fortunately, was oblivious to Shannon's subsequent comment of 'Christ! Whose fanny stinks?'

When Sunny had confirmed with Tim, the speaking clock, that his full quota of forty-five minutes' break had elapsed, we got back on the coach and made our way to our afternoon's venue. The Big Pit was a disused coal mine which had been turned into a museum, allowing coach parties to experience a little of what life must have been like for miners generations ago. There were a few disconcerted faces as we entered the shaft for the 150-foot descent into the mine below. Fortunately, the small group in my cage included Rachel, who looked terrified, so I could put on the manly 'hey, what's all the fuss about?' front as we reached the depths below. A brief tour followed, in which Rachel clung, not unpleasantly, to my side, and she was actively squeezing my arm when we experienced complete darkness as the lights were momentarily turned off.

After the mandatory photograph with the children dressed as miners, we set off for our guest house in Tenby, near the coast. When we finally arrived we were greeted by the owners, Jim and Irene Ward, a plump, jolly-looking, middle-aged couple with a plump, jolly-looking daughter. The children then struggled with their cases and were shown their rooms. My first impression of the guest house was that it had been preserved in a Seventies time warp. From the outside, it resembled a Welsh Fawlty Towers, whereas the inside, remarkably, had been recently refurbished. Where on earth they'd managed to purchase red flock wallpaper and carpets with orange and maroon swirls heaven only knows. What could have been a stunning Edwardian villa, with its fireplaces, cornices and beautifully proportioned, high-ceilinged rooms, had been systematically butchered with the clumsy addition of partitioned walls and ill-matching furniture.

As I watched the children scurry past paying no heed to such detail, it crossed my mind that only six months ago I would have done the same. Alison, however, was an avid viewer of countless home improvement programmes on obscure satellite channels, and this had clearly and unwittingly rubbed off on me.

The children had an hour or so to unpack before dinner, during which time Rachel discovered that her cunningly hidden bottle of red wine had broken inside her suitcase, the contents irreversibly staining all in its way. Sunny had been rather aggressive in his handling of the cases, clearly with another tea break imminent, although I don't suppose he would have considered the possibility of red wine being stowed away in one of them. Had this happened to anyone else at any other time, I would have found it quite hilarious, but it was actually quite a disaster, and unless she wanted to look like an extra from *The Texas Chainsaw Massacre* she had very little left. Leah sorted her out some essentials to last until a trip to the shops could be arranged and the crisis lessened somewhat. However, during the whole incident, not one person mentioned the rather more serious consequence of us being a bottle of wine short.

Tea consisted, perhaps unsurprisingly, of vast quantities of burgers and chips, which the children guzzled down with gusto. A quiz followed and then came the unenviable task of trying to get twenty-seven hyped-up children into bed. We knew it would be a nightmare and although we had a 'lights out and quiet at ten' policy, this was clearly an unrealistic one. Elizabeth got another attack of homesickness, which Leah dealt with admirably, and it was nearly eleven before we felt it safe to crack open one of the remaining bottles of wine. We drew lots as to who would be on duty each night and it was a bitterly pissed off Frank who said a final goodnight to each room, giving his room as their emergency port of call in the night.

We had promised the staff at Green Acre that we would send them a postcard every day, but none of us felt like writing boring summaries of the day. After discussing various formats, Rachel came up with the winning formula:

Dear All
Twenty-seven children
Boarded the bus in glee
Four got poisoned eating lunch
Then there were twenty-three.

Twenty-three small children
Saw what miners used to do
One went off to fetch some coal
Then there were twenty-two ...

I awoke early the following morning and met Frank on his way back from the shower, grinning and announcing that he had had a completely undisturbed night's sleep.

'I promised the kids that if they were good and didn't disturb me, I'd give them loads of coke and orange smarties on Wednesday night when, I do believe, one of us will sleep soundly and the other one won't.'

Bastard.

After eating our slab of lard at breakfast, Frank announced the two groups, who would be alternating activities during the day. When he announced that Leah and I would be leading one group and he and Rachel the other he did so with a straight face, but I bet the little bastard did it deliberately. I contemplated getting a majority vote to determine group dynamics but figured that Leah wouldn't be too impressed. The more I'd got to know Leah Jones the more I'd got to like her, but she wasn't Rachel, whom I'd privately resolved to flirt with as much as possible all week.

Tuesday was our activity day; trained instructors were to lead us through the delights of abseiling and pony trekking. When our group arrived at the abseiling session we were met by Dean, a cocky-looking eighteen-year-old with long, bedraggled hair, who started by giving us a demonstration of how the equipment works. He then slowly and carefully explained the techniques for climbing down a wall, and there were many anxious-looking faces as he leaned back casually from the top before starting his descent.

A slightly evil look passed across his face as he asked, casually, who was volunteering to go first. Somehow the malicious sod seemed to know that all the children would, at this point, shuffle uneasily, and said, 'Well, sir, it looks like it's got to be you.'

Relieved and mocking voices of assent echoed around the hills as I was thrust forward. I had always been scared of heights and had, so far in life, avoided such stupid activities as parachute jumping, bungee jumping and, of course, abseiling. I was also, though, left in no doubt that I was expected to run this particular gauntlet if I had any chance of getting the children to do the same.

So I walked up the steps of the hill with Dean who, by this time, was looking so arrogant that I simply wanted to hit him.

'Right then, sir,' he laughed, 'now let me see if I can remember how to put on your harness correctly. I get it right most times.' Shannon, in particular, found this hilarious so, rather than causing a bit of an incident by hurling him to a speedy death, I smiled sardonically as he pretended to fumble with my harness. Eventually I was standing on the edge of the Grand Canyon with my back to the void and being told to lean backwards. In short, I was being asked to put my life in the hands of a spotty adolescent, and I was absolutely terrified. This wasn't helped by Sean shouting, with great mirth: 'Oi, Mr Gray. Do we still have to come to school after half-term if you're dead?'

With as much courage as I could muster, I let my body weight fall backwards and slowly began to walk down the wall. It wasn't exactly Mount Everest, and it didn't take me long, but by the time I reached ground level I felt a little like Sir Edmund Hillary as the children sportingly clapped.

My unexpected survival certainly gave the others confidence and Sean quickly volunteered to go next. If he was nervous, he didn't show it, and his descent was impressive. Richard, Sanjay, Cherry, Robert and Prakesh all followed without incident and Shannon would have done if Dean hadn't taken one look at her and proclaimed:

'My, you're a big girl, aren't you?' I really thought she was going to deck him. Her look of malice as she told him to shove his bloody harness was vicious in the extreme and I actually felt quite sorry for her as she seethed privately in the corner.

There were a few more anxious moments – both Simon and Elizabeth had to be coaxed into donning the harness, but the moment I had dreaded from the start occurred shortly before the end of our session. Leah Jones, for whatever reason, was at least sixteen stone and had sat slightly awkwardly at the back of the throng since the beginning. It took Robert, who else, to volunteer her when it was announced that there would be time for one last go. Even Shannon, who by now had calmed down, had had her turn and, short of someone going again, only Leah remained.

'No, it's all right, thanks,' she replied and I hoped that would be the end of it. Unfortunately, as soon as one of them said 'Oh, go on, miss, it's fun' others followed suit and, despite me chipping in with 'not if she doesn't want to' she clearly felt pressurised and eventually stood, to great applause. I don't think any of them, with the possible exception of Robert and the twins, specifically wanted to see an obese lady struggle down a rope, I think they just wanted the sport of watching her have a go.

Even Dean looked slightly concerned as he tied on her harness, and Leah began to look more and more uncomfortable. As soon as she started leaning backwards, silence engulfed us and, as the rope clearly began to stretch and groan, there were audible gasps as Leah froze. So there we were, suspended in a moment of time, with Leah Jones unable to move. Dean, realising he ought to coax her down, tried to talk her through walking step-by-step, but she had obviously suffered a major loss of confidence and would not budge. The rope was quite clearly straining by now and, while there was no real possibility that it would snap, it only heightened the tension.

Eventually, Dean had to tie himself to the spare harness and virtually move her feet for her. When she eventually reached the floor, there were no loud claps or sarcastic comments. The look on her face silenced all of us and many of the children were visibly shocked.

Fortunately, packed lunches were ready and waiting and, as everyone tucked in, the situation was somewhat diffused. I felt I needed to speak to her though, but beyond my 'You OK?', to which she gave a curt nod, I couldn't find anything remotely suitable.

After lunch, with the mood a little more buoyant, we set off in the coach to the stables for our pony trek. A jolly horsey type named Judy talked us through some basics before finding suitable horses for everyone. Again, this could have been an awkward process if the wrong thing was said, but Judy was obviously pretty skilled at dealing both with children and horses, and when Shannon was given a horse nearly twice the size of David's, nobody flinched. Leah was again looking rather nervous when she was given a friendly, docile beast, and her mounting skills weren't exactly elegant, but she got on and you could practically hear the collective sigh of relief.

I was last to mount, and there was an instant mistrust between Jupiter and myself as our eyes met. There was a definite 'don't mess with me' look on his face and, such was his wriggling, I felt like a contender in a rodeo as I mounted him.

The few times I've ever ridden horses, I've never quite got it right. Judy kept telling us to 'rise with the horse', whatever that meant, but however hard I tried to ride smoothly, when Jupiter started trotting, my backside was forever coming down as his back went up. Consequently it began to get very sore, very quickly, and I didn't really like to ask Judy if we could stop so she could rub my bum better. It was a quite tortuous session and, by the time we got back to the stables, after what seemed like hours later, my backside was on fire and I could barely walk.

'Teach you to try to ride me,' snorted Jupiter, unkindly, as I limped away.

I must have looked ridiculously constipated as I walked painfully back to the coach, and the moment was not lost on Shannon.

'You hurt your bum, Mr Gray? Never mind, I'm sure Miss Sanders will sort it out for you when we get back.'

I couldn't really ask her whether this was simply a throw-away comment or whether she'd noticed my puppy-like adoration of Rachel over the months, but it certainly got me thinking. If it was that obvious then it wouldn't have been lost on anyone, not least Rachel.

Everyone was exhausted when we arrived back at the Hilton and the children were given some time to write postcards and relax. As our group were first back, I opted for a hot bath which, after the initial protest from my backside, was lovely.

During tea, we swapped stories, although neither Leah nor I mentioned her abseiling. The two major incidents in Frank's group both involved Charlie. First, her horse had shied at something and nearly thrown her off and then, perhaps due to this fright, she'd had an attack of the Leahs on the rope and had thrashed out unwittingly at Dean as he'd tried to help her down. Good old Charlie.

Jim and Irene organised some games in the evening, and getting the children into bed was considerably easier than the previous evening.

Dear All,
Twenty-two small children,
Went abseiling with Dean,
Three ropes snapped and four took flight
Then there were just fifteen.

Fifteen little children,
Went riding on the glen,
Five wild horses disappeared,
Then there were only ten ...

Wednesday dawned the hottest day of the year. After breakfast and suntan cream, we set off for our day's six-mile hike. It was an energy-sapping experience, and many of the children, not to mention a very sweaty Leah, were beginning to lag behind as we approached lunchtime. We had arranged to walk down to one of the coves for our picnic lunch and when we arrived we sat down to eat without noticing the signs surrounding the beach. A shriek of laughter from Kate made us all turn, but by then it was too late.

Walking towards us was a group of naturists, who were clearly trying to decide whether to adopt *the 'Hell, we're naturists, this is a naturist beach and we've got nothing to be ashamed of'* approach, or the '*Shit, there's a bunch of school children, bollocks to my principles, I'm covering myself up'* approach. In the end, most of them bravely opted for the former, apart from the only woman in the company, who attempted, without much success, to protect her modesty.

Before ever stumbling across a British nudist beach, I'd always imagined that there would be something faintly erotic about them, with beach-loads of nubile young women looking at you suggestively. The truth, however, is that the majority of naturists are aging men, with nothing even vaguely erotic about them. Such was the case with this group and the children, perhaps unkindly, simply laughed. How we had managed to settle on this tiny naturist cove was a mystery, but it was a moment that the children would not forget in a hurry. As the group walked past, it became clear that the woman, at least, was beginning to look rather embarrassed. Perhaps if she'd had another woman to walk naked with her, it might have eased that embarrassment. Rachel always loved to please ...

Nudist jokes were abundant as we continued our walk and any flagging souls had been recharged by the food and entertainment. It was a long, hot afternoon, however, and by the time we got back to Tenby, with a steep ascent awaiting us, many of the children had had too much sun and were slowing considerably. I had horrible visions of being up all night, on my duty evening, tending the aftermath of sunstroke.

There were some dreadfully tired faces that emerged for tea a couple of hours later, and it was just as well that we had decided to put on a film for them in the evening – any sort of physical exertion, from a triathlon to a tiddlywinks competition, would not have been a good idea and, again, they went to bed eventually without fuss.

I was now pretty confident that I'd get a peaceful night's sleep, even when Kate came to find us during our third glass of wine.

'Sorry to disturb you, but I've got a really bad headache ... Jesus, where did all those bottles come from?'

It was a horrible role-reversal of the child being discovered smoking behind the bike sheds, and we all looked pretty guilty until Frank, rather weakly, announced that only one of them was ours, and the rest had already been there when we'd arrived. Kate's expression made it clear that she didn't believe us, and she was obviously making a mental note of the seven empty bottles that stood guiltily on the window sill. If her maths had been a little better, she might have worked out precisely how much we had drunk over the previous three evenings.

I was asleep within a few moments of going to bed and was completely disorientated when I was awoken by continued knocking on my door. Eventually I put on my dressing gown and opened my door, to find a sorry-looking Marcus standing there.

'What's the matter?' I asked, with far less sympathy than I should have done.

'My hair.'

Even at that hour, I couldn't resist it.

'I know it's getting a bit long, Marcus, but I'm afraid I've left my scissors at home.'

'No – you see – Josh – he's put shampoo in it.'

'What?'

'I was asleep and felt something funny and when I looked up, he was pouring it on my head.'

'Oh, for God's sake! Can't it wait till morning?'

As he shook his head and started crying, I realised how unfair I was being, so I gently led him back to the basin in the corner of the boys' room. As I started rinsing his head, the subsequent frothing and bubbling would have done justice to a manic washing machine. It took several minutes to clear what must have been half a bottle's worth and I finally went back to bed dreaming of reprisals for Josh in the morning.

Dear All,
Ten little children
Ignoring the danger sign
One fell off the cliff
And then there were only nine.

Nine little children
Saw naked men walk by
Four shed clothing there and then
Leaving only five ...

'What do you mean, Sean told you to do it?'

'He said I had to.'

'Well, I say you're going to write a letter home to Marcus' mum tonight, explaining what you've done to her son. How does that sound?'

We were sitting at breakfast the following morning and

Frank and I were giving Josh the grilling of his life. When we had finished with him none of us was in any doubt that he wouldn't repeat such a trick again.

After breakfast, we all headed down for our beach study day. In the morning the children had great fun with their rock pool studies, identifying and, in some cases, throwing about a variety of sea life. Part way through the morning, Elizabeth complained to Rachel that she felt sick. She had found something to complain about at every possible occasion all week and Rachel, in a rare unsympathetic moment, told her to pull herself together and enjoy the sea air: 'You'll be home tomorrow, Elizabeth. Why don't you at least try to enjoy yourself until then?'

By 11.30, however, when we began a sand sculpture competition, Rhiannon, William and Sanjay were also complaining of feeling unwell, and the first tinkles of alarm began to ring. By the end of the competition, which was won by Shannon and Kate's unfeasibly buxom mermaid, ten of the class were feeling ill and William had been sick. We made the decision to get back to the hotel quickly and abandon the afternoon's activities but, even as we began the slow ascent, the children were visibly worsening.

Halfway up the hill, we stopped and reassessed our situation. We were by now using seaside buckets as sick buckets, but there simply weren't enough to go round. I was given the easy job of taking the twelve able-bodied children up to the guest house, while Leah, Rachel and Frank tried to somehow juggle buckets and children for the longest half-mile journey of their lives. There had been no reply at the guest house when we'd phoned, Sunny was busy entertaining other travellers and taxi firms wouldn't risk contaminating their cabs.

When my party arrived back, Prakesh, Charlie and Donna went straight to bed, and I was feeling distinctly queasy. The Wards had now returned and you could almost hear the words 'Oh my God, what have we done to them, they're going to sue,' screaming in their brains. Not surprisingly, they flung themselves into preparing sick bays while their daughter drove down the road to rescue the most stricken.

It was a short-lived but particularly vicious airborne virus that got to just about everybody. I was in bed for two hours in the afternoon but, by six o'clock, the worst of it was over. The Wards, needless to say, were extremely relieved to hear that the illness was airborne, rather than brought on by overdoses of unhealthy artery-clogging food.

'That's the good news,' said the doctor jovially. 'The bad news is that you're going to have to practically fumigate the place before you can let anyone else stay here.'

The children were still determined to have their end-of-holiday disco that evening and, as only a handful were still in bed at 7.30, it was agreed that it would go ahead as planned. I never quite found out who Shannon was trying to impress, but her combination of deodorant, hairspray and perfume actually managed to set the smoke alarm off.

Nobody really appreciated how much the virus had taken out of them, and the disco barely lasted the duration. Many of them were begging to be allowed to go to bed by nine o'clock, and everyone was asleep by ten.

Dear all,
Five little children
Went fishing in the sea
Two got jumped by jellyfish
Then there were only three.

Three little children
Began to collapse and fall

As the airborne virus struck them down
Till none were left at all.

There was a great sense of fatigue as we boarded the coach for our return journey the following morning. Not even Sunny's cheery countenance could raise their spirits – they just wanted to go home. Even the thick black smoke that emanated from the coach halfway up the M4, causing a half-hour delay, seemed more of a nuisance than a prospect of high excitement. Josh managed to blurt out 'Look, everyone! The coach is going to blow up,' but his words were largely ignored.

By the time we arrived back at Green Acre, the whole school and all the parents had heard about the virus, and Chinese whispers had elaborated the truth markedly. Apparently, three of the children and one member of staff were dead, with several others fighting for their lives in hospital. There were some disappointed faces, among the Year 5 children in particular, when we all emerged, relatively unscathed, to the over-protective bosom of close family. I was then subjected to a grilling by Mrs Vaughan before I finally managed to slump into a staffroom chair. It was only then, when they were gone, that I realised just how tired I was. So I forced myself into my car, drove home and finally collapsed into bed ridiculously early. I slept for a thoroughly deserved fifteen hours.

'Mr Gray, could I have a word, please?'
'A word?'
'Yes, please. About Elizabeth.'
'Is it a nice word?'
'I'm sorry?'

'Your word. Is it nice? Is it something along the lines of "thank you" or "I'm grateful"?'

'Er – well, Elizabeth seems a little upset. Now, you did promise you'd take good care of her, and she's told me that when she was homesick this week – the poor little flower – the staff weren't very sympathetic. Now, if she feels that no one is looking after her, well, it just makes it worse and – '

'Mrs Vaughan?'

'Yes?'

'I've just been in the coach for the best part of five hours listening to our driver drivel on about how terrible life is. Yesterday I was literally passing sick-buckets from one child to another and getting splattered with some fairly unpleasant stuff into the bargain. The night before that I was woken at some Godforsaken hour to perform a rinse and blow-dry, and I spent all day, every day dealing with some problem or another.

'As for your delightful offspring, she has barely stopped crying or whingeing ever since she kissed goodbye to Mummikins. Despite hours of TLC and encouragement from me and my colleagues, she seemed resolute on hating every minute of the trip and making everyone else's life a misery.

'And now I'm tired, Mrs Vaughan, and I want to go home to bed. Please then, would you do me the honour of taking your spoilt little brat away from me, and shoving your complaint somewhere where it will never see the light of day again.'

22.

Rupert had warned me, before the school trip, just how draining it would be. It was not so much the specifics that had taken it out of me – the sickness, or being woken in the night – it was more the constant feeling, for twenty-four hours a day, that you were on call. It felt wonderful, then, to wake up late on Saturday morning knowing that the rest of the weekend belonged entirely to me. It would have been nice if half-term had come a week earlier, but I rather figured that I'd be able to go through the motions somewhat for the last few days, and keep a more sustained rest on hold.

By Monday morning, I felt sufficiently rested and was raring to go when the class arrived at nine. Despite the problems and the exhaustion I'd really enjoyed the week and I was pretty sure that they had too. I had especially valued the fact that we could be relaxed together. Apart from Josh's misdemeanour, there had been very few times that I had felt that I needed to be an authority figure and I rather hoped that this less formal state could continue.

I'd decided that we'd spend the mornings doing follow-up work from Tenby – diaries, letters and the like, and begin rehearsing in earnest during the afternoons.

At first all was well – the mood was lively and convivial as we shared our favourite moments from the week and our photographs. Even when they started working they settled reasonably quickly to the task, but it became apparent, quite soon, that they didn't really want to be writing diaries. They'd worked stoically practising writing techniques for SATs, when they could see a purpose in their efforts. Now, clearly, they were seeing this for exactly what it was, a tokenistic piece to pass the time and they quickly got bored.

It was an awkward dilemma, as I found myself shushing them at ever more frequent intervals. I really didn't want to go back to being an authority figure, yet I wasn't going to let them dictate proceedings. The crunch point arrived when Shannon said, bluntly: 'Do we have to do this? It's boring!'

Now Shannon and I had got on pretty well in Wales and I had found out the capacity she had for making people laugh. But this wasn't a sandcastle competition on the beach, this was my classroom, this was an activity that I had told them to do, and she was challenging it. I had no choice:

'I'm sorry, Shannon, yes, you do. I bet you'll look back at this diary in years to come and it will serve as an excellent reminder of your holiday.'

'I bet I don't. It's going in the bin when I get it home.'

I knew Shannon far too well by now to react to this rather provocative statement, and my non-committal 'whatever' signalled an uneasy truce.

It suddenly hit me that I had been extremely casual in my preparation of this week – I had rather assumed that they would happily settle to any task I set them but the general mood, when we packed away for break time, was not convivial anymore.

'Are we going to have to do writing like that all week?' asked Alice, of all people, and I felt a horrible sensation that I hadn't really thought this one through.

A quick rethink had them drawing their favourite scenes from the week after playtime, but it was such a badly delivered lesson, with no real stimulus or direction behind it, that the work produced was rubbish. What's more, they knew it was rubbish and there wasn't the usual sense of enjoyment that characterised most art lessons.

By the end of lunchtime it was clear that a new virus had swept through 6G, commonly known as Year 6itis. I'd been warned about it, of course. I'd been told to expect a cockiness, rudeness to ancillary staff and a general feel that they were simply too big and tough to endure the childish regime of primary school anymore. Both Sean and Shannon, apparently, were dreadful during lunchtime, and Kate and her cronies were downright rude to one of the dinner ladies. Even lovely kids like Cherry and Miranda, who were perhaps getting just too mature for junior school, showed signs of surliness.

The mood was softened, somewhat, in the afternoon, with our first full rehearsal of *Oliver!* Here, at least, was something that the children were actively looking forward to and the session passed happily enough. At the end of the afternoon, though, the simmering tension, evident throughout the day, finally erupted. As they filed back into class from the hall, there was clearly some rumpus developing between Shannon and Alice. I missed the specifics but by the time I reached them it had obviously begun to turn nasty. Alice was crying as an irate Shannon hurled abuse at her and gave every intention of being about to physically attack.

I was fed up with Shannon, she'd been a pain all day, looked like being a pain for the rest of term, and now she had made Alice cry without thinking. I stormed over and got between them, unwittingly banging Shannon's shoulder as I did.

'What on earth do you think you're doing, Shannon? You've been spoiling for trouble all day and now you've found it. Look at Alice. I hope you're proud of yourself.'

Of all the mistakes I had made during the year, this was probably the worst. I had made no effort to find out what had enraged Shannon, which just doubled her anger.

'Oh, that's right. Side with Alice why don't you, as usual!' Her shout was vociferous in the extreme, as she grabbed her bag and slammed out of the door. As it was already hometime, I let her go, but there was a deathly hush now, broken only by Alice's sobs.

Too late, I tried to find out what had happened. It seemed that, for whatever reason, Shannon had been teasing Alice all day, and she had finally reacted. When I heard that the words 'at least I'm not fat' had been said, I drew a deep breath. Shannon had shown, on many occasions, how sensitive she was about her mature physique, and she would have taken my remarks as an endorsement of Alice's outburst.

I resolved, as the others went out, to speak to Shannon in the morning, and try to be as conciliatory as possible, even to the extent of apologising for not establishing the facts before jumping in. I was just beginning to calm down, some half an hour later, when an irate Mr Williams strode in to my class.

I'd half prepared myself for the possibility of him coming in, but not for what he then said: 'What's all this about you manhandling Shannon?' he said, with the look of someone who was about to manhandle me. 'She told me that you pushed her and bruised her arm. You can be sacked for that, Mr Gray.'

While I wanted to throw my hands up in the air and run out screaming, I just about managed to maintain my calm. Even though I could remember brushing passed her arm, it had not even crossed my mind that she might somehow twist this to look like a violent assault. I explained to Mr Williams that I had run to the scene as I was worried that one of them might get hurt and in doing so had accidentally knocked his daughter's arm.

'That's not what she says – or Sean. She says you deliberately pushed her.'

I didn't know which of my feelings, at this point, were the strongest. Of course I felt threatened and concerned where this might lead but, more than this, I felt angry and betrayed that someone who I thought I was getting on well with could do this to me.

'If she said that, Mr Williams, then I can understand your annoyance, but I can assure you that that is not what happened. There were plenty of children around who would vouch for that, if it came to it.'

This seemed to subdue him somewhat. He clearly thought that if it were a 'his word against hers' scenario, he could back her up. The fact that I had volunteered children as potential witnesses made him change tack.

'Hmm, we'll see. But isn't it your job, Mr Gray, to listen to both sides of an argument, rather than sticking your oar in? As far as I can see it, Shannon got annoyed because some girl called her fat, and you sided with the girl. How does that work?'

'I was cross with Shannon because she had been awkward all day. I don't know if she's told you how she's been in trouble today, and now she was involved again. Yes, I should have established what had happened first and I will apologise to her for that, but I was exasperated with her behaviour, which has to improve.'

It was a fair attempt to twist things around but he wasn't having any of it.

'I'll talk to Shannon about her behaviour, don't you worry about that, but this isn't about her, it's about you, and how you dealt with it. I think I need to speak to the headteacher about this one.'

I was seething and shaking in equal measure by the time he left. Part of this disastrous day had been my fault – I had approached it in the wrong manner and was woefully underprepared. But part of it had been due to a girl that I now knew I would never be able to fully trust. If I had learnt anything from the day it was to never take children or teaching for granted – however predictable the job may appear to be getting. The change in atmosphere from the day's beginning to its end was quite chilling.

I had a pretty miserable evening, although I did rethink the week. I resolved to talk privately to Shannon in the morning, and then to the whole class. I felt we needed to agree a few compromises. Sometimes, I figured, it was important to bow to a general consensus, especially when there was nothing important riding on the tasks I was setting.

I walked into school on Tuesday with a slightly uplifted air, which lasted for less than thirty seconds before I was told by the secretary that Sandra Little wanted to see me. Images of accusations and suspensions echoed around my head as I sheepishly entered her office.

Before she could speak, I started blurting out my side of the story and my plans for trying to erase the mistakes I had made the previous day. I'd hardly begun my planned defence, however, when she silenced me.

'Adrian, listen. I spoke to Mr Williams after you'd gone last night and he left reasonably appeased. I think he probably accepted that Shannon's version of events was a little bit exaggerated. He'd had his pop at you and I don't think anything more's going to come of it. You didn't do a huge amount wrong apart from to act impulsively after being exasperated. We've all done that.'

It was only when she said this that I fully appreciated how anxious this incident had made me. I took some deep breaths as I felt a surge of emotion run through me.

'Actually, Adrian, though I'm glad that's cleared up, that's not the main reason I wanted to see you. I've had a long chat with Frank and our chair of governors yesterday and we want to offer you a permanent contract. You've had a good year in what could have been difficult circumstances, and we think you can become a great asset to this school. What do you say?'

I had no hesitation in accepting the full-time post there and then. I wouldn't work at Green Acre for ever, but I was very happy to have the opportunity to continue next year.

Feeling considerably happier than five minutes previously, I left Sandra's office and watched as the children arrived, hoping to clear the air with Shannon before the day started. If I was half expecting penitent tears, hugs and a 'let's both promise never to be horrible to each other again' moment, it was obvious, when I called her in, that I wasn't going to get it. She folded her arms, looked at me sourly and, summoning up what she had clearly gleaned from reading 'A beginner's guide to how to be a bastard of a teenager', let out that immortal word: 'Yeah?'

Had I not been in such a good mood I might have reacted, but my only concern today was getting my class back on my side and I didn't care how I did it.

'You were right to be angry with me yesterday, Shannon. I should have listened to you first and I'm sorry.'

I could see her desperately hoping that I would qualify that statement with a 'but', so she could renew her antagonistic posture and, when I didn't, it clearly threw her somewhat. I even allowed myself a self-satisfied smirk as I then said evenly, 'I'll see you in class in a minute,' before turning and walking away. I had apologised unreservedly to a girl who probably deserved a detention, yet I was undoubtedly in the ascendancy. She simply didn't know what to say.

I continued this approach with the class when they arrived a few minutes later.

'You're quite clearly not in the mood for writing up diaries this week, and I think that's fair enough. Instead, I want you to imagine that you've been approached by an advertising agency, who want you to sell the holiday in Tenby to next year's class. You've been asked to produce an information pack, with posters, leaflets and so on that'll appeal to ten-year-olds. When you've finished, I'll show your work to Miss Luck's class and ask them to see which one looks most interesting. The one with the most votes will be the winner.'

'Can we do it on the computer?'

'Can we make a PowerPoint presentation?'

'What do we win?'

Apart from this last question, a rather mercenary one from Josh, there was, as hoped, a sense of interest and excitement as I put them into groups and got them working. The change in atmosphere was palpable and I felt that I'd gained their respect because I'd listened to them, rather than lost it by sticking rigidly to my ill-prepared plans.

A noticeable side effect of their regained interest was that the spread of Year 6itis during breaktimes was far less evident. This continued throughout the week and, while I was happy to see it, the unmistakable link between their behaviour and what I set them to do put an undoubted degree of pressure on me for the remaining weeks of their primary school life.

On the last day of the half term we completed the mini-topics in the morning and presented them to Ellie's class just before lunch. I had felt irrationally nervous about asking her if we could do this, considering it effectively gave her an hour off teaching as the presentations and voting took place. I needn't have worried; she was more than happy to oblige and even mustered a smile, saying that it sounded like a good idea. She was quite clearly demob happy, knowing that in six weeks' time she could say farewell to teaching forever.

On Friday afternoon there were to be no rehearsals; instead, it was time for that dreaded moment that I had been putting off all year: sex education. Again, I had spoken to Frank and his advice was to treat it all as casually as possible, while appealing to their sense of maturity. He said that he always started these sessions by telling the children that they were going to be hearing words such as 'sexual intercourse', 'penis' and 'vagina'.

'If you can cope with that, Adrian, and actively encourage them to get their giggles out of the way first, then the rest of the session will be a cinch.'

I tried it in the mirror in the gents at lunchtime. 'Peee-nusss', 'va-gi-nah', 'Sex-u-al in-ter-course'. God, that was difficult. And if it was difficult in front of a mirror to, let's face it, a comparatively forgiving audience, what would it be like in front of Shannon, Kate and the rest?

If they had been studying my body language as much as I was studying theirs at the beginning of the lesson, they would have noted countless signs of terror and anxiety. For their part, they fell into four quite distinct categories. The first, which encompassed by quite some margin the majority, was the 'silly giggles' category, advocated by the likes of Andrew and co., Josh and Charlie. Then came the earnest-faced mature group, led by Alice, Miranda and William. There were a few who seemed completely disinterested by the impending lesson, chief among whom were Patrick and Daniel. Finally, there were those, headed by Kate and Shannon, who quite clearly felt that it was show-time – the show being the slow and complete denigration of their teacher. Oh yes, and there was a fifth category, consisting of one child who just looked down his nose at me like a supercilious twat.

Sitting alongside me was the school nurse, a rather imposing figure in her early fifties named Edith. Her appearance was both reassuring and terrifying. I was infinitely grateful that she would be taking the girls for the 'question and answer bit' after the video – I don't think I could have coped with Alice's earnest questions about menstruation. However, having to deliver the lesson in front of an experienced nurse who would be, no doubt, mentally scoring my performance, was unnerving in the extreme.

'OK, everybody. As you know, we've got our sex education session this afternoon. Yes, Josh, get your giggles out of the way. I'm sure you've all met Mrs Winterburn, who's very kindly offered to speak to the girls after the videos and answer any questions they may have. Now, I know this all may feel a little uncomfortable at first – that's only natural, so let's get the giggles out of the way, shall we? You're going to hear words on the video such as, er, as – well ...'

'What words, Mr Gray?' asked Kate maliciously. It was a hot day, and I was now sweating profusely as I squirmed in my seat. But it was no good, the brain was relatively willing, but the mouth was having none of it.

'Well, er, you know, Kate. Words that make you giggle – a bit – a lot, maybe – you know, such as – er – "bottom".'

The hilarity that greeted my 'bottom' was not due to the word itself – there was nothing of a 'penis' or a 'vagina' in a 'bottom', so to speak – but the fact that it had so obviously been such an embarrassment for me to utter.

'Yes, all right, calm down,' I said, noticing Edith Winterburn's eyebrows rising in a 'What is this guy doing?' sort of way.

So I managed to achieve relative calm and gladly passed the buck to the cool young dudes on the video, who managed to mention the taboo subjects without stuttering or squirming, and the children listened attentively enough.

As soon as the video had finished Rozinder put up her hand, but I simply wasn't going to risk it.

'Not now, Rozinder, you'll have an opportunity to ask whatever you want when Mrs Winterburn takes you into the music room.'

'It's just that ...'

'Did you hear me, Rozinder? All questions are to be written down. It's much better if these things are kept anonymous.'

'Mr Gray?'

'Oh Alice, what now? I've just said ...'

'I think she wants to go to the toilet.'

It was another horrible moment. Never before had I forbidden a child to speak on the off-chance that they might unwittingly embarrass me. I muttered something to Rozinder and quickly sent the girls packing. By now, Mrs Winterburn was looking with concern at the boys, clearly wondering what damage I was about to unleash.

I watched as the boys wrote down their questions, folded them neatly, and placed them in the box. The act of unfolding and reading was probably worse than having to give the answers. I had a couple of gentle openers about voices breaking and hair growing, before the fun started. I even managed to stutter my way through wet dreams and had given a suitably brief summary of basic male contraception before Allard put up his hand. The problem, of course, about a hand going up, is that you can't pretend you can't read it and throw it in the bin.

'Can you feel anything with a condom on?'

Shit. Shy away from it, and risk them assuming that I don't know because I've never been lucky enough to find out; or start giving details, and risk allowing the session to get personal.

'To be honest, Allard, that's not something you really need to worry about at your age.' It was a complete cop-out, and they knew it, but at least the moment passed.

I'd deliberately planned to give this lesson the day before half-term, so that any awkwardness would be forgotten nine days later. As the children finally left at 3.30, after an excruciating session, still giggling and passing sideways glances at me, I wondered whether nine days would be enough. I had learnt a lot in my first year at Green Acre, but I had not learned how to deliver sex education to eleven-year-olds. As the last of them disappeared from view, I shivered with a mixture of guilt, inadequacy and relief.

'What words, Mr Gray?'

'Well, er, you know, Kate. Words which make you giggle a bit – a lot, maybe. You know, such as – er – "bottom".'

'Oh, come on, Mr Gray, bottoms don't make us giggle. I'm sure you can do better than that.'

'Er, well Kate, I'm not sure that – er – oh look! Here's Mr Bell! Now 6G, as I've never taught sex education before, I asked Mr Bell earlier how I should approach it, and he told me that the best thing to do was to get the words that make us all laugh out in the open straight away. Isn't that right, Mr Bell?'

'Er, I don't remember exactly what I said, but ...'

'But you do remember the words?'

'Well, obviously ...'

'Oh, I'm so glad, because they've slipped right out of my mind. All I could come up with was "bottom". Perhaps you'd remind the children for me.'

'Well, I'm in a bit of a hurry, actually. I only came in to borrow your CD player. I've left my class and they're ...'

'Oh, never mind about them. Now, what was that first word? Another name for your todger, wasn't it? P-something?'

'Pee ... pee ... Look, Mr Gray. They know what I mean.'

'Yes, but you told me you have to say it. Who wants to hear Mr Bell's words? Oh come on, Mr Bell, don't let them all down.'

'Pee ... pee ... niii ... sssss.'

'Now, that wasn't too bad, was it? What was the next one?

'Er ... va – va – va – front botty.'

'Front botty?'

'Front botty is, I believe, the technical term, yes. Can I go now?'

'Not till you've said the last one. Come on. Open wide.'

'Er, sexual – inter ... er – Horsy – horsy. That's it, yes. Horsy horsy.'

'Thank you, Mr Bell, for your excellent advice. It certainly, as you predicted, got them giggling.'

23.

For a variety of reasons, our Friday night pub sessions had ceased to be since the wedding, so it was lovely, then, when Liam and Naomi joined Tony, Graham and me for a few beers that evening. After the week that I'd had I was more than in the mood to over-indulge and when we entered the pub I actively looked out for someone who might object to our Friday night banter.

It was fascinating to listen to both Liam's and Naomi's interpretations of married life. Naomi was unreservedly happy about the whole set-up but I sensed, watching Liam's smile as she described their domestic bliss, that his interpretation might not be quite so rosy. Indeed, when Naomi went to buy a round he said, with feeling, that while he wouldn't change it for the world, if she went on about him leaving wet towels around or not closing drawers one more time ...

Graham was a great addition to our throng and entertained us with tales from his travels but he was single, I was single, Tony was always single, and Naomi wasn't around to mother us any more. Thus the flat was beginning to revert to the untidy bachelor pad and desperately needed a woman's touch; or, more accurately, the three of us desperately needed a woman's touch.

I hadn't seen Alison since we'd split up six weeks previously and I missed her. I felt irrationally nervous, then, when I phoned her up on Sunday evening for a chat. She seemed really pleased to hear from me and proceeded to tell me about Phil, a rather shy zoologist she had met through a dating agency. Of course I told her how pleased I was for her but after we had spoken, with the prospect of a largely unaccompanied week ahead of me, I did feel rather lonely and somewhat jealous of this faceless figure who had managed to make Alison happy.

I'd been looking forward to half-term so much, after the exertions of Tenby and the subsequent week, but when Monday morning arrived I found myself wondering how I was going to fill my time. By the end of the break I'd become thoroughly bored and was looking forward to the start of the final half term as much as I had looked forward to the end of the previous one.

So the last six weeks began, with a variety of 'get on with it while I supervise the play' activities, as *Oliver!* began to take shape. Fortunately the nine days' holiday had allowed my attempts to teach sex education to fade slightly into the background, although the word 'bottom' did emanate from Kate's lips when she knew I was listening.

While some of the rehearsals were a bit of a slog, and some of them required me spending most of the session quietening those without a main part, it soon became obvious that there was scope for a really special production.

I had never thought it possible for a child to get close to what was required to play the part of Fagin, but Allard was clearly a natural. As I watched him twist his body and face with ever-increasing skill, I simply could not fathom how he and his father could be related — unless a friend had dared an extraordinary actor to attend his son's parent consultation as a creepy Donald Pleasance-like figure. I knew that Allard lived alone with his father and assumed that he would have received some help from him in learning and even delivering his lines; thus either Dad had more about him than I'd credited him for or Allard had considerably more about him than I'd originally thought.

As the weeks wore on and the play took shape, I noticed how much more confident some of the leads had become since rehearsals had started. Both Alice and William, for instance, while intelligent and outwardly confident with me, had always taken a more passive role in large group discussions, but both were becoming considerably more assertive as a result of their acting. This was wonderful to see, so when Mr Cox, our school's advisor, came for his annual visit, I invited him to come and watch a rehearsal. He couldn't have been less interested. As far as he was concerned, Year 6 had now done their SATs, and he only wanted to see if Year 5 looked as though they would meet their targets for the following year. Indeed, when our results had arrived, shortly before his visit, they were almost anti-climactic. We did about as expected, exceeding targets in maths and science and being slightly down in English, but now, somehow, they didn't seem too important any more. The children were nervous enough when they received their results but turned their focus remarkably quickly back to the play. Mr Cox's whole raison d'être, as far as I could see, was to ensure that all children reached their 'entitlement' of a level 4 in maths, English and science. Beyond that, he showed apparent disinterest.

It must be difficult for such people to show interest in specific children, because they visit so many different schools. Each child that I had carefully nurtured throughout the year was, almost literally to Mr Cox, a number. If that number was a 4 or 5, then that was just fine, but if it was 3 or below, we had clearly sold them short and he would want to know why.

Had Mr Cox been even vaguely interested in names then I

would have told him about Robert. I would have told him how Robert had joined my class as a screwed-up and unpredictable but highly intelligent child. I would have told him how this boy had lost any sense of emotion during the previous four years and had found forming friendships virtually impossible. And how gradually, from about March, he had slowly but surely begun to inch out of his shell, to the point where he auditioned and got the part of Mr Bumble in *Oliver!* And how, since then, his mother had been in, with tears in her eyes, telling of how her wonderful boy had thrown himself into a role in a way that she'd never have believed possible.

'*That's as maybe,*' Mr Cox would have replied, '*but what's his number?*'

Of all the children in my class I had probably watched and worried over Robert the most. He was the first child I had had any dealings with, the first to test my authority and the most complex boy I had ever known. Each time, over the first six months or so, that I felt that I was getting somewhere with him, he would somehow contrive to throw it all back in my face. To watch him show real enthusiasm for something as trivial as a lateral thinking quiz was lovely, but to watch him throw himself into a role that required emotion and commitment to his peers was simply wonderful. Despite this, though, I still didn't feel that I could quite trust him. On more than one occasion, with less than a week to go until the opening performance, I woke up in the middle of the night visualising Robert refusing to go on stage for no discernable reason whatsoever.

Before the final week's festivities, however, there was the little matter of Ellie Luck's retirement party to negotiate. She'd requested a drunken rave at a London nightclub, but we'd managed to persuade her that a quiet, stripperless party in the hall would suffice. Sandra had asked her for names of people she wanted to be invited and ideas of what she might like to receive as a leaving gift.

I could tell, from the outset, that the whole process was going to be a horrible one for Sandra. It clearly fell upon her, as headteacher, to organise everything, which included inviting teachers whom she had effectively forced out of Green Acre years before.

'Mrs Timms? It's Sandra Little here. Remember me? I was the one who told you, in no uncertain terms, that your teaching was crap. As it didn't improve I made life so awful for you that you eventually gave up and left. Fancy coming to a party?'

As ever, Sandra made no references to the potential awkwardness of reuniting with her ex-colleagues or, indeed, of the speech that she would inevitably have to make. Even though the relationship between Sandra and Ellie had been more civil since her return, there was clearly a feel that this was purely because Ellie's retirement was imminent and hence there was no point any more in Sandra criticising Ellie's teaching. This uneasy stand-off would not have been lost on either of them, yet Sandra told the rest of us that, whatever our personal feelings towards Ellie, it was her special night and we must all go out of our way to ensure that she enjoyed it.

The first major hurdle to overcome was her present. Ellie had requested vouchers to buy an expensive range of garden furniture from an up-market chain store. The problem, however, was that when the donations from staff, parents and guests had been counted, there was only enough to finance less than half of what she clearly wanted to purchase. To simply give the total donation in the form of vouchers would have been akin to writing on her leaving card: *'Here's enough money for one garden seat, which is all you'll need because you're less than half as popular as you clearly thought you were.'*

The problem seemed insurmountable, as any course of action, save asking everybody to double their donation, would clearly show Ellie how little had been collected. Fortunately, however, Leah Jones noticed an almost identical range at a much cheaper store, at half the price. After lengthy discussions it was agreed that this range, with a top-up from the slush fund, would be bought and wrapped 'to save you the trouble of buying it yourself'. Even after this course of action had been agreed it was clear that everyone was fearing the same nightmarish scenario in which Ellie noticed the forgery in front of sixty guests and asked why she hadn't been given the set she had asked for.

The evening of the party began after school with Ellie being shepherded home and everyone else helping organise food, blowing up balloons and laying tables. Frank was given the task of buying a bouquet of flowers to be presented with the present and returned, five minutes later, with a manky-looking array of carnations and chrysanthemums hastily purchased from the local petrol station. The look of sheer disgust on the face of every woman present suggested to me that he might just have done it on purpose, especially when it provoked Sandra Little into what, for her, was a major outburst.

'Oh for God's sake, Frank, what the hell are they? If that's what you give to someone who's about to retire after thirty-four years' service, heaven knows what your wife gets on anniversaries.'

'So that's why you were picking daisies the other day,' I piped up. 'No wonder you're not getting any.'

'Yes, all right, Adrian. Irene, would you go to Tesco and spend at least twenty pounds on a decent bouquet? Frank, see if you can manage to blow up a few balloons.'

While this was all good-humoured, I could sense uneasiness in Sandra's voice that went beyond a wrong bunch of flowers. Frank, Rachel and I were actively looking forward to the evening. Sandra, patently, was not.

I finally got home at about 5.30, after promising Rachel that I'd pick her up two hours later. I was on the verge of leaving again when she phoned:

'Hello, Adrian? Listen – I'm not going to be able to make it tonight – at least not at first.'

'Why, what's wrong?'

'It's Alan. He says he needs to see me. He's back off to Africa in the morning and says it can't wait.'

'What can't?'

'I've no idea. Look, save a seat for me and if Ellie starts kissing everybody, no tongues – OK?'

With this rather hideous image in my mind I left for the party with a slightly uncomfortable feeling gnawing away at me. I simply couldn't remove the thought of Rachel arriving later to announce that she would be moving to Africa with her new fiancé.

Most of the guests had already arrived when I reached school and already little cliques had formed. Ellie was sitting at a table with a group who I knew, even without asking, were her old colleagues. All now fifty or over, each had a sticker stapled to their head reading *uncharismatic and set in my ways* and, even though they were chatting merrily among themselves, one could almost feel the levels of boredom that they would generate in front of a class.

'You haven't signed this,' Irene said as I joined our clique. I looked at the sensible retirement card in front of me and read the sensible messages but, after perhaps five seconds in which inspiration failed to strike, I opted for that master of the insincere: 'All the best, Adrian.'

When Frank and I went to get some drinks a while later, he surreptitiously showed me the little bottle of vodka stowed in his pocket.

'What d'you reckon, eh? Shall we spice up Ellie's evening?'

'Frank, not only is that completely unprofessional, it's not in the least bit big, or in the least bit clever. Let's do it.'

He was a charming old sod, I'll give him that. Without a hint of hesitation he sidled up to Ellie and smoothly asked what the belle of the ball was drinking. A couple of minutes later saw Ellie sipping, perhaps for the first time ever, a large Vodka and Coke.

For the next half hour or so we reverted to boyhood, watching for the moment when our teacher would sit on the drawing pin.

'Go on, Ellie, one more sip. There's a good girl.'

'Oh, see that? That was a definite hiccup.'

'Was that me, or did she just fart loudly?'

All this time Sandra was looking distinctly nervous. The party itself was going well and everyone seemed to be enjoying themselves. Time, however, was relentlessly ticking towards the moment when she would have to get everyone's attention and begin the speeches.

By the time that Ellie had finished her drink she was definitely giggling more than I had ever seen her, which, I suppose, was not that much of an achievement given the giggle-free year that I had just been party to. We were just discussing whether we should risk her vomiting over the guests by spiking a second drink when Sandra called for quiet.

'Many people would like to speak tonight, including old friends, colleagues and pupils. I'm sure if we ask her really nicely we may even get Ellie to speak a few words too, but I think it falls upon me, as headteacher, to start the show.'

There were many people, myself one of them, who at this point listened attentively to how Sandra would go about making her speech. Of course I needn't have bothered. There was no way that Sandra was going to say anything beyond polite platitudes and if we had hoped, secretly, that she might have slipped in a double entendre for our benefit, we were disappointed. It was a good speech, humorous and kindly meant, but without the over-enthusiastic garnish which would have smacked of hypocrisy.

'I'd now like to hand over to Mrs Carrington who, as some of you may know, was in Ellie's class, well – one or two years ago.'

'Shit, that's Danielle's mum. You know Danielle Carrington, in my class?' For some reason, Frank looked rather perturbed by the thought of the mother of one of his charges about to eulogise about Ellie Luck.

'I'd first like to apologise to Miss Luck,' she began, brandishing an exercise book. 'This piece of homework was due in twenty-three years ago. Still, better late than never! No, seriously, this is a really special evening for me. I was really honoured when I was asked to speak because I remember your teaching so well. I know it's all too easy to come up here and say nice things on a night like this, but I can honestly say that you were the best teacher that I ever had. It seems to me that in this day and age children spend most of their time talking during lessons, and I had teachers who encouraged that sort of stuff, but I found that I simply couldn't concentrate. With you, Miss Luck, we all knew where we stood. You taught us and we listened – quietly.'

By now I could see Frank's veins sticking out from his wrist as he gripped his pint glass tighter and tighter. How we'd laugh, on the way to casualty, if this woman actually caused him to lacerate his fingers.

When she finished, to slightly drunken applause, Frank spoke through gritted teeth.

'That bloody daughter of hers wouldn't say a word when she joined my class. Now, after a year of getting her to talk about her work to the class, she's come right out of her shell. If she didn't mean it as a direct criticism of me, it would definitely have sounded like one.'

It certainly seemed incredible to hear someone speaking of Ellie in such terms. I could only assume, therefore, that before choosing Mrs Carrington to talk Sandra must have personally interviewed the thousand or so people that Ellie would have taught, before forming a shortlist of one. This, however, was just the beginning. We watched, with ever-growing incredulity, as a former colleague, a friend and a relative took the stand and spoke of the inspirational Ellie Luck. And then finally, after a little stumble en route, the hero of the hour herself got up to speak. An expectant hush filled the room before, with perfect timing, a mobile phone started ringing.

Manufacturers of mobile phones deliberately make them gradually increase in volume, to maximise the embarrassment of the owner in a circumstance such as this. At first, a tiny noise floats around the room, loud enough to attract everyone's attention, yet subtle enough for no one to know if it's theirs. As the noise increases, just as the owner realises that they are the guilty party, the phone itself cleverly moves to the deepest depths of its master's bag, causing them to rummage frantically down through the jumble of other objects as any last vestiges of dignity leave them. By this time the noise is so deafening that a few elderly folk start evacuating the building. Just as the phone is finally switched off its owner does all they can do in the circumstances, and utters a woefully inadequate 'sorry'.

It was somewhere between the second and third stage of this scenario that I realised, in a moment of horror, that the phone was mine. I very rarely use my mobile and certainly didn't recognise the ring tone that screeched from my bag under the table. With an almost tangible glare bearing down on me, I was just about to press the 'off' button when I noticed the word 'Rachel' on the display.

All social etiquette, as well as sixty people, demanded that

I switched it off but, for whatever reason, Rachel had not arrived at the party but was phoning me instead. I had absolutely no hesitation.

'I'm really sorry, everyone, but I need to take this call.' And with a whole range of emotions battering me from inside, I strode out of the room.

'Hello, Rachel?'

'Adrian.'

The tone of that one word spoke volumes.

'Are you OK? Where are you?'

'I'm at home. Can you come round, please?'

'Er, yes – of course – er, I must first just, er, Ellie's speaking. Look, I'll be with you in a minute.'

I edged back into the hall in time to see Sandra giving Ellie a suitably grand bouquet, and calculated that her speech must have lasted for no longer than thirty seconds. A horrible vision of Sandra actually having to curtail the speech because Ellie was slurring too much appeared, fleetingly, in my mind as I explained the call to Frank and asked him to pass on my apologies.

Ten minutes later I was sitting on Rachel's sofa listening to her telling me how Alan had decided to break off their relationship. She was clearly fighting back tears as she explained.

'He was quite matter of fact, really. He just said that it was unfair on both of us to be involved with someone when you hardly ever see them. He said he's likely to be in Africa for the best part of next year – he didn't ask me if I wanted to go with him.'

'Would you have gone?'

'Yes, probably. Being separated for most of the last few months has made me realise how much I – '

As words failed her and she gazed into a point well beyond the confines of the room, a single tear escaped from her eye.

'I'm really sorry, Rachel,' was all I could say, and I meant it.

Feelings of excitement that she was now available were, at this moment, completely overshadowed by feelings of pity, helplessness and guilt – guilt at being so relieved that she was not telling me of her impending engagement.

The silence was broken when, fortunately, she started asking about the party. I cheered her up a little by relating the drink-spiking episode, but it was clear that she was not in the mood for partying, even the gentle type which would still be going on at school, and after a while she suggested that I should go back. It was clearly one of those 'I just want to be alone' moments, and I was running out of different synonyms for 'sorry'. After checking that she'd be OK over the weekend – she'd hastily arranged a trip back home to Leicester – I gave her a hug and left.

Even though the party would still be in full swing and I may not yet have missed the present-opening, all party spirit had deserted me, so I slowly drove home.

'I wanna jus' say a huge thank you to everyone who's said nice things about me – oi! Could someone turn that facking phone off?!

'Right, yeah, 'cos you're all really special, yeah. Ya know what I mean? Thirty-four years, yeah, and it don't seem like yesterday – and stuff. And now you're all here and – hic – saying lovely stuff about me and now I'm thinking maybe I should stay on for another thirty-four.

'That would be good, wouldn't it Sandra? Oi, Sandra, come and give us a hug why don't yer? This lady – this lady 'ere, she's gone to all this bother tonight just fer me, and you know what? I love 'er, I do. Me and Sandy, we're like that, we are, aren't we Sandy? You thought you were going to get rid of me when you joined Green Acre, didn't you? You naughty girl. An' you know what? You know what?

'Aw, look, some lovely flowers. Are they fer me? They're lovely, they are. Just like you, Sandy. Thing is, though, when I retire again, properly like, in thirty-four years, d'you think you could see yerself clear to some carnations and chrys-chrysanthemums – They're my absolute favourite, they are.'

24.

And so the last week of my first year at Green Acre Primary School began. I had looked forward to this week, with mixed feelings, for most of this year. On the one hand there were the excitements of the play and the leavers' party to look forward to, as well as the six weeks of freedom that would follow. On the other hand, though, I had to say goodbye to the children who I had got to know so well over the last year. Many experienced teachers have told me that their first class is their most special, and I knew that I would always remember them.

I arrived on Monday morning with a bunch of flowers for Rachel, having first asked Frank his advice on a suitable bouquet. It was very difficult to know how to pitch it with her. I'd been the one who she had turned to on Friday night, something that I was very proud of, and she quite clearly valued me as a close friend. I had phoned Naomi the previous evening for advice and she had effectively repeated what she'd said before.

'Take her some flowers and tell her that if she wants a punch-bag, she'll just have to phone, but leave it at that, at least for the moment. If she even sniffs that you're trying to muscle in on her loss, it could be disastrous, so play it cool.'

So I did as Naomi suggested and Rachel thanked me and smiled, but she was clearly very numb. If I had secretly hoped, and I had, that she was going to throw herself at me, as her knight in shining armour, then I was disappointed.

I spoke to Frank to see if I had missed anything exciting at the party.

'To be honest, Adrian, it was all pretty dull. Ellie's speech went something along the lines of: "Thank you, everyone, for coming", and then it all went quiet. It was actually fairly embarrassing when we all realised that there wasn't going to be any more. Sandra thrust the flowers at her purely to fill the void – the producer had clearly budgeted for another few minutes before the advert break. I really think we should have given her that second shot of vodka.'

'What about the present? Did she notice?'

'Well, if she did, she didn't say anything, not even when one of the cheap plastic legs fell off.'

I even plucked up the courage to speak to Ellie herself and apologise for my hasty departure. She actually smiled at me, I think for the first time, while saying that of course she understood, before asking after Rachel. Maybe she should have retired more often.

My classroom was a flurry of activity from the moment the children arrived, with the dress rehearsal planned for ten o'clock. I had one moment of panic when Mrs Carlton arrived, without Robert, as I visualised her telling me that he had decided against it after all. She assured me that, after a doctor's appointment, he'd be in in time for make-up, and he was.

I'd been very concerned that because the dress rehearsal was to be shown to a virtually empty hall it would be a bit flat. I had at least expected a few elderly folk to come and be an audience, but, of the five who did make it, only two were in a position to respond when Alice started singing 'Who will buy?' Of the other three, one had mysteriously disappeared some twenty minutes previously, and the other two were asleep. Indeed, when the artful dodger had to go among the crowd and pretend to steal a wallet, the phrase 'candy from a baby' sprang to mind.

I'd warned the children that it would seem difficult trying to act, in costume, without audible response from the crowd, apart from a few embarrassingly loud snores of course. While they made a pretty good fist of it, there was a definite lack of 'oomph' about the whole show, and a few of them were a little down at the end.

'This really is part of the process, Alice, believe me. It's impossible to "bowl 'em over" when there isn't actually anybody there to bowl at. You wait until Wednesday night. You'll feel completely different after that final curtain call.' She didn't look very convinced.

I think I was as nervous as they were when, the following evening, the parents started arriving for the first of two performances. I knew that a really good performance would reflect well on the school. I was also pretty confident that a poor showing, with lots of fluffed lines, would reflect badly on me. Year 6 children would have long since used up their full quota of 'bless 'ems'. Hence, while I knew that the children had it in them to shine, I also knew that a few mistakes or accidents would attack self-belief and the show could decline into a woeful spectacle.

I so much wanted them to do well but as soon as the curtain opened their performances would be out of my hands. So when, early on, Alice had an attack of stage fright and needed several prompts, I feared the worst.

'Please, sir, can I have some more?'

'Not with acting like that, boy. If you want more soup tomorrow night, damn well learn your lines.'

Though she recovered somewhat, she needed a lot of pick-me-ups during the interval, and I had a horrible feeling that she was only a few muffed lines away from a collapse of confidence. Until this moment I had never doubted that she was the right child to play the pivotal role of Oliver, but now, several weeks too late, I began to wonder.

Miranda and Allard came into their own in Act Two as Nancy and Fagin and, with rapturous applause for 'Oom-pa-pa' and 'Reviewing the Situation', this helped to gradually regain Alice's composure. By the end of the performance, everyone was all smiles and, although there was definite room for improvement, it had been a good show.

A good show turned into an outstanding one the following evening, where everything went well. When we had won the 7-a-side football tournament in March, I had thought that nothing could beat the thrill of the highs and lows of such an occasion. I was wrong. The generous applause, the complimentary speeches and the looks of sheer joy on the children's faces brought tears to my eyes. In the space of twenty-four hours Alice, in particular, had journeyed from the fringes of despair to the ecstasy of achievement, and when I came backstage to congratulate them, she ran over to me and gave me the biggest of hugs. It was a truly magical moment.

It was not just Alice though, who reacted so well to success. When Sean had shone in the football tournament he had had a cockiness and a 'look at me, aren't I wonderful?' air about him. There was a subtle change, however, in his response to another good performance, this time as Bill Sykes. Somehow his countenance seemed only to show pride in a group achievement, rather than a belief that he was the star.

Nobody really doubted that the real star of the show was Allard. As I saw him modestly accepting praise lavished on him from all quarters, I remembered the surly and uncooperative child who I had taken an instant dislike to back in September.

And then there was Robert who, while possessing nothing

First Class!

like the acting talents of Allard or Miranda, had played his part well. Now here was he, smiling and interacting with his peers as naturally as the rest of the class.

Everyone was on such a high that an impromptu and completely unplanned party evolved, with most parents happy for their children to remain, chatting, until 10.30, when the caretaker, showing all his usual charm, unceremoniously threw us out. But the best part of the whole evening occurred shortly before the party, when Rachel, who'd been helping clear the stage, came backstage to congratulate the cast.

'That was absolutely brilliant, Adrian,' she said, kissing me on the cheek. 'You must be really proud of yourself.' Of course, the kiss wasn't lost on Kate and Shannon, who delighted in telling anyone who would listen.

'Did you see that? Miss Sanders kissed Mr Gray! I bet he asks her out now – I told you he fancied her!'

But I didn't care. It was good-humoured enough and it would have taken much more than their gentle jibes to ruin such an evening.

It was difficult, the next morning, to find something for them to do that did not seem a complete anti-climax. In the end, I offered them a choice of activity: either a 2,000-word critical essay comparing and contrasting the characteristics of the book and stage versions of *Oliver Twist*, or yet more quizzes. I could see Timothy actually contemplating the rival merits of the two options and thought I'd better tell them that I was joking before he got out his English book and became the butt of even more jokes.

Our leavers' party was due in the evening, and we spent a large portion of the afternoon discussing games and activities. A 'guess the baby' competition was to be one of the highlights, and they'd spent the last week or so bringing in photos of themselves as babies or toddlers. When

Shannon gave me hers, I had to double-check that she had not opted for a photo taken slightly later than toddlerdom, showing her, in all probability, trying on her first bra.

Had an Ofsted inspector been on hand to evaluate my day's teaching, I'd have failed spectacularly. The last few days of a child's primary schooling should be about fun and memories, and this was carried over into the leavers' disco that night. It was remarkable how grown-up the children looked, dressed and made up. Many of them could pass as teenagers and it made me think, a little sadly, how ready they were for secondary school.

The evening was great fun. Games, music and a barbecue occupied their attention and there was a real sense of unity about this group of children who, after tomorrow, would never see each other, en masse, again. I'd brought along a CD of tribal African music and the children looked around in a mixture of disbelief and disgust when the DJ put it on. When, however, I asked them all to form a circle and instructed Shannon to give her rendition of a beating heart in the centre of it, the sneers turned to smiles. Shannon, to her credit, hammed it up superbly, and by the end of her impromptu improvisation, everyone was in fits of laughter. The mood was wonderfully buoyant from there on in, and there were a lot of tired faces on children who left school, for the third night running, well past their bedtime.

I barely slept at all that night. The adrenalin, carried forward over the last week, had me buzzing with thought, and I was still wide awake when I arrived at school for the final day of the year.

Again, I was inundated with presents when the children came in and, again, the nature of these was telling. I was given a box of chocolates by someone calling himself 'Daniel' and, after asking him to identify himself, duly thanked him. Timothy gave me a science kit and I couldn't resist asking him if you could make a periscope from it. The joke was so obscure that I knew it was safe, although I did notice Robert smirk as I mentioned it. While he wouldn't have got the exact reference, he knew well enough that I was taking the piss.

One of the highlights was Miranda's still-unwrapped-but-slightly-bigger bag of jelly babies. This seemed, at first, like a vote of confidence, until I read the words '50% extra free' in large black letters. A hastily put-together DVD of Wednesday night's performance from William was probably the best present, but a bottle of vintage port from the Carltons ran it a close second.

A morning of tidying, games and shirt-signing followed, and by lunchtime there was still none of the infamous crocodile tears that tend to sweep through Year 6 on their final day. On the contrary, secretive whispers and giggles led, inevitably, by Kate, suggested that they were up to something, and that histrionics could wait.

At lunchtime, Rachel came into my room brandishing an impressive-looking bunch of flowers. My first thought was one of embarrassment – I had considered buying her something but did not want to risk overkill – and yet here was she with a lovely … It was only then that I realised that women don't tend to buy flowers for men – bottles of wine, perhaps, or a football, but hardly flowers.

'Adrian?' she asked awkwardly, 'Are these from you?'

My expression of bewilderment answered her question for her, and we both looked even more surprised when we read the simple inscription: 'All my love.'

'They were on my desk when I came in this morning – I'm sorry if I thought – I just … well … who on earth could have sent them?'

There were simply no candidates. They had to have come from a man, unless Ellie had gone completely mad in her last-day euphoria, and they certainly wouldn't have come from Frank.

But then I knew. With an uncanny sense of certainty I wheeled round to see Kate, Shannon, Charlie and Rozinder, with massive grins on their faces, blatantly staring at us. Kate even had the nerve to give me an unambiguous thumbs-up sign, and I was fully expecting her to double-check, loudly, that she still knew her sex education vocabulary when fortunately they were herded in for lunch.

I felt thoroughly embarrassed and didn't know what to say, but as soon as they were out of sight Rachel burst out laughing.

'You've got to admit, Adrian, as last-day practical jokes go, that's pretty good!'

'I will kill her,' I replied, grinning broadly. 'That girl is incorrigible. You seem in a better mood, Rachel. How are you bearing up?'

'I'm OK. I'm OK. It's been kind of weird this week knowing he's no longer around, but I'll get over it – plenty more fish and all that.'

There was a silence. I really, really, really wanted Naomi at this point. Plenty more fish ... Was that supposed to mean anything?

'So what are your plans now for the summer, weren't you two supposed to be going away?'

'To Greece, yes. We cancelled it. So, I – I don't really know now. Six weeks is a long time. I expect I'll spend some time in Leicester. What about you?'

'Like you – not much. To be honest, with the play and all the leavers' stuff I haven't really thought beyond today.'

Another silence. How would I feel if, after a long, uncomfortable lull, she were to say something along the lines of: 'Well, have a good one. I'll see you in September'?

Take a deep breath, Adrian.

'I, er, I don't know whether you fancy, you know, doing something, sometime – I mean, if you're not too busy of course.'

'What, together?'

'Well, yes – I mean, just good friends of course.'

'Just good friends?'

'No, I'm sorry, you're probably still getting over – I mean – you're not going to want to – '

'That sounds lovely. Anything in mind?'

By now my heart was racing and Naomi's 'play it cool' advice seemed impossible as I stammered and fidgeted.

'Er, I don't know – anything, I suppose.'

'Why don't we go abroad for a week, eh? As you say, just good friends. I was looking forward to some sun. What's wrong, Adrian? You look like you've just seen a ghost.'

'No, no, honestly, I'm fine. I'm just a bit surprised you wanted to – you know – with me.'

'Would you rather not then?'

'Oh no, Rachel, I think it's a wonderful idea. Let's – next week – get down to a travel agent – you know – see what's about.'

'Excellent. I'll look forward to it.'

And then she smiled. The first time I ever met her, when Sandra Little was showing me around the school, she smiled at me courteously, as a complete stranger, and I felt that that smile was specially made for me. And now, one year later, she was still smiling at me in the same way after just suggesting a holiday together, and I was in heaven.

'Anyway, better get on. Thank Kate for the flowers for me. They're lovely.'

I then had three or four minutes sitting motionless at my desk, before the door burst open and Kate abruptly brought me out of my trance.

'Were those flowers from you, Mr Gray? They were very nice.'

'You know, Kate, if you weren't leaving in two hours, I'd

have you expelled. You really are quite disgraceful.'

So we laughed, I congratulated her on her choice of practical joke – and she had no idea how glad I was that she had played it – and she disappeared to find someone else to sign her shirt. I would miss Kate Robinson, I thought, as much as I would miss anyone.

And so we all filed into the hall for the final assembly and Sandra gave a wonderful 'moving on' speech. I think it was Sophie and Alice who were the first to start wiping their eyes, but very soon it spread as fast as an airborne virus, and most of Year 6 was in tears. Most of these were genuine; indeed, a few children were obviously very upset, although some of the boys, especially Josh, were trying their hardest to force tears out, to be part of the scene. By the time we all returned to our room, with just a few minutes left, I too was struggling to hold back the tears, but I was determined to say my piece.

Despite the mixture of euphoria and sadness in pretty equal measures, they still managed to settle on the carpet to listen to me for the last time.

'Well 6G, this is it. In a couple of minutes' time you'll be free from Green Acre for good, and can spend the next six weeks looking forward to life at your new school.

'As you all know, you lot are my first ever class – Mrs Little clearly decided to throw me in at the deep end – and I think, for that reason, you will always be special to me.

'You probably worked out that I was pretty nervous back in September, and I'm sure I've made lots of mistakes along the way, but I have to say that I have thoroughly enjoyed teaching you. There are so many things I'll remember, especially the play, and I hope you have enjoyed your last year here just as much.

'So I just want to say two things to you. First, thank you so much for being a great class and secondly, I really, really hope that you all get on well at secondary school. Please come back to see me next year, I'd love to hear how you're getting on.

'Well, it looks like it's two o'clock, make sure you've got all your stuff, and you can go.'

I'd thoroughly expected some good-natured jibes or fingers stuck down throats during that speech, but they all just sat there and, when I dismissed them, none of them seemed to want to go. Alice, in particular, was beside herself, tears freely running down her face. Eventually, I managed to shoo them out, and was just about to fetch a cup of tea when I noticed Robert standing alone by his peg.

'What's wrong, Robert? You not going home?'

He continued to stare at the floor so I walked up to him and noticed that his face was desperately grimacing as he tried to avoid tears. I gently put my hand around his back as he leaned his head towards me and started sniffing.

'Let it out, Robert, let it out.'

And gradually the sniffs turned to sharp intakes of breath, and finally to tears – huge, uncontrollable tears. I held on to him tightly as he shed tears of change, tears of four years' worth of pent-up emotion, and tears for a little girl called Hannah.

For a full two minutes the tears flowed, before he slowly pulled himself free of me, murmured something incomprehensible, and walked out of the door. It was a moment, I knew, that I would never forget.

Later that night, I opened my diary and started rereading my entries, which I had been keeping all year. It was only when I reread the first few that I realised how much things had changed during the year – wariness of Sandra Little, indifference towards Frank Bell, and a thorough dislike of Kate and Allard, to name but a few.

I looked back over all those things I would have loved to have said, or would have paid money to watch happen – outlets for my frustration towards the likes of the Caldwells, Ellie Luck, or Sheila Warnock.

And after I'd read my latest entry, I sat back and tried to · picture what I would like to make my imaginary punch-bag for today. But nothing came, so I put down my pen, loaded the Oliver! DVD and poured myself a glass of port.